Perspective

Francis Semazzi

Francis Semazzi

E BOOK: 978-1-966131-75-5

PAPERBCK: 978-1-966131-76-2

HARDCOVER: 978-1-966131-77-9

Published by **Author Publications**: 2025

https://www.authorpublications.com

+1 (771) 203-5560

Dedication

To my mom, dad, my sister Dora, and my brother Joshua—thank you for being with me throughout my mental health journey.

Acknowledgment

I would like to thank my mom and dad for all their love and support throughout my life. My mom has recently been like an angel. When I'm feeling low or sad, I talk to her and she gives me tremendous emotional support. My dad has been an exemplary role model, guiding me through life and reminding me what it means to be a man. He is both intelligent and honest.

In this book, I've been brutally honest about the emotions that people with mental illness experience. I thank my sister for her comical personality, and my brother for the beautiful conversations we've shared.

I'm grateful to Mike Hollard and Mike Alson for being wonderful sponsors in my AA program. This program has helped me emotionally and in other profound ways that have enriched my well-being. I also thank all the other members of my AA group—I love you more than you can understand. You've helped me through many crises, and together, we've found solutions to the challenges I faced.

There are too many names to mention from AA, but you all know who you are. You've helped me tremendously and given me dynamic faith in God.

About the Author

Francis Semazzi holds a degree in Electrical Engineering from North Carolina State University. But what he enjoyed most were the books he read during his college years. Ralph Ellison's Invisible Man was a groundbreaking novel that opened his eyes to the power of words and how they can beautifully activate the imagination. That particular book reminded him that he has much to offer the world—if he works hard and believes in himself.

Francis has spent time in and out of hospitals, tried various medications, and worked with numerous psychiatrists and therapists, often without much relief from his symptoms. However, those hospital experiences shaped his character in ways he never thought possible. He has developed a deep faith in himself—one that only God can instill.

During his hospital stays, he met remarkable men and women—deeply human individuals with complex challenges. These people touched his heart and inspired him to write this novel. He has read countless books on mental illness, which have not only helped him manage his symptoms at times but also cultivated his understanding of the subject.

Francis has been diagnosed with schizoaffective disorder, which he has spent years trying to explain to professionals. Many say he has strong insight into his condition. His faith in God has sustained him through the hardest times.

Table of Contents

Perspective

Chapter 1

Jake was consumed by a blind rage. The voices, which usually aggravated him during work hours, had now taken full control of his mind at 10 p.m. Their irrational torment fed on his emotions, distorting them into something dark and uncontrollable. These voices didn't just intrude; they dominated, pushing Jake to the edge. He couldn't fathom why this part of his consciousness was so overly abusive. Suicidal feelings, once fleeting, now clung to him with an intensity he'd never known. It felt as if he were no longer himself but someone very dangerous…

The angrier Jake became, the louder the voices grew, orchestrating a cacophony of torment. They wanted him to act, to succumb, to lose control. He tried to resist, but the rage coursing through him left no room for reason.

"If you change your face, I will stop," one voice taunted, cryptic and cruel. Jake froze. For months, he had been plagued by an inability to control his facial expressions—twitches, fleeting smiles, and movements he didn't command. It was as if his own face had turned against him.

A guttural, hellish scream erupted from him, a desperate plea for silence. But the voices persisted, their manipulation of his emotions amplifying his fury. Moving with robotic aggression, Jake stormed into the living room. He reared back his arm and drove his fist into the wall, punching a hole right through the wall. The drywall crumbled, and blood began to drip from his knuckles, staining the floor.

The voices didn't relent, pushing him further to the point of senseless torture. Another screamed another animalistic sound from his throat as his fist struck the wall again, leaving a second bloody hole.

"Jake, what's going on? Why are you doing this?" his brother shouted, running into the room. But Jake couldn't hear him; he was beyond comprehension. Another blow, another hole. Blood now poured freely from his torn skin.

Their parents rushed downstairs, their faces pale with fear. "Jake, stop! Please!" his mother begged, her voice breaking. His father joined in, pleading for him to calm down. But Jake couldn't respond. He was a storm of rage and pain, disconnected from the world around him.

Spotting the family's big-screen TV, Jake grabbed it with both hands. "Jake, no! Don't push the TV—we need that!" his mother cried hysterically. Ignoring her, he shoved it. His brother caught it halfway, but the corner cracked off, the screen irreparably damaged.

Jake turned back to the wall in his violent spree, his fists trembling. His brother tried to restrain him, grabbing his arm, but Jake broke free and slammed his knuckles into the wall once again. His skin peeling away with each strike, exposing raw flesh.

Not being able to control Jake any longer, Jake's mother dialed the police while he punched three more holes in the wall. Then he saw the magnum opus on the wall. The picture included Jake, his brother, his sister, mom and dad all dressed up in elegant clothing when Jake was 10 years old. He vaguely recognized what the picture represented at that moment, but the abusive voices kept talking and the emotions of rage were flowing through his mind and body. Jake picked up the huge gorgeous picture of his family, and broke it on his knee, causing blood to patch from his knee. The picture broke in half and Jake broke the remaining pieces with his hands. The picture was elegant and priceless, because It was the only picture of his family which showed what magnificent people they were. That picture for them was like picking up the first made picture of the Mona Lisa and snapping it in half. Everyone was looking splendid, such a beautiful family. Jake was wearing a sophisticated sweater which had majestic lines going up and down methodically, on the far end on the right of the picture. His brother was next to him with another elegant sweater with a brown shirt underneath; it had diverse intricate shapes built on top of each other. His mom was in the middle with a beautiful golden gown. The gown looked like it came from the land of the Pharaohs in Egypt. The gold gown was so beautiful it looked like dozens of men traveled around the world to find it. His dad was sitting down on a chair wearing a sweater that had elegant fork-like shapes with blunt ends. One could tell it was very cleverly designed to look exquisite. Jake's Dad also had a checkered collar within the sweater. Jake had his hands on his dad's left shoulder in the picture. Jake's sister had her hands on Jake's dad's right shoulder, she was wearing a sweater with a vest. The sweater was multicolored with unique shapes and varying patterns. She had a necklace with a pendant on it. The pendant looked priceless, Jake once thought she must have borrowed it from someone. She also had a graceful long skirt which matched her sweater. Jake used to joke to himself he was in a family who liked their sweaters.

Piece by piece, he broke the frame, tearing through the memories it held. The once-pristine portrait was now a pile of splinters and torn paper. The destruction was absolute, yet Jake felt no relief—only the ceaseless, burning rage.

A loud knock startled the room. The police had arrived. As the door opened and officers stepped in, something shifted in Jake's mind. The rage ebbed, replaced by a hollow stillness. For the first time that night, the voices were silent.

Through some fleeting grace amidst the chaos, Jake began to grasp the reality of his surroundings. His bloodied hands trembled as he noticed the police officers' guns, their voices cutting through his mental fog. "Stop!" they commanded. Slowly, the rage that had consumed him ebbed into something more manageable, a simmering anger still tainted by desperation.

When one of the officers cautiously approached, Jake looked up, his voice trembling yet forceful: "Take me to the hospital! *Now!*"

The officer hesitated, clearly uncertain. People in Jake's condition rarely expressed a desire for help. More often, they resisted, lost in the moment, unable to see beyond their spiraling emotions. The officers exchanged glances before one finally instructed Jake to turn around. "We're putting cuffs on you," he said firmly but without malice.

Perspective

Jake didn't resist. He felt the cold metal around his wrists and allowed the officers to guide him upstairs, through the front door, and into the backseat of their patrol car. His tall frame struggled to fit in the cramped space, knees pressing awkwardly against the seat in front of him.

Inside the car, Jake's heart pounded violently. His head bobbed against the seat, his voice low and trembling. "God, please, make the voices stop. Just make them stop." But the voices didn't cease. If anything, they grew louder, their venomous whispers tearing at his fragile sense of self.

"It's your ego, it's your pride," they hissed, their tone dripping with scorn. He felt like a machete was going through his sense of stability within his mind again.

The words were secondary to the emotional assault that followed. It wasn't what they said—it was the unbearable weight of the emotions they injected into him, intangible yet excruciating. It felt as if his very essence was being pierced by invisible daggers. The torment was visceral like a surreal Vulcan mind meld gone horribly wrong, where insanity and malevolence bled into his psyche.

Jake clenched his fists within the cuffs, his anger swirling uncontrollably in his mind, a vortex that suffocated any remnants of peace or reason. The helplessness stung the most—there was nowhere to run, nowhere to hide. His reality had become an unending nightmare.

"Why don't you hit the police officer in the face?" one voice sneered suddenly, its tone razor-sharp.

Jake froze, the command slicing through him like a spear. He felt the emotion attached to it—a violent, searing sensation that gripped his chest and radiated through his entire body. He whispered back to the voice, his tone filled with a mix of defiance and weariness. "I can't do that. I'd go to jail. Besides, I'm in handcuffs, asshole."

The voice laughed, mocking him with a chilling detachment. "Yeah, you forgot one thing. We don't care about anything." A little frenzied, the voices detected the hostility dripping in Jake's voice.

Jake shuddered as their laughter echoed in his mind. They recognized the hostility in his voice and latched onto it, exploiting the opening to stir his anger further. Their sinister energy swirled around him, trying to drag him back into the abyss.

He closed his eyes, trying to steady his breathing, but the voices continued their relentless assault. Every word, every twisted emotion felt like another step deeper into a hell he couldn't escape. Jake knew he was teetering on the edge, fighting to retain the faintest shred of control in an already compromised state.

Jake was separated from the police by a metal barrier, the noise from the outside world muffled. He heard one of the officers muttering, trying to reassure him. "Everything's going to be okay." The words barely reached him. The voices in his head roared louder, drowning out everything else.

"No! You lie! We won't stop until you end your life!" they screamed, their words cutting through his mind like jagged glass. Jake's thoughts swirled in confusion. Why was this happening to him? Why had God forsaken him? What had he done to deserve this hell? He tried to grasp the reality of his existence, but it slipped through his fingers. *I've never hurt anyone,* he thought, *never committed any crime.* The worst thing he'd done, in his mind, was stealing fruit snacks from a friend in kindergarten.

His chest tightened as the rage from the voices intensified. "God, please help me... help me... If I've done anything wrong, please forgive me," he whispered, his head swaying rhythmically as the torment inside him grew.

Jake began to recognize the highway signs through the car window. They were on their way to the mental institution. The voices in his head twisted and contorted like puppets, pulling at the strings of his emotions. Though he wasn't religious half the time, today he felt something else— *maybe* this was the devil. Or perhaps it was just his mind, twisted and broken beyond recognition.

A part of him, the skeptic, clung to the idea that these were just auditory hallucinations, that with the right medication, he could be freed. But a deep fear gnawed at him: none of the antipsychotics had worked. He had built a tolerance to mood stabilizers, antidepressants, and anti-anxiety medications. His past efforts to understand cognitive behavioral therapy had yielded few answers. The one thing that had given him any peace, though, was a book on Dialectical Behavior Therapy someone had given him at the hospital during his first visit. But even that had only calmed him slightly before the voices took over once again.

Jake had been to the hospital *fifteen* times. He had been in and out of institutions for years, always hoping for a solution, a cure. This time, though, was different—it was his third time at Zion, the mental institution that had become a grim part of his reality. Again he was being taken there. He didn't know this time he would be able to manage its expenses since his father had exhausted almost all of his resources during those grueling hospital stays.

As the officers drove for what felt like an eternity, the voices began to subside, though their influence remained lurking beneath the surface. Jake didn't know how to explain it, but at the sight of the mental institution, something within him eased. His mind, once a war zone, felt like it was finally entering calmer waters. The voices spoke in disarray, muttering something about the hospital being "mystic."

Jake wasn't sure what they meant by that. He wasn't trying to mock God—he was just bewildered. Was this divine intervention? Could this place really offer him the peace he so desperately needed?

The officers helped Jake out of the car, still in handcuffs, and guided him through the emergency entrance of the hospital. They were gentle with him, offering quiet words of encouragement. "Are you more relaxed, buddy?" one officer asked. Jake nodded, the first sign of relief he'd felt in hours.

"I feel a little better," he said, his voice hoarse from exhaustion and emotion.

But the voice in his head wasn't done. "This isn't over. So you think they're really going to help you here? You remember what happened last time?"

The dread flooded Jake's chest, and he tried to cry, but the tears wouldn't come. The officer's voice cut through the tension. "We're almost there. Just a little longer."

Jake couldn't process it anymore. His mind was spinning, his body overwhelmed by the never-ending waves of confusion, fear, and frustration. He just wanted the voices to stop. Just once, he wanted peace. But as the elevator doors began to close, he wasn't sure if he was any closer to finding it.

Jake couldn't cry. It felt as though a part of him was being held back, locked away by the voices in his head. He knew they would follow him into the mental institution, just like they always did. No matter what medication he tried, nothing seemed to work. He had been through it all.

The officers guided him to the elevator, and for a brief moment, Jake managed to regain a small amount of control over himself. He wasn't completely lost yet. He could still answer their questions, even if his mind felt like a twisted labyrinth.

As usual, they asked him the same things. But one question always stood out, no matter how many times they asked it. "Do you have any desire to hurt yourself or anyone else?" Jake found it oddly intriguing how each person asked that question differently. For those who had worked at the institution for years, it was more of a formality, a tired question that seemed to lose its weight with each passing day. For others, it was full of care. But no matter how it was asked, it always felt like the same question.

The nurse who asked him this time was punctual and professional, though Jake couldn't help but notice something else about her. Her exotic, Arabic appearance had a timeless quality—her black, mystical eyes seemed capable of seeing deep into his soul. But that wasn't what was on his mind at the moment. His focus was on the voices, the rage, and the overwhelming desire to make everything stop.

Jake didn't want to talk about his appearance, his past, or the hospital's routine. He didn't need questions—he needed answers. Answers to the chaos in his mind. He felt like something was manipulating his expression, forcing him into a grotesque, cartoonish version of himself. He tried to express the anger and frustration on his face, but whatever it was that controlled him wouldn't let him. Every time he tried to focus on concrete thoughts, they scattered like broken pieces of glass.

He couldn't even remember the last time he shaved. His mind was racing with negativity. It was like his thoughts had taken on a life of their own, spiraling downward no matter how hard he tried to stop them. *God, what's going on?*

"What was that?" the nurse asked, glancing at him with a mixture of concern and professionalism.

"I'm confused… I feel like I just exist to suffer," Jake muttered, his voice hoarse.

"Do you feel like you're in a safe place?" the nurse asked, her voice soft but steady.

"Sometimes…" Jake replied, his words trailing off. He wasn't sure anymore. He wanted to believe he was safe, but the storm inside his mind made it feel like anything but.

Jake looked into the nurse's eyes, feeling a strange pull, a momentary connection. *She's so beautiful,* he thought, distracted. *She probably has a husband and kids. She'd never be interested in someone like me—someone with schizophrenia.* He could feel his face shift, a change he couldn't control. The nurse noticed and smiled, her expression warm yet professional.

"Well, at least I'm talking to a beautiful woman," Jake muttered to himself. He felt a little lighter, a small break in the heaviness of his mind.

"What's your name?" he asked, his voice softer.

"My name is Yamel," she replied, her voice calm and soothing. Jake could see that she noticed him relaxing, the tension in his face easing, though the voices continued their relentless assault in the background.

The entity is still doing something to my face, Jake thought. *This feels so uncomfortable. So awkward.* Normally, in a situation like this, he'd joke or try to flirt, maybe ask for her number. But the constant barrage of negative voices clouded his mind, preventing any thoughts of attraction or fantasy.

Yamel glanced down at Jake's fists, noticing they were bleeding. "Can I take a look at your hands?" she asked, her concern palpable. She put on gloves and gently examined his hands.

"Do you need bandages or something?" she asked, her tone soft yet practical.

"I'll be fine," Jake muttered. "I just want to have control over my symptoms." His thoughts were fragmented, like shards of glass, and every time the voice spoke in his head, it made him feel even more detached from reality. *How do these voices work?* He wondered. *Can I somehow get ahead of them and brace myself before they strike?* He wondered if the voices were demonic in nature, but the thought barely formed before being swallowed by the chaos in his mind.

Yamel smiled again, this time with a deeper warmth, and Jake felt the stirrings of desire rise in him. For a brief moment, he entertained the idea of saying something inappropriate, something sexual. *Maybe I could make a move now while she's here.* But the voices became louder and more demanding, insisting that he act on these thoughts.

He tried to smile back, but the voices grew angrier, tearing at him. Yamel noticed his discomfort and backed away, her smile faltering before she left, speaking a few words that Jake didn't even register.

He sat in the medical chair, his mind spiraling out of control. A police officer appeared at the door, keeping watch. Jake could feel the weight of his presence, the officer's gaze cold and indifferent. *What do you want?* Jake thought, speaking to the voices. *Why do you keep hurting me?*

For a moment, there was silence. *Why do you keep hurting me?* Jake repeated, his words desperate. He recalled something he'd read in a book about hearing voices: *If you can communicate with them, they lose their power.* But no response came. He still felt like he was teetering on the edge of something, a threshold to hell. His thoughts stagnated, growing more frustrated and angry with each passing second.

The officer began talking to another nurse. *Why won't they help me?* Jake thought bitterly. *I'm right here, and no one is listening. The voices won't stop, and I feel like I'm losing my mind.*

His mind was a blur, and his body felt detached from reality, as though someone was manipulating it, controlling his every sensation. *Why am I feeling this way?* He wondered. *Why are my emotions so chaotic, so bent on destroying me?*

Suddenly, the sensations in his body shifted, feeling eerily sexual—humiliating, invasive, and entirely beyond his control. His mind screamed at him to stop it, but it only made it worse. *This isn't me,* he thought. *I've never been touched this way. Why is this happening?* The sensation felt like a violation like someone was forcing these feelings into his body against his will. It hurt his pride and his sense of self-worth. *I feel like someone's cutting me open and throwing salt in the wound.*

"AAAAHHHHHH!" Jake screamed a guttural cry of frustration and pain, his body trembling with the effort of trying to contain the overwhelming sensations.

"I feel like someone is molesting me, and it won't stop. It hurts." These words made Jake angry in a very strange way. The emotions stopped to some degree when the nurse came back, but deep inside, Jake didn't know what triggered the shift. What caused the radical emotions to calm?

"We're going to take you to the holding cell," said the nurse. This was Jake's fifteenth time in the mental hospital. He didn't know what was so special about this place that sometimes made the voices quiet down. The voices kept saying the police officer was a mystic as he walked Jake through the halfway hallway to the holding cell. *If that's true, why didn't the voices stop when I first saw him?* Jake wondered.

He looked to his right and saw a wall of pictures of doctors. *What about me is so complicated that none of these men in the hallway can fix my problem?* Schizophrenia…

Schizo-affective disorder… Bipolar, or whatever they wanted to call it these days.

The nurse, the police officer, and Jake entered a narrow elevator. They went up to the third floor and walked through another hallway to a secure door with an electronic lock. The officer typed in the code, and a man suddenly jumped in front of Jake.

"The day of reckoning is upon us," the man said. "There's going to be an Armageddon… The chosen one is upon us."

Jake froze, staring at the blood dripping from the man's wrists onto the floor. *Aren't you going to do something about him?* Jake thought. He spoke up. "Aren't you guys going to help him? He clearly needs help right now."

The nurse didn't seem alarmed. She just walked to the big window at the front of the room to get help. "Save the women and children, my friend. The demons will be camouflaged this time," the man continued.

The officer led Jake into a room with eight indentations, each with a bed and a TV protected by plastic. The officer told Jake to change into hospital scrubs, which he did without protest. He lay on the bed, staring at the ceiling.

"So, here we go again. I'm back in the psych ward for the fifteenth time, I think. Don't know what meds they'll give me this time; I've tried them all."

"The only thing that can help is some sort of God-like therapy. Or Jesus talking to me in the flesh." He tried to cry but couldn't. It felt like there was some sort of entity inside him that wouldn't let him cry. *Maybe they'll take me to Zion this time, and I might have sex with someone. It still seems like my voices want some sort of sex.* He thought back to the time he had sex with a prostitute last year and how unexciting it was. The prostitute had a high-pitched voice, like a kid, but her body was okay. It was a dark, dusky room.

Jake closed his eyes, thinking of one of his fantasies: having sex with Supergirl, played by Helen Slater. That did the trick. But then he quickly became frustrated because the voices had been saying that if he hadn't had sex, they would stop and go away. *That means it was never about the sex in the first place. That means I'm royally fucked,* he thought.

Chapter 2

It was late at night when someone brought food. Jake got so angry with the person who brought it that he didn't say anything at all. He didn't even eat, in full rebellion. "Why hast thou forsaken me?" he whispered. He remembered Jesus saying something like that and thought it would make a good joke with God.

Through all of Jake's thoughts, he forgot that the man who had said "The day of reckoning" had disappeared. A young woman with golden blonde hair, who looked like a nurse, came in with a man who had jelled black hair. They came with the usual procedure. They asked him about the event at his house, but Jake could only recall bits and pieces. He was also having a hard time focusing on the male nurse because a face hallucination popped up mysteriously, almost constantly. He tried to figure out how to explain the cartoon face on top of his face but had a hard time doing so.

He said the same things he had told his psychiatrist and therapist before. "I feel like someone inside me is contorting my face to be cartoon-like, and I've tried all the main anti-psychotics."

"Well, how about clozapine?" said the male nurse.

Didn't he hear me? I said all the fucking medicines, Jake thought. *I tried that too, but I don't remember why I stopped it. Oh, that's it—it slowed down my speech.*

"How about Zyprexa?" the nurse asked, grinning like he had solved some ancient riddle.

You're a fucking idiot, thought Jake. *Didn't you hear me? I've tried all the medications, and none of them worked.* Jake was about to give the male nurse an "Are you serious?" look. He answered the questions like a robot, obviously declining both Zyprexa and clozapine.

When the nurse left, Jake closed his eyes. The virtual face was everywhere he looked. The voices started talking to him again as if they didn't want him to have a moment's rest. The whole room felt quiet, unlike the man's voice saying, "It's time for reckoning," somewhere close. In a normal scenario, Jake would have been able to sleep.

But the sexual emotions started up again. He felt like someone was raping him, forcing him to feel sexually aroused through telepathic means. He had no idea how to make it stop. With each sensation, he groaned in discomfort. After five minutes, nothing worked. So, he started to say a mini prayer to God. That helped a little.

"God, please help me. This feels so uncomfortable."

He kept praying in that way, and then it popped into his head: *Benadryl. That might help me sleep.*

Usually, at home, Jake had the six pink pills of Benadryl. He saw a nurse walking right by him. "Hey, could you help me out… I need some Benadryl to help me sleep," Jake said.

"We can make an order for you to get some, but we have some Zyprexa onsite that you can take," the nurse replied, her face unchanged.

Jake thought he might be losing his mind for a moment, but he kept his cool, knowing he had to stay calm to get what he wanted. After several sensations of feeling violated, he was able to wait for the diphenhydramine. They gave him two pills. He had to settle for that.

Through the grace of God, he was able to sleep.

When Jake woke up, he found a police officer and a nurse standing over him, with a tray of unreal eggs on the floor near his bed. "It seems that they've found a bed for you at Zion. You can eat your breakfast so that we can take you to Zion." He'd been there before, so he didn't know what would be different this time. *Maybe God incarnate might be there and help me recover,* he thought. *At least I won't hurt myself from these sexual impulses now.*

Despite all the thinking he had done, he still hadn't figured out how to make those sexual feelings less unbearable. He had never been raped, so he didn't know what that was like unless the memories had been suppressed. He remembered back when the sensations first started. He had gone to a sexual therapist, trying to understand what was going on. When he mentioned the voices in his head, the therapist stopped him in his tracks and told him she'd try to get him a psychiatrist. She was alarmed by the voices.

The psychiatrist she found told him they could give him a shot of Invega, but Jake wasn't inclined to take it at the time. It struck him as strange that today he had taken the shot. *If the pills don't work at all, how can the shot suddenly work?* He couldn't understand why doctors didn't see the simple logic.

Jake felt stuck between a rock and a hard place, but he could never quite build the courage to kill himself. He loved life so much. This was all he knew. He couldn't imagine hell or heaven for eternity. He could only imagine what was right in front of him: cause and effect. But his emotions seemed void of that—just confusion and irrationality.

With all the therapists he'd had in the past, he had told them exactly how he was feeling in the most eloquent way he knew, and he'd received some good answers, but they were never knowledgeable enough to make those overwhelming emotions disappear or become controllable. It felt like there was an invisible, powerful, yet sturdy force pushing him toward insanity.

I guess, Jake thought, *if I don't know God, I'll meet him in the first few days.*

The things psychiatrists say to their patients should be documented. I never thought my old psychiatrist would say something so disrespectful and degrading to me. Whenever I reminisce about such incidents, I feel my demons taking over me all over again.

Perspective

It was a Wednesday, and I was having a terrible day. The voices in my head wouldn't stop. The medication wasn't helping. My eyes were blinking uncontrollably, and my tardive dyskinesia was wreaking havoc on my entire body. This was before I had Ingrezza, which made the condition somewhat more manageable.

I met with the doctor, who always sounded like he was hiding something—like he was doing something harmful to me but didn't want to admit it. He suggested medications I was popping into my system. When I told him they didn't work, he simply shrugged and said, "You know what, Jake? One thing you have to understand about yourself is that you're broken."

It wasn't just the words; it was the way he said them. My whole world shattered. For the rest of that day, I felt like a diseased person—someone with an incurable condition, set apart from society, placed into a category of rejects. It cut me to my core.

A mental health professional should never take away a patient's hope; that is the only thing which keeps us going. His words pushed me closer to the edge. I questioned if life was even worth living—if I would always be trapped in this reality, haunted by an invisible malevolent presence. I was already near the breaking point, and Dr. Prometheus' words only made it worse.

But the next day, something shifted. Despite everything, I felt a need to live. Yes, what I was going through was unbearable, but life was too precious to give up on. My family and friends loved me. They would miss me. And besides, I didn't know how God judged suicide. I had seen YouTube videos of people managing their schizophrenia, finding ways to cope, and still living good lives. I had to believe I could do the same. I just needed to find my own way—whether simple or complex, there had to be something that worked.

Afterwards, we talked briefly about whether I was suicidal. I was, but I knew better than to admit it. If I did, he'd send me to the hospital, where they would pump me full of more medications—ones that wouldn't help and might even make things worse. When our session ended, he smiled, but there was something off about it—something almost sadistic.

Now, I'm not saying all psychiatrists are evil. But some have tendencies that make you wonder. When your whole career revolves around prescribing medications you **know** will eventually cause problems for your patients, how much of your humanity do you lose along the way?

The rattling of the handcuffs brought him back to reality. The nurse and the police officer took him downstairs to a small room where he was handcuffed. That's when he saw her. She had beautiful blonde hair that shone in the light, looking like an angel. She looked like a Victoria's Secret model, but she had scratches on her arms, which made Jake sad. He concluded she must have abused herself. It was strange to see such a beautiful woman in handcuffs.

"So, what's your name?" Jake asked.

She looked at him with a quizzical expression. "I'm Rachel."

Jake was about to say more when a man stepped in between them and started talking to Rachel in a sexually charged manner.

Jake wasn't even mad at him. The symptoms were creeping in again, threatening to drown him in their intensity. The voices in his head, the faces flickering in his vision—it all felt like he was floating somewhere between reality and something darker. If he was losing touch with reality, then where was he? It wasn't like he could call out to anyone for help. The feeling was suffocating, like he was trapped in a void, a space between life and death.

He tried to focus on something the *Dialectical Behavior Therapy for Bipolar Disorder* book had taught him: *live in the moment*. Don't think about the past. Don't worry about the future. Just focus on what's around you. He tried. He really did. But his mind wouldn't stop pushing him forward, demanding answers to questions he didn't even know how to ask.

He felt the fear and anger bubble up inside him, validating his emotions as the book suggested. It didn't help as much as he hoped, but it was something. At least, it was a small reminder that he wasn't entirely lost.

Jake was trying to figure out how to explain what he was experiencing to the doctor when he saw them. The faces weren't really faces at all, not the way you'd expect. They were twisted, glitching like an old TV channel, half-formed images that didn't make sense. It was like some sort of voodoo emotion. It was like his brain had gone rogue, creating these disjointed visions for reasons he couldn't understand. He thought it was his imagination, but at this point, who could tell?

As they loaded into the van, Jake felt a sharp sense of déjà vu. He and Rachel were among the patients being transferred. His legs were shackled, and he could feel the weight of the metal around his ankles. He sat in the back of the van, stealing glances at Rachel, who sat up front. She seemed lost in her own thoughts, her face in confusion, as if she, too, was wondering how she had ended up here.

Around him, the other patients looked mostly normal. There were always one or two with wild hair or unsettling eyes, but the rest of them could have been anyone. He was a little disappointed that the 'Day of the Reckoning' guy wasn't in the van with them. He probably couldn't handle the trip. Jake figured he was too suicidal to be with the others.

"I'm ready for the big ride, baby!" the man who'd been talking to Rachel sang as if he'd made this trip a hundred times.

Jake snorted, his frustration easing just a bit. It reminded him of the other times he'd been in the hospital, meeting people who became fast friends for a brief, surreal moment. He'd gotten their numbers but when he called them they never picked up. It was like the bond was only temporary, formed in the chaos of shared pain. Some people volunteered to go to the hospital. Others were sent against their will. Jake didn't know when he'd leave this time. His problems felt more intense, sharper than before. Would the right meds help him this time? He didn't know. He just wanted the voices to stop.

Maybe I'll get sedated, and when I get out, try to find sex again, he thought. *Maybe I'll go see a shaman or something. I don't care. Just make it stop.*

They finally arrived at Zion, the psych ward. The van pulled up to the building, and the police officer chatted briefly with the nurses. Then, one by one, they uncuffed the patients.

They were grouped into fours by one of the nurses. Each patient is assigned a specific caretaker. The nurses ushered them to different areas of the hospital. Jake felt a small sense of relief when he found himself in the same group as Rachel, who was deep in thought. The mental hospital had a calming atmosphere, with soft brown and white tones that seemed to blend into the background. In the common area, people were scattered around—some watching movies, others playing games, and a few engaged in quiet conversations.

Jake was led to his room and told he'd meet with the doctor soon. After the nurse left, a new face appeared: Steve, a nurse Jake recognized from his previous visits. Steve was one of the few hospital staff members Jake felt comfortable with.

"Hey, Jake. It's good to see you again. How's it been going?" Steve asked, giving him a warm smile.

Jake gave a half-hearted smile in return, feeling the weight of his recurring visits. "Same old, same old," he muttered, signing the required documents. He could tell Steve didn't want to dig too deep into what had brought him back for his third stay in eleven years. No one ever did.

With a heavy sigh, Jake mumbled to himself, "Here I go again." The routine felt endless.

Steve told him lunch would be served in a few hours and that he'd be off to assist other patients. As Steve left, Jake sat down on the bed, his chest tightening. He wanted to scream—something raw, something barbaric—just to release the frustration of feeling so trapped. His mind was no longer the same as it had been in college. Thoughts no longer flowed freely or coherently. They bounced around, disconnected, leaving him feeling lost. But at least the voices were quieter now, only murmuring that this place was "mystic," whatever that meant.

Wanting to escape the silence of the room, Jake walked to the common area, hoping for some distraction. There, he spotted Rachel sitting by herself in a chair, staring off into space as if trying to solve an impossible puzzle. She looked distant, as if her mind was miles away, tangled in a web of paradoxes.

Jake walked over to her, his long legs taking slow, deliberate steps. He wasn't used to feeling self-conscious, but he wondered if he looked as lost as he felt. He wasn't ugly. In fact, he thought he was quite handsome—tall at six-foot-four, dark-skinned with sharp features, though a subtle bump in the middle of his nose always caught his eye. He had a certain presence, or at least, that's what he liked to tell himself.

"Hi, Rachel. How are you doing?" Jake asked, sitting down next to her.

Chapter 3

"I've been here before. And I'm so confused right now. I don't know what to do with myself, but I know he cheated on me. He must have. Why else didn't he answer my calls last week?" Rachel's thoughts spiraled, but before Jake could say another word, she suddenly widened her eyes, staring past him.

"I can't believe it's him. But... What if this is some sort of hallucination? I need to remember what the doctor said about my illness—it pulls me in all kinds of directions," she murmured to herself. Rachel abruptly got up from her chair and jogged toward a young man with bright red hair, barely out of college.

"What are you doing here, Jason?!" she demanded.

Jason looked just as shocked. "I can't believe it. They put me in the same section as you," he said, then turned to the nurse nearby. "Is there any way I can be moved to another room? She's my ex."

The nurse, a middle-aged man with a weary expression, shook his head. "There's no more room. You'll have to stay in this section."

Jason exhaled sharply. "Rachel, this won't work. You're trouble," he muttered.

Rachel's voice quivered. "Why didn't you answer my calls? You didn't call me back for an entire week! We break up all the time, but we always get back together!"

"So you guys know each other. I never witnessed this before. There is no more room, so we have to put you guys in the same section," said the nurse. Jason didn't respond, his face tight with frustration. The nurse, noticing the growing tension, intervened. "Rachel, discipline yourself, or we'll have to send you to the seclusion room," he warned.

Rachel froze, her thoughts racing. *Maybe this is part of my sickness. I need to relax.* She took a deep breath, turned, and walked back to Jake, who watched her with a puzzled expression. Meanwhile, the nurse escorted Jason to his room, the anguish clear on his face.

"What was that all about?" Jake asked as Rachel sank back into her seat.

"That's my boyfriend... or ex-boyfriend. I don't even know anymore." She looked at Jake, her eyes heavy with emotion but somewhat empty. "I still love him. Is it wrong for someone like me to love?" she whispered.

Jake winced. Hearing Rachel describe herself as "someone like me who has schizophrenia" unsettled him.

Rachel shrugged. "It's the truth. Besides, I've been called worse."

Jake tried to shift the conversation. "Where did you meet?"

"At college," Rachel replied softly.

"What was your major?"

"Psychology."

Jake smiled faintly. "Then you must be familiar with the id, ego, and superego."

Rachel nodded. "Of course. The id is the primal part of the mind, full of hidden memories and conflicts between sexual and aggressive drives. The superego represents our moral conscience, and the ego balances the two, keeping us grounded in reality."

Jake leaned back, impressed. "You're clearly smart. But something tells me this isn't your first time here at Zion."

Rachel narrowed her eyes. "Why don't you tell me about your first time here instead?" she countered.

Ok, but it will be kind of embarrassing… I don't know if it would do justice for you to outdo me once you hear my story. I was a senior in college, carrying a full load of classes, including a senior design project that I didn't understand. I was very depressed and had been drinking heavily the day before. My mom called to check on me, and I told her I wasn't doing well. She decided to take me home.

When she picked me up from my college apartment, my head was lolling back and forth, and my eyes were rolling into the back of my head in the car. At the time, I didn't fully grasp what was happening, but years later, I came to call it a nervous breakdown.

We drove to the nearest hospital, which was right next to my college. For some reason, the staff told me to wait in the common area until the doctor could see me. While I sat there, racing thoughts flooded my mind—thoughts I'd never experienced before. Looking back, I believe it was some kind of bipolar episode. If you want the blurry medical term, that's what I'd call it.

"Explain in detail about your thoughts. I need detail, man," said Rachel.

"That's just it, Rachel. Whenever I think back to those days, I have a hard time remembering. I do recall having end-of-the-world scenarios running through my head. They were bizarre, disjointed thoughts. For instance, I went outside to get some air, and there was a lady sitting nearby, speaking in this strange gibberish. She wasn't forming complete sentences. I automatically thought my mom had abandoned me and left me outside."

I know why you're looking at me and laughing right now. Why would my mom bring me to the hospital and then leave me outside for no reason? It's ridiculous, I know. But you're laughing because maybe, just maybe, you know how it feels.

"So far, nothing is embarrassing. I think I've still got you beat in the 'most embarrassing story' department," Rachel said.

Anyway, my mom eventually came outside and told me the doctor was ready to see me. The doctor performed a routine check-up and said everything seemed fine. With my mind still racing, I asked the doctor if he believed in God. I couldn't hold on to one solid thought, and that question just spilled out. The doctor said he did.

To speed up the story, Rachel… They gave me a room in the hospital. That's when things took a turn. My muscles started to tense up—it felt like a mild electric current was coursing through my body. They put me in a hospital gown, which became my uniform through what felt like a descent into hell.

I lay down in the bed, and my family brought KFC. Eating the chicken helped me feel a little more relaxed for a while. But when my family left, the racing thoughts came back, stronger than ever. I couldn't sleep. The doctors or nurses gave me nothing to help me relax. My body became almost completely tense, and I remained in a hyper-alert state all night.

Wearing only the hospital gown, I decided I had to escape.

"Now we're getting somewhere," Rachel said.

Perspective

In the morning, around 9 a.m., I jumped out of bed and sprinted down the hallway to the emergency exit stairs. I had no shoes or socks, but the adrenaline coursing through me dulled the sensation of the cold, hard surface beneath my feet. When I reached the parking lot, the chill of the cement jolted me back to reality. I sprinted across the lot toward the woods, feeling unseen eyes on me, but I didn't care. I had to escape the hospital.

When I reached the woods, I slowed to a brisk walk, the crunch of leaves and the sharp edges of stones pressing into my feet. Ten minutes later, I found myself at the edge of the forest, facing the highway. As I glanced back into the woods, I spotted a snake, its head raised in warning. The sight sent a shiver down my spine as if it were a harbinger of things to come.

My thoughts spiraled into paranoia. If I stayed in the hospital, a millionaire CEO might harvest my heart for himself. These absurd, life-threatening ideas consumed me. A year ago, I'd been jogging daily, keeping my heart in perfect condition—prime for someone to steal. People with power and money could do anything, I thought. Then another wild idea struck: robots and AIs had taken over the world.

I needed to change my face. Grabbing a rock, I tried pressing it against my skin, hoping to scar myself. But the pain was unbearable, and I gave up. Looking at the highway, I realized there was no nuclear explosion, no sign of an apocalypse. The world wasn't ending. I decided to ask someone for directions to my college, which I believed was nearby.

Walking along the path, I approached a young couple and asked how to get to my college. They said they didn't know, but as I walked away, I glanced back to see the man on his phone, staring at me. Paranoia gnawed at me again. After ten more minutes on the trail, I found a cardboard box and thought about carving it up with a metal pole rooted in the ground. Just as I picked up the box, a cop appeared and shouted, "Freeze!"

Fear consumed me. The next thing I knew, I was on the ground, handcuffed, with my ass shunning the police officers. They took me to jail, where I sat in a holding cell, my thoughts racing uncontrollably. Eventually, they transferred me back to the hospital. Once home, I had another episode. My parents watched me closely as if I were on suicide watch. It felt like an exorcism. I screamed and begged Jesus to take away the intense emotions. At one point, I thought I could see the insides of my body—a hallucination, perhaps, or something worse.

I asked my parents for water, but when they brought it, I was convinced it was poisoned. I refused to drink it. Later, I wet the bed and had to shower while my father stood guard in the bathroom. The next day, I told my parents to take me to Zion on my own accord.

This was all when I was 23 years old. Of course, I would be coming back here and to many other hospitals several times. When I got to Zion, it was pretty much all gone to hell. My parents and I were placed in a room, and I was taken to the third floor for evaluation. Initially, I felt calm and relaxed, but as I followed the nurse and security officer to the ward, apocalyptic thoughts flooded my mind. I imagined I was in a dungeon, navigating a cave-like building. My muscles tensed, and the hairs on my neck stood on end. My head darted around, scanning my surroundings like a headless chicken.

At the unit, I saw nurses behind a desk. "We should have a party here," I blurted, attempting to mask my distress. A male nurse replied, "We need more girls," his expression tinged with fear. My vision narrowed like a racer looking at the track, the periphery darkening. A woman approached me with a pill in her hand. "Take this; it will help you calm down," she said, her dark, enigmatic eyes staring into mine. I hesitated but eventually took the pill. The next thing I knew, I woke up in Zion, which felt like Wonderland.

"That was terrifying. I don't know if I should give you an Oscar or what," Rachel said. "Now that I've spilled the beans, it's your turn."

"Well, okay," Rachel began. "I was dating this guy, Jason. We'd been together since my freshman year of college. We were happy at first, but then I started suspecting he was cheating on me. I never had concrete proof, but I couldn't shake the feeling. I checked his phone and tried catching him in the act but found nothing. Despite my suspicions, I couldn't let him go. Jason eventually broke up with me, but I always managed to pull him back.

"During my junior year, one of my major classes required attending a NAMI talk on schizophrenia. I'd done internships with NAMI, so I was familiar with their work. That day, Jason and I had a fight about my accusations. I didn't know if I was in a different dimension or reality. Flustered, I went to the meeting, feeling out of sorts. I loved Jason. That was true. Maybe the reason why I kept saying he had cheated on me was because I was a little obsessed and could believe that we had something like that. With my chronic suspicions, I was searching the big crowd of people at the NAMI meeting for the woman Jason was cheating on me with, and A professor of psychology was doing a talk about schizophrenia at the same time. I was already familiar with the jargon around the word schizophrenia. He talked about hallucinations, delusions, voices, positive symptoms, negative symptoms, and catatonia. Then, that's when it happened. As the professor spoke about schizophrenia—hallucinations, delusions, catatonia—a girl sat down next to me. She stared at me in a way that felt intrusive, like she knew me. I zoned out in a trance that only God and my higher power knew about, and I stood up, yelling, 'You're the one cheating with Jason!'

"The girl was vexed, but I kept shouting. People gasped in disbelief; some chuckled nervously. The psychologist stopped his presentation, calling for someone to help me. A woman and a man near me in the audience came to calm me down and take me out of the building. At this point, I calmed down a little bit. I sat on a bench, trying to calm down. They told me they'd called the police, who would take me to Zion. I'd never been to a looney bin before. The police were kind, and the staff at Zion labeled me paranoid schizophrenic."

"That must have been embarrassing," Jake said.

"Your story is embarrassing, too. Someone you knew could have seen you running into the woods," Rachel teased.

"I'm sure someone in that presentation must've been in your class or someone you'd seen before, Jake countered, smirking.

"The strangest part," Rachel continued, "is Jason visiting me in Zion when I thought the relationship was over."

The story deepened Jake's perplexity, putting him in further vexation. How could a beautiful, intelligent, and charming woman like Rachel find herself in such a predicament? Since that day, she had visited Zion several times, often for reasons involving Jason. Yet no one had helped her enough to stop her recurring stays in mental hospitals.

"That's some story," said a man standing behind them, his voice startling Jake and Rachel.

"You've been here the whole time?" Jake asked, visibly surprised.

"Yes," the man replied. "I'm Pedro. Let me tell you my story."

"Join the 'Unusual Experiences Club' and share," Rachel said with a wry smile.

"Well, this is my first rodeo," Pedro began. "I've always struggled with anxiety, especially after my parents became verbally abusive toward each other when I was in the fourth grade. I wouldn't call myself shy, but I've had my moments. I eventually saw a psychiatrist, hoping to manage my anxiety. Nothing worked—not the therapy, not the medications—until my doctor suggested I might have a form of bipolar disorder. He thought an antipsychotic might help. The problem was... I didn't think I was psychotic.

"Anyway, my anxiety hit its peak the day before my GRE exam. I didn't do great on the English part of the SAT, though I scored slightly above average in math. But I worked hard in college and maintained a high GPA, so I didn't feel stupid. Still, the pressure of the GRE—a test that would determine my future—was immense. It's just that the clock looks so big when you're doing a national test of that caliber to get into Grad school. The test was being held in the university right next to mine.

"The night before, I couldn't sleep. My thoughts raced. When morning came, my hands wouldn't stop shaking. I prayed, hoping for calm, but the tremors persisted. At the test site, surrounded by other young people who were nervous but not as much as me, I felt like I was about to explode. My hands were sweaty. Then, to my utter horror... I farted. Loudly.

"The woman in front of me whipped around, glaring. I wanted to disappear. I sat down, trying to focus, but my thoughts were a whirlwind. Writing my name on the answer sheet became a Herculean task. I knew it was Pedro, but my hand wouldn't listen to my mind and relax. My body shook uncontrollably. Suddenly, I screamed.

"Everyone stared as I was the star attraction. The facilitator approached, alarmed. 'What's the problem? Are you okay to take the test?' he asked.

"At that moment, I felt like I'd stepped into the Twilight Zone. Or maybe I was on Star Trek in a malfunctioning holodeck. My arms locked, stretched out in front of me, trembling.

"'Calm down,' the facilitator urged. 'Try breathing.'

I must've looked like I was about to perform some kind of magic trick. "Clear the area around him. I think he is having a nervous breakdown. I already called the ambulance to come get him. Now, what's your name?"

"Pe Pe Pe Pe Pedro" was all I could manage. "Ok, Pedro, I want to know if you can sit down and try to breathe steadily. I sat down, but then my eyes got wide open, and I started to breathe erratically. I noticed all the students backed away from me with the facilitator the only one next to me. At this moment, my mind started to do weird things, but for the most part, each second felt like an hour.

Each second felt like an hour. Then the ambulance arrived. They placed a breathing mask on me, and for the first time that day, I felt a sliver of calm.

"The facilitator was kind of undecided about canceling the test for everyone in the room. He gave them the option to stay or reschedule. I don't remember what the students did after that ordeal but I remember the look on one woman's face when I walked through the door of sheer utter shock and the utmost contempt as I was wheeled out.

"In the ambulance, I finally began to relax. And now, here I am... in Zion."

Pedro paused, his story hanging in the air. Jake and Rachel exchanged glances, both moved by the raw honesty of his experience.

"Life has a funny way of bringing us to places like this," Jake said finally, his voice low.

"Indeed," Rachel agreed. "We're all just trying to find our way."

"Well, it seems like we all have issues," Jake said, exhausted from listening to everyone's stories. He yearned for a meal and the solace of sleep, hoping to escape the constant voices in his head. It amazed him how so many people, like Rachel and probably in the future Pedro, were trapped in the same cycles of despair, ending up in mental wards repeatedly.

"Isn't the mental hospital supposed to be rock bottom?" he thought. "Once you're here, this should be the place to get real help."

Perspective

Still, Jake felt a flicker of curiosity about the man and woman he had just heard stories from. He noticed striking similarities between their struggles and his own. Like him, Rachel and Pedro were ensnared in their own fabricated realities, unable to fully grasp their circumstances.

Chapter 4

Jake couldn't shake the sense that something needed to change—not just for them but for everyone suffering from this decay or the way people call it, "mental illness" plaguing the country and the world. This is just ridiculous how intelligent people were put in these scenarios. Jake was familiar with the hearing voice network, which was a good source to get help. In HVN he formed lovable good relationships. How can one feel so helpless about their situation every day? The decay of mental health systems was glaring. He wasn't a psychiatrist, so he didn't know the details of ongoing research, but he was certain something was deeply flawed.

Jason walked into the common area just as Rachel lost herself in thought. From all the stories she had heard, she had almost forgotten her own. She was gridlocked—unsure if her struggles stemmed from normal emotions or a full-blown schizophrenia episode.

When she was first diagnosed, the very name of the illness sounded terrifying. She didn't see herself as catatonic or experiencing the negative symptoms often associated with schizophrenia, though she supposedly had delusions about another woman having sex with Jason.

"Could it be that I love him so much that it's clouding my judgment?" she wondered. "How does someone medicate love? That doesn't make any sense."

Despite her diagnosis, Rachel had maintained a 4.0 GPA while majoring in psychology. Even after her first stint in Zion, she performed well academically. She couldn't help but wonder, *Can't I outthink this illness?*

The emotions came and went like waves, leaving her disoriented.

"Hello, Jason. How's it hanging?" she greeted him, forcing a smile.

"Rachel, I don't have time for this," Jason snapped. "We're both in the psych ward. Let's just stay out of each other's way."

"I'm curious, Jason," she pressed. "What brings you back here? I know you've been here before. What happened?"

Jason noticed the others at the table, all eyes fixed on him with anticipation.

"Oh, this must be show-and-tell," he said sarcastically.

"We all think there's something wrong with the way mental health is handled in this country," Jake interjected cautiously.

Jason sighed. "Fine. I'll share a little. First, have any of you been to Zion before?"

"All of us, except Pedro," Jake replied.

"Well, here's the deal," Jason began with a smirk. "I have obsessive-compulsive disorder. I am a germ-cleaning freak. I'm one of those people who obsessively clean—everything all the time. It's not just a habit; it feels like life or death if I don't."

He leaned back in his chair, gauging their reactions.

"It started when I was a kid. Well, it all started when I was a child, and I fell in a sewer covered with toxic waste on me for 3 days. I'm just kidding, I've never ever had that happen to me.," he joked, "but just… I don't know why. It's like if I don't clean something before using it, the universe might explode."

Jason went on to describe his experiences with various medications. "My psychiatrist tried several medications. Prozac might be helping a little now, but I've tried everything—even antipsychotics, which I hated. They made me feel like I was in another dimension, and I gained a ton of weight."

He paused, his tone shifting. "Anyway, I was at the gym one day, doing my usual routine—wiping down equipment before and after using it. I'm slow and methodical, so it takes me longer than most people. Not because I didn't do it right, but it is like a life and death situation for me."

Jason described an encounter with another gym-goer who grew visibly annoyed with his cleaning habits.

"The guy cleaned the machine for me—longer than usual—while glaring at me," Jason recounted. "When he was done, he said, 'You don't have to wipe it down today, Jason. I already did.' But I couldn't help myself. I wiped it down again."

I finished cleaning and started using the machine. I did three sets of five. The man chatted with his friend for a little bit and I could see they were watching me the whole time. Jason's voice grew quieter as he relived the confrontation. "His friend cut in front of me as I went to clean the machine again. 'Don't worry about it; I don't care if it's clean,' he said, smiling at me like it was some joke."

Jason sighed, the frustration evident on his face. "I tried to explain, 'Let me just wipe it down. You don't understand.' But he didn't care. No one ever does."

"Get away from me, you freak!" the man's friend shouted. He didn't understand that the balance of the universe depended on me cleaning that machine. If I didn't clean it, my entire thought process would spiral out of sync. I'd be stuck in some parallel universe where normal things ceased to make sense—a mist of confusion engulfing everything I knew and plunging it into disarray.

In this confusion, the mind plays strange tricks with time. A memory from 7:30 a.m. could vanish, or a fabricated memory could appear at 4:30 p.m. The man's friend didn't grasp the catastrophic stakes of my actions, so I kept cleaning the machinery.

The man's friend grabbed my arm and slapped me across the face. Instinctively, I punched him in the stomach, forcing him to stumble back, gasping for air. His companion charged at me, seizing my arm to strike again, but I quickly popped him in the face, banging his head on the metal piece I had to keep cleaning.

I turned back to the task at hand, grabbing sanitizer to clean the blood off the machine. The room was heavy with eyes watching me, murmuring about what they'd just seen. I scrubbed harder, determined to finish despite the rising tension. Five minutes later, a man announced himself as the police. But I couldn't stop cleaning—not yet.

The officer said he would take me to the hospital, where the people from Zion would help me. My breath became labored as handcuffs clamped around my wrists. As they escorted me to the police car, I learned that the two men had been arrested for aggravated assault. Witnesses at the gym told the police the men had struck me first.

In the back of the police car, I retreated into my mind, far away from the officers' questions. My answers were brief and detached. But I knew things would be different once I got to Zion.

"I love you," Rachel said, her gaze fixed on Jason, mesmerized.

"Whatever, Rachel. So now you all know the story," Jason replied.

"I need to stop coming to these mental hospitals. They don't seem to be working," he added with a laugh. Everyone else joined in.

Steve appeared through the double doors and announced, "Lunch is ready! Everyone, line up!"

"Oh great, back to lining up like school children," Rachel muttered as she, Jason, Pedro, and Jake joined the other patients in a single-file line.

The cafeteria was large and spacious, the tables and chairs bolted down to prevent anyone from throwing them. Each patient waited for their tray. The menu was meatloaf and mashed potatoes. After collecting their meals, the group sat together at one table.

"There's something seriously wrong with the mental health system in this country," Rachel began. "They throw us in here, adjust our meds, make us sit through art therapy or group sessions, and expect us to be fine when we leave."

"Maybe our problems are so personal and complex that no one knows how to help," Jason suggested.

"Or maybe the system is broken," Jake added.

"What we need is an organization outside of this system—something that actually helps people," Rachel said.

"There are groups out there," Jason pointed out, "but none of them seem to do the trick."

"The Hearing Voices Network can be helpful," Jake said, "but they don't dive deep into how to make the voices stop. Sure, they talk about coping mechanisms, but the discussions sometimes veer off track, but I do love HVN."

"I've read books about bipolar disorder, schizoaffective disorder, schizophrenia—none of them offer real solutions for making the voices disappear," Rachel said. "You'd have to read academic dissertations for that, but those are so complicated."

"Movies don't do a great job representing our lives, either," Jason said.

"How about *A Beautiful Mind*?" Rachel asked. "That was good."

"It was okay," Jason replied. "But I'm talking about a movie where young people like us recognize the flaws in the mental health system and do something to fix it. And maybe we can even win a Nobel Prize."

Pedro chuckled. "This reminds me of *It's Kind of a Funny Story*. It's basically what we're going through now."

Rachel nodded. "True. Maybe we should do some research on NAMI. We could tweak what they are doing—turn it into something new."

"I don't suppose any of you want to do a walk for mental illness," Pedro joked.

Some of them laughed, but Jake shook his head. "Don't mock those walks. They raise awareness and are a good fundraiser for research."

Jake sat quietly, thinking. Something needed to be done—something that could inspire researchers and advocates to work harder and smarter. He didn't know exactly what, but he felt that this group, despite their flaws, had the potential to make a difference. Something to encourage the ones doing dissertations on it to work harder and to think more about the solutions.

"Maybe we can just do speeches and inspire people with our stories," said Jason.

"Perhaps we should do more research on the issue and what's being done to fix the problems," said Pedro. Jake knew that there were some good things discussed that could be exploited in a good way.

When lunch ended, the patients lined up again to return to the unit. Steve led the line, his face a mix of apprehension and relief as he glanced back at the group following him.

"We need to take blood pressure readings, and then we'll have group therapy," said one of the nurses.

The common area was modern and spacious, with a predominantly white aesthetic softened by neutral tones like beige and light brown—colors meant to create a calming environment. Everyone in the unit lined up for their blood pressure checks before gathering for the group session.

A recreation nurse facilitated the session, starting with introductions. Each person was asked to share their name, their goal for their hospital stay, and their mood on a scale of one to ten.

Jake went first. "I'm a five," he said, "and I'm here to figure out how to silence my voices and manage my intense emotions."

Rachel followed. "I'm also a five," she said. "I want to stop having paranoid delusions about my partner."

Jason shared that he hoped to overcome his compulsive thoughts, and Pedro explained that he wanted to understand his bipolar episodes, particularly the one he had during his GRE test.

When it was Ayn's turn, she simply stated, "I want to understand why I have so many suicidal thoughts." Her tone was matter-of-fact, almost detached.

"Wonder what her story is," Rachel murmured after the session.

As the group dispersed, Rachel rallied the others. "I think we've found our fifth member," she said with determination.

The group approached Ayn and introduced themselves. Her face was expressionless, her voice somber as she spoke.

"Would you like to tell us a little bit about your story of what brought you into the mental ward for the first time or this time in particular?" She was hesitant at first but agreed.

"I don't mind since I feel less suicidal now," Ayn began. "I was doing an internship at a Fortune 500 company, competing for a permanent job. The person with the best performance and portfolio would win the position. I worked tirelessly—my 4.0 GPA, every late night, every sacrifice, all led to that moment."

Her voice wavered slightly as she continued. "On one Monday, I opened my laptop to work on my portfolio only to find out my portfolio was gone. I called the IT department to search for the file but they confirmed it had been deleted. I remembered that Andrew had used my computer before leaving on Friday. He must have deleted my work accidentally or done it on purpose to get ahead of me to get the job. I lost my USB drive on Friday, which had some of my portfolio, and I brought it over the weekend to have a backup of my work. I worked my whole life to this moment at the internship. Whenever my parents fought, I would work on my homework more. When my grandma died, I would work on my homework. When my Dad got cancer, I would study harder. I worked so hard to get that internship I had a 4.0 GPA."

Ayn paused, visibly grappling with the memory. The suicidal thoughts started to enter my mind when I started the internship. I would be concentrating on a project then I would think to myself, wouldn't it be good if I died right now? I started to have fantasies of hanging myself or jumping off the building. I couldn't explain why I was having those emotions at all. I just wanted to die. During the internship, I would have these mental blank spots where I don't remember what I did for certain parts of the day. I thought to myself after the internship, I would have a vacation, that's what I needed. The day when I found that all my information had been erased I decided to jump off the building. I tried to think of my mother and father and family, but there was a mental block. I tried to cry but couldn't. I was in perpetual depression that I could not logically understand. I started a mechanical walk to the ends of the building, huffing and puffing, trying to let it out but couldn't. I got to the edge of the building and just stared down at the parking lot. I got a little dizzy and almost fell off. Andrew came through the building door.

She stopped for a moment, then added, "Ayn, don't do it if it is because of your work. It was an accident. I was trying to delete all of my information off the computer and deleted yours instead. I even accidentally deleted the backups" said Andrew. He begged me to step away and talked me off the ledge. I cried, not just for the lost work but for everything—the hopelessness, the chronic depression I couldn't escape. I agreed to get help and checked myself into Zion. And here I am."

The group listened in silence, absorbing her story. Finally, Rachel broke the tension. "That's a scary story."

"Please, Rachel, stop with the sarcasm," said Jason.

. "Well, I think it's safe to say we've got a new member for our mission."

"Mission?" Ayn asked skeptically.

"To rid the world of mental illness," Pedro chimed in with a grin.

The group laughed, sharing lighthearted banter before diving into deeper conversations about their lives— childhood, college, and the challenges they'd faced.

Later that night, Jake lay in bed, apprehensive about the voices that often plagued him as he tried to sleep. It was as if his mind became an open arena for them to torment him.

When they talk to him in his head, he feels like it's just him and the voices. He was also sleeping with his contacts on, which he couldn't get out without a suction cup. Jake tried something different tonight. With all the force he could use, he tried to remember the good times that he and his voice had together.

He thought about the visions that he used to have of getting a blue-collar job, and meeting his wife. He thought of the deep, exotic emotions of love for his wife. He doesn't know how his voices put those emotions into his mind or how his mind orchestrated it, but at that time, he was very happy. The voices about Jesus, the devil, and God were so intense in a good way in the beginning. They all played the part of being his friend.

It was fun when fake Jesus used to joke around with him instead of now hurting him emotionally almost at every moment. The good Jesus drops in every now and then and treats him like a friend, but that's very seldom these days. Jesus would masquerade as cool people that Jake heard from on TV and have fun with him. With the essence of him disappearing the voice or whatever it was having a hard time communicating to Jake. It was very uncomfortable to try and fall asleep when you never knew when a voice was going to interject with something annoying to say. Also, it was weird, but as he closed his eyes, he could feel like someone was changing his face and doing something. Putting a distorted face on top of his doing stuff to make him very angry. It felt like someone was interjecting on his privacy.

After about an hour, the trazodone medicine kicked in a little, and he felt a little sleepy. Before going to sleep, Jake felt the emotion of someone touching him again then he fell asleep, almost like having a real demonic spirit in his body. Jake had ok dreams. Then, at about 6:00 am, one of the nurses came to take his blood pressure. After Jake got his blood pressure, he tried to go to sleep, but the voices kept playing haphazard games in his mind, keeping him awake whenever he felt sleepy. Why were the voices so demonic in his mind in the first place? How did they function? It made sense that he had to be in a particular mood, but who started that particular mood for him, the voices or some type of anomaly? They seemed to not want to be there, but what made them come and talk and do things in his mind in the first place? Jake would constantly feel this complicated emotion as if someone was forcing Jake to think that he wanted to feel those negative emotions. There was one time he was moving his face from spot to spot, and the thing inside him kept changing his face from moment to moment. Why the entity or whatever it was in him, it seemed to get his attention that way.

Jake had a feeling that there was something underlying wrong under his conscious emotions orchestrating all this in his mind. There was a part of him in a desperate plea for help, as if that part of him was somewhere where death was imminent. There were so many unknowns for his situation that he felt like he was going insane. When he first heard the core voices, he didn't snap or anything. He didn't feel like he was in a weird state of mind. The only thing he remembered was this kind of split consciousness. He could feel the emotions of another presence in his body but at a distance. The entity felt things according to Jake's prior emotion, and Jake felt things in accordance to the entity's haphazard emotion.

Chapter 5

When Jake woke up, it was time for breakfast. Even though he felt trapped in hell, something told him this stay in the mental institution would be different. He stepped out of his room and found Jason waiting in line.

"This thing inside me—it keeps tormenting me," Jake said, his voice low but strained. "It's like I'm telepathically forced into this awful mix of intense sexual arousal and crushing suicidal emotions. I want it to stop, but it feels like I'm being raped in a strange way."

"Have you talked to a doctor or nurse about it?" Jason asked.

There was a time when I had a psychiatrist named Dr. Confucius. I walked into his office expecting a new prescription and a conversation about my voices. He always had samples, so he let me try them out instead of making me buy them.

"Hello, Dr. Confucius. I'm still hearing voices. They feel hardwired into my brain. I don't know if medication is going to help," I said.

"We have a medication called Caplyta. It might help," he replied.

"Don't you want to hear about my voices and face hallucinations? Maybe if you had some insight, you could suggest coping mechanisms other than medication. It might also help you make better choices about my treatment. Maybe I need a strong antidepressant or a mood stabilizer," I suggested.

"Your voices are caused by a chemical imbalance in your brain," he said.

"Well, if that's the case, then why doesn't medication solve the problem?" I asked.

A long, eerie pause followed. He just stared at me with a poker face, as if silently declaring the conversation over.

"My voices say they are the Devil and an evil Jesus Christ. They act like they're helping me, but they hurt me instead," I continued.

"Yup," he muttered.

"The Devil mocks Jesus Christ, saying things like, 'If Jesus is there, then where is he?' He also accuses me of trying to be Jesus. Then, to confuse things further, he'll suddenly claims I'm not Jesus, as if he knows him and was lying before," I explained.

"Yup."

"They always have something to say whenever I feel even a little happy. They throw in a few words to punctuate my emotions with negativity," I added.

"Yup."

"Were you even listening to a single thing I said? I think this is important," I snapped.

"I was listening to every word. It's just that all that information isn't important. You have a chemical imbalance. Those voices will say anything," he replied.

"I can't believe you don't care at all. Fine, I'll take your pills and get out of here. I don't think you can help me anymore," I said.

And that was the last time I saw Dr. Confucius.

Psychiatrists in the Western world rarely discuss the details of what someone is actually going through. I doubt they can create real change. He was just a pill dispenser. I don't think he even cared about me as a person. To him, I was just another case file. The thoughts of going into a whitewashed room with a statue of a man sitting on a chair. Though, he seems human with breathing lungs and a pumping heart but they are statues—hard, rocklike.

"I did, last time I was here. They didn't help. All they did was up my antipsychotics. I feel so helpless, Jason. I'm not getting help here, and I wasn't getting help out there either. Once, I went to a shaman. She just told lies to get more money out of my dad."

"Seriously?" Jason said, raising an eyebrow.

"Yeah," Jake replied. "She switched her focus to my dad after some pointless ceremony. She claimed people were jealous of his success. It was a scam. I thought about trying another shaman or a voodoo priest—maybe in New York—but honestly, I'm losing hope. I even went to a hypnotist, and that didn't work either. I didn't feel anything after the whole ordeal."

From across the hall, Rachel's voice interrupted them. "Your voices—are they getting any better, Jake?"

"I slept, Rachel," Jake said, "but as soon as I woke up, they started manipulating my emotions again. It's exhausting."

"My voices didn't bother me at all last night," Rachel said. "I had sweet dreams. Maybe you have a different type of schizophrenia than me—if that's even what you want to call it."

"I can't shake it, Rachel. It is playing havoc on my face," Jake said, his frustration mounting. "It's like I'm not even in reality most of the time. Whatever this thing inside me is, it's humiliating and relentless. It's like it wants something, but I can't figure out what."

Before Rachel could respond, Pedro and Ayn approached. Ayn, wearing a long Michael Jordan jersey, had dark black hair, striking black eyes, and pale skin. Jake couldn't help but notice how gorgeous she looked. Pedro, with his Hispanic complexion, curly black hair, and strong jawline, gave a casual nod.

"How'd you guys sleep?" Jake asked.

"I slept okay," Pedro said. "But after taking Zyprexa, I'd wake up and couldn't move. It was terrifying."

"Same thing happened to me," Jake said. "I had to stop taking that stuff."

Steve, one of the staff, stepped to the front of the line to escort the patients to the cafeteria. As they shuffled forward, a doctor in her forties called Rachel aside.

"Rachel," Dr. Tolstoy said with a professional but guarded expression, "can we talk for a moment?"

Rachel smiled faintly and followed her into a secluded conference room. The atmosphere grew heavy as the doctor studied her. "How are you doing these days, Rachel?" the Doctor asked with a poker face which only could be read if one pays close attention to the subtlety of her face.

"I don't know, Doc. Maybe I'm just stressed out," Rachel said, avoiding eye contact.

"How are the voices?" Dr. Tolstoy asked.

"They're still there," Rachel admitted. "They keep saying they're going to steal Jason away from me. It feels so real, like someone's trying to kill me over him."

"I hear Jason is here with you. What are the odds?" Dr. Tolstoy said.

"Yeah, he's here," Rachel said. "And honestly, I know we talked about this before. You said it might all be a delusion, and part of me believes you. But the emotions—they feel so real. Like, overwhelmingly real. Sometimes I think he cheated on me, and other times I don't. It's exhausting."

"Do you still love him?" Dr. Tolstoy asked.

"Yeah, I do," Rachel said softly. "We've had our rough patches, but we always find a way back. If love is a sickness, then everyone should be in a straightjacket."

Dr. Tolstoy allowed a small smile. "Have you ever considered that you might be right? That he could have cheated on you? What would you do if you were certain?"

"I'd probably leave him," Rachel said. "But I'm not sure I'll ever know for sure. Tell me, Doctor—do you think I'm schizophrenic?"

"You were diagnosed with it a few times, but to me, you have proved to communicate very clearly about your issues. You have great insight into your problem, whatever it is," said Dr. Tolstoy.

"How about the voices? What am I going to do about them? They're very cruel and mean to me. I hear voices of people that Jason has cheated on me with. They say that if I don't leave Jason alone, they will kill me. They're aggressive and sound like very jealous women," said Rachel, her expression twisting with distress.

"Well, I was thinking we could try Thorazine to address that problem," said Dr. Tolstoy.

"That's just it, Dr. Tolstoy! I've tried all the medications, and none of them work for the voices. I'm beginning to believe that someone is using telepathy to say those mean things about me," Rachel replied, her voice escalating with anger.

"We can try a combination of medications," Dr. Tolstoy said reassuringly.

"Stop it right now, just STOP!" Rachel screamed. She stood up and began pacing the room. Dr. Tolstoy remained calm, though momentarily startled.

"Don't you guys have all my records by now? I've been here on, like, one hundred thousand different combinations of medications. I've tried all the antipsychotics and other drugs. I can almost name them by heart," Rachel said.

"Okay, Rachel, calm down. You don't have to take anything you don't want to, but I strongly suggest you take something. Imagine what might happen if you get off all your medications—you could relapse," Dr. Tolstoy said sternly.

Rachel was about to yell back but stopped, realizing there was no winning the argument. She sat down in her chair, defeated, and let Dr. Tolstoy continue discussing higher-dose injections. Her mind wandered, thinking, *Jake's right. Something has to be done about the mental health system in this country. It feels like I'm just going in circles.*

Meanwhile, Jake, Pedro, Jason, and Ayn were having breakfast in the modern, neutral-colored cafeteria.

"I wonder what's going on with Rachel and Dr. Tolstoy. I know Dr. Tolstoy is nice; she just doesn't know how to solve these hard problems, like me and my volatile emotions," Jake said, lost in thought. *It doesn't make sense. People can go to the moon and back, build computers, do heart transplants, but they still can't make voices disappear or manipulate emotions to make them livable.*

"Well, I've tried like five different therapists, and none of them have helped since I started hearing voices," said Jake.

"I know what you're thinking about. Why don't you try hanging out with Buddhist monks?" Pedro suggested.

"I would, but the airfare is kind of expensive," Jake replied.

"Radical acceptance," Ayn chimed in. "There are some great concepts in DBT. Although my voices sometimes catch on to what I'm doing, mindfulness—living in the moment—helps when they don't. It works for all mental illnesses. You're not stuck in shame about the past or apprehensive of the future." said Jake.

"The idea isn't necessarily to master the nuts and bolts but to exploit the helpful parts," Jason said with a half-smile.

"I know DBT works for depression, OCD, bipolar disorder, and psychosis, but there's nothing specifically tailored for schizoaffective disorder or schizophrenia," said Jake.

"When I read the DBT books, I felt a little better, but applying the worksheets to real-life scenarios is hard," Jason added.

"Yeah, I read the one for depression. It was good when it showed pros and cons, but you can't make a pros-and-cons sheet for every negative thought. Distress tolerance isn't bad, though. If you rate how you feel before and after an activity, it might help," Ayn said.

Rachel walked briskly toward the group.

"So we can agree DBT is helpful for mental illness. I've read all the DBT books, and I think they're great," said Rachel.

"The only problem with DBT is that it's just like NAMI, promoting established therapies like CBT," Jason said.

"NAMI is already running educational classes to help people manage their mental illnesses. Some therapists are just better than others. It shouldn't be about how much money you have," Pedro said.

"I went to a great outpatient program with group therapy. The therapist was amazing. If I'd had her one-on-one, she could've helped me more. She really got to the root of our problems," Jason said.

"Maybe it's about therapists figuring out what you truly need deep down. Once you have that, your symptoms might disappear," Jason continued.

"I don't know. Even if I get something I want, my depression lingers. It's hard to pinpoint what I need to make it go away. I've tried different medications for what they call a chemical imbalance, but nothing has worked," Ayn said.

"I haven't taken an antipsychotic for my severe depression. Maybe one would help," Ayn added thoughtfully.

Jake listened, knowing they were all right in their own way. He'd thought about these things before, running through every scenario about mental health solutions. *If only there were more awareness about what we go through. Maybe some brilliant minds could create new medications or therapies,* he thought. *For people with severe issues, these therapies can help tremendously.*

As the group continued talking, Ayn suddenly felt a wave of suicidal emotions crash over her. It hit like a ton of bricks, the depression slicing through her self-esteem like a razor blade. She was in so much pain she just wanted it to stop. The thought of cutting herself crossed her mind, but the pain felt so deep that even that didn't seem like it would be enough.

Ayn started to feel a creeping paranoia. *How the hell did that emotion come about? What can I do to prepare myself in case it comes again?* At that moment, her thoughts were fragmented, breaking into one-sentence intervals. Confusion consumed her.

Jake noticed something was wrong. A shadow of sadness eclipsed his face as he observed Ayn's frozen expression—a mask of severe distress.

"Ayn, are you okay? You don't look good," he said cautiously.

"I just had an earth-shattering, suicidal emotion," Ayn replied, her voice trembling. "When it hit, I couldn't think. It felt like an eternity. I'm going to lie down and try to sleep it off."

She walked to her room, but the thought lingered, an unwelcome guest in her mind. She couldn't stop obsessing over the suicidal feelings that had gripped her so tightly. A knock on the door interrupted her spiral.

"Hey, Ayn, may I come in?" asked Dr. Tolstoy.

"Yeah, sure," Ayn responded, her voice subdued.

Dr. Tolstoy entered briskly, her expression stern. Ayn's face tightened, and tears spilled uncontrollably as the weight of her emotions overwhelmed her. Without a word, Dr. Tolstoy hugged her and guided her toward the doctor's office.

"Ayn, what's going on?" Dr. Tolstoy asked gently.

"I feel suicidal, and I don't know what to do," Ayn admitted. "The emotion came out of nowhere. It overloaded me. I've tried medications for depression, but nothing works."

"How often do you experience these feelings?"

"Sometimes. But even when they're gone, I'm paranoid about the next wave. It's a cycle," Ayn said, her voice quivering. "The medications don't help. I've tried everything."

"Have you tried Latuda?" Dr. Tolstoy asked.

Ayn's disbelief was palpable. Tears welled up again as she spoke. "It's like the whole world is pushing me to end my life. I'm holding on to the ledge with paralyzing fear. When the emotions hit, I freeze. Then I'm paranoid, stuck in a cycle. Can't you tell me something to make it stop?"

Dr. Tolstoy sighed. "Your situation is complex."

"How?" Ayn demanded. "I don't understand. Earlier I thought it was my grades but still after a 4.0 GPA the void is still there. I've tried everything. Changing my environment, helping others, even service work—nothing works. I feel empty."

"Do you have a family history of mental illness?" Dr. Tolstoy asked.

"Not like this," Ayn said. "I was depressed when my dad had cancer, but that felt normal. This is different. It just comes out of nowhere."

"I was considering ECT for you. It might help," Dr. Tolstoy suggested.

"What about TMS?" Ayn interjected quickly. "I've read about it."

"We don't offer that here," Dr. Tolstoy said. "You'd have to be an outpatient."

"But I don't feel safe outside. The suicidal spells are too unpredictable and frequent sometimes," Ayn said, her voice rising in desperation.

"Don't worry. I'll consult with my colleagues and superiors to explore options," Dr. Tolstoy reassured her. "In the meantime, I'll prescribe a combination of Zoloft and Ativan. Zyprexa will stabilize your mood, and Ativan will address your anxiety."

Ayn nodded, her mind grasping at the faint hope these words offered. She inhaled deeply and muttered a prayer under her breath. "I feel a little better," she said, rising from her seat. "I'll go rest now." Dr. Tolstoy watched Ayn go back to bed with a poker expression on her face.

After an hour-long nap, Ayn felt restless. She found Rachel sitting with Jason, engrossed in a game of chess.

"So, she did it to you too?" Rachel said, smirking. "Judging by your face, you must have been crying. I got angry instead."

"It's like she's lost her soul," Ayn said. "She doesn't care about our emotions."

"Jake was right. Something has to be done," Rachel said, standing to hug Ayn warmly.

Meanwhile, Dr. Tolstoy approached Jake feverishly. "Jake, can we talk?" she asked.

"Sure," Jake said, glancing at Ayn before following Dr. Tolstoy. Jake walked side by side to Dr. Tolstoy, sort of expecting what was about to happen next.

Chapter 6

In the office, Jake sat in a fixed chair across from Dr. Tolstoy.

"So, what brings you back to Zion?" Dr. Tolstoy asked.

"I had an episode at my dad's house," Jake began. "I trashed the first floor mostly—holes in the walls. It felt like some entity inside me was distorting my emotions. My face… it didn't feel like mine. It felt as if someone was intruding on my privacy of what makes me me. It was as if a distorted, cartoonish face replaced it."

Dr. Tolstoy leaned forward. "That sounds terrifying. We'll try adjusting your treatment."

"Don't you get tired of saying that?" Jake snapped. "Out of all people, you know that I've tried every combination of medications. None work. Just admit you don't know how to help me."

"Jake, calm down. You're in a safe place," Dr. Tolstoy said firmly.

"No! You're not listening," Jake said, his voice rising. "Don't you have something to say to make me understand the demonic emotions that I was going through? If you don't know how to stop these voices or the rage, just say so. Don't give me empty words."

Dr. Tolstoy met his gaze. "You're dealing with schizoaffective disorder. It's a mix of bipolar disorder and schizophrenia. That explains the manic highs, depressive lows, and the rage."

"I wasn't manic or depressed," Jake countered. "Just angry. Explain that."

Dr. Tolstoy paused, searching for the right words. "Your case is unique, Jake. We'll continue exploring options to help you manage these symptoms."

You may have pent-up emotions that you're keeping deep inside of you," said Dr. Tolstoy.

Jake stood up, locking eyes with Dr. Tolstoy's poker face.

"If you believe in judgment day, I feel worse for people like you," he said before walking out of the room. He felt like crying but couldn't. The voices wouldn't let him. Even when he tried with all his might, the tears refused to come. His emotions at that moment were raw anguish—a storm of feelings he couldn't escape. He had no idea how to seek help for whatever he had.

Paranoid thoughts crept into his mind, spinning wild theories about who could be responsible for the havoc in his head. At one point, he considered the Illuminati but then dismissed the idea. "Just because someone's rich doesn't mean they're telepathic," he thought. He realized these thoughts were the seeds of delusion. While he knew he was stuck in a pickle himself, he couldn't help but feel empathy for others experiencing the same—or worse. If he got trapped in this emotional state again, how would he ever escape? Would the hospital even know how to handle it if it became acute and unrelenting?

Jake saw the crew sitting together in the common area and approached them.

"So, you went through the drill," Rachel said, her tone dripping with sarcasm.

"Something has to be done, but I just don't know what. These mental institutions are getting out of hand. We've been through this before with psychiatrists and doctors. The only thing I can think of is raising awareness. People need to know what's happening with mental health in this country. Otherwise, we'll just keep cycling in and out of these places until our minds can't take it anymore."

"I don't even know if I can give a speech about my depression," said Ayn. "It's just so damn hard when I'm having a depressive episode."

"It doesn't matter," Jake replied. "We have to try our best to help ourselves and others who are suffering. One thing is for sure: psychiatrists here need better training in therapy. They need to learn how to talk to patients who've experienced trauma. Dr. Tolstoy was basically a robot. She probably cared in the beginning but lost her soul along the way," Rachel added.

Perspective

Suddenly, Jake was hit by an overwhelming sensation. It was as if someone was simultaneously arousing him and flooding him with suicidal emotions. He kept feeling like he was at the final ejaculation act, every repetitive cycle in his mind. He prayed under his breath, begging for relief, but the feelings didn't stop. The pain was excruciating. He felt as though someone was telepathically controlling his emotions, though part of him knew it was all in his mind.

His brain refused to relax. Tactile hallucinations—or "faces," as he called them—plagued him. He tried to listen as Pedro spoke, but the words were empty sounds; they held no meaning. Concentration was impossible. Whenever he tried to force a positive thought, it twisted into something dark and negative. It felt like an entity occupied every corner of his mind, amplifying his anguish.

The voices were relentless, chanting the same phrases over and over. But it wasn't just the words—it was the emotions they carried, emotions that pushed him toward suicide. Desperate to escape, he walked to the bathroom. Yet, even there, the voices placed him on the edge of a metaphorical cliff, making him feel as though he was losing control of his own mind. He felt like a puppet manipulated by some unseen force. The paranoia was suffocating.

When it wasn't the voices, it was the hallucinations. When it wasn't the hallucinations, it was the invasive, sexual molestation feeling in his dick. And when it wasn't that, it was the image of an evil Jesus having a field day in his mind. Looking at Rachel's face, he felt an unnatural compulsion to look away. The entity controlling him no longer suggested where to direct his attention; it used brute force. If he resisted, he felt utterly humiliated—a demonic shame that tore at the core of his existence.

He tried to recall past traumatic events involving the voices but couldn't summon the details. He remembered only fragments, moments of unbearable emotional pain. He'd been to the hospital many times but couldn't piece together the entirety of his experiences. It was all too intense to grasp fully.

Jake was terrified. He wanted desperately to live but felt as though something within him was trying to push him toward suicide. He couldn't understand why. He loved his family and couldn't fathom any reason to take his own life. Yet the emotions the voices used against him were layered with complexity, saturated in despair.

"I feel like something is trying to make me end my life," Jake said, his voice trembling. "But there's no one inside me. So what's going on? I'm scared this will be my reality forever."

"Don't think like that, Jake. This may sound corny, but you're not alone," Ayn said softly. "You have to keep going. Even if it's hard, even if it feels impossible, if we do awareness speeches, we can help so many people."

"My voices get angry when I try to think about helping others," Jake admitted. "I don't know if I can be a leader. I have so many problems, I don't know what to do anymore. Deep down, I know I'm depressed, but I don't know how to suppress these suicidal emotions. I might have spent hours searching online for a fix. I've found good advice, but nothing that truly helps. I'm tired of living on the edge, moment to moment. I'm so confused. Why haven't I found the help I need?"

"We have to support each other," Rachel said firmly. "You don't have to do this alone. And yes, we're all struggling with severe mental health issues, but that doesn't mean we can't make a difference. Together, we can raise awareness and help others. And, Jake, you're stronger than you think. We've got your back."

Jake nodded, though the storm in his mind still raged. Deep down, he hoped that one day, he could find peace— not just for himself but for everyone battling the darkness.

"I don't know, you guys. I might just go to my room and sleep," said Jake.

"No, don't, Jake. What's going on with you right now can be worked through," said Pedro.

Jake hesitated, then replied, "I feel like someone is copying my face and manipulating it. I try to have a normal expression, but it's like someone's turning it into a cartoon."

"Well, I can honestly say there's nothing wrong with your face," Rachel said earnestly.

"I can vouch for that," said Pedro and Jason simultaneously.

Jake's voice grew heavier. "It's weird. It's like there's something inside me that keeps saying it's Jesus and the Devil, and they're messing with me. When I try to cry because I'm in so much pain, whatever it is inside me twists my face into anger. Then I actually feel angry and want to lash out.

"No matter what I do, it's there, saying the same things over and over. It's driving me crazy. Even when I try to think clearly, paranoid delusions come into play out of nowhere.

"And these urges to hurt myself..." He paused, swallowing hard. "They're so strong. They hurt a lot. I don't know how to stop them or even manage them. They seem to take over on their own accord. Any distress I feel gets twisted into a rage so intense it's unbearable.

"It's only by God's grace I can function as I am now. But you guys have to understand I'm going through absolute turmoil inside. I feel so paranoid, and it's so hard to shake off. I don't know when the next wave of suicidal feelings will hit."

"You're not alone," Pedro said softly. "There are others going through this, just in their own way."

Jake lowered his head into his hands, despair shadowing his face. His thoughts raced: *If something doesn't change soon inside these walls, I don't know how much hope I have left.*

Perspective

Pedro was the one who was able to comfort Jake. They seem to relate to each other a lot. Each one of them helps the other in their moments of despair. One of the things that helps Pedro get through his GRE episode and the relentless storm of racing thoughts is the simple fact that he knows he's not alone. He's seen YouTube videos, read books—stories of people who have been through the same thing, some even worse. And somehow, that knowledge settles him. He doesn't compare himself to them, doesn't fall into the trap of measuring his pain against theirs. Instead, he identifies. He understands.

And Jake helps. More than anything, Jake helps.

When Jake was first admitted to the mental hospital, the doctors told him he had bipolar disorder—the same diagnosis Pedro carries. That shared experience became a bridge between them. They trade notes, talk about what it feels like, about the days when it's unbearable and the days when it's just a whisper in the background. Jake had found solace in a book, *DBT for Bipolar Disorder*, and when he passed it on to Pedro, it was like passing on a lifeline. For the first time in a long time, Pedro felt like maybe—just maybe—things could get better.

But it wasn't just books or shared diagnoses that pushed Pedro forward. It was seeing his friends change, watching them grow stronger in ways he hadn't thought possible.

"I've got a perfect idea to get us out of our mental despair," Rachel said suddenly. "How about a game of charades?"

"That's a good idea," Pedro agreed.

Rachel walked over to Sara, the nurse monitoring the unit and taking notes of everyone in that particular unit. "I was wondering if we could play a game of charades with everyone in the hospital."

Sara gave her a kind smile. "If the activity nurse approves, it should be fine."

With a wide grin, Rachel returned to the group, who waited eagerly. Ayn, however, seemed less enthused. She sat slumped in her chair, the weight of her depression evident.

"I want to play," she muttered, "but at the same time, I don't."

Jake noticed her discomfort and moved to sit beside her. "I see you're not excited to play charades," he said gently. "I don't know if this will help, but the voices in my head don't want to play either. They just hit me with one of their prideful, suicidal blows. For a moment, I wanted to end it all.

"When I think of what I just felt, I don't even know how I'm sitting here with you guys. Usually, I'd be stuck in bed after something like that."

Ayn nodded slowly. "I've never had voices, but I know what you mean. It's like my depression takes control of my emotions completely. The tiny part of me on the sidelines that's still there just tries to survive."

Jake placed a hand on her shoulder. "Let's stick together, Ayn. I've never been connected to a group of people like I am with you guys. I know it's tough, but we have to coexist with the system to get better."

Ayn managed a small smile and leaned in to hug him.

As the activity nurse moved through the unit, asking everyone if they wanted to play, Jake sat back in his chair, reflecting. He felt a sense of pride—he had stepped up for someone else, a small victory amid the chaos within him.

Jake was surprised. He was grappling with a storm of uncomfortable feelings, like someone was twisting his emotions and exploiting his vulnerability. Despite the discomfort, he felt an unusual sense of camaraderie—a new support system made up of people just like him. They were all tired of the endless hospital visits and wanted a big change. While Jake doubted he could defeat the system, he figured he could at least make it bleed a little. He had never seen himself as a leader before, but the feeling was exhilarating. It wasn't the power of a dictator but something closer to the strength of Malcolm X—inspired, purposeful, and determined. For once, he felt like he could be one of those benevolent leaders he had read about in books or seen in movies. Still, the idea of manipulation didn't sit well with him.

After a lively game of charades, the group was in high spirits. They had stumbled through the game, laughing at their mistakes and enjoying the moment rather than focusing on how to conquer the nation's mental health crisis. Rachel's voice whispered incessantly about Jason's supposed girlfriend trying to kill her. Jason's OCD nagged him to obsess over cleaning his chair, convinced it was covered in germs. Ayn's depression crept in with flashes of suicidal ideation. Yet, despite their individual struggles, they ended the game with a shared sense of fulfillment. The activity nurse had been patient and encouraging, and the group carried that warmth into dinner, chatting and relaxing until it was time for their medications.

Jake wasn't even upset about taking his meds that night. For once, he believed he could help bring about real change in mental health care. "Something has to change," he muttered. The system wasn't all bad; some unique approaches were helping patients. Who would have thought that a group of young adults, burdened by their own mental health battles, could inspire one another to make a difference—not just within the hospital walls but possibly out in the world?

As Jake walked back to his room, the voices returned, a relentless barrage of negativity aimed at breaking him. They amplified his insecurities, trying to diminish the joy he had felt with his newfound team. Jake called the nurse to help him remove his contacts, took a shower, and lay down in bed, hoping for peace. But the voices persisted, stirring up thoughts and emotions he struggled to control. He tried using the skills he had learned in Dialectical Behavior Therapy, telling himself he didn't care about the thoughts. But the feelings were too strong, particularly the invasive, sexualized sensations that tormented him.

Perspective

Desperate to make sense of it all, Jake's mind wandered to his past. Had he been molested? He couldn't recall anything like that, unless there was a suppressed memory. Why were the voices so aggressive now? Was it some broken part of his mind, fixated on these intrusive feelings?

The voices just didn't care or maybe there was a loose screw in his mind consciously, that didn't care about anything but just getting more sex. It doesn't make sense though he already had sex. Well maybe it's the sex he wanted which didn't have to do with paying people to have sex with him. It didn't make any sense to be suffering like this on a daily basis. Anyway, I guess he had no choice. He would do the sex search like the voice wanted but also try to work through the voices and understand how they existed in his mind in the first place. Somehow, Jake fell asleep.

A nurse woke him at 5 a.m. for vitals. Annoyed, Jake snapped out of his brief reprieve, frustrated that even his dreams—his only escape—were now intruded upon. As soon as Jake opened his eyes, he could feel the different perceptions of the world around him that the voices evoked. As the nurse checked his vitals, he asked, "What can I do to make these symptoms go away?"

"What do the voices look like?" she asked.

"They look like me but devilish," Jake replied.

The nurse offered some advice, but Jake, too consumed by his turmoil, barely registered her words. The sexual emotion came that made him feel like he was being raped passed through his body. He doesn't even get a heads-up anymore, and he didn't know what the triggers were that made them come like that. It was like a part of his mind forced him to feel those sexual emotions that kept damaging his pride. He didn't know where to start to make the sensations he felt disappear.   He tried grounding techniques—naming things he could see, touch, hear, smell, and taste—but they only heightened his frustration. "The voices are winning," he thought. How could he lead this group of incredible people when he couldn't even take care of himself?

Still, hope flickered. A young patient had mentioned something called Response Relief Therapy, and Jake decided it was worth a shot. He had dismissed similar ideas before, but maybe this time, it could help. If he could just reduce his symptoms, even by half, he could be a better leader. Perhaps if he were symptom-free, he could focus on getting a job and moving out of his parents' house. But for now, he was stuck in the cycle of confusion and despair.

Chapter 7

He got up and headed to breakfast. The gang was already there, except for Ayn. "So, how did everyone sleep?" Jake asked, forcing a smile.

Jason woke up with a lingering frustration. "I slept okay, but when the vitals lady woke me up, I kept thinking about the fact that someone hadn't cleaned my room before I woke up." He was visibly irritated, his anger radiating in the small room. But as his eyes scanned the others, he noticed a shared defeat among them—each weighed down by their own struggles.

"I'm at a loss for words, my friends," he admitted. "My voices really messed with me last night. I was this close to going to the nurses' station and demanding some experimental medicine or tranquilizers to make me feel better. But I didn't. I just prayed to the man upstairs, and somehow I fell asleep."

"You'll get through it, Jake," said Ayn. "I once heard someone say that emotions like this are temporary. You're not destined to feel this way forever."

Pedro added, "Yeah, you know where this leads. That feeling we're not even supposed to mention here. It's taboo and draining. But in this place, we're not supposed to feel suicidal emotions." He chuckled bitterly. "There's supposed to be some mystic force that fights against the voices."

Rachel nodded. "That's another thing my voices talk about. They say there's some kind of mystic keeping us from going over the edge here. I don't know how it works, but they're convinced it exists."

"Too bad Zyprexa doesn't work for me anymore," Jake replied. "I'm on an Invega injection once a month, and it's useless. I only take it because my doctor insists. These psychiatrists and therapists don't help. The only time I felt real hope was at a hospital where three psychiatrists saw me at once. I don't remember exactly what they said, but it gave me just enough hope to get out of bed."

As Jake stood in the breakfast line with the others, a psychiatrist approached him from across the cafeteria. Her gait was uneven, as if she had an issue with her leg, but her face was strikingly beautiful. "Jake, can I talk with you for a moment?" she asked.

Jake followed her to a small room where he used to read. They sat down, and he immediately recognized her. He remembered the flirtation between them—her smooth voice, steady eye contact, and calming demeanor. She had a way of making him feel comfortable in his own skin, a rarity for Jake.

Their ten-minute session wasn't groundbreaking, but when it ended, Jake felt neutral—not depressed, not angry. Just a little sliver of hope. Dr. Kaytalin, with her mystical words and messed up leg, had given him enough motivation to consider trying new medication combinations, even if he doubted their effectiveness.

"Thank you," Jake said as he left. She responded with a playful retort that lingered in his mind, though he couldn't recall her exact words. The others saw her one by one, and they all agreed—she had a unique ability to instill just enough hope to get through the day.

"There's something about her," Jason said. "It's not that she's smart—it's more like she has some divine creativity or manipulation. I wish she were my therapist outside this place."

Despite the brief uplift, Jake's reality soon came crashing back. A crushing sense of disconnection overwhelmed him. It felt like someone was invading his body, manipulating his emotions with telepathy. He tried the breathing exercises his therapist had taught him, but they only made him feel as if someone else was breathing with him. The rage was suffocating, leaving him powerless.

Jake went to his room, shut the door, and lay down. The voices were back, pulling him further from reality. Whatever he had inside of him had manifested itself in complexed form. Each word echoed deeper into his psyche, tangling him in a web of despair.

"Jesus, Devil, or God," he muttered. "Take your pick. They all bring the same damage."

The thought of suicide resurfaced, though he had no plan to act on it. His last attempt had been a reckless overdose of caffeine pills—a desperate bid to either end it all or gain the clarity he craved.

Why couldn't he make peace with the voices like he once had? They used to be good friends with all the beautiful expectations for the visions. Now, most of the time, it was like an offensive beat down by the entity that made him feel less of a man, or maybe less like a human being.

He recalled a time when the voices pretended to be God. Together, they had imagined themselves web-slinging through the city like Spider-Man. It had been a blissful escape, complete with a loving wife and baby waiting for him at home. But those moments were fleeting. The voices rarely allowed him to remember the good times anymore. When God wasn't there, and it was hell. Jake had a hard time remembering the good times most of the time when he was in the damp mist of all the bad times.

There had to be a way to regain control, to outsmart his own mind. He remembered reading in a CBT book that disarrayed values could trigger problems with voices. But what values were causing this chaos? And even if he identified them, how could he change something so deeply ingrained?

Jake closed his eyes, hoping for a solution, but the only thing that greeted him was the relentless storm of his inner world.

He was told by one of the patients that he would soon see a psychologist. Maybe this time, it would be different. Patients were only allowed one visit with a psychologist during their stay at the hospital. They were always nice to him, but none had given him a definitive answer to combat the voices or whatever entity seemed to dwell in his soul.

As Jake sat alone, his thoughts wandered to the team he had agreed to lead. Were they really the "Mental Health Power Rangers" now? Did that mean he had to put his own problems aside, march up to Congress, and fight for laws to protect people with mental illness? The thought felt overwhelming. He was tired of living in constant fear—real, relentless fear. He tried to focus on regaining control of his emotions, but the effort left him drained. After 15 restless minutes, Jake gave up on napping and headed back to the common area to meet the group.

"Well, that was quick. Did you see Jesus or something?" Pedro asked with a smirk.

"No, I just saw hope. Real, powerful hope," Jake replied. "If no one helps us, we'll have to support ourselves with this little clique we've created. We're all knowledgeable and capable of making a dent in this enemy called mental illness. And for the record, I mean no disrespect to Jesus," Jake added, glancing at Pedro.

"We have to stick together, no matter what our therapists, psychiatrists, or counselors say. We need to become a collective, malleable force—something perpetual. Most of us have been through the mental health system, studied therapies, and tried medications. But something more has to come out of this group. Maybe we won't find all the answers, but we can inspire those who have the resources to do so. There are others like us who are losing hope, and we can't let that happen," Jake said.

Jason leaned forward. "So, what's the plan? Are we going to be some kind of perpetual machine, giving speeches around the country to raise awareness about mental illness?"

"We can start there, but God knows we need to do something big that actually works. This is my 15th hospital visit, and it's getting out of hand. Medicaid doesn't cover these visits anymore, and I have no idea how I'll pay for treatment that barely works," Jake said, his voice heavy with frustration. "We could also go to Congress and bring this issue to the senators and representatives. Meanwhile, we'll keep attending HVN (Hearing Voices Network) meetings, NAMI groups, yoga—anything that helps, even a little."

Jason nodded. "You're onto something, Jake. What you're saying gives me hope. Maybe we can find new ways to help—substantial ways. We're young; we have the energy to make real change."

Rachel smiled at Jason and blew him a kiss. "Right, my love?" she teased.

Jason rolled his eyes. "The only reason I'm doing this is to make real changes in the world. And for the record, Rachel, I'm not into you. That said, you're smart and definitely bring value to this group."

"Speaking of groups, what should we call ourselves?" Pedro interjected. "I was thinking something like the

Animorphs. It's kind of fitting since we've got a Jake and a Rachel, just like in the books. They were trying to save the world, too. For those who don't know, the Animorphs fought aliens called the Yeerks. These aliens would enter through your ear canal and control your mind and body. You were still there, but you couldn't move—the Yeerks did everything."

"That book was amazing," Ayn said. "Not only were they fighting aliens, but they were also battling their own fears and doubts. We're doing something similar—fighting the establishment and our inner demons. At least they won in the end."

"We'll win, too," Jake said with conviction. "I've never been this sure or excited about anything in my life. I may have a degree in electrical engineering, but advocating for something I believe in is more fulfilling than any engineering job could ever be."

"Where should we meet?" Ayn asked.

"For now, we'll stick to meeting at our parents' houses or cafes. If we grow, we'll rent an office for privacy. First, we need to understand what's already being done. Let's research what Congress is doing about mental health. Not everything they're doing is bad, but some things definitely need to change. As we help others, we'll help ourselves," Jake said.

"That's it," Ayn said. "We'll call ourselves 'The Perpetuals.' We'll keep going, running on our collective willpower. It's going to be tough. As we help others, our own problems will flare up and disrupt our goals. But we're human, not superhuman. We just have to remember that."

Rachel grinned. "I was thinking maybe we could go to a club or something after we get out of the hospital. It'll help us bond as a group."

As she gave Jake a high five, three doctors approached him. "Jake, we need to talk about what brought you to the hospital," one of them said.

Jake nodded and followed doctors into the room.

Inside, Jake noticed a professional smile from one of the doctors, Dr Real. Recognizing her from a previous visit, Jake returned the gesture. Another doctor, Dr. Bernard, observed the interaction and offered an earnest smile, seemingly pleased by the unspoken connection between Jake and the woman doctor.

Jake forced himself to refocus. *I can't let myself get distracted by this group,* he thought. *I'm here to figure out what's wrong with the mental health system so we can help.*

His emotions churned. Pure, unadulterated rage simmered beneath the surface as he struggled to process the doctors' conversations. It felt almost like an out-of-body experience.

"So, what brings you to the hospital, Jake?" Dr. Real finally asked.

Jake hesitated before speaking, his voice low but firm. "It started at night. I felt like my face was being contorted, like someone else was controlling it. I was so angry I started making holes in my dad's house. It wasn't just anger; it was rage I couldn't control. It felt like someone was infringing on my private emotions. I was terrified.

"My family was yelling at me to stop, but it sounded like they were miles away. I didn't care about the damage I was causing, the cost of repairs—none of it mattered. For a moment, my mind was clear, but then I spiraled back. Can you tell me what was happening to me, Doctor?"

Dr. Real leaned forward slightly. "It sounds like you were experiencing a mixed episode. Intrusive thoughts likely triggered it, but the symptoms also align with schizoaffective disorder. Did anything happen earlier that day to upset you?"

Jake contorted his brow, trying to recall. "I was working at Rack Room Shoes, just dealing with my usual voices. Nothing stood out. Well, there was a girl at the store—a cute one. I tried to talk to her, but she turned me down."

"You felt humiliated," Dr. Real observed.

Jake glanced at the woman doctor, and she offered a kind smile. The subtle exchange didn't go unnoticed by the other doctors, who shared a look acknowledging the quiet exchange.

Dr. Bernard broke the moment. "Your voices likely heightened your negative emotions until your usual coping mechanisms couldn't keep up," he said gently.

"You're probably right," Jake admitted. "It's hard to say exactly what was happening in my mind. If I could watch myself from the outside—see what was going on—that might help. Maybe remembering the day without all the chaos clouding my thoughts is the key."

Dr. Real nodded empathetically. "I'm sorry to ask this, but it's important. On a scale from 1 to 10, with 10 being the worst, how would you compare the episode to how you feel right now?"

Jake sighed. "During the episode, it was a 9. Talking about it now, I feel like I'm at a mixture of anger, fear, and humiliation. Maybe an 7. I can't even feel my normal face anymore. It's like someone else is manipulating it—turning me into some kind of cartoon, forcing emotions on me. And the sexual emotions… they're relentless."

Dr. Real exchanged a glance with Dr. Bernard before speaking. "After reviewing your previous files, we've noted consistent patterns. While you don't exhibit the physical rituals of OCD, your constant intrusive thoughts seem to overpower everything else in your mind. This could be a variant of OCD coupled with other underlying factors."

"It may seem like schizophrenia and OCD thoughts are taking precedence in your mind," said Dr. Real.

Perspective

"That makes sense," Jake replied. "It's probably why it's so hard for me to focus for long. My attention span is terrible now. I used to concentrate for hours, constructing my thoughts clearly. These days, I live one sentence at a time, overwhelmed by intrusive thoughts—about sex and other trivial things. I used to think it was nonsense—thinking about sex is so natural, so normal. I thought everyone thought about it. But the way my voices think about it... it's terrifying. It feels like that desire consumes everything—my family, my books. When I read, I feel as if someone's watching my private consciousness. Does that make sense? It's as if someone is observing my core emotions. Like I'm naked, my pride ripped in half, and salt is being rubbed into the wound. It hurts, and I don't know how to make it through each moment."

Jake paused, eyes wide with the weight of his words. "What do you think I should do?"

"You should continue the injection," Dr. Benard said. "Sometimes it takes four to six months for it to really start working. You need to be patient with us."

Jake shook his head. "You and I both know I've tried so many antipsychotics. I seem to have a high tolerance for them."

Dr. Benard looked sympathetic. "I'm sorry to say this, but you must continue the injection. We may also need to adjust your medication, perhaps adding some new therapies. Exposure therapy, or psychoanalysis. These intrusive thoughts seem tied to past traumatic events, events that need to be understood. A good therapist can help you process them, Jake."

Jake managed a small smile. "How do you do it? You guys always manage to give me hope. Especially you, Mr. Benard. It's incredible. You manipulate words, and somehow... it works. But I have a question. When I leave here, I always fall victim to my voices—or whatever you call this illness. If I had someone like you as my therapist outside, I don't think I'd have this problem. But they mainly want you guys for emergencies." He stood up, his voice suddenly brimming with conviction. "Well, don't worry. I'm starting an organization to tackle mental health problems in this country. It won't be as biased as what I've experienced here."

He gave the doctors a final smile before turning to leave. Dr. Real had been in the middle of a sentence about medication, but Jake was already out the door.

He walked straight to his room and lay down, hoping his voices would subside enough for him to talk to his new friends. His mind was buzzing with excitement about his organization idea. With a burst of energy, he stood and made his way to the common area, where everyone had gathered.

Upon entering, he saw a short black woman being restrained by the nurses.

"What happened?" Jake asked.

Ayn, who was nearby, spoke up. "She walked up behind Pedro and hit him in the back of the head while he was reading. Pedro got up and slapped her across the face. Then she went wild, knocking his drink to the floor."

"Pedro, are you okay?" Jake asked.

"I'm fine," Pedro said, shaking his head. I don't feel safe anymore."

Rachel chimed in, her excitement palpable. "I would've done the same thing! Nobody should be treated like that, especially with everything we're going through."

"It'll be okay, Pedro," Jason said, his face filled with anguish. "You've got to understand, we're in a mental ward. Anything can happen."

Ayn didn't share the same reactions. Unlike Rachel's enthusiasm or Jason's sympathy, she was deep in a depression spell. The world around her felt distant like there was a thick, dark cloud blocking her from reality. She struggled to feel connected to the moment, her emotions heavy with a sense of isolation.

"Will I ever feel like myself again?" she wondered silently, the weight of her emotional state pressing down. She tried to think of something to lift her spirits—TV shows, movies, familiar faces—but the depressive force weighed on her mind, making it impossible to escape. She sank into a chair, her eyes fixed on the woman who had hit Pedro.

Why can't I just be present? She thought. I should be using all five senses to take in what's happening. Five things I can see, four I can hear, three I can touch… but it all felt so far away.

But when she reached the three things she could touch, she lost her train of thought. Maybe she wondered if she could do the intense exercise, like the third tip the psychologist had mentioned. She glanced at Rachel, who was smiling right in front of her. Something about Rachel's smile made her feel better. It was a reassuring smile, as if telling her everything would be okay. Her face embodied what they were planning to do in the world—to help herself and, in turn, help others. Maybe she could stop a girl from committing suicide. Maybe she could help several girls like her—or even thousands. Who knew? She smiled back at Rachel.

"Pedro did surprise me kind of hard," Ayn said, smirking.

"So, Jake, what are we going to call our group? Something like the Animorphs?" Ayn asked.

"We'll figure that out after dinner," Jake said earnestly.

They lined up single-file and walked to the cafeteria, with Steve, the lead male nurse, leading the way. The meal was pasta, mashed potatoes, and gravy—not bad by hospital standards.

"Weird, right, Jake? I'm afraid of myself and also afraid of the people in this ward," Pedro said.

Jake nodded, grabbed his food, and sat down next to Jamie, one of the other patients. Jamie was one of the most social people in the ward. Everyone got along with him, and he got along with everyone else. He'd bring drinks to people and help push handicapped patients in wheelchairs— basically an all-around altruistic person. Jake had learned from a brief conversation that Jamie had been a counselor at a prison, gave drug-awareness speeches, and even owned his own business. Jake told him about his organization and asked if he wanted to join. Jamie didn't say no but mentioned he could come in and out to help Jake's group of freedom fighters.

"So, Jamie, what brings you to the paradise of Zion?" Jake asked.

"I had a fight with a cop. He broke my hand," Jamie said. "After they hurt me, they took me to the psych room, then moved me into a padded room with some crackheads and a transvestite. It was very weird. I ended up talking to the transvestite a little. Afterward, they put me in another padded room. I wasn't going to hurt anyone or myself. I was still mad about what the cops did to my hand, and it was hard to adjust. They left me a blanket, so I lay down on the floor and went to sleep. I was trying to figure out why I was even in the hospital. Maybe I did something wrong—I didn't remember. All I did was put trash in a can and make a fire. Next thing I knew, the cops were roughhousing me and putting me in a car. I also remember them shoving my head down, and my forehead hit the top of the car. I figured they took me here to keep me from going against them in court."

Jake listened to Jamie, then heard the nurse's assistant shout for everyone to line up to return to the common area.

"It's happening again," Jake muttered.

The voices started, accompanied by the face—first, always the face. He tried hard to think of how to explain what he was going through to the doctors and nurses, but it was difficult for anyone to understand if they were just looking at his face and not in his mind. Once he got used to the face, his mind seemed to inflict some kind of telepathic, disturbing, sexual emotion that made him want to cry. It felt like someone was molesting him—intensely, like a powerful man doing it. He tried to think about sex with a woman, but the voice inside his head would always divert his attention with powerful emotional force. One thing Jake knew for sure: the sensations were tied to humiliation and powerlessness. Those words flashed in his mind, and with them came a heavy presence within him.

"Damn," Jake whispered angrily. "The combination of medicine doesn't work at all. I can't think of anything to weaken this voice. The voice is king in my head."

Maybe he was in some sort of hell, he thought. There seemed to be no one to help with this problem. If he had schizophrenia, why didn't any of the medications work? He began to fear for his life. He couldn't live with the constant sensations of being touched and humiliated by something inside him. At least when he drank, the voices were more tolerable, and he could have some fun. The only problem was the hangover—the deep depression that followed, which made him drink again to keep the high going. He thought about how good a beer would taste right now. After getting out of Zion, he could buy a twelve-pack and spend the day watching music videos on the computer.

"I thought I was smart," he mused. "I thought these problems only happen to dumb people, not someone like me. I may not be a genius, but I'm smart enough to know what's going on... or do I? Like, if someone asked me who the President of the United States was, I'd say Obama. Hold on... Maybe he was never the president. How could someone with a last name like that be president? That doesn't make sense. This country is still run by old white men. What if I'm not in America? What if I'm in some mega mental institution and haven't realized it?"

"Damn, Jake," he scolded himself. "Don't mix facts with imagination. Of course, Obama was the President. DBT... CBT isn't really working for me anymore. It worked a little at first when I was diagnosed with bipolar disorder, but then it stopped. When I was diagnosed with schizophrenia, that's when the voices started. That's when everything changed. Another thing that doesn't make sense—why does one of my dominant voices sound like Jesus Christ? Last I heard, Jesus isn't supposed to not care for me. He's supposed to save me. Why is the Jesus in my head so evil, and why does He want me to have sex all the time?"

Sometimes, Jake would be reading a book only to see a visual hallucination or imagine a face that didn't align with his desired expression. He would feel the onset of an emotion pushing his primary instincts toward sex, trying to force him into it. He wasn't sure if it was his id, superego, or ego controlling his emotions.

One thing is certain: sex is a desire driven by the id. Perhaps it stems from primal, even barbaric, impulses buried deep in Jake's subconscious. Maybe the id harbors suppressed emotions—shame or guilt for events he doesn't want to confront—not right now. Jake often felt as though the world revolved around him, even before the voices became prevalent.

He used to believe in a bizarre conspiracy: that women were talking about having sex with him throughout the school on the internet. Standing at 6'4", with dark skin as an African American, Jake stood out in preponderantly white crowds. He always thought these impulses were merely a subconscious yearning for connection—a desire for a woman that he didn't know how to pick up for just sex. Looking back on his college days, Jake concluded it was unlikely that many people even knew who he was. He hadn't attended many parties, football games, or basketball games. The idea of being some sort of famous figure in a sexual conspiracy theory, a so-called "sexual legend," seemed absurd in hindsight.

"I'm sure some people saw my face online and recognized me when I walked certain routes back in college," Jake reflected. He, too, recognized certain women when he passed them in buildings or on pathways to class.

Still, one question haunted him and fucked up with his mental state: why had he only managed to engage in foreplay with a woman when he was 21? He graphically remembered those daily make-out sessions one semester with Becky—an Ibo woman, if he recalled correctly, from a tribe in Nigeria. Hooking up with her had been a desperate act. "I just want to be with an attractive woman," Jake thought. "Is that too much to ask?"

The prostitute he once hired didn't help. She had been naked in front of him, yet something was missing. Maybe what he craved was a "real" woman—clean, intellectual, and a little sex-crazed like him. He knew he had to address these impulses because they were constant—didn't budge like a stubborn little child. He'd be thinking about one thing, and then the entity or voice in his head would redirect his attention to emotions that made no sense.

One thing was clear: these desires existed long before the voices began.

After a long, relaxing shower, Jake found some relief when the voices stopped tormenting him. Yet he felt irritated by mundane problems—like not having floss or the right toothbrush. He decided to sleep it off, but his irritation flared again, triggered by what he perceived as a prideful move by the entity inside him.

Jake managed to finish his yoga routine and lay down in his room. He was about to pray but hesitated, frustrated by the idea of talking to a God who didn't respond. As he lay in bed, he felt a strange force on his face, as though something was plastering specific expressions onto him. It felt like someone was carving those subtle guises on his face with a little crafting knife. Simultaneously, he sensed a creeping intrusive focus on his body's private areas, as if someone was telepathically arousing him by force.

The emotions that accompanied these episodes were always the same: **humiliation, powerlessness, and pride.** Every time, he would use these three simple nouns to describe his state. With the voices taking over, Jake often felt as though his pride was being violated—a manipulation that often terrified him. Even though he always called it telepathy, he knew, deep down, it wasn't real.

Eventually, he drifted to sleep. When he woke, he went to the bathroom, washed his face, and brushed his teeth, preparing to face another day.

Jake left his bedroom and went to the nurse to put in his contacts. As he stepped into the hallway, he noticed Jason standing in line with a few others, waiting for breakfast.

"How did you sleep last night, Jason?" Jake asked.

"I slept okay. How about you?" Jason replied.

Jake hesitated for a moment, then told him the truth.

Jason nodded thoughtfully. "Well, if you ever need someone to talk to, you can ask me. What's been bothering you?"

Jake glanced away, trying to find the words. "My voice… it keeps doing stuff to my face. It's really uncomfortable. It's like they wait until I'm in a vulnerable emotional state, then they attack and make me feel like the biggest loser in the world. When I tell them to stop, it's like they just keep going. It feels like the only one who could make them stop is God."

Jason looked at him with concern but said nothing, letting Jake continue.

"Sometimes CBT slows it down a bit, but these days, the voices use the words I'm trying to force into my head. When I get to the behavior part of CBT, I get stuck between my thoughts and emotions." Jake paused, his hands fidgeting. "And then there's the thing with my head. For the past five months, it keeps going down, like I'm trying to physically dodge emotions. I have to force it back up, but when it happens constantly, I can't even breathe right."

Jason's brows contorted. "That sounds exhausting. I was just wondering, what if there were people who could do telepathy, hypothetically speaking?"

Jake shrugged. "What if there are people who can do telepathy? I've thought about that. Most of the time, the voices sound like Jesus and the Devil. Maybe Jesus didn't do miracles for people the way the Bible says. Maybe he used telepathy to help them figure out their problems. But then… Jesus wouldn't use evil tactics, right? He's supposed to be good." Jake's voice faltered. "He's there when bad things happen, though. He helps people through their problems, big or small."

Jake sighed deeply. "But I can't talk to fake Jesus like I talk to you. I can't find a compromise with the voice. It wants what it wants, whenever it wants. And when it comes, it brings… these suicidal, sexual, and intense emotions. It's like being trapped in hell."

Jason didn't interrupt, sensing Jake needed to get it all out.

"When the Devil's voice shows up, it's worse. It's constant, enraging—it is actual evil. The emotions are so intense I feel like breaking something or hurting myself. I didn't feel this way before… not four years ago, when the voices weren't as strong. But now, when I'm near a knife, and those emotions hit, I actually feel like I could cut myself or do something worse." Jake's voice cracked. "That's why I hate doing dishes at home. If those emotions come, anything could happen."

Jason leaned forward slightly. "Have you told anyone about this? Your ACT team, maybe?"

Jake nodded slowly. "Yeah, once. I called the crisis line. The counselor convinced me to go for a walk. I wasn't even a quarter mile into the neighborhood before I turned back. On the way home, I tried talking to the voices, and I must've looked like I was talking to myself. Thank God no one was around to call the police."

Jake managed a faint smile. "It's not the first time, either. Once, I was at the store, buying something, and I started talking to the voices while paying the cashier. The look she gave me…" He shook his head.

"I'm so confused, Jason. I feel powerless," Jake admitted, his voice heavy with frustration. "How's your OCD been lately?"

Jason hesitated but then managed a small, feeble smile. "It's been tough but manageable. We're all fighting our own battles, Jake. You're not alone in this."

"It was uncomfortable, but I got through it. I managed to clean the bathroom, though it was difficult because I didn't have the right tools to make a real difference. I kept feeling like if I didn't clean the bathroom after the cleaning lady did, I would die or something. But I finished it. They gave me some medicine to help me sleep because I was having a hard time knowing someone else had used this room before me," said Jason.

"They say people like us are supposed to be smart…" Jake began.

"I know what you're about to say, Jake. You feel like the dumbest person in the whole world," Jason interjected.

"I think I have some form of OCD with intrusive thoughts, but I don't have the compulsive behaviors to act on them," Jake replied.

Jake suddenly remembered someone once saying that people with their condition often have it for the rest of their lives. His face started to feel strange like someone was beneath the layers of his skin controlling it. He looked directly at Jason, but he couldn't shake off the sensation of his facial muscles changing on their own as if being in control of some robotic artificial intelligence. It felt as though some force was seeing the world through his eyes, trying to communicate through his expressions. Whatever this was, it hurt his sense of well-being. It almost felt like another person resided inside him like a parasite, feeding on his energy and thoughts and slowing claiming power over his body. Jake was turning into a mere puppet of this entity.

Jake kept imagining a confused face superimposed over his own as he talked to Jason. He had no idea how to stop the voices or the facial spasms. Before coming to the hospital, he had tried researching what the spasms might mean. He couldn't tell if he was hallucinating or if it was all in his imagination. He understood only that whatever was inside him had manifested in different forms.

Sometimes, the entity or voices would attack him seemingly at random. He tried to engage the threatening emotions in a positive way, but it was difficult. One of the voices often said, *"You are using force."* Jake never felt himself using any force—at least, none he was aware of. It seemed like a subconscious ploy he couldn't control.

The emotions felt real as if deep down, Jake himself was asking the voices for help. But their only way of helping was by hurting him emotionally, causing rage and fear. He thought, *If I could get rid of these two emotions, I'd finally be free.* There was a glimmer of hope in that realization, however small.

Chapter 8

Jake sat alone in his room, halfway through reading *A Promised Land* by Barack Obama. Staring at the cover, he saw Obama smiling, though to Jake, it resembled a Halloween pumpkin grin. Nostalgia washed over him as he remembered helping Obama win his campaign. He had gone door-to-door in his neighborhood, encouraging people to vote for Obama, even when few knew much about him.

Back then, Jake had anxiety but felt he was doing something good for the nation. Politics hadn't particularly interested him; he couldn't imagine himself as a senator or president. He just didn't have the affinity for it. The idea of power intrigued him, but he didn't care enough about the country's problems to take such a role seriously. Nowadays, he feels disillusioned by the lies in politics. When he used to fantasize about power, it felt like being drunk—wild and out of control. He would imagine his finger hovering over the red button to launch nukes at Russia. The thought made him laugh now, and something clicked in his mind.

Jake walked to the common room, where Rachel, Jason, Pedro, and Ayn were playing Uno. "You guys, I've been thinking. One of the things we need to work on is our organization's core beliefs—especially when it comes to demystifying the stigma of mental illness.

"Whenever you tell someone who's never been to a hospital about having bipolar disorder, schizophrenia, or whatever it is, their mind automatically jumps to movies, shows, or documentaries. They think it's a death sentence. That's what we need to change."

One of the challenges with mental illness is helping people relate to those experiencing it. A notable portion of the population, for example, mistakenly believes that bipolar disorder is the same as having a split personality. "When we give speeches or try to raise awareness, we must relate to the public," Jake said. "People need to understand how normal we are—we just happen to have mental health challenges."

"We should research NAMI since they're one of the biggest mental health organizations in the country," Jake continued. "I remember browsing their news section and seeing articles about people working to change legislation on mental health. Once, I read about initiatives to create housing for people who have nowhere else to stay."

"That's a good idea," Jason said. "But I think most people don't want to share a house with random strangers. For instance, I'd rather stay at my parents' house until I feel better."

Jake nodded. "One thing we really need to focus on is the precision of our messaging."

Jason hesitated. "I guess, since I'm suicidal most of the time, giving a speech can't be much worse. Still, I do feel a sense of relief when we brainstorm ways to genuinely help this country—maybe even the world—address mental health issues. If we can get on platforms like TED Talks, it would really amplify our message. We can start small and build up to larger audiences through TV and the internet."

Jake's enthusiasm was soaring. "So, you're saying we need practice? We could try joining Meetup groups that focus on public speaking or just rehearse together."

"Exactly," Rachel chimed in. "Just like how we shared our stories with each other, we should start sharing them with a larger audience. The more we practice, the better we'll get. I know we're all dealing with our own struggles—severe emotions that threaten to overwhelm us—but we can support each other as we grow this organization. For instance, I cope with voices that try to humiliate me, and Jason deals with OCD symptoms. Together, we'll keep pushing forward."

Rachel paused, her tone thoughtful. "We should encourage people to detect mental health issues early to prevent insurmountable problems later. Our organization could collaborate with scholars to share valuable information with the public."

As Rachel spoke, Jake sat quietly. His focus shifted inward as an unsettling sensation crept over him. He felt as if someone was altering his face in his mind, twisting it into a buffoonish caricature—a cartoon, basically. The intensity of the experience left him unmoored. It felt like someone was raping him telepathically, which made him embrace death right there.

"I think I'm going to my room to relax a bit," Jake murmured, standing abruptly.

Jason glanced at him, concern etched on his face. "It happened again, didn't it?" he whispered. "That... feeling?"

Jake nodded slowly. "Yeah, it hit me like a ton of bricks. When it happens, I can't do anything. I just want to close my eyes. And when it's not happening, it feels like someone is probing my emotions, searching for a weak spot to exploit."

His voice dropped, heavy with confusion. "I've never been molested, so I don't know why I feel this way—like someone is molesting me. Maybe instead of reading books on schizophrenia and OCD, I should look into books on sexuality. Sometimes, my brain is so on edge that when I stand up, I feel dizzy, like I'm about to collapse."

"I wish I knew the right words to tell myself or the thoughts that could make those sensations less intense," Jake said, his voice heavy with frustration. "The voice in my head says I use force when trying to get help. Maybe this is its way of forcing me to act."

Rachel snickered. "I'd do you if I wasn't engaged to Jason."

Jason rolled his eyes. "Who said we were getting married? Whatever... Jake, just remember, if you want to talk about anything, we're here for you. So, do these sexual emotions feel like they're tied to anyone in particular?"

Jake hesitated before answering. "It feels like a man. To be precise... it feels like it's the Devil. He only has a tiny space to help me, so instead, he hurts me. The lewd sensations are so intense I get numb and zone out. The main voices in my head are the Devil and fake Jesus Christ. And, strangely enough, the Devil seems to help me more in this jungle of a mind.

"When I get those feelings, it's as if the entity, or whatever it is, says, 'If you don't find a woman to have sex with, I'll have to do those sensations myself.' It's so intense I can feel it in my toes. What's odd is that I've never been religious—never even believed in anything like this—until I started hearing voices back in 2013.

"I started having visions of Jesus and the Devil, and they were... bizarre. What confuses me the most is how Jesus, in my mind, has to hurt me to help me. It doesn't make sense. I'm left powerless, unable to fight back. The voices are so evasive and overwhelming that I can't stop them when they attack. And those sexual pride sensations? They hurt the most. When I feel them, it's like an eternity of pain, cutting into the core of my being."

Rachel leaned forward, her tone softening. "Have you thought about talking to a sexual counselor?"

Jake nodded. "I did. When I told the counselor about the voices, she suggested I see a psychiatrist. She even looked one up for me, but that didn't help. They just prescribe medication, and it doesn't work. Once you're on antipsychotic injections, you've hit rock bottom—you've tried everything. Honestly, though, even just telling someone how I feel makes me feel a little better. But when I tell them it feels like someone is telepathically raping me... well, they don't know what to do.

"I've seen several therapists, but no one's been able to ease these emotions. Another symptom I have is this chronic second-guessing about my facial expressions. It's like someone's constantly changing my face, and when I try to express myself, I get hit by these dangerous sensations.

"Just now, while we were talking, it hit me again—like someone is toying with my prideful emotions. Pride, humiliation, powerlessness... those words haunt me. But even with all this, I still feel a sliver of hope, and I hold onto it, trying to push back against the suicidal emotions. If it weren't for these sensations, my attention span would be tenfold worse."

Jason sighed. "Well, at least we're talking about it. Jake, when you feel those emotions, try naming them: 'I feel humiliated,' or 'I feel like hurting myself.' It might help, even just a little. As for the sexual emotions... maybe you're right. Maybe because you can't find someone you're attracted to, your mind conjures that person, creating those sensations as if the voice in your head is trying to seal the deal."

"Yeah, you're right," Jason said hopefully.

"Before I leave this mental institution, I wonder if it's possible for someone to help me feel a little more normal— without all these weird emotions," Jake said.

"I would have sex with you, but it's hard for me to get in the mood. Maybe if I felt like it, I'd tell you," Ayn replied.

Everyone laughed.

"The thing is, what am I going to do to make this less potent? If I could find someone with the same thing I have—someone who could tell me what to think about or what to do—it would be great. I already had sex with a prostitute, but these emotions are still playing a demonic tune in my soul," Jake said.

"You had sex with a prostitute? Good one," Rachel said.

"I wasn't joking. I did," Jake replied.

The tech nurse called everyone to the common area. Once they gathered, she asked if anyone wanted to play charades. Jake didn't really want to play, but something hopeful in what his friends were saying made him feel more like a person.

As he sat down, he felt like someone was scanning his crotch, but he managed to be a good teammate. To his luck, Rachel, Jason, Pedro, and Ayn were on his team.

Jake could feel someone looking through his eyes at whatever he focused on, yet he still managed to enjoy playing charades with his new friends.

Afterward, dinner was served, and everyone returned to the common area to get their blood pressure checked. Ayn winked at Jake as he left for his room, and Jake smiled playfully back.

Jake stopped by the nurse's station to take out his contacts, then took a shower and did some yoga. Despite his efforts, the voices—or whatever they were—continued to unsettle him. He felt like someone was distorting his face every time he closed his eyes. The voices weren't talking much, but the unsettling emotions remained, especially in his dick.

Still, he felt a slight hope that it wouldn't last. Waiting for his medication, Jake decided to ask for an Ativan. He reasoned that it might help ease the anxiety caused by his disturbing sensations.

When the nurse arrived, Jake asked in a pleasant voice, "Can I take an Ativan with my medication?"

"That's fine," she replied.

She handed him 300 mg of Seroquel along with other pills he couldn't remember the names of.

Jake returned to his room, closed his eyes, and pressed his legs together, hoping to stop the sensation of being touched. These days, he noticed the discomfort lessened when he fell asleep.

As he lay there, the voices continued to interfere—twisting his face and leaving him uneasy—but he recognized a rhythm to his nights. The first stage was a hazy drowsiness, and then he drifted into a deeper, dreamlike state.

Jake forced himself to think about his favorite book, *The Invisible Man* by Ralph Ellison. How did Ellison write such a masterpiece without a computer? He wondered.

Jake reflected on the powerful themes of Ralph Ellison's *Invisible Man*. The protagonist's struggles and insights resonated with him, particularly the theme of race. Jake reminisced about how real it felt when he read about the racial profiling faced by Black men in society, but he also recognized the parallel crisis of mental health. He recalled a quote from the rapper The Game: "Fuck Jesse Jackson because it's not about race anymore." This reminded him of an article stating that one in four Americans struggles with depression or mental illness. The media's promotion of antidepressants felt pervasive, and he thought about the time he had taken Prozac, a drug heavily advertised on TV.

His thoughts drifted to a specific memory—the night the police stopped him. He had been running into the road in a hospital gown. Initially, he feared the officers, but their kindness quickly disarmed him. One officer's casual conversation helped calm his racing thoughts. It was a moment of surprising humanity that stayed with Jake. Perhaps, instead of trying to create a new organization, he could join an existing one and work to change it from within.

The protagonist of *Invisible Man* had genius-level insights that Jake found really cool. Although he didn't see himself as a genius, he knew he wasn't stupid. After a shower, Jake climbed into bed, and through what felt like the grace of God, he managed to fall asleep. When he woke, voices greeted him. "Hello, it's us," announced a team of psychiatrists as they entered his room. Jake waited impatiently for them to finish their introductions so he could share his side of the story. A nurse entered alongside them, handing Jake his contact lenses.

"When you first arrived, you said you wanted to die," one of the doctors began.

"I wouldn't be in a mental hospital if I didn't feel like dying," Jake replied.

As the conversation unfolded, one of the psychiatrists informed Jake that he would be discharged. While he appreciated the doctor's attempts at an inspirational speech, Jake concluded that the hospital hadn't helped him much despite scribbling down prescription after prescription. Instead, it was the friendships he had formed during his stay that gave him hope.

After the doctors left, Jake brushed his teeth and headed to the common area, where he joined his friends for breakfast. He shared the news about his impending discharge and exchanged phone numbers with four of them. They discussed staying in touch through social media and future plans. "Our fearless leader leaves us first, and we will surely follow," Rachel said with a smile.

"What's the plan when we're all out?" Pedro asked.

"We need to join NAMI and see what they're doing to support people with mental health challenges," Jake suggested. "And you should all experience HVN, the Hearing Voices Network. It's a group that could add more structure to what we're trying to achieve."

"Maybe HVN can inspire us to build something impactful," Pedro agreed.

As they spoke, Jake noticed his reflection glitching for a moment, a subtle distortion no one else seemed to see. For half a second, he felt the urge to cry but quickly composed himself.

"We have to find solutions," Jake continued. "Half of us have been hospitalized multiple times. It doesn't make sense to leave here without addressing the root causes of our struggles. Membership in NAMI is affordable, and it's a step toward creating real, lasting change."

Before the conversation could go further, a nurse approached Jake. "It's time to pack your things," she said. Jake followed her to his room, gathering his clothes and belongings into a plastic bag. As he prepared to leave, he felt a mix of hope and uncertainty about what lay ahead.

As Jake walked to his room, he felt like he was treading on eggshells. A light, sly smile crossed his face, but the entity within him twisted it into a full grin, a gesture that pierced the core of his remaining pride. Surprisingly, pride was something he still held onto.

Perspective

The nurse entered with his safety sheet, explaining it was for writing down actions he could take in dangerous situations. Jake signed it, and she added, "Jake if you ever feel overwhelmed or have acute suicidal thoughts, you know where to go. We're always here to help."

Jake paused, considering her words. It was true—they had helped him feel less suicidal during his stay. Yet, as he packed to leave, the dark thoughts lingered. He didn't feel safe.

Living with the voices in his head felt like sharing emotions with a madman. They were erratic and intrusive, often overwhelming. Jake followed the nurse to the parking lot, where his mom stood waiting by the car.

"Hey, Jake, how are you doing?" she asked.

"I'm doing okay," he lied. "Glad to be out and ready to eat some real food and get back on my phone."

As he hugged his mom, the entity tried to twist his expression into a scowl, another blow to his fragile pride.

In the car, Jake's mind raced. He thought about the voices and the four friends he'd made at the hospital. For a fleeting moment, he felt the urge to hurt himself. If there had been a knife in his hand, he wasn't sure he could resist the impulse to make it final.

Pulling out his phone, he searched for "schizophrenia" on Google. The images and terms—flat affect, hallucinations, delusions, bizarre behavior—were all familiar. On a Wikipedia page, the words *there is no cure* stared back at him in italics.

Jake couldn't accept it. He couldn't live like this—cycling in and out of hospitals. Something had to change.

He visited the NAMI website, finding information about legislation, walks for mental health awareness, and support groups. While it was reassuring, he wasn't in the mood to read further. Instead, he stepped onto his treadmill, hoping exercise might clear his mind.

In college, he could run six miles effortlessly. Now, he struggled to walk even one. The voices had eroded his confidence. He used to think he could conquer the world; now, he doubted if he could even hold his old job at Walmart.

Returning to his computer, he searched for ways to combat mental illness in the 21st century. The articles explained disorders like schizophrenia and bipolar disorder, but no one seemed to have a concrete plan for fighting them.

As he browsed, the entity invaded his body again, scanning his most private thoughts. The sensation was humiliating, leaving Jake desperate to reclaim control. Sometimes, these intrusions triggered terrifying urges to sprint to the kitchen and use that large knife his mom keeps under the cabinet to mutilate himself. The hallucinations worsened. Faces appeared, mocking him, while the voices blocked his ability to think clearly. Even when he tried to read aloud what the voices were saying, frustration consumed him. He never understood his triggers, though. He could be just chilling over an episode of Boondocks, and moments later, these obscene images would flood his mind.

His vision had also gotten worse. Before getting contacts, he'd visited an eye doctor for new glasses. After weeks of waiting, the prescription turned out to be wrong. He had to reorder using his old prescription. Still, his eyesight remained blurry.

In the days after leaving the hospital, Jake's thoughts often drifted to his new friends. Jason was the first to call.

"Hey, Big Jake! How's it going? Nice to be out, huh?"

"Yeah," Jake replied. "It's nice to be outside. So, are you sticking with the meds?"

"No," Jason said. "They tried to put me on antipsychotics, but I don't think they're the answer. I feel the same as before—except now I have a little more hope. But the suicidal thoughts? Still there, and still intense."

Jake could relate. As they talked, the entity seemed to smile at him through his own face, mocking him. How could the same voice torment him and occasionally try to comfort him? It was a riddle he couldn't solve.

"I found a NAMI meeting online," Jake said. "I was thinking we could all go—me, you, and the others. It might help."

"That's a good idea," Jason agreed. "There's also a bipolar group that meets on Tuesdays at 8 p.m. They welcome people with other mental health issues, too. The woman who runs it is a saint. She'll be glad to see me again."

Jake smiled at what he said, feeling a flicker of hope. Maybe these meetings could help him and his friends find a way forward.

Chapter 9

Ayn sat in the common area, staring blankly at the wall, trying to sort through the storm of thoughts in her mind, but clarity eluded her. Her depression felt like a phantom hovering just above her, intangible yet suffocating. Every time a positive thought tried to surface, her depression crushed it, twisting it into something dark and heavy.

She thought about Jake and Jason's departures and realized her own time at the facility was nearing its end, as her doctor had hinted. The idea weighed on her. She considered taking an extra dose of antidepressants to ease the overwhelming burden. Though the doctor had suggested antipsychotics to manage her suicidal thoughts, Ayn had refused them.

"Hey, Ayn. How's it hanging? Looks like my fiancé and Jake got discharged," Rachel said, walking toward her with an easy stride.

"I'm hanging in there," Ayn replied with a weak smile, her voice tinged with sarcasm. "Thinking about walking off a building or maybe shooting myself just to quiet these emotions. Other than that, I'm looking forward to catching up with Jake. He's kind of cute, right?"

Rachel gave her a soft smile. "Yes, he is. Tall, dark, handsome, and brave. He's a good guy."

"Yeah, but I can't have sex with him. I'm waiting until I'm married. I could be his girlfriend, but I think he wants more than that," Ayn said, shrugging. "He's nice, though. Even if he does want more, I think we could still be good friends."

Rachel nodded thoughtfully. "Yeah, he is a good guy."

Ayn stood, pulling her oversized Michael Jordan Bulls shirt into place. "I'm heading to see the doctor. Maybe he can help me deal with these negative emotions." She scanned the room feverishly, her nerves frayed, until she spotted a nurse.

"Excuse me," Ayn said, approaching the nurse. "I was wondering if I could have some medication to help me feel less depressed."

The nurse glanced at Ayn's chart. "I can give you Zyprexa or Ativan, based on what's prescribed."

Ayn hesitated but decided on the Zyprexa. The weight of her suicidal thoughts was too much to bear alone. After taking the medication, she wandered back to the common area to find Rachel but felt an overwhelming wave of drowsiness. She turned toward her room instead, the nurse's words echoing in her mind: *Zyprexa can make you feel very sleepy.*

She collapsed onto her bed and fell into a deep, unbroken sleep that stretched through most of the day. Meanwhile, Rachel sat in the common area, chatting with Pedro.

Perspective

"Pedro!" Rachel called out as she saw him.

"Hey, Rachel," Pedro replied with a grin. "You look chirpy today."

Rachel sat beside him. "The doctor said I might be able to leave soon. The weird thing is, I don't feel ready. There's still so much wrong with me. But I've been thinking about my fiancé a little less, and Jake got me interested in this organization we've been talking about in group sessions. I'm starting to wonder if our problems are so personal, so individualized, that it's impossible to solve them collectively—whether as a nation or even as a small group."

Pedro leaned back in his chair. "Well, before we set out to save the world, maybe we should focus on something fun. Soon, there's going to be a Galaxy Con in the state capital. We should all go. It'd be good to relax before we dive into world-saving plans."

Rachel laughed. "That sounds like a great idea."

Meanwhile, Ayn woke groggily, her body heavy with exhaustion. Dr. Tolstoy entered her room, clipboard in hand.

"How are you feeling?" he asked gently. "Are the suicidal thoughts easing up?"

"A little," Ayn admitted, stifling a yawn. "But I'm so tired all the time. Right now, I feel like I could sleep all day. Still, I really want to leave this place. I need to see if I can salvage my internship."

Dr. Tolstoy offered an encouraging smile. "I'm glad to hear that. We're planning to discharge you tomorrow. Does that work for you?"

"I guess," Ayn said, shrugging. "I'm not sure this place can do much more for me."

Dr. Tolstoy gave Ayn a bright smile, one that seemed to say, "Everything is going to be okay," though behind her cheerful expression, there was a flicker of something else—an unspoken warning, almost as if she was silently saying, *Your life is going to be turned upside down.*

Ayn sighed and headed to the bathroom. She brushed her teeth, splashed cold water on her face, and tried to shake off the lingering unease. Outside her room, she joined the line for breakfast and spotted Pedro ahead of her.

"When did Rachel get discharged?" Ayn asked, stepping closer.

"She left last evening," Pedro replied. "She knocked on your door to say goodbye, but you were still asleep."

Ayn frowned. "Oh, I wish I'd known. How are you feeling, Pedro? Are you ready to be discharged?"

Pedro hesitated. "Honestly, I don't feel like I'm getting any better here. The medication is helping with the racing thoughts, sure, but now I wake up and can't move. It's like some kind of sleep paralysis. I told the doctors, but they didn't really have much to say. They didn't prescribe anything for it, either. Plus, this medicine makes me feel like I want to sleep all the time."

Ayn nodded in understanding. "I know what you mean. I'm so tired all the time, too. I slept most of the day yesterday and through the night."

Ayn noticed the angry glare of the person standing behind Pedro. She didn't want to cause trouble by cutting ahead, so she moved to the back of the line. The patients, including Ayn and Pedro, shuffled into the cafeteria to grab their trays of breakfast. Pedro sat at a table with two other patients—one with a perpetually blank expression and another who had the hardened demeanor of someone who'd spent time in prison.

The next day, Ayn was discharged and finally went home. A day later, Pedro followed.

At her dad's house, Rachel stretched out on the couch, turned on *Dawson's Creek*, and idly scrolled through her phone. She'd just finished a conversation with Jason about Comic-Con when an idea struck her. She dialed Ayn's number.

"Jake wants us all to go to Comic-Con," Rachel said with a laugh. "He thinks it'll be a great way for us to bond outside the walls of the hospital."

"What's Comic-Con?" Ayn asked, curious.

"It's where people dress up as superheroes or comic characters and show off their costumes. I'm going as Supergirl."

Ayn chuckled. "I guess I'll go as Poison Ivy—or maybe Rogue from *X-Men*."

After saying their goodbyes, Rachel called Pedro to share the plan. Pedro's voice lit up with enthusiasm as he agreed. "I'll go as Batman!" he exclaimed. "I already talked to Jake, and he's dressing as Captain Picard from *Star Trek*. Oh, and Jason told me he's going as Spider-Man."

As the days passed, the group worked on their costumes. Some ordered theirs online, while others, like Jason and Jake, used Amazon. On the day of the event, Jason drove his SUV to pick up Jake.

Jake spotted Jason through the window and opened his front door, striking a playful, exaggerated pose in his Captain Picard costume. His stomach protruded slightly, and the tight fit of the costume made his chest look puffier than usual. Seeing Jason in his Spider-Man outfit brought a grin to Jake's face.

Jason's suit hugged his toned physique, the fabric outlining his defined muscles. He looked like Spider-Man straight out of the comics.

"Ready for this?" Jason asked with a smile.

"As ready as I'll ever be," Jake replied, climbing into the car. "You know, I was just thinking—it's kind of weird imagining Spider-Man or Captain Picard with a mental illness. Star Trek's one of the few shows that touches on mental health, but they usually explain it away with aliens or some kind of chemical microbes."

Jason nodded. "Yeah, true. Spider-Man has a photographic memory, but they never really show him struggling with anything like that—unless you count him talking to himself while swinging through the city."

"Don't forget about Venom," Jake added. "When Venom bonded with him, his emotions were all over the place, almost like schizophrenia. And then there's Eddie Brock—Venom amplified his darker thoughts, too."

Jason grinned. "Good point. All right, let's go pick up Rachel. She says she's going as Supergirl, and I bet she's going to look amazing."

The SUV roared to life, and the duo set off, excited to meet the rest of their group and see how the day would unfold at Comic-Con.

Jason eased the SUV to a stop in front of Rachel's house. She stood on the sidewalk, her usual air of bold confidence unshaken. Her outfit hugged her figure in a way that commanded attention, the skirt revealing long, graceful legs and the costume emphasizing her curves. Jake caught himself staring, a memory of a certain adult film flashing unbidden in his mind. He shook his head, determined to redirect his thoughts. When Rachel climbed into the back seat, her energy filled the space, momentarily pushing aside Jake's unease.

"Jake, you okay? You look... off," Rachel said, her brow contorted with concern.

Jake hesitated before responding, his voice edged with tension. "My voices... they're acting up again. It's like they're messing with my face, making it feel weird, like it's not even mine. It's humiliating."

Jason glanced at him briefly through the rearview mirror. "Your face looks fine, man. I don't see anything wrong."

Rachel chimed in, her tone reassuring. "Yeah, seriously. You look totally normal to me."

Jake exhaled, frustration lacing his words. "I already took some Benadryl, and before I left Zion, they gave me an injection of Invega. But it's still happening. I don't know how to make it stop."

Jason attempted to lighten the mood. "Well, Rachel, you do look incredible in that outfit. Total cosplay goals right there."

"I second that," Jake added, forcing a half-smile despite himself.

Rachel grinned, slipping effortlessly into character as she gave them her best Harley Quinn impression. "Thanks, boys. Now let's go pick up Pedro and Ayn. By the time we're done, we'll be the Justice League meets Marvel with a dash of Star Trek for flair."

Jake couldn't help but admire her confidence. She was stunning, yes, but she was also with Jason, and any thoughts of her beyond friendship were off-limits. He shifted his attention to Ayn instead, wondering if she might be a better match—someone who could help him navigate the strange emotions bubbling under the surface.

The next stop was Ayn's house, a sprawling estate nestled in an affluent neighborhood. When Jason called her, Ayn stepped out, moving with the deliberate poise of someone fully aware of the attention she commanded. Her curves were more understated than Rachel's, but she exuded her own quiet allure.

"Hey, guys!" Ayn greeted them, her smile radiant. "Wow, your costumes are incredible. Rachel, you're going to sweep any cosplay contest you enter tonight."

Jason gave her a mock pout. "What about my Spidey suit? Don't I get some love too?"

Ayn laughed. "I'm just kidding. You all look fantastic." She turned to Rachel, adding with a playful grin, "But seriously, Miss Sexy Poison Ivy, you're stealing the show."

Rachel laughed. "Look who's talking, Miss Seductive Poison Ivy. You're stunning."

Ayn smiled, but beneath her outward joy, a wave of emptiness surged. She knew she should feel excited about the evening ahead, but the phantom of her depression loomed, waiting to pull her down. She considered opening up to her friends but stopped herself, unwilling to burden them.

Jason, meanwhile, was managing his own challenges. His obsessive-compulsive tendencies tugged at him, but the small bottle of hand sanitizer tucked into his Spidey suit provided a comforting anchor. He focused on the positive: a fun night out with friends, immersing himself in a world of fantasy and camaraderie.

Their final stop was Pedro's house, a modest two-story home he shared with his mom and grandmother. Pedro emerged in a Batman costume inspired by *The Dark Knight*, his movements precise and deliberate, almost mechanical. The group erupted in cheers at his entrance, their admiration for his outfit obvious.

"You look amazing, Pedro," Rachel said, her enthusiasm genuine.

Pedro nodded appreciatively. "Thanks. You guys look awesome too. This is going to be epic."

With everyone assembled, Jason steered the SUV toward downtown, the excitement in the car growing as they neared the ANC Arena. The parking lot buzzed with activity, and the group stepped out one by one, falling into formation like a team of superheroes. Their mismatched Justice League-Marvel-Star Trek ensemble drew amused smiles and nods from passersby.

Jake's earlier discomfort began to melt away as he took in the vibrant atmosphere. The weight of his struggles seemed lighter, and for the first time in a while, he felt a sense of belonging. Tonight, they weren't just individuals navigating their own battles; they were a team, ready to face the night's adventures together.

As they were grooving on the music, Jake turned to Rachel and Jason. "The cost of mental healthcare in this country is insane. Most middle-class families can't afford it. People just keep going deeper into debt.

"When I was at Zion, it was $1,000 a day. I can't afford that anymore. Medicaid won't cover it, and my credit is probably ruined after fifteen hospital stays."

At first they all contorted their eyebrows on the sudden change of atmosphere. Everyone seemed to be enjoying the mellowed down environment after facing those whitewashed doctors. "My mom gave me really good insurance," Rachel said. "So I can afford it."

"Well, the rest of us can't," Jake shot back. "And it's not our fault we can't pay for hospital stays. Something has to change. They only help a little, mostly by keeping you from doing something drastic. If you're out of control, they sedate you or restrain you so you don't hurt yourself. That's it."

"You're right," Jason said. "Something has to be done. Most people can't afford these bills, insurance or not. If I could control my OCD, I would. But it's not something I can just turn off."

"I was only at Zion twice," Rachel said, "and even that one stay was expensive, even with good insurance. There has to be a better way to pay for this. The government should be doing something."

"And when you leave, the problem isn't even solved," Jake added. "You just live in fear, waiting for the next breakdown, the next trigger. I wonder if NAMI or the government is even trying to fix this—or if they even care at all."

While they were all pondering over their cause and stumbling over roadblocks, a billboard with large flashy words, "HELPLINE" passed on their way.

Jake was part of an ACT team, which includes a therapist, psychiatrist, and nurse. One of the most valuable resources available to him is the crisis line—a phone number patients can call when experiencing an emotional crisis. Jake finds this service particularly helpful. When he speaks to someone on the crisis line, whether a therapist or nurse, his voices and face hallucinations tend to lessen.

Perspective

It's as if the voices—or entities, whatever they are—recognize that this is his last resort. Jake only reaches out when things are really bad. Usually, the mental health professional begins with a grounding exercise to help him relax, such as deep breathing or identifying five things he can see and four things he can touch. They then ask if he has used any of his distress tolerance skills, like placing something cold on his face, taking a cold shower, or splashing ice water on himself to regulate his emotions.

The voices seem to believe the crisis line has mystical qualities, often whispering that it possesses some kind of power. This belief alone dials them down a notch or two. The professionals on the line are always kind, caring, and reassuring, helping Jake feel more at ease.

Once, Jake was talking to someone online about Thich Nhat Hanh, a Buddhist monk. They had a long conversation about his books and how they helped Jake feel calm, easing his nerves. Similarly, texting and speaking with counselors on the 988 Suicide & Crisis Lifeline also provides relief. Again, the voices insist the hotline is mystical. Perhaps it works because it's Jake's final line of defense against them—something he turns to when he feels truly suicidal.

Though he doesn't usually have a plan, fleeting thoughts of suicide creep in—hanging himself, shooting himself, even though he doesn't own a gun. Calling the crisis line or 988 doesn't make the voices disappear completely, but it softens them enough so he can sleep or push forward with his day.

135

Beyond professional help, opening up to friends about his voices and hallucinations also helps. They may not have the answers, but some are great listeners, offering comfort when he needs it most. One friend, in particular, shares Bible verses with him, grounding him in faith and giving him hope for the future.

Jake instantly felt a sliver of hope that finally there might be something they could do to get their cause running.

Chapter 10

After about 30 minutes, they arrived downtown at the ANC Arena, where Comic-Con was being held. Stepping out of the car, they walked in a line as the new Justice League/Avengers/Star Trek clique. As soon as they entered through the double doors, a swoosh of cold air washed over them, keeping` them cool.

Inside, the event was buzzing with excitement. Costumes were everywhere—Spider-Men, Batmen, Robins, Wonder Women, Star Trek officers, Star Wars characters, X-Men, and more. Pedro knew he was in a public event but was afraid of having an anxiety attack in front of everyone. His thoughts were structured, and he wasn't having racing thoughts, but his anxiety was peaking. He knew he looked like a pretty good Batman, and people would likely want to take pictures with him and the group.

When he got home, he thought about his episode during the GRE test a few times. He feared that somehow he was stuck in that mindset, reliving the episode. The right environmental factors had been in place during the test to trigger his anxiety, but this situation was different—he was surrounded by good friends. Reassuring himself with that fact, he walked alongside his group, weaving through the incredible costumes and superhero merchandise.

Jake, meanwhile, noticed the number of attractive women at the event but didn't want to make things awkward in front of his new friends. He also wasn't sure if Ayn would follow through on whatever pact she had made with him.

They had spoken on the phone a few times, but whenever he tried steering the conversation toward sex, she would cleverly change the subject. The day before Comic-Con, she had finally told him outright that she couldn't have sex with him because she had to be married first. Jake didn't react with anger—he wanted to maintain their friendship. He understood that Ayn was someone struggling with severe depression, and they needed someone like her in their group.

Ayn, on the other hand, saw the world through a different lens. Though she could see perfectly, it felt as if the colors of her day had been drained away. Even the most vibrant costumes seemed mundane. It felt like a shadow—her phantom—hovered over her. Thankfully, she had some pills in her pocket. She took one in the bathroom and returned to meet the group.

"You guys, let's get some pictures," Jake suggested.

He found someone to take their photo, and the man shrugged indifferently before agreeing. "Say cheese, everybody," he said.

They all smiled, though the smiles were forced. Each of them was privately thinking about their struggles.

"You guys want a beer?" Rachel asked.

Not everyone agreed, but they did decide to sit and relax. Jake and Ayn opted for sodas, while Rachel got a Corona, and Jason and Pedro ordered tall Bud Lights.

"I wonder how many people here just smoked pot. I know there are a lot of drunk people, but I wonder how many are under the influence of Miss Mary Jane," Rachel mused.

As she walked back to the table with her drink, she caught a lot of stares, though she barely noticed. Instead, she found herself wondering about Jason's motives when it came to women at the event. There were plenty of attractive women around—ones Jason would normally be interested in—but she struggled with the thought that she looked better than most of them. She took a sip of her beer and hugged Jason tightly.

"Just like old times, huh?" she said.

"Yeah, whatever makes you feel good, Rachel. I'm tired of fighting you," Jason replied.

Jason rubbed Rachel's shoulder, making her smile widely, almost like Harley Quinn from *Suicide Squad*.

"So, there's this bipolar disorder support group that meets every Tuesday. I want all of us to attend, even though only one of us has been diagnosed with bipolar disorder. We should take notes and pay attention to the discussions. It's a good group—I used to go before I started hearing voices," Jake explained. "The lady who runs it has bipolar I, just like Pedro."

Jake could never forget how he had treated a woman with schizophrenia at a past meeting before he, himself, had started hearing voices. She had approached him after the session, confiding in him about her hallucinations, but he had panicked and walked away. It felt like karma had come full circle.

Jake had noticed that when he was occupied with leadership responsibilities, his voices became quieter, less aggressive. He tried to think more about it, but as soon as he focused on how the voices tormented him, he saw a fleeting hallucination—a distorted face. He had come to believe the voice wasn't just in his head but part of a larger entity. When speaking to his psychiatrist, he would simply say, "I see hallucinations."

"I wonder how many people here have depression," Ayn murmured.

"I wonder how many people hear voices. There's got to be a lot of supposedly depressed people in this country," Jake added.

Just then, a man dressed as a Cardassian from *Star Trek* walked past, holding hands with a woman in a Uhura costume. Jake nodded toward a random man. "Maybe he has schizophrenia. You can never tell—it's not like people walk around with labels saying 'I'm depressed' or 'I hear voices.'"

"I hate the word schizophrenia—it sounds disgusting," Rachel said with a quirky smile.

The Cardassian cosplayer approached Rachel, asking for her number. She simply smiled and glanced at Jason, silently signaling that she was taken.

"That's the third person today who's asked for your number," Jason noted.

"Well, it's not like we're walking around holding hands or anything," Rachel teased.

She smiled at Jason. "I'm still in love with you, hubby."

"I'm more in love with your body," Jason admitted bluntly.

Pedro cut in, steering the conversation away from Jason and Rachel's drama. "It would be cool if we had a booth to recruit people for our club."

They got up and wandered around the event as a group. Jake started to notice something strange—his head was subtly moving up and down involuntarily. As they walked past a man, Jake's head dipped slightly, and the man nodded back, as if acknowledging him. The movement was subtle, but it reminded Jake of the time he had involuntarily nodded at a man inside a place called *Massage Envy*.

Then, an unsettling sensation crept over him—a strange pressure in his lower body, as if someone was trying to invade his mind. It felt like a telepathic attack, a mental violation. He grimaced but didn't say anything. He was tired of telling the group about his symptoms. No one said anything about his discomfort, but he figured they all had their own struggles.

Would he still be strong if he admitted he wanted to leave? The thought lingered, but instead of voicing it, he excused himself and went to the bathroom, where he took a propranolol pill.

Usually, it takes about 20 minutes for the drug to take effect. So, he does something he has done a few times when he's in a rut with the voices—he goes to the toilet, gets down on his knees, and prays to God to ease his symptoms. He doesn't feel anything immediately, but a thought crosses his mind: *If I have an episode here, at least I'm among friends. And maybe this will push me to do something about the mental health problem in this country.*

He really doesn't want to go back to the hospital, but his thoughts keep intruding, popping in and out of nowhere. *The annoying thing,* Jake thinks, *is that I don't feel safe at all at Comic-Con. I feel like I'm standing at the edge of a cliff.*

"You guys ready to get out of here?" Jake asks.

They all nod in agreement. As they walk through the crowd as a group, one last person asks Rachel for her phone number. She declines and continues outside with the others.

Meanwhile, Pedro sees a vivid image of himself hanging from a tree in his mother's yard. The thought triggers an onslaught of racing, suicidal thoughts.

"You guys mind if I go to the bathroom?" Pedro asks.

They acknowledge him, and he heads inside, popping a Zyprexa in his mouth.

"Jason, can you take me home first? I feel like I'm in the middle of an attack," Pedro says.

In the car, he tries to focus on a single object, but his mind won't cooperate. He feels like his head is jerking around unnaturally, like a chicken, as if he's trapped in some paranormal state. The moment he gets home, he rushes to his room and takes more medicine. About thirty minutes later, he feels a little calmer and lies down in bed.

How is it that my entire life revolves around pills just to ground me back to reality? he wonders. *If there were a war or something and no one was making these medications, I'd be royally fucked.*

"You guys think we can pull off this organization?" Ayn asks. "Because I'm pretty sure Pedro wasn't the only one having problems at Galaxy-Con."

Everyone agrees.

"We can do this. Everyone should go see their psychiatrist, and then we'll meet again at the bipolar disorder group to discuss our organization. And when you talk to your psychiatrist, don't dismiss everything they say. I'm sure they'll tell you both good and bad stuff. They usually don't know what to say when someone keeps going in and out of mental hospitals."

Pedro walks into the clinic. The psychiatrist, Dr. Beck, stares at him uncomfortably. After the usual formalities, he says, "I thought I had an attack at Comic-Con, but that's getting ahead of myself. I don't even know where to start."

He exhales and runs a hand through his hair.

"I was about to take the GRE when I started having these racing thoughts that scared me. They weren't tangible—just rapid, chaotic. It started before I even went inside to take the test. I sat down, picked up my pencil to fill out my name, but my hand was shaking so badly. With patience, I managed to bubble in my name and birthdate, but I knew at that rate I wouldn't finish the test. It took me almost five minutes just to write my name.

I started to panic.

I had done so many practice tests at home—I was ready. But when the real test was in front of me, I couldn't even read a full sentence and understand it. I got up, and suddenly, my whole body locked up. My back went stiff, my arms stretched out like a robot, and I started shaking and gasping for air like something was constricting my throat. After that, everything became a blur. I remember the facilitator trying to calm me down. Eventually, I managed to control my breathing, and when I got to Zion Hospital in the ambulance, I was able to settle."

"That was a manic attack," Dr. Beck says. "Classic bipolar symptoms. Racing thoughts that spiral out of control."

Pedro feels a thought pass through his mind: *If my brain could think that fast but in a structured way, maybe I would've aced that test.* He immediately shakes it off. *No, I'd rather have slow, normal thoughts than this chaotic mess.*

"The pills seem to be working," he admits. "I thought I was going to have a full-blown episode at Comic-Con. The only problem is that when I wake up after taking them, I can't move. It's terrifying. I'm considering taking sleeping pills or something else in case I get those racing thoughts again."

"That's not a good idea," Dr. Beck says firmly. "If you have a psychotic break, you need antipsychotic medication to combat it."

Pedro clenches his jaw. "Is there another medication I can take instead of Zyprexa? Something with the same effect but without the side effects? I don't want to wake up paralyzed."

"You should stay on the medicine," Dr. Beck insists. "Every medication has side effects."

"Have you been listening to anything I've said?" Pedro snaps. "I *can't move* when I wake up. It's terrifying. Is there an alternative or not?"

"If you don't stay calm, you'll end up back in Zion," Dr. Beck warns.

Pedro glares at her, his fists tightening. He's about to explode but forces himself to sit back down.

"Fine," he says through clenched teeth. "I'm calm. I'm asking again—very gently—is there *anything else* I can take?"

Dr. Beck sighs. "You can try Seroquel. I'll write you a prescription. But if you experience acute anger like you did just now, don't hesitate to go back to Zyprexa."

Pedro exhales in utter defeat. He sticks with Dr. Beck for now because she's the only psychiatrist his mother can afford.

Whatever.

He walks outside, the heat hitting his face as he drives home, trying to think of a way to get another doctor. Nothing comes to mind. He remembers searching with the social worker at Zion—this is the only doctor who takes his insurance.

Frustrated, he picks up the phone and calls Jake.

"These psychiatrists are insane. They don't listen," Pedro vents. "I guess they just want to slap a label on me, shut me up, and make me take the meds. And they especially don't give a fuck when they're not the ones paying the bill.

Anyway, I'm looking forward to this bipolar disorder meeting. It'll be good to see what other people are doing to cope."

"I suggest you buy *DBT for Bipolar Disorder*," Jake says. "It's a good book on mindfulness and distress tolerance. Helped me before my bipolar got worse and turned into schizophrenia. Man, I *hate* that word."

"I hate the word *bipolar* too, but I guess I'm stuck with it until someone finds a way to change my DNA with a pill," Pedro mutters. "The doctor at Zion actually said something about my DNA being responsible for these symptoms."

"That's funny," Jake says. "My psychiatrist's name is Beck too."

"Good luck," Pedro scoffs. "Don't let her get under your skin. She'll make you lose yourself in rage."

Jake goes upstairs and has dinner with his family.

Jake's family was from Washington, D.C., and had lived in the district since he was five years old. His dad taught algebra at the community college, and his mom was a registered nurse. When he was a kid, his parents argued aggressively, but they calmed down once he went to college. He majored in electrical engineering.

As he sat at the table, he felt like there was a sixth presence there—something unseen but oppressive. None of his family members asked about the mental hospital or what had happened. Almost as soon as he sat down for dinner, his aunt called. She spoke unusually slowly, enunciating each word carefully. Jake's anger flared—she must think he was completely crazy. Midway through the conversation, frustration boiled over.

"I'm tired, Auntie. I'm about to eat dinner and go to sleep," he said curtly, cutting the call short.

He was certain someone in the family had told her about his hospital stay. He wanted to express his anger openly, but he held it in. He knew that if he showed too much emotion, the entity lurking inside him would make him feel unbearably uncomfortable. His voices tended to attack him when he was engaged in something—and also) when he was idle or about to sleep.

"My voices are making me really uncomfortable," Jake muttered. "Why do I keep getting these weird sexual emotions, like someone is violating me telepathically? I've never been raped before."

"If you feel that way, go to the downstairs bathroom and masturbate," his mother suggested bluntly.

"I've tried that," Jake said, frustrated. "But the voices make it impossible. They don't stop. They just start right back up again. Can you imagine trying to masturbate while a male voice is in your head, watching you?"

Perspective

His voices always seemed to take advantage of moments when he was feeling better, only to return and drain the life out of him. He didn't know what to do.

After dinner, he took a shower and went to his room, only to notice shattered glass on his table. His mind raced. The voices kept telling him to cut himself. What if one of them took over his body? What if he walked up to that glass and attacked himself? The mix of suicidal and intrusive sexual contorted feelings overwhelmed him, making him momentarily forget where he was.

"Why can't these doctors fucking help me?!" he screamed, his voice raw and desperate.

His mother rushed to his door. "Jake, do you want to take a Zyprexa?" she asked cautiously.

"I already did! It doesn't do anything. My voices don't react to antipsychotics anymore."

"Well, I'm not taking you back to the hospital. They don't help," she said firmly.

"So what the fuck am I supposed to do?" Jake yelled.

"You could take propranolol as a PRN. If you take it with the Zyprexa, the combination might help."

Jake hesitated but decided to try it. Before swallowing the pill, he prayed. *God, please make these feelings stop.*

He wasn't sure if it was the medication or the prayer, but after a while, the voices backed off, giving him a brief moment of relief. He dozed off, but before sleep took him completely, an intrusive thought crept in—*What would it feel like to slit my wrists?* He had never done it before. Would it distract from the sensations the voices inflicted on him? He didn't know.

But somehow, he made it through the night.

The next morning, his nurse arrived at the house to administer his injection. She was attractive, but Jake had already asked if she was married. The pretty ones usually were. She quickly gave him the shot and left.

His next stop was the hospital to see his psychiatrist. Running five minutes late, he parked his 2001 Nissan and hurried inside. He had seen different psychiatrists over the years but had recently returned to Dr. Beck. In the end, he figured it didn't matter who he saw—real help always seemed out of reach unless you had money.

After checking in at the front desk, he was called in to see Dr. Beck. She was slim, with a serious, unreadable expression—a poker face. She gestured for him to sit.

"So, what happened that led to the hospital, Zion?" she asked, her tone brisk, as if she already knew the answer.

Jake exhaled. "I was trying to sleep, but the voices kept humiliating me. I got out of bed and trashed the downstairs. I was about to do the same upstairs, but my dad stopped me.

I remember looking in the mirror and seeing my face—it wasn't mine. It looked… cartoonish. I punched the walls and cut my knuckles.

"Before that, I'd tried all sorts of medications with my last psychiatrist, and nothing worked. And please, don't tell me to try some combination of pills. I've tried antipsychotics, antidepressants, anxiety meds. If one doesn't work, a combo isn't going to either."

Dr. Beck's lips tightened. "I'm the psychiatrist here, Jake. I went to school for several years to do this."

Jake ignored her comment. "Most days, I feel like someone is telepathically touching me sexually—forcing it. It's mixed with these suicidal emotions. The entire time I was in the hospital, it felt like I was being raped. And it… it hurt to the core of who I am."

As he spoke, a wave of emotion hit him, a familiar and violent sensation. The rape feeling came first, then the face distortion—like someone wanted to humiliate him again. The sexual intrusion was brief this time, but the humiliation lingered.

Dr. Beck studied him carefully. "If there were a magic pill to fix everything, I'd give it to you, but there isn't. What did your therapist say?"

"She gave me TIP skills—temperature change, intense exercise, paced breathing. The ice packs help sometimes, but I can't exactly carry an ice pack with me everywhere I go."

Dr. Beck nodded. "How's your love life? I remember you saying you watched *The Original Star Trek*. You thought the Black woman in it was beautiful."

"Yeah, Uhura—Nichelle Nichols. She was beautiful."

Jake hesitated, then added, "My voices talk about sex all the time. It's like that's all they care about. I had sex last year, but I think what they want is for me to sleep with someone I'm actually attracted to. Maybe they want me to pursue a woman, not just pay for it."

Dr. Beck leaned forward slightly. "And the voices themselves? Who are they?"

"The main ones are fake Jesus and the Devil," Jake admitted. "Sometimes, they act like they're challenging me. It's terrifying. The Jesus voice is the worst—he's the most aggressive. Yesterday, he tried to force me to cut myself. It scared the hell out of me.

"The thing is, no one even knows what Jesus really looks like. But when that particular emotion hits, it's overwhelming. It's more than a voice. It's like... pure terror."

Dr. Beck nodded but said nothing. Jake stared at her, waiting for an answer he knew she wouldn't have.

"Is there any time when they're not that bad? I mean, to the point where you feel at peace with them?" asked Dr. Beck.

"Sometimes I laugh at them, but only when I feel on equal footing with them. Most of the time, they scare me and make me feel rageful. As soon as I wake up or right before I fall asleep, they're there. The only time I don't see them is when I'm in deep sleep.

When I was taking Saphris, I had weird, paranoid, detailed dreams. Since I stopped drinking, I've experienced a spectrum of emotions—good and bad. Most of the time when I drink, I feel fine, but those rage emotions are terrifying when they hit. It's like I could do anything when I'm that angry. Even right now, I feel rageful—mostly in a powerless way," said Jake.

"Do you feel like hurting yourself or someone else?" asked Dr. Beck.

"I feel like hurting myself a little, but not anyone else." Jake hesitated. "What about ECT? Could that work?"

"That's usually for people with acute depression—so severe that they can't get out of bed or even shower," Dr. Beck explained.

"Well, I feel depressed because of my voices. But anyway, I probably won't do it—I don't want permanent brain damage."

"I haven't ruled it out," Dr. Beck said. "You could still consider it. I was thinking—why don't you try a low dose of Clozapine? It could help with the voices without causing too much slurred speech."

"I already tried a low dose with my previous psychiatrist. Don't you have my records?" Jake's face tensed with frustration.

"Oh, okay. I'll talk to your therapist from the previous ACT team and find out what you haven't tried yet. Have you been eating alright?"

"Yes, but I've been gaining a lot of weight. I'm 6'4" and 304 pounds. When I jog, my voices get louder—they're very powerful. The last time I jogged was a year ago. Whenever I do vigorous exercise, they strike back," Jake admitted.

Dr. Beck's expression changed. "Do you have any guns in the house?" she asked, alarmed.

Jake didn't like the way she asked. He lowered his gaze while she studied his face. Without making eye contact, he picked up his prescription and left.

For some reason, his voices gave him nostalgia. It was rare, but every now and then, he thought about the good times he had with them. It was all part of a certain frame of mind he sometimes fell into, and Jake felt like he had no choice but to follow those thoughts.

He remembered when the voices used to play God— how they would act out scenes of him being Spider-Man in his imagination. It almost felt like heaven. Back then, he would have visions—glimpses of the future—that filled him with excitement. He believed them. He was certain he would get a big job. The voices promised that once the vision came true, they would disappear.

But the job never came.

Then the voices shifted. They told him he would meet the love of his life—his soulmate—at a *Bath & Body Works* near his town. But that didn't happen either.

They told him not to think about time when it came to these visions.

For years, Jake leaned on the voices. They reassured him that they'd disappear soon, and he believed them. But they never did.

Eventually, their promises changed. They told him he needed to find sex—any kind of sex—and then they would go away. That became his new mission.

During that time, Jake was drinking every day with a college friend. They went to bars constantly, chasing women. His friend had his own apartment and slept with women all the time, so Jake convinced himself that was the missing piece—his own place. He believed, because of the voices, that he didn't need a job, a car, or an apartment. The only thing that mattered was sex.

When the voices first started in 2013, they convinced him he would have two sons—one would be a comedian, the other would go to Harvard and drop out to land a high-powered job. They even described his future wife: a woman with a lazy eye, a nice ass, and a gentle heart.

But in the present, thinking back on all those visions, Jake didn't even feel angry anymore.

He was still hearing voices. He had part-time jobs—one at Rack Room Shoes, another at Walmart. He also worked for a low-end IT facility. That job was hell. It wasn't the prestigious job the voices had promised, but it was *something*.

At work, he spent most of his time talking to the voices in his cubicle, waiting for customers to call for help with their computers. His main task was password resets. That was all his mind could handle. His supervisor routed all password reset calls to him. Even then, he struggled.

The only good thing about the voices back in 2016 was that when he talked to women, they stayed quiet. There was one time he went on a date with a woman he found hideous, and the voices were silent the whole night.

These days, though, the voices wanted him to kill himself for no reason at all. Sometimes they changed when he spoke to women, but not as often anymore.

Jake had been in the hospital so many times he lost count. He would have to call the mental hospital just to find out how many times he had been admitted.

As soon as Jake got home, he picked up his phone and called Ayn.

She answered cheerfully, her voice a small comfort. They talked about his session with Dr. Beck, and she made him feel a little better.

Ayn had an appointment with Mr. Carey the next day.

"Is there anything I should say to the psychiatrist that I might forget?" she asked.

"Just tell the truth," Jake said. "Nothing but the truth. Even if you think it'll get you sent to the mental hospital or jail—just tell the truth."

Ayn puts on black spandex pants and a tight T-shirt in the morning. She goes through her usual routine, no different from any other red-blooded American woman. She flosses, brushes her teeth, and eats very little—just some eggs her uncle made. Then she gets in the car and heads into town to see her psychiatrist.

All the while, the suicidal phantom hovers around her, creeping into her thoughts. It's almost as if Death himself is enjoying his time lingering over her. Unlike Rachel and Jake, she doesn't hear voices or see things, but she feels an overwhelming sense of despair. She pops her antidepressant medication into her mouth, stops at a gas station, and buys an orange juice to wash it down.

She's a little early for her appointment, so she pulls out her phone and goes on YouTube. She searches *how to make a noose* and starts watching a video. Halfway through, fear grips her, and she stops. *All I need to do is buy a gun*, she thinks. *A shot to the head would be quick—no pain.* But then another thought interrupts: *My friends are counting on me. They're dealing with their own struggles too.*

When she arrives at the psychiatric office, Dr. Carey steps into the waiting area. "Hey, how are you doing, Miss ______? You can come in now."

His face reminds her of Jim Carrey, and in the beginning, he always treats her kindly.

She sits down, shifting slightly in her seat. "I feel this huge cloud of emotion over me. I can't ignore it. It's like this weird kind of depression. The phantom just... sucks all the happiness out of me and makes me feel like a loser."

Dr. Carey leans forward, his voice earnest. "Do you feel like hurting yourself or anyone else right now?"

Ayn stares at the floor. "I feel like committing suicide," she admits. "Right before I came in, I was looking up ways to kill myself on YouTube."

Dr. Carey exhales, nodding as he flips through her records. "I've been reviewing your case, and I want to recommend TMS or ECT. One of these therapies might help. Both are relatively safe. With ECT, you could experience some short-term memory loss, but it's usually mild. We give medication to help manage any side effects."

"I'll do it," Ayn says. "Whichever one is safest. I don't have many options."

She smirks slightly but doesn't let herself smile too much. *The phantom would only suck it away,* she thinks, *humiliating me, always wanting more.*

As soon as she leaves Dr. Carey's office, she calls Jake.

"So, it looks like I'm going to do TMS or ECT," she says.

"I heard they're both good. Actually, I've been considering ECT myself because my voices make me really depressed," Jake replies.

"Talk to your psychiatrist about it," Ayn suggests.

"I tried, but they said I'm not severely depressed enough," Jake says bitterly.

Ayn sighs. "Well, I'm going to bed. I've salvaged what I can out of this internship."

"Yeah," Jake mutters. "Might as well sleep, I guess."

Chapter 11

Jason woke at eight o'clock on the dot. He had a meeting with his psychiatrist and wouldn't miss it for the world. Before heading out, he cleaned his toilet, scrubbing every nook and cranny, and wiped his room three times over. It was like a little workout session for him. Then, he got into his SUV and drove into town to see Dr. Applegate.

He wasn't sure what to tell her. The medications weren't working at all. In fact, he seemed completely resistant to them. They only made him feel slower. He arrived a little earlier than expected, and before turning the doorknob, he sprayed his hands with antibacterial cream. He always sanitized his hands after touching any doorknob.

When he sat down in the waiting area, Dr. Applegate appeared at the door and invited him inside. Jason gripped his hand sanitizer tightly, just in case. He had been here before and already knowing his diagnosis—OCD. As he settled onto the comfy couch, he tried to gather his thoughts. He was determined to tell Dr. Applegate everything without holding back.

Dr. Applegate sat down next to him.

"Hey, Jason. I hope all is going well. I'm sorry, but it's mandatory for me to ask you this..." she began.

"I don't feel like hurting myself when I'm mostly doing my rituals," Jason interjected quickly.

"I still have to ask—do you feel like hurting yourself or anyone else right now?"

"Myself, a little," Jason admitted.

"What do you mean by a little'?" Dr. Applegate pressed.

"Every now and then, I think about it. Sometimes, it even makes me feel a little better. I think it's because if I touch something dirty, I could get germs and die," Jason explained.

"I need you to tell me, from beginning to end, what exactly happened at the gym?" Dr. Applegate asked.

Jason met her gaze seriously, and the entire episode flashed right before his eyes. He recounted the entire story— how he had gotten into a fight and how he had double-cleaned the exercise machines before using them. As he described cleaning the equipment, his face exaggerated the intensity of his words.

"So, when did you first start feeling suicidal?" Dr. Applegate asked.

"When the guy told me he had already cleaned the machine. I felt like hitting him or hurting myself at the same time," Jason admitted.

"Have you ever tried Zyprexa?" Dr. Applegate asked.

"Why are doctors always so eager to prescribe antipsychotics?" Jason scoffed. "To answer your question, yes, I've taken it before. It makes me feel sleepy more often, but I still do my rituals. See? I even know some of your terminology—'ritual.' That's it. Yeah, I haven't fought anyone since high school."

"Do you know why you have OCD?" Dr. Applegate inquired.

"If I did, I wouldn't be here. Your guess is as good as mine," Jason replied.

"Some people have an idea of why they developed OCD..." Dr. Applegate trailed off. "I'll just increase your dose of Prozac."

"Aren't you supposed to connect dots in my life? Trace something back to when I was a kid to figure out why I'm such a clean freak?" Jason asked.

"Not unless you have anything to tell me today. I got a message from the doctor inside Zion, and he said you were doing okay, except for taking five showers a day and repeatedly cleaning the toilet with shampoo," Dr. Applegate responded.

"That wasn't helpful. I guess you lost your soul when you stopped caring about people's lives," Jason muttered.

To his surprise, Dr. Applegate simply smiled—a wide, unsettling grin stretching from cheek to cheek, almost villainous.

Jason left the office flabbergasted. He drove straight home and called Jake, who was at his house.

"Oh my god, man, I think there is a serious problem with healthcare in this country. This psychiatrist was terrible. I've seen her three times before today, but she's not helping at all. I am starting to believe that these people are completely devoid of souls. She just keeps asking if I'm a danger to myself or someone else before every session."

"I kinda told her I'm a danger to myself, and she didn't even acknowledge it. It felt like my words went right through her head. Then, in the end, she did something really evil—she smiled after I called her useless like she had me trapped. And my parents pay for this expensive-ass insurance." Jason sighed. "The only way I can stay in the house is if I keep doing what Dr. Applegate wants. At least, that's what the people I live with say. It's really scary when you think about it."

"My psychiatrist, Dr. Beck, was on that same bullshit. Pedro and Ayn said the same thing," said Jake. "The last person left is Rachel. She's seeing Dr. Camus at the edge of town." He glanced at his phone. "She's blowing up my phone as we speak."

"Later, man."

"Later."

Jason stared at Rachel's incoming call but didn't pick up. He thought about how beautiful she was, even though her accusations about him and other women were a little crazy. With a sigh, he switched off his phone and went through his nightly rituals before sleep.

Rachel woke up to a bright morning. She had stayed up late the night before, hitting the gym and watching *Star Trek*. She recalled Jake showing up at Comic-Con last week and wanted to brush up on her *Next Generation* knowledge.

At the gym, some guy had tried to get her number—it happened all the time. She knew she looked like a Victoria's Secret model with curves. But she brushed him off, thinking she'd reconnect with Jason eventually as the group kept meeting.

Afterward, she went home, took a shower, and drove to Dr. Camus's office, about twenty minutes away. Rachel dealt with paranoia and heard voices, though the paranoia only surfaced when she was deep in thought about Jason. Most of the voices were about him. Occasionally, she didn't hear them at all, but when they did come, they were cruel. More and more, she was beginning to believe they were tied to something deep inside her. She wanted to talk to Dr. Camus about the aggression in the voices rather than just the paranoia—she felt there was a connection.

The next day, Jake called everyone in the group to remind them about the bipolar disorder meeting that evening. Even though not everyone in the group had bipolar disorder, they figured the meeting could still be helpful.

That night, Jake arrived first at the church where the meeting was being held. The building, constructed in the late 1980s, had a distinct Catholic feel. He introduced himself to the group leader, Caroline, who welcomed him warmly.

Jake had attended countless meetings—both online and in person—but tonight, he was curious to see how his new friends would react.

Caroline called the room to order and had everyone introduce themselves.

After everyone introduces themselves, Rachel follows suit. Caroline smiles warmly at the group. After a long hesitation, she says, "The floor is open to share your experiences, Jake."

Jake looks at Caroline, who meets his gaze with full eye contact. "I guess I'll start. Just in case nobody heard before, I'm Jake. I've been told I have schizoaffective disorder—or at least that's what the doctor at the mental hospital diagnosed me with. But I think it's something worse."

He pauses before continuing. "I constantly hear voices—fake Jesus Christ and the Devil. They talk to me all the time. Sometimes, it's good, but mostly, it's bad. Their voices come in rhythmic intervals, and as time passes, the gaps between them grow longer.

"Sometimes, I feel like someone is telepathically raping me. It's painful—a forced emotion trying to induce arousal, but instead, it makes me feel suicidal. It's like an evil version of Jesus Christ is violating my mind. It's disturbing and confusing. The only way I slow it down is by saying mini prayers or repeating the voices out loud.

"The voices are forgetful, manipulative, and prideful. They mock me constantly. The Jesus voice sounds like someone speaking in a stadium—powerful, profound. Satan's voice sounds exactly how you'd expect it to. Sometimes, whatever this entity is inside me restricts my breathing, making me feel like I'm suffocating.

"I also feel like my face is constantly being distorted as if someone is using immense force to contort my expressions. There are moments throughout the day when my facial emotions seem to be in conflict. The doctor in Zion called it 'tactile hallucinations.'

Jake looks around the room. "I'm really glad to see you all again. It's been a long time. I have a question for the group: Does anyone else experience conflicting voices of Jesus and the Devil? And if so, how do you control it?"

Jeremy responds first. "Well, I assume you've prayed and read the Bible, but they're still there?"

"I've read the whole Bible, and nothing has changed," Jake admits. "Sometimes, while I'm reading, I hear a voice claiming to be God. I pray on my knees every morning and night, begging for these voices and emotions to disappear, but they don't. If anything, they get worse." He sighs. "I'm starting to think it's more psychological."

"What about when you talk to people, read, sing, or exercise?" Jeremy asks.

"They still find a way to manifest," Jake says. "They use my face instead." He shrugs. "Thanks for the advice, though."

Just then, Jason and Pedro enter quietly. Pedro wears a T-shirt with an ape on the front, paired with Nike basketball pants. Jason wears a Ralph Lauren shirt with brown khakis. Jake shifts his attention to the window for a moment, taking in the clear blue sky and the warmth of the sun. It's incredible how beautiful the day looks while inside my head, it's like hell on earth.

He glances at Jason and Pedro, nodding in acknowledgment. As he scans the room, he wonders how many others here struggle with auditory hallucinations as intense as his. He recalls all the dead ends he's faced in the bipolar disorder network and sighs.

In despair, he sighs at the thought that there may be no cure for his voice problem at all. If that's the case, he can't fathom what it would be like to live forever with these demonic voices in his head. Jake diverts his attention to the middle-aged man speaking—Andrew. He missed the beginning of Andrew's story but quickly realizes he's describing a recent episode.

"I just put my head down and tried to block out what the voice was saying. It sounded just like the Devil himself, telling me to do things I didn't want to do," Andrew says. "The voice kept telling me to smack my wife across the face for lying about where she was yesterday. I thought she had to be cheating on me. I called the gym—she wasn't there. I called the arts and crafts place, but she wasn't there either. I even called a couple of her friends, but none of them had seen her.

"The voice, in this deep, baritone tone, kept repeating: *Smack her in the face as hard as you can.* To be honest, I wasn't even sure if she was cheating or not. I had no proof. But then, as I was heading to the Food Lion to grab some beer, I saw her. She was standing outside Sugar Ale, kissing some young guy—flirting, laughing, kissing again. I felt this overwhelming anger, but at the same time, I was shocked. The voices were right.

"I decided not to confront her. Not to hit her. Because the despair was stronger than the rage, so, I just got my wine, drove home, and cried while I drank. I was in the living room when she came back home—with him. And from what I could hear, they couldn't keep their hands off each other. I stood up, my face drenched in tears. She saw me, and the groceries in her hands dropped to the floor."

Andrew looks at the facilitator, Caroline, and suddenly breaks down. "I can't believe it," he says over and over again.

Caroline rushes over, wrapping him in a hug. "It's gonna be okay. You didn't know. And you're doing the right thing by talking about it."

The room is heavy with whispers—not necessarily because Andrew's wife cheated or because he's crying for the tenth time—but because of the eerie fact that the voices were right. This realization changes something in Andrew. Maybe, he thinks, they aren't as evil as he once believed. After all, they had figured it out, even if it was just a hunch.

A few minutes pass before Ayn finally speaks. "I'd like to share."

A brief pause follows before Caroline nods. "Go ahead. Ayn, right?"

"Yes," Ayn confirms. "I wanted to talk a little about my depression. I've found that talking about it helps me. The feeling usually creeps up on me slowly, but once it settles, I feel it in every part of my body. It's like a force—a mystical, overwhelming force.

"When it hits, I feel like I'm the only person in the world. Utterly and completely alone. It's strange. It's like I have no soul—just an empty shell with nothing inside. I can't even feel my own heartbeat, as if my life force is gone. People's voices sound distant, like a radio signal from a planet far away. My eyesight stays the same, but emotionally, everything looks dull, drained of life.

"Medication doesn't usually help. And I don't want to take so much that I turn into a zombie. I wouldn't wish this feeling on my worst enemy—the despair is just... unbearable."

A short pause follows, stretching into what feels like an eternity. Then Jonathan speaks.

"Yeah, I know how you feel, Ayn," he says. "It's frustrating. I've tried so many medications, and on top of that, I have some type of bipolar disorder. DBT has been helping a little, so I'm sticking with that. I like it because I don't have to analyze every emotion—I can just acknowledge it and let it pass without diving into it. I also started yoga, and that seems to help a bit.

"The hardest part is getting out of bed when I'm depressed. And my depression is unpredictable—kind of like how Jake's voices come and go. I can be fine for a while. Then suddenly, I'm spiraling into suicidal thoughts."

"Yeah," another voice chimes in. "I think we all relate in some way. We've all experienced mania, intense depression, and extreme emotional swings. But for me, it's different. I don't just feel sad—I feel *frightened* and *angry* all the time."

"A few years ago, when I talked to people, the voices would stop. But now, they talk in between my conversations," said Jake. "It's strange—like, in a sacred state of mind, I find it hard to think about certain subjects. When the voices are in a good mood, I feel okay. But sometimes, it's difficult to talk about the bad times I've had with… whatever entity or voice is inside my body. I just call it the Devil because he can be very cunning."

"I think we all have the Devil inside us to some degree," Caroline, the host, chimed in. "But when you actually hear his voice in your mind… So, I want everyone to raise their hand if their voices or emotions are somehow related to religion—like Christianity. This is interesting."

Everyone raised their hand except for two people, who looked visibly confused.

"With my emotions and several hospital visits, it feels like I have a badge on my forehead that says I'm mentally ill. God, I hate that word," said Johnathan. "If I meet a woman I want to be with, I have to tell her I've been to a mental hospital—and there's a chance I could go back if I don't figure out how and why I experience these intense emotions."

"I recently attempted the GRE," Pedro added. "It had me feeling like a satanic MC Hammer—time slowed down to milliseconds that felt like hours. My bipolar mania attack was so intense I couldn't even write my name on the answer sheet. A daunting feeling took over as if this test was going to determine my entire life. Some might say I was in a fight-or-flight state like a lion was right there in the room with me. I know God is always there, but in those moments, it felt like only the Devil was. No God, just him.

"I wouldn't wish that feeling on anyone—not even Adolf Hitler in the flesh. But I have to admit, the medicine helps to some degree. At least I don't have as many racing thoughts."

A woman named Sara joined the conversation. "I wonder if I should even tell someone I'm in a relationship with about my mental health issues. So, I just keep quiet. My psychiatrist told me that dating someone with similar problems wouldn't be a good idea. She said I should be with someone who has never been to a mental hospital or struggled with mental health issues."

"I beg to differ, Sara," said Rachel. "I believe love conquers all, and we're meant to be with who God wants us to be with." She cast a quick glance at Jason, who looked uncomfortable.

"Maybe Rachel is onto something," Sara said quickly. "Maybe I *could* be with someone who has the same mental struggles."

"That's exactly right," Rachel agreed, smiling at Jason.

Jason finally spoke. "Honestly, I can't even think about relationships until I find a way to quell my compulsive thoughts. Hey, everyone, I'm Jason, and I've been diagnosed with obsessive-compulsive disorder. I constantly think I'm in a germ-infested room and immediately start figuring out ways to sanitize it. I've already used hand sanitizer three times and offered it to the people next to me.

"My doctor told me there might have been a pivotal moment in my life when my brain decided it was okay to have obsessive thoughts. But to this day, I can't pinpoint a single major event that justifies my condition. Sometimes, my thoughts are so overwhelming that I struggle to follow simple TV shows—like *The Fresh Prince of Bel-Air* or *Family Matters*. You know, the one with that nerdy guy… what's his name? Oh, right—Steve Urkel. There was this one episode where Steve built a transformation machine and came out as a smooth, confident version of himself.

"I'm not saying I'm smooth, but I feel like I'm living a double life—one half consumed by my mental health issues, the other just me trying to be normal."

"I think once someone acknowledges they have a mental health problem, they have to live like superheroes with secret identities," Jason continued. "To blend in, they have to hide their struggles and pretend to be flawless. But every now and then, their secret identity gets exposed."

"I concur," Caroline said. "There's definitely some truth to what you're saying. Out of curiosity—if you feel like you're living a double life, raise your hand."

Everyone raised their hand.

"Can I try something real quick? This is fascinating," said Jake.

"Jake, we need to give others a chance to speak," Caroline replied. "But go ahead."

"Everyone, raise your hand if your current therapist is helping."

Only a third of the group raised their hands.

Jake noticed but tried to suppress a reaction. Still, his face twitched into a slight smile—no, not a smile, more like hesitation. A sensation ran through him, like something inside was forcing his emotions into an expression he didn't intend.

"You're not Jeeessssuuuussss," a voice whispered in his head.

Not here. Not now, Jake thought. The meeting was getting interesting, and he wanted to focus on the conversation, but the voices were back.

Well, I guess I'm in the right place if they're talking to me again.

There was something about Jesus that obsessed the voices—something Jake didn't understand. When he was in the hospital, the voices wouldn't stop talking about Jesus. Even before that, they spoke of him constantly.

He remembered one time the Devil's voice said, *I want Jesus.*

And Jesus' voice responded, *I want the Devil.*

But it felt like the Devil wanted Jesus more than Jesus wanted the Devil.

Maybe the voice in his head *was* Jesus. Maybe.

Jake had always seen Jesus as a grand figure, someone good beyond question. And yet, the voice inside him—the one that sometimes claimed to be Jesus—was manipulative. At times, even evil.

Before the voices, Jake had no issues with Jesus. But now… now, the Jesus in his head didn't always feel like the one from the Bible.

And that thought terrified him.

Chapter 12

He remembered the first time he met the Jesus figure in his head. He wasn't feeling happy or mad. In reality, he didn't know what he was feeling. He was at the movie theater with his dad when suddenly, a figure resembling him in a brown outfit appeared in his mind. The background was dark and mysterious. The Jesus figure tilted his head to the side and asked, "Who are you?"

Automatically, some gag reflex of emotions surged in Jake's consciousness, making a strange sound as if trying to kiss Jesus. Jake knew it was a show of deep love—one he had no capacity to process slowly. How and why the emotion surfaced, Jake didn't know. The brown Jesus, who looked just like him, was infectious. He said, "Well, if you feel that way about me, and I feel something like that about you…" Then, the voice began a diatribe about Jake's future—his wife, his kids, his life. At first, it wasn't so bad, but when none of the visions came true, that's when the Jesus figure started to toy with him in an almost cruel way—yet he could also be kind. The figure would make him laugh, make him content as if he was trying to clean up the mess he had created.

Sometimes, Jesus spoke with a solid, authoritarian voice. Other times, his voice was soft, almost angelic. But for the most part, he was consistent with the five voices he used to communicate with Jake. A year before this unique Jesus appeared in his head, Jake had attempted to write a memoir about the first time he ended up in Mt. Zion Mental

Hospital. He typed it out without much thought, yet he managed to get 100 pages on paper. Weeks later, he brought bits and pieces of the memoir to a critique group at Barnes & Noble. The critics didn't hold back in their edits.

Somehow, after Jake met this so-called Jesus in his head, the figure told him not to put the memoir away. According to Jesus, in the distant future—about 500 years from now—humans would do something unique with the internet and even transform their skin to be lizard-like, green, and silky. The most frustrating thing was that Jake believed him one hundred percent. Even to this day, Jake still kind of believes in what the first unique Jesus told him.

When Jesus was bad, he was really bad. But when he was good, he was funny. He told Jake about his future—his family, his siblings, his parents. He even described his future children's careers. In a strange way, Jesus had to be careful not to become too emotionally connected to Jake because if he did, he would apparently turn into another Jesus himself. The Jesus figure created such a beautiful narrative for Jake's entire life.

Jake often thought to himself that it could be a really good life—if only he got an engineering job and married the woman Jesus had promised. Jesus assured him of endless love and intimacy, something Jake had never experienced before with a woman he had never even met. The promises of a job and the love gave Jake hope for his future. Maybe Jesus did this to many people like him, and once they got what they wanted, he disappeared in a way that wasn't frightening.

After years of joblessness, Jesus switched the trajectory of Jake's future. Now, he said that once Jake had sex with a bombshell, he would vanish. It was unsettling. The way the voice acted, it was as if the Jesus figure was actually the Devil in disguise. Jake thought that would be the perfect disguise for someone as good and altruistic as Jesus.

Jake could never forget the day he held a knife to his arm while his dad stood at a distance downstairs. At that moment, Jake heard the Jesus voice in his head—laughing like an emperor on the verge of victory, pleased with the unfolding chaos. Yet Jake still had time. He could still be a family man, live an average life, or he could become a mental health advocate, helping millions of people suffering from psychological distress. He could die like Ralph Ellison, a literary crusader bringing awareness to mental health through his novels and books. He could be a CEO and earn honorary degrees from distinguished universities worldwide for his advocacy. The possibilities were endless.

Jake wanted to use all of his good and bad experiences—the ones tied to exotic emotions—to help others who had suffered the same struggles. He knew it would be a lot of work, but he imagined it could also be more fun than he expected, giving speeches and spreading awareness about mental health in America and beyond. It would take backbreaking hard work, but the journey might be worth it to the hundredth degree.

Now, he needed his group members to solidify the organization he had created at Zion Mental Hospital. He wanted to spread awareness about mental health in this country and how to improve mental health services. One thing Jake knew for certain: something was seriously wrong with the mental health system in North America, and it had to be fixed.

Among the emotions Jake had experienced, there were some so exotic they touched his very soul. These emotions made him question his reality. Perhaps they could be forgiven but never forgotten, especially when they stemmed from the voices in his head. After a while, Jake snapped out of his thoughts and tuned in to what was happening in the group.

"Sometimes I wonder if I should even be the leader of this organization I just formed. There are times when I feel like my problems are worse than my friends," he thought. "In a way, my situation overlaps with all their struggles. I have a touch of depression, obsessive-compulsive disorder, bipolar disorder, and, last but certainly not least, schizophrenia. I've had an experience with everything."

At that moment, he was in some kind of depression, weighed down by the daunting hill he would have to climb to lead his friends from Zion. He thought about Ayn and how lovely she looked in a Michael Jordan dress. If he had just met her, he would have never imagined she had depression. Her depression was steady, sure of itself. Once it sank its tentacles into her consciousness, it took a long time to go away. Jake, on the other hand, could be depressed for five minutes and then suddenly boiling mad. There was no in-between.

The only friend whose struggles closely resembled his own was Rachel. She had been diagnosed with schizophrenia, a label Jake had been plastered with by doctors at least a dozen times. It was strange. Ever since the voices started to feel like an entity of their own inside him, his entire perception of life had changed. He felt more trapped, more at their mercy. What if one night, the voices became too aggressive, and he struggled to go on a date with that perfect woman Jesus had promised?

Jake's eyes landed on Rachel. She was so animated— her voice seemed to give her power. When her voices became louder, she became more paranoid, convinced that one of Jason's so-called girlfriends wanted her dead. Jake felt as if he was missing that *umph* he used to have. The prideful push that had once given nuance to his every step seemed to have vanished.

Back in college, when he got drunk to the point of belligerence, he would sometimes bark at his friends—or even at the apartment complex staff—that he was going to be the President of the United States. When inebriated, he would feel this sudden surge of power. In those moments of intense euphoria, he had seen extreme visions—visions of grandeur, of control, of possibility.

He would say to himself in those moments that he just wanted power.

During his senior year in college, Jake would run six miles a day on the treadmill in under an hour. Back then, in his young adult years, his legs were muscular, and his body was toned. While jogging, he would chant in his mind: "Power, power, power," at the low frequencies in the backdrop of his thoughts. Could this have been the reason—or part of the reason—the voices manifested? Even now, every once in a while, when he was experiencing an emotional rollercoaster, he would imagine himself as the President of the United States. Though, he could honestly say those thoughts of power occurred far less now.

The voices made it very difficult for him to maintain the determination to run long distances. Whenever he did something physically exhausting, they made him feel extremely angry. Also, because of the sheer number of times Jake had been in mental hospitals, the visions he had made it increasingly unattainable to become President of the United States.

"I've never heard of a President of the USA going to the nuthouse ten-plus times and having all those visions," he thought. Actually, he couldn't even imagine a president being admitted to a psych ward once. Sure, George Bush had been president, and Jake thought he was dumb as a doorknob. But he wasn't crazy. Obama was half-Black and half-white and had a near-perfect record in his life, with no negative instances. He was the furthest thing from someone who had been to a psychiatric hospital. Although, when Jake read his book, he learned that Obama had once slept on the street while looking for the person he was supposed to stay with in New York. That might count for something crazy.

What Jake could see himself being was someone like Elyn Saks or Eleanor Longden—spokespeople for the mentally ill. They traveled the country, getting paid to raise awareness about severe mental health cases. The best part about that job was that he would be discussing something he was already passionate about while learning more about how to fix his own problems. Touring the country with his new golden friends and their budding organization would allow him to meet some of the top names in the mental health field, people who were genuinely trying to make substantial, positive changes.

Jake glanced at Pedro for two seconds and was instantly reminded of the problem he had faced on his GRE test day. That summer, he had been staying in his sister's apartment with his brother. His mother had told him not to forget to take his lithium medication, which was supposed to help with bipolar mania. This was before the voices. Before coming to D.C. for the summer, he had undergone frequent blood tests to check whether the lithium levels in his bloodstream were within the "Goldilocks zone." His doctor found them to be at the lowest end of the acceptable range.

Jake had read on the internet that lithium could cause prefrontal retardation. This terrified him. He didn't want to be mentally impaired. So, he took the lithium in front of his sister, but once she left for work, he drank cup after cup of highly caffeinated tea to counteract what he feared was its effect. He could feel his heart doing strange things from all the caffeine in his system. That night, he had bizarre dreams and delusions—visions of the FBI running experiments on him, stationed right outside his sister's apartment.

He woke up around 7:00 AM, and the delusions persisted. A severe mania was creeping in. Again, he took the lithium in front of his sister, but as soon as she left, he drank more caffeine. An emotion dawned on him—he believed he had magical abilities and could hack into Google.

Days before, he had met a woman at the pool. Now, along with the Google delusions, he felt as if someone was prying into his consciousness with brute telekinetic force. In his mind, he could see the woman's face tearing through the very fabric of his consciousness, looking inside. The paranoia intensified. The FBI was outside, watching him with special technology. That thought terrified him enough to stop drinking caffeinated drinks.

That evening, his parents drove from another state to visit him, his brother, and his sister. While sitting on the couch, a sudden burst of adrenaline shot through his veins. He got up, extended his arms, and his back stiffened. He was frozen, unable to move a single finger. His eyes were wide open, and his breath came in rapid, shallow inhales and exhales.

Somehow, Jake's father managed to coax him into sitting on the floor, but the adrenaline still surged through his veins. Someone must have called an ambulance because paramedics arrived within minutes. They placed an oxygen mask over his face, trying to regulate his breathing, but it didn't help much. The paramedics slowly helped him down the stairs and into the ambulance. His dad rode with him, speaking gently, trying to reassure him. But Jake was too paranoid—he was convinced his father was working with the FBI, delivering him to some unknown fate.

When they arrived at the hospital, a doctor came in to speak with him. The adrenaline had begun to subside. Out of the corner of his eye, Jake saw a demon. But when he turned to face it, it was the doctor. He shifted his gaze again, and in his peripheral vision, the demon reappeared. When he turned directly toward it, it was just a man.

That particular incident landed Jake in the mental ward. And the rest was history.

A woman named Sara shared her story of mania during the preliminary intake process at Zion Mental Ward. Afterward, the facilitator, Caroline, spoke a few words, and the meeting ended.

Chapter 13

Out in the parking lot, Pedro, Jason, Rachel, Ayn, and Jake regrouped.

"So, how did you guys like the group meeting?" Jake asked.

"I enjoyed it… but there should have been more organization," Rachel replied.

"Well, this is kind of the best there is in the country for people with mental health problems."

"These groups, I take it, were adopted from the ones in mental institutions," Jason added.

"It's better than nothing, I guess, for people like us," Ayn said.

Everyone laughed out loud.

As the conversation continued, Ayn's eyes darted toward a car painted with race car lines. A dark emotion eclipsed her immediate thoughts. The depression was looming over her again. She was confused—why was it creeping in at this moment? She had just told a funny joke and made everyone laugh. She should be happy about that. But it was as if something was forcing her to feel depressed.

She tried to force a smile but couldn't. Though Ayn was slim, lightweight, and somewhat athletic, she felt like it took extreme effort just to walk to her car with her friends.

"You guys want to grab some dinner? Maybe some burgers?" Jake asked. "We can talk about our next move while we eat."

Everyone agreed.

"You okay, Ayn? You look a little disturbed," Jake said, looking directly at her.

Ayn wasn't okay. But she knew that the organization she was now a part of could help her. She forced a fake smile and quickly responded, "I'm okay."

They met up at a burger joint and sat down at a booth.

Jason's face changed. His obsessive thoughts began to set in.

"This table must have a gazillion germs on it," he thought.

Jason wanted to clean. Clean, clean, clean. The thought gripped him suddenly.

He looked to his left and noticed a woman wiping down the table next to him and his friends. Why should I clean when the staff already disinfects the tables after customers leave? The thought was irrational, yet another one followed—*If I don't clean anyway, I could get cancer and die.* It was quick and intrusive, accompanied by similar thoughts.

When Jason forced himself to think logically, he knew it was impossible to get cancer from an unsanitized table. *I better clean the surface anyway.*

"If you guys don't mind, I need to grab some sanitizer from my car and clean the table," Jason said abruptly.

"They already cleaned the table, babe," Rachel said, casting him a sensual glance.

"I don't care. I have to clean it again," Jason insisted.

"We're like the mentally handicapped Power Rangers," Ayn jokes. A few laughed, and Jason snickered.

"I'll be back," Jason said before briskly walking out of the restaurant.

At his car, he opened the glove compartment, grabbed a large bottle of sanitizer, and pulled out a few tissues. When he returned, everyone was laughing at something, but he barely noticed. Ignoring the curious glances from other patrons, he cleaned the table with obsessive precision, ensuring he didn't miss a spot.

Jake, looking slightly uneasy, subtly signaled everyone to stay quiet. Jason continued cleaning for three solid minutes before finally sitting down with a long sigh, as if he had won a battle but was still strategizing for the war ahead.

"I can honestly say everyone is doing an exceptional job managing their symptoms as best they can," Jake said. "I know some days, people just want to scream because their symptoms are relentless."

As Jake spoke, Pedro's gaze drifted toward a TV in the restaurant displaying a commercial about a GRE prep course. His heart leaped into his throat.

I don't know if I can take the GRE again, he thought. Just the mere sight of the ad gave him goosebumps.

I was terrified when I took that test. It felt like life or death. Like a beast staring me down, ready to devour me. He had decent grades, but the idea that this single test could dictate his entire future was suffocating. He didn't have the money to keep retaking it.

How do some people just sit there and take it without breaking a sweat? He felt a sense of failure—something he hadn't experienced since his hospital stay.

"Will I ever take the GRE again and go to graduate school?" he muttered to himself. *I don't think I can. I spent so much time studying before. I can't go through that again.*

But despite everything, Pedro liked this group. They all had struggles, but they also wanted to see change—in themselves and in others.

"I was just thinking about the GRE," Pedro finally admitted. "I had an episode during the test. I feel like such a failure."

"You're not a failure. A lot of people have been through similar things," Jake reassured him.

"I think we should establish a charter or something, like the Hearing Voices Network," Rachel suggested. "Something that defines who we are and what we stand for. We also need to research NAMI—see what they're doing right and what they're getting wrong."

"There's a NAMI convention downtown next week," Pedro said, perking up. "We should check it out."

Rachel stiffened at the mention of a convention. Memories of her public breakdown at a mental health seminar resurfaced. A psychiatrist had been giving a speech and something—she wasn't sure what—triggered her episode. Now, the thought of another convention filled her with unease. But it could also be an opportunity to help the group. As a psychology major, she could contribute in a meaningful way.

After finishing their meals and sharing laughs about Dave Chappelle's stand-up routines, everyone headed to their cars.

Jake sat in his car and felt a strange mix of pride, pain, and something almost primal. His mind drifted to the dark times—when suicidal thoughts loomed over him like an emperor dictating his fate.

He recalled a day at the pool with his brother and a friend. The voices inside him had deepened, taunting him, stirring something dangerous within him. He had no immediate intention to act, but he toyed with the idea, hoping the thoughts would dissipate.

Later that night, he sat in his room, staring at a bottle of Clorox on his desk. The voices urged him to drink it. A deep, Jesus-like voice tempted him directly.

"What are you doing with that Clorox, Jake? Are you trying to drink it?" his mother's voice cut through the fog.

Her words snapped him out of it. "I was just cleaning," he lied, quickly putting the bottle away.

Another time, in the early days of hearing voices, he had nearly overdosed on caffeine pills. He had felt slow—his mind sluggish—so he wanted an adrenaline rush. Within thirty minutes, panic set in. He confessed to his father what he had done.

His father, unfazed, simply told him to go to bed.

That night, Jake felt like he was in another world—a strange, mystical fantasia. A high unlike anything he had experienced before, as if he had stepped into a surreal, animated dream. *Like the VHS version of Fantasia—the one with Mickey and the enchanted brooms.*

On his drive home, Jake reflected on all of it. *It's like when I get close to suicide, my mind shifts—pulling me into another realm, another state of being.*

He remembered the time he had bought a rope from Walmart, planning to disappear into the woods behind his house.

He had come so close.

So, he bought the rope and went on YouTube to learn how to tie a noose. Before buying it, he recalled seeing a blue demon saying he didn't want to put Jake in that suicidal realm but had to put himself in it. Then, by some acknowledgment of the gods, Jake's mother saw the rope. She was furious. Jake quickly made up a story, claiming he bought the rope for his friend Bryan to use while moving some furniture.

He got in his car, drove to Bryan's apartment, and tossed the plastic-wrapped rope near the garbage cans. Jake realized that to go through with suicide, his entire mind had to be committed. He would need absolute determination. All those times, he had flirted with the idea, but he had never crossed the threshold. A wave of sorrow washed over him for those who had. They must have been in unimaginable pain. The thought was unbearable.

Jake was no stranger to emotional pain, but even he had never experienced that level of inconceivable agony. When overwhelmed by emotions, he would think briefly about the end, only to feel stuck, trapped, and confused. Usually, time made the pain more tolerable. To break free from that confusion, one would need an unshakable resolve. There had to be constant, consuming thoughts about it. He understood that if such pain ever lingered long enough, he might have been one of those who followed through.

Once, while browsing in the library, he stumbled upon a book titled something like *The Essence of Suicide*. He chose not to read it, realizing that suicide was deeply personal. There was an unspoken taboo around those who went through with it. He came to a realization—he didn't want anyone to experience that kind of pain regularly.

His new friends had all battled their own mental health struggles, each of them having flirted with suicidal thoughts. He sometimes wondered if he should encourage them to keep private notes about their emotions, helping them better understand themselves. Reading a book wouldn't help much—everyone was different. Therapy might offer insights, but ultimately, people had to find their own way to understand what made them tick.

If anything could earn him a place in heaven, perhaps this was it. By exchanging ideas with his friends, Jake hoped to figure out how to avoid such intense emotions. A sudden rush of pride coursed through his veins. Maybe he could even make a living from his organization, never having to work a nine-to-five job. His desire to conquer these emotions was fueled by both personal ambition and a selfless drive to help others. His friends would have to engage in deep thinking—after all, no one could read every book on mental health. Only God possessed such knowledge, but they could do their best with what they had.

Fifteen minutes later, Jake arrived home. Under the trickling drops of water out of the shower hose, his mind fixated on turning his organization into a true force in America. Power. The more powerful he became, the more people he could help. And perhaps, in doing so, he could also solve his own problems.

Alexander the Great, Barack Obama, Malcolm X, Mahatma Gandhi, Marcus Garvey, Aristotle. These men had power. Some were killed young, but more or less, they all achieved their goals. Alexander the Great conquered most of the known world in his twenties. Jake wasn't particularly drawn to his military conquests, but he admired how these titans conquered men's hearts.

Jake and his friends would need to forge an intimate connection with the people, much like Malcolm X. Not to preach about race relations but to highlight mental illness as the next great challenge in America. He wasn't denying that racism still existed. Of course, it did—he knew that firsthand. As a 6'4" dark-skinned Black man, he had been stopped by the police for no reason other than the color of his skin.

But when he thought about Malcolm, it seemed like Malcolm genuinely loved the people he spoke to. Jake, if he was being honest, only loved his family and friends. Would he have to love everyone, like Jesus Christ, to achieve his goals? It was true—speaking to someone you love is far easier than talking to someone toward whom you feel animosity or indifference.

When it came to people who heard voices, Jake cared for them more than others because he had something in common with them. Maybe he could be like Elanor Longhorn, a woman who had a dozen voices in her head yet still traveled the country, giving speeches about different approaches to managing them. One thing Jake and his friends knew with absolute certainty was that change needed to happen in the mental health world if people were to truly recover.

It was true, Jake thought. I used to be power-hungry—before I went into a mental hospital. He once believed he was as talented and intelligent as Barack Obama and could become the first truly Black president, with no hint of white ancestry. But after multiple situations in mental institutions, he realized how unlikely it was for someone with his history to become president. Reading Barack Obama's biography made him understand that even if he did reach that position, he would be preoccupied with matters far removed from the mental health issues he was passionate about. Instead, being a force like Elanor Longhorn, Elyan Sacks, or Kate Whitfield was the kind of power he could realistically aspire to—if he was genuinely making a difference.

To Jake, attainable power equaled change in the mental health world. He also remembered a friend mentioning that people like Elyan Sacks were paid quite well. As long as he was doing something he was passionate about—and within the scope of his intellect—that was enough for him.

That night, he visited the NAMI website to learn more about their efforts to support people with mental health challenges. To join group discussions or classes, he needed to register and pay a fee or become a member. He didn't have the money at the moment but planned to pay once he received his disability check. From what he read, NAMI was clear and concise in defining mental illness within the framework of Western medicine. However, he disliked the term "mental illness"—it felt like a curse, a label that condemned a person for life. He preferred the term "unique mind" or, as a compromise, "mental health problems."

One undeniable fact was that, no matter how uncomfortable it made them, people in his organization would need to give speeches and be knowledgeable about the state of mental health care in the country. Jake clicked on the "Support and Education" section, then on "NAMI Helpline." He noticed a number to text for immediate support. A line on the page mentioned volunteers who guided individuals through steps to feel better. The only word that unsettled him was "volunteer." Hopefully, these people were trained in some form of peer support program.

Jake thought about his new friends and the organization he was trying to build. Wow, we have a long battle ahead of us. Not only do we have to fight to change others, but we also have to battle our own personal struggles. He recalled a quote from a book or somewhere: "God uses broken people to fix the world."

Picking up the phone, he called Rachel. "Hey, Rachel, could you tell everyone that we'll meet at The Box Car before getting down to official business? I think we should get to know each other's mental health struggles in more detail."

"That sounds like a good idea. As soon as I finish painting my toenails and fingernails, I'll do it," Rachel replied.

She called everyone, and they all agreed—some hesitantly, others with caution.

That night, as Jake closed his eyes, distorted images of his own face filled his mind. It felt as though his very essence was being forcibly transformed. Before drifting to sleep, he remembered praying about it. Usually, when he prayed, he would get a few images now and then, but not frequently. Maybe my problem with my voices has something to do with religion, he thought. Every now and then, his voices mentioned God, as if to say that God was helping him. Jake mostly believed in God, but at times, he questioned what kind of God would allow him and his friends to suffer so much. Then again, couldn't anyone facing hardship ask the same question? Once a person hit rock bottom, no matter the reason, they were bound to wonder, "Why isn't God helping me right now?"

Tomorrow, I'll ask my friends what they think about Jesus, God, the devil—basically all religions, Jake decided. Thinking about religion somehow calmed him, and he drifted off to sleep.

Perspective

The moment he woke up, the voices were already talking in his head. He was frustrated because just when he had grown accustomed to them, they would say something different yet somehow familiar.

Jake loved to read, and he had until five o'clock before Pedro picked him up to go to The Box Car. He was a big fan of Russian literature, particularly Dostoevsky. The book he was reading was *Notes from Underground*. He wasn't fond of the first part, *Apropos of the Snow*, but he identified with the main character. The protagonist was intelligent in his own way, sometimes believing he could figure everything out. In the book, he was humiliated by former classmates at a reunion.

Jake remembered how lonely he had been in high school, mostly keeping to himself. Girls occasionally approached him, but he was too shy to talk to them. In *Notes from Underground*, one of the protagonist's classmates was having a farewell party at a bar-restaurant, and the protagonist ended up there. He spent time with them but kept drinking until he was unaware of his intoxication. He began hurling monstrous insults, believing himself to be smarter than everyone else.

Jake sighed. He understood that feeling all too well.

Before Jake went to the mental hospital for the first time, he was very prideful in college. Even though he didn't have high IQ test scores or a high GPA, he still felt superior to those around him—smarter. Sure, he could have gotten a D in one of his engineering courses, but that didn't mean his classmates were more analytical than him. Even with the voices, some part of him believed he was above most people in the world.

Chapter 14

His once-unshakable pride has softened now, dulled by the weight of his mental health struggles. There was a time when his voices were more creative, once telling him he was just average. The way they said it reminded him of how God spoke to Moses through the burning bush. For a few years after that, he actually believed he was just average—until, somewhere in the crevices of his subconscious, that unshakable pride resurfaced.

Jake finished his book just in time to get dressed and head out to the Box Car. For those unfamiliar, the Box Car is an arcade where people go to play video games. As he was about to leave, Pedro sent him a text. Jake responded, letting Pedro know he'd be outside in a few minutes.

When Jake stepped out, he noticed Pedro looking anxious, staring at something on his phone.

"You okay, Pedro? You look kind of anxious," Jake said.

"I'll be okay. It's just that ever since the episode with the GRE test, I've had trouble going into public places. Whenever I'm in one, I'm afraid I might have another episode," Pedro admitted, his voice filled with concern.

"I don't know if you're religious or anything, but sometimes I say little prayers. It helps, I guess, because it's a last-resort thing. Before we go inside, let's have a prayer together," Jake suggested.

"I was raised Christian, non-denominational," Pedro replied.

They bowed their heads, and Jake recited the Saint Francis Prayer.

"You feel a little better, man?" Jake asked afterward.

"Yeah, a little. It's weird—during the test, I could kind of recognize my surroundings, but inside, emotionally, I was in pure hell. My thoughts were racing in a single heartbeat. The Zyprexa helps slow them down, but it makes me feel sluggish. It also paralyzes me. When I wake up at night, I can see, but I can't move my eyes. It lasts for like two full minutes."

"Yeah, that happened to me once too."

They met up with their friends and had a good time at the Box Car, avoiding discussions about their struggles or the organization. At the end of a very casual night, which was really rare for them, they said their goodbyes. The next morning, Jake went to the nami.org website. As a member, he wanted to check when and where the next convention would be. While browsing past conventions, he realized how much good work was being done for mental health—yet he couldn't shake the despair of having been in and out of hospitals without ever hearing about these programs.

For example, he hadn't known about the peer-to-peer program until last year when someone from the Hearing Voices Network mentioned becoming a peer worker. This woman heard voices and struggled with paranoia, yet she was still a peer specialist. When Jake asked her what they did, she explained that they help people with mental health issues—similar to therapists, except they mainly listen for dangerous thoughts. Jake couldn't see much difference between peer-to-peer support and therapy, so he dismissed it as something that might help others but not him.

As he continued browsing, he found group therapy sessions for depression and anxiety. He remembered a friend who had attended an anxiety group. Over the phone, the friend told him he had tried to understand the connection between his voices and anxiety, but the other participants couldn't relate.

After more searching, Jake found discussion boards buried deep within the website. About five months ago, he had posted a question in one of them: 'How do you explain to people what it feels like to hear voices?' He had waited two months, but no one ever responded. Instead, he found the same generic topics he had already come across on Google searches: 'How do you cope with voices?' 'What medications help with voices?'

Reading those generalized discussions made him so angry he felt like screaming.

He searched for more conventions. He had been to one before, but he wanted his new friends to experience it, too. He watched past convention videos, finding them informative—yet many relied heavily on statistics to highlight problems within the mental health system. That frustrated him. What frustrated him even more was hearing presenters make sweeping statements like, "The reason people are depressed, anxious, or have panic attacks is because of the culture."

Jake scoffed. "What about the culture, exactly, is causing all these so-called mental illnesses?"

Of the three videos he watched, not a single person provided details. Just more vague generalizations: 'social media,' 'video games,' 'technology,' 'weather.'

"Weather?" Jake muttered to himself, shaking his head in disbelief.

The presenter mentioned that during winter, many people experience depression, and in summer, some struggle with it due to the sun. Jake felt like he had stepped into the Twilight Zone hearing such statements. NAMI was supposed to be a leading advocacy group, yet few people knew what they actually did, and even when they did, the details were often unclear.

Jake liked the Tulip Group, an organization dedicated to breaking mental health stigma by encouraging people affected by mental illness, either personally or through loved ones, to plant tulips across America while discussing mental health. The only issue was the lack of clarity—what exactly did they discuss to combat stigma?

Jake wanted to reach out to a friend and share what he had learned from his years as a NAMI member. He called Ayn.

"Yeah… there's quite a lot happening around depression. I heard a statistic once that said about one in five people experience it," Ayn said.

"I know that's true. I feel like NAMI mainly focuses on helping people with depression and anxiety. If you call with a question about schizophrenia, there's not as much information available. And statistically, people with schizophrenia are significantly more likely to die by suicide," Jake replied.

"I once saw a book titled *CBT for Schizophrenia*," Ayn said.

"CBT is good, but it needs to be explained better. Just drawing a triangle with arrows connecting behavior, thoughts, and emotions isn't enough. CBT is a way of life—it can reshape how we think, but only with the right guidance. Then there's DBT. We've talked about this before, but I came across a book called *DBT for Bipolar Disorder*. Simply reading the book, even without memorizing everything, can bring a sense of peace. But when I started hearing voices, mindfulness—which is all about staying in the present—didn't help much. The voices constantly second-guessed everything I did," Jake said.

"I'm familiar with DBT. It's very helpful, though, during depressive episodes, emotions can feel too deep for words," Ayn replied.

"Whenever I start drifting toward depression, my voices work overtime to make me scared or angry. Before I started hearing them, my depression lasted longer, but I never really did anything to address it. Back in college, I used to run miles on a treadmill in my dorm. I'd run and run, then collapse in exhaustion. Gatorade back then felt like honey to a bear. But now, when I try to jog, the voices make it impossible to focus. Sometimes, I almost believe they're real—like actual evil spirits. A woman once told me that negative energy feeds on vulnerable people. She said if someone is prone to anger, a spirit might amplify it."

Jake changed the subject. "So, are you free right now? Want to go bowling? Maybe grab a bite to eat?"

"Yeah, I'll go. When?" Ayn asked.

"Right now."

"Okay."

Jake got dressed, entered the bowling alley's address into Google Maps, and asked his mom to borrow her car. She agreed immediately—probably because he had just returned from the hospital. He arrived at the bowling alley in twenty minutes and waited at the entrance. Five minutes later, Ayn arrived, and they exchanged a hug.

"You might have what people call severe depression, and I might have what they call schizophrenia, but let's make this date work," Jake said.

Ayn felt good in that moment. Jake was charming—tall, dark, handsome, and intelligent—but she wasn't sure she was ready for a relationship. A familiar gloom settled over her, yet she also felt happy. As they walked to get their bowling shoes, she tried to pinpoint the source of her sadness. Was it her suicide attempt? The internship she never finished? She ran through a dozen possibilities, but none clicked as *the* reason.

Jake, meanwhile, was present but also distant. Something inside him—an entity, a voice, or whatever it was—was playing tricks on his perception of his face. He could feel minute changes in his facial muscles, an eerie sensation as if he were sharing his face with someone else. He had told multiple psychiatrists and therapists, but none had a clear answer. The last one had dismissed it as a "tactile hallucination."

"Is my face doing weird things?" Jake asked.

"Your face looks fine. I haven't noticed anything strange," Ayn reassured him.

"I don't know if it's psychosis, a hallucination, or just an overactive imagination, but I feel like someone is trying to express themselves through my face. Like we're fighting for control over it."

Ayn subtly shifted the conversation back to NAMI, and Jake caught on. He continued their discussion from earlier, but his thoughts remained unsettled.

It's not fair, he thought. *Before I heard voices, I never had to worry about this face or voice stuff. Do I really have to be part of the one percent who lives like this?* Most of the time, he lived in fear. He didn't think the way he used to in college, back when he read Dostoevsky and Ellison. Those books made him feel *smarter*—they made him think about Truth, Morality, Love, Pride, and Justice.

He recalled a scene from *Invisible Man* where the protagonist delivers a passionate speech while an elderly couple's belongings are thrown onto the street. Jake loved that moment—it was the birth of a hero. What kind of hero would he have to be to improve the world's mental health system? What could he say to inspire intellectuals and policymakers to take mental illness more seriously?

He glanced at Ayn, a brilliant and intriguing woman battling her own darkness. And he wondered: *What exactly does it take to help someone heal?*

Jake told himself that Ayn was far more than just depressed. She had many admirable qualities. The entity within Jake acknowledged his strange expressions as if it were agreeing with him while simultaneously causing him pain.

Jake playfully pushed Ayn's shoulder, and she giggled. He knew the voices in his head wanted him to pursue something physical with her, but he wasn't sure how to approach it. Ayn was beautiful and intelligent, and he recalled her joking about having sex with him in the hospital. But that was the hospital—people say all kinds of things in those situations. He was almost certain that Ayn wanted to contribute to improving the world's mental health crisis, but he wasn't sure if she wanted an intimate relationship with him. He was too afraid to kiss her.

Somehow, their conversation drifted to how saliva remains in a person's mouth for some time after a kiss. Was that a sign? Jake wondered. Was that the moment to go for it—with a simple kiss? But the fear of losing an ally in the fight for mental health awareness held him back.

After bowling, they went to a bar and ordered cheeseburgers with fries. Ayn got water, and Jake opted for fruit punch.

"So, what do you think this is—what we have going on here?" Jake asked.

"I really like you a lot, and I'm all in for the movement," Ayn said. "But I don't think I can commit to a serious relationship right now. To be honest, I have no idea how to control my depression. Every time I try to pinpoint a reason for it, I end up going in circles. Exercise helps sometimes. Reading helps sometimes. Just living life helps sometimes. I like you a lot, but I don't want to make things weird— especially with you being the leader of the movement and all," she added with a laugh.

Jake laughed, too. *Movement—that's a cool name for our mental health group*, he thought.

"Yeah, I really think we can help push for better mental healthcare in this country—maybe even the world," he said.

Ayn smiled playfully, her eyes and lips glowing under the dim light. "I can say one thing for sure—you're the coolest and most attractive man I've ever been on a date with."

"Thanks," Jake said. He may not be having sex with Ayn that night, but that was one hell of a compliment. Since becoming the leader of the group, he felt a sense of pride that affirmed his self-worth. He was charismatic, intelligent, and confident. The fact that he was the only Black member of the group never crossed his mind as a challenge—his friends followed him because they believed in him and their cause.

The only other time he had been a leader was during a summer basketball league in college. He and his friends had formed a team, and he was one of the best players, trusted to make the right calls. But this was different. He wasn't leading because he was a great speaker—he simply cared deeply about mental health. He was tired of being institutionalized three times a year. Since leaving Zion, he had vowed to do everything in his power to avoid being placed in a hospital again.

As the night came to a close, Jake and Ayn hugged in a lingering embrace before heading to their cars. His phone rang, and he saw Jason's name on the screen.

"Hey, Jason, what's up, man?" Jake answered. "Ayn and I just went on a date."

"How was the big date?" Jason asked.

"It was alright. A little flirtation but not much action. I kind of feel like I shouldn't pursue a relationship with Ayn since she's trying to recover," Jake admitted.

"Why not? Rachel is on my case like white on rice. And I have to admit, she looked *very* sexy at the Galaxy Con event."

"She sure did," Jake agreed. "She's a little eccentric, but deep down, she's a good person. I guess I'll just take things slow and see where life leads us."

"That's a good idea."

"Hey, if you're free tomorrow, maybe you, Pedro, and I can play some basketball. Just to chill," Jason suggested.

"That sounds cool. I need to get some cardio in."

"I'll call Pedro and see what he says."

After saying their goodbyes, Jake scrolled through his contacts and called Pedro. Pedro agreed.

Later that night, Pedro knelt beside his bed and clasped his hands in prayer. "Dear God, it seems like the Zyprexa causes the paralysis most of the time, but sometimes it doesn't. Please help me wake up without being unable to move my body. And help me find peace with the GRE episode. Amen."

The next morning, Pedro woke up and immediately noticed he could move. A smile spread across his face. But when he looked in the mirror, he saw he had gained weight—one of the side effects of Zyprexa, as his psychiatrist had warned. After a quick breakfast, he got in his car and drove to the basketball court to meet Jake and Jason.

Jason wore a large Larry Bird jersey and generic basketball shorts. Jake had on a moisture-wicking workout shirt and loose-fitting basketball shorts.

Jason dribbled lazily near the three-point line before launching a high-arching shot. *Swish.*

"So, Pedro, how was your sleep? I remember you saying Zyprexa was giving you trouble," Jake asked.

"When I take it, I usually wake up paralyzed for a couple of minutes. But last night, I prayed, and I woke up able to move right away. It felt like a miracle. Even ten seconds of that paralysis is terrifying," Pedro admitted.

"Great," Jake and Jason said in unison.

"I keep thinking about the GRE episode," Pedro continued. "It's like I'm stuck in a cycle of fear as if it's going to happen again."

"I don't know what to tell you," Jake admitted, "but I have a fear of losing control again—of doing what I did at my dad's house. Or worse. It's strange. When that happened, part of me was aware but powerless, while most of me was consumed by uncontrollable rage. You were stuck in fear. I was stuck in fury. My psychiatrist won't even ask about my childhood to understand why it happened."

Jake tossed Pedro the ball. Pedro took a shot from where Jason had stood earlier—airball.

"I'm more of a soccer guy than a basketball player," Pedro laughed. "But I *can* do a layup!"

They all chuckled and played three intense games of 21. Jason and Jake played with the smooth precision of NBA players. Jake, being the tallest, dominated with blocks and dunks. He often told his friends that if he had played AAU or high school basketball, he could have made it to the NBA—if only he hadn't injured his shoulder in college. Watching him, one could see glimpses of Michael Jordan in his moves.

After the games, they sat down to drink water and catch their breath.

"So, I did some research on NAMI," Jake said. "They're doing good work, but they're not detailed enough. Not everyone can afford a $500 psychoanalyst session, so they turn to NAMI. But sometimes, I feel like these professionals use complicated language just to sound credible and keep their jobs. Maybe the only thing that can truly heal mental illness is a miracle from God. I was thinking—we should go to NAMI in person and see what they really have to offer."

Pedro sighed. "The medicine seems to be helping me, but I don't think as quickly as I used to. And like I told you guys, sometimes I wake up paralyzed for a few minutes. I think the only way I can feel better is if I get psychoanalysis from someone truly talented—but that would cost $500 a session."

"I can relate a little to how you feel, Pedro," Jason said. "For me, there's no medicine for what I have. I probably need a psychoanalyst, too, but I can't afford one. Maybe it's from some childhood trauma that explains why I have OCD traits. I've looked into something called exposure therapy. It might help, but it's a hit-or-miss situation."

"We'll go to three or four presentations and see what makes sense during the NAMI convention," Jake suggested. "Last time I went, it was interesting, to say the least. I remember this guy promoting his book. Apparently, he didn't even write it; someone ghostwrote it for him. They must have had some kind of Malcolm X and Alex Haley set up to get it done. Though to be fair, Malcolm X's autobiography was way better than that guy's book. For those who don't know, Malcolm and Alex would have these meetings where Malcolm talked about his life, and Alex made both mental and physical notes to write the autobiography. But this guy at the convention? His memoir wasn't that earth-shattering. What stood out was that he managed to document his episodes in a logical way. He ran naked through Paris, ended up in a hospital there, and later in North Carolina—Duke University, I think."

"Maybe someday someone will write a book about us," Jason mused.

"Maybe," Jake agreed. "There seem to be categories for the presenters at the NAMI event: research psychiatrists, enthusiastic youth talking about suicide, therapists, advocates, and people connected to pharmaceutical companies."

"Yeah, it's going to be a long day, but worth it," Jason said. "We should go through the convention program before attending. There's information on the NAMI website about their current projects."

They talked a little more about NAMI before heading home. As Jason drove, his phone rang. It was Rachel.

"Hey, sugar poo," she cooed.

Jason sighed. "I thought I told you not to call me unless it's about the organization. There is no 'us.'"

Rachel scrunched her face in frustration, though no one could see but God. "Yeah, it's business, baby. There's a fee for the NAMI event coming up."

"Don't call me baby, Rachel. We're just friends. Look, it's true you're gorgeous and borderline a genius, but I can't have a romantic relationship with you. Pedro, Jake, and I played basketball earlier and talked about the research Jake found on NAMI. Apparently, there's good and bad, but overall, they're trying their best to help people with mental health issues. It should be interesting, especially for you as a psychology major."

"I should probably be there when some Sigmund Freud type tries to find fine wording to keep his job," Rachel said, laughing.

They exchanged goodbyes and hung up.

Chapter 15

Lying in bed, Jake stared at the ceiling, lost in thought. He took his sleeping pills and 300 mg of Seroquel. It might work, or it might not. His psychiatrist insisted he take them, so he did.

He thought about the *Hearing Voices Network* book—a collection of journal-like accounts from people who heard voices. Some lost them over time, while others learned to live with them. The more they engaged with their voices as friends, the more they disappeared. But one disturbing pattern stood out: most of the people in the book had been sexually abused.

Jake hadn't been, or at least he didn't think so. But his voices tormented him in a sexual nature. They talked about wanting sex. Once, they would stop when he spoke to a woman, but now they harassed him even during conversations. It was getting worse.

He struggled to explain it, but he felt his consciousness slipping away like he was losing himself. When he had first read the book, those sexual pains hadn't been there. The people in the book came from all over the world, mostly Europe. He once read an article claiming American voice-hearers were more aggressive than European ones, likely because of America's culture of violence.

He'd had violent episodes involving his voices, but he feared diving too deep into them. He wasn't strong enough to handle those emotions. During those episodes, reality felt different—like another dimension. Maybe it wasn't psychosis; maybe his mind actually transported him elsewhere. There was one dimension he dreaded: the misty place his voices sent him whenever they said he was suicidal. He hated it.

Thinking about the quantum realm, he dismissed it as nonsense. He didn't understand the math behind it, anyway. How could anyone will themselves into another dimension? The more he thought, the more questions arose.

What hurt most was being labeled psychotic. He hated the term *mental illness*. It made him feel less than human. The people in the HVN book never described themselves as schizoaffective or schizophrenic.

He remembered the day he was first diagnosed. He had searched "schizophrenia" on YouTube and found videos about people doomed to live like children, needing constant supervision, cycling in and out of hospitals. It felt like a curse.

"I'm so tired of this crap. Why do I have this problem? It's so hard to live with these thoughts, God," he whispered aloud.

Jake knew he'd go to the hospital a thousand times before considering suicide. He'd call the ACT crisis line a thousand times, even if the person on the other end rarely knew what to say to help him.

He couldn't talk to his voices the way those in the book did. He could only respond with automatic thoughts. Most of the time, the voices had nothing of substance to say; they just wanted to enrage him.

One thing was certain—he felt another presence inside him. It was like someone else was in his mind, humiliating him, knowing exactly how his brain ticked. He had heard the voice of the devil before. Maybe the devil was real. Maybe heaven and hell were real, and this dark presence was a fallen angel. He had heard that the devil only appeared when some kind of agreement was made. Maybe he had unknowingly made a deal.

But for what? And why wouldn't it go away?

He longed to feel normal again. He wanted to cry, but something in his mind wouldn't let him. He climbed out of bed, sank to his knees, and began to pray. Five minutes passed, and exhaustion overtook him. His words turned into rambling—he didn't know what else to say, didn't know how to frame his plea to God.

As Jake closed his eyes, he felt something controlling his facial expressions again, as if an unseen force were manipulating the muscles in his face. He wanted to scream— bloody murder. He just wanted to express an emotion, to feel it naturally through his face, but it seemed as though the devil had a vice grip on his consciousness.

Still, a small glimmer of hope flickered in his mind. It was faint, but it was there. There had to be someone who could help him with this. It didn't make sense that not a single person in the world could offer him a solution.

Paranoia was a powerful state of mind. When he was paranoid, it felt impossible to think his way out of it. He had experienced multiple episodes, each more consuming than the last. He used to believe that if he thought hard enough, he could break free from them. But the more he tried, the deeper he fell into paranoia.

The circumstances leading up to his hospital visits were never clearly connected. One delusion he had was the belief that Duke students, so intelligent that they had discovered a way to telepathically communicate, were controlling his mind. When his mother and brother brought him to Duke University Hospital, his paranoia convinced him he had been hypnotized by the students. He thought that if he looked at his mother or brother for too long, one of them would disappear.

This was before he started hearing voices. Back then, he had been diagnosed with bipolar disorder and given a high dose of Zyprexa to combat the paranoia. These days, his paranoia was more subtle. One of his recurring delusions was the belief that he had been mentally controlled by an evil version of Jesus over 2,000 years ago. In Jake's mind, when Jesus became a man, he somehow connected with everyone who wasn't even born yet.

How could Jesus be telepathically communicating with him from the past or from heaven? At one point, Jake entertained the thought that Jesus came from the year 3000 when time travel technology existed, and that was how he performed miracles. He was familiar with time travelers from sci-fi books, but this theory felt beyond comprehension. Jesus was as much a mystery as God himself. No one truly understood how Jesus worked, not even through prayer.

"So, theoretically, if Jesus has all these powers, then maybe I'm not in psychosis every time I hear his voice," Jake thought. "But that's insane—Jesus is good," he muttered aloud.

Jake had been paranoid to the point of putting himself in danger, yet he never understood why people took drugs to induce paranoia like weed. He had smoked weed about seven times in his life. The first time was an ecstatic, surreal experience, but the last five times had been filled with unbearable paranoia. A neighborhood friend assured him that the more he smoked, or if he found the right strain, the paranoia would disappear. But the last time he got high, he was drinking at a bar with a man he had just met. The man was nice, smart, eccentric, and wealthy. The first few times Jake smoked with him, he was fine. But the last time, when his mom picked him up from the bar, he became so paranoid he thought she was secretly taking him to a mental hospital.

He felt like an alien again. But then, when he thought of Rachel, Jason, Ayn, and Pedro, he didn't feel so alone. These were the few people who liked him for more than just his mental health struggles. He concluded that it was almost impossible for someone to live their whole life without experiencing paranoia. People often equated paranoia with irrationality, but fear could easily trigger it. He also recognized that some people who heard voices were geniuses—but that didn't mean all were. The flaw in that logic, he thought, was that paranoia itself was inherently illogical.

Jake sat at his student desk and pulled *Kindred* from the shelf. He had already read the first third and was enjoying it. In some ways, he felt like a slave to the devil within him, much like how Dana, the main character, was trapped under the control of Rufus.

Jake understood that slavery was a horrific experience—living in constant fear of beatings, death, sickness, or punishment for trying to escape. The devil inside him had caused him immense turmoil, and he wanted to make it suffer. It had stripped him of any sense of normalcy.

It was strange. When Jake felt emotions, he also felt the emotions of the devil. The devil seemed protected by pain, which Jake experienced as an overwhelming sensation. His emotions would sometimes shift unpredictably—if he felt the devil was stupid, he would suddenly feel that he himself was ten times more foolish. At times, he would see visions of himself with horns atop his head, a demonic reflection staring back at him.

Even while watching YouTube videos, he would feel an unbearable humiliation coursing through his body, tightening his muscles. It seemed that every muscle contraction was another wave of shame pulsing through his veins. Even when he and the devil found something amusing, he felt like he couldn't fully express his laughter. He often talked to the devil in his thoughts.

"Maybe I am in hell," Jake thought. Most of the time, he was miserable. Even time itself felt different when he was hearing voices. It didn't move in a linear way—it froze, rushed, or dragged unpredictably. He would watch a 55-minute video but experience time jumping, pausing, or stretching.

Alone at home, Jake spent much of his time repeating the devil's words in his mind. This helped him become more aware of his own thoughts. Half the time, the entity—or devil, or whatever it was—came and went in a rhythm he recognized but had no control over. He felt utterly powerless against it.

Some days, he wished the devil inside him would take physical form so he could fight it. He recalled an episode of *Black Mirror* where a woman paid a corporation to create a copy of her consciousness, placing it in a computer that controlled her house. She could press a button to make the copy of herself disappear into a white void with nothing to do.

Jake often fantasized about doing the same to the devil in his head. When he went to bars, he would drink and imagine torturing the devil the way that woman tormented her digital copy. But Jake didn't want to torture himself— just the part of him that represented the devil.

He rested his head on the desk, remembering when the devil used to tell him it would disappear one day, that he would feel stable, get a good job, and have a family. Even after a year, Jake still found himself believing that particular lie. Most days, the devil pretended to prepare him for job interviews, only for the phone calls to be about something else entirely.

But how had the devil kept him believing for so long?

Then he realized—it had always been the same trick. False dreams, false hope, built up and shattered time and time again.

The only thing that seemed to help was prayer. Jake prayed several times a day, and whenever he did, a voice would reassure him that certain things happening throughout the day were God's way of helping him—especially after he prayed. Whenever Jake heard this, he felt a sense of relief, almost as if he knew the next few minutes would be okay.

Jake understood from his research that the devil often preyed on vulnerable people, especially those experiencing rage, intense fear, or depression. But even if the devil exploited his emotions, why was he completely unable to eliminate the voices in his head? From what he had seen on YouTube, some people with similar experiences referred to their voices as "people," while the medical term for them was "non-hallucinatory."

"I'm not crazy," he thought. "There's more to me than these voices."

Deep down, Jake knew there wasn't a pill that could simply switch them off. He was already taking Invega Sustenna, a shot he received at the beginning of each month. Once, he had stopped taking it for three months and noticed no difference in his symptoms. When he spoke to his psychiatrist about it, the doctor told him it would take six months for the medication to become effective again. Jake wanted to call him an asshole but held his tongue—his parents had raised him with manners.

Whenever Jake expressed his feelings to his psychiatrist, the response was always the same: more antipsychotics. But if one pill didn't help, how could a combination work? His therapist, on the other hand, was kind and a great listener, but she had no real solutions for controlling the voices. She probably had too many cases like his—people who were even more suicidal.

One thing Jake knew for certain was that the voices were manipulative. They could make him angry in an instant and, on rare occasions, even happy—but that happiness was always tied to an undercurrent of depression.

"Damn, these voices," he muttered. "They make me feel like the dumbest, most worthless person in the world."

He clenched his fists. "Fuck, man. I feel like my emotions are being controlled."

Frustrated, Jake lay down on his bed, trying to think of ways to free himself from this psychological bondage. It felt like someone was imprisoning his mind—but that didn't make sense. There was no one else there. Before he started hearing voices, he had thought telepathy was fake. But maybe it was real. Maybe it was some kind of mysticism he didn't understand. Professor X from *X-Men* was a telepath. Dracula was a telepath. Even Jesus sometimes seemed like one.

He felt a little better and picked up *Kindred* to read. Eventually, he slept most of the day.

At about 2:30 AM, he picked up his phone and called Rachel.

"Hey, Rachel, I'm signing us up for the convention. That okay with you?" he asked.

"Yeah, that's fine. There are a few people I really want to see," Rachel replied.

After saying their goodbyes, Jake registered the whole group for the convention. Everyone agreed it fit their schedules.

Rachel was home alone—her parents and siblings had left. She lay on her back, thinking about what had led her to the hospital in the first place. She could have sworn the woman Jason had cheated with had been right there in that presentation room.

She turned on the radio.

"He's mine, bitch. Jason is mine. If you come near me when I'm with him, I'll kill you."

Rachel's eyes widened. She rushed to the radio and slammed it off. "It's not real," she chanted to herself over and over.

She turned on the TV, hoping for a distraction. But the newscaster's voice made her freeze.

"Rachel, you are surrounded. We have cameras in your house. We are watching you. Jason is ours, bitch."

Fear gripped her, and she quickly turned off the TV. Her mind was racing. She walked to the bathroom, opened a drawer, and took out a few sleeping pills. She swallowed them with water, took a shower, and went to bed by 8:00 PM.

"There's no one talking to me through the radio and TV. It's just a hallucination," she reassured herself.

But a nagging thought crept in. *What if Jason really did cheat on me?* That wouldn't explain why these women would plant cameras in her house. The paranoia was suffocating.

She got up, grabbed a bottle of antipsychotic pills—Seroquel—and took 300 mg before lying back down. With the grace of God, she finally drifted off to sleep.

That night, she had a nightmare. She was tied to a chair, hands bound behind her back. The woman she suspected of being with Jason loomed over her, holding a knife. The blade gleamed as she raised it high and brought it down.

Rachel's eyes flew open. Her heart pounded, sweat dampening her skin. Without thinking, she grabbed her phone and called Jason.

After three rings, he picked up. "Hey, Rachel. Why are you calling me?"

"I just… I wanted to know if you love me."

Jason sighed. "I love you as a friend. Depending on how well things go with the organization, maybe we could rekindle our relationship. I haven't dismissed you. And I've never cheated on you. You're the only woman I've been with intimately."

Rachel swallowed hard. "What about your prom date on Facebook? She's beautiful. Are you seriously telling me nothing happened that night?"

"Nothing happened. For one thing, you know you're more beautiful. And another thing—we didn't do anything physical. We just danced."

Rachel let out a breath she hadn't realized she was holding. They said their goodbyes, and for the first time in a while, she smiled and fell asleep like a baby.

Chapter 16

The next morning, Pedro wakes up but can't move. His eyes dart around, struggling to focus. He concentrates hard, willing his arm to move, but it feels impossibly heavy. He tries his other arm—same result. Panic sets in. He waits for thirty seconds, silently begging God to let him move. Then, somehow, he manages to twitch his right index finger. Summoning all his will, he slowly extends his hand. Suddenly, with one long exhale, his body jolts back into motion. He sits up in bed, cursing under his breath.

"What the fuck am I supposed to do?" he mutters. "I need Zyprexa to stop the racing thoughts, but if I take it, I won't be able to move."

He grabs his phone and calls Jake. Jake picks up almost immediately.

"Hey, Pedro, what's up, man?"

"Hey, Jake, man, it happened again. I woke up and couldn't move. I could barely move my eyeballs," Pedro says, his voice still shaky.

"This might sound out of left field, but have you ever tried lithium? It might help," Jake suggests.

"No, I haven't, but I'm scared to take other antipsychotics. I don't want to feel slow like I do with Zyprexa."

"You might need to see your psychiatrist. Maybe try a lower dose or the version of Zyprexa that doesn't cause weight gain. There could be a connection between the weight gain and the paralysis."

"Yeah, that's a good idea. I'll try a lower dose," Pedro agrees.

They exchange goodbyes, and Pedro picks up the book *DBT for Bipolar Disorder*—something they had discussed back in the hospital. He spends three hours engrossed in it, reading from cover to cover. By the end, he's in awe. The book is incredible. The more he reads, the calmer he feels, as if he's drinking serenity like alcohol, getting more intoxicated with each page. He especially loves the four core principles: interpersonal effectiveness, distress tolerance, emotional regulation, and mindfulness. Mindfulness captivates him the most. The idea of fully immersing himself in the present moment intrigues him. He tries not to dwell on his past episode during the GRE or worry about it happening again. For the first time in a long while, his mind feels at peace.

Picking up the phone again, he calls Jake.

"I read that book we talked about in the hospital, and it really helped. I might not remember every detail, but I *know* I'm not on the edge. Just reading it makes me feel more in control."

"I'm so happy for you," Jake says. "It helped me, too, when I first started hearing voices. By the way, I saw something on the NAMI website—there's a sign-up for doing a presentation."

"Sounds great. You wanna hit the gym? I think we both have memberships."

"Yeah, give me an hour."

Then, suddenly: *Jesus.*

The voice rings in Jake's head, eerie and cartoonish. He tries to keep his face neutral, but the entity contorts his expressions, making him feel humiliated.

"Not now. I just wanna go to the gym and hang out," he mutters to himself.

Whenever he goes to the gym, his voices wreak havoc on him. They always start with the Jesus talk. *You're not Jesus. That's not Jesus. Wait.* He braces himself—this pattern always leads to some kind of repetitive woe. The words echo, looping, making it impossible to think clearly. His paranoia heightens. As he moves his hand, it feels like someone else is controlling it. He tilts his head slightly to the right, but just *thinking* about moving it left triggers paranoia, as if his brain has lost control over his body, and now it is dancing at someone else's tune. The facial hallucinations are the worst. It's like a projected image over his own face as if someone else is subtly controlling his facial muscles, cowering behind the thin layer of his skin, passing around signals to either twitch or relax, just enough to unsettle him. His anger boils.

"What the hell can I do about this?" he grits his teeth.

Lately, the voices have been adding a new bane into the mix—scrambling his focus. When he tries to concentrate, they flood him with thoughts that make him feel like the most confused person in the world. If he stays stuck in this cycle, he'll never get a girlfriend and never get off these high blood pressure pills. At 6'4" and 304 pounds, his frustration spikes. He *wants* to work out, but something inside him resists, something that *wants* him to stay away from the gym.

"What the hell—how can a voice tell me to get laid but then say, 'Get help now'?"

On the treadmill, he knows what will happen. The voices will chant *Jesus, Jesus, Jesus.* Then, suddenly, a new phrase: *Wait for help.* It's a bizarre relief. That second chant usually means they'll ease up. When that happens, they say, *That's God.* And for some reason, that calms him—just a little, like a thin shield against the storm.

Maybe I shouldn't go, he thinks.

He kneels down and prays. "God, I'm about to go to the gym. Please make sure I don't have disturbing thoughts, hallucinations, or emotions. Protect me from myself."

After praying, he feels a slight comfort. The facial hallucination still lingers, but it's manageable. He watches music videos on YouTube to distract himself. *Racks on Racks on Racks* by YC blares through his speakers. He's about to pray again when his phone rings. It's Pedro.

Perspective

"Hey man, you ready?" Pedro asks.

"Yeah, let's go. I'm having hallucinations. I keep thinking if I saw a witch doctor, I could be free from this. But the problem is, not all witch doctors are legit," Jake admits.

He laces up his gym shoes, grabs his headphones and iPhone, and heads out. Pedro is waiting in the car. They shake hands.

"I hope I don't have any episodes at the gym or while driving there," Pedro says.

"That's okay. I feel safe with you. It's crazy—my voices are talking to me at the same time I'm talking to you. They communicate through facial expressions and intrusive thoughts. Let's start with one mile of cardio on the treadmill."

When they arrive at the gym, they stash their wallets and keys in a locker. As they step onto the treadmills, Jake's voices switch tactics. Now, instead of shouting, they communicate through automatic thoughts laced with remnants of emotion and through subtle changes in his facial expressions.

Jake has been coming to the gym on and off for about a month. He sets the treadmill to three miles an hour. If they keep this pace for twenty minutes, they'll complete a mile. He used to have a treadmill at home, but his brother broke it by going full speed on sprints.

"Yeah, this used to be so simple before I started hearing voices. Now it's a psychological labyrinth," said Jake.

"I never really needed to work out at all. I still have a high metabolism," said Pedro.

As they walked for ten minutes, Jake's voices started chanting "Jesus" every time he tried to express himself. The voices began doing the face thing—projected faces appearing whenever he looked away from Pedro. He felt completely trapped, powerless in his own mind. He wanted to scream, but he knew that even thinking about screaming excited the voices.

"Oh man, I think I sprained my ankle," said Pedro. Just when Jake was trying to read his mind he heard Pedro whimper in pain.

He stepped off the treadmill and grabbed his ankle. Jake was about to get off as well to check on him, but Pedro stopped him.

"You finish the mile. I want you to defy those demonic-ass voices," Pedro said.

Jake finished the mile and felt a sense of accomplishment. The treadmill was always a challenge for him.

As he cooled down, Jake noticed a woman talking to herself. At first, he thought she was crazy, but when he looked closer, he saw she had cordless white headphones on.

She was a Black woman. This got him thinking about what it meant to be Black and struggle with mental health.

His thoughts about America stalled because he realized he hadn't been to many places in the country as an adult. He couldn't use his own state as a model. Through research, movies, and conversations, he had learned that white people were more likely to seek professional help for mental health issues, while Black people often dismissed them.

"That's just the way Jermaine is, always saying crazy things," was something he often heard in the Black community. Hearing voices and experiencing paranoia were often seen as just part of a person's personality. He had heard stories from the hood of people self-medicating with alcohol or weed instead of seeking help. He also heard claims, though he wasn't sure if they were true, that psychiatrists put less effort into treating Black patients with mental health issues.

I just want to go on vacation, Jake thought, *somewhere like Jamaica, where I might not hear any voices. Just enjoy the sunshine with some down-to-earth friends.*

Most of the time, he realized his mental state never felt stable for more than five-second intervals. Different communities experienced mental illness differently, but Jake wanted to create an organization that looked past race and focused solely on the mental health issue itself.

He once talked to his father about Uganda, where people could stop each other on the street and openly share their problems. African cultures had traditions to help people with mental health struggles. For example, if someone claimed to hear the voice of Jesus Christ, they weren't immediately dismissed as mentally ill. In the U.S., mentioning private struggles to a stranger would likely make them walk briskly away. He also believed people with mental illness in the U.S. were more aggressive compared to those in Europe. In Europe, people were more open about their emotions, whereas in America, men especially were conditioned to hide their feelings.

"You okay, Jake? Ready to do some weightlifting?" Pedro asked.

"Yeah, I'm ready." Jake hesitated for a moment, then looked around the gym. He noticed three attractive women he wouldn't mind getting to know. One particular white woman in front of him had wide hips, a plump butt, and medium-sized breasts in a sports bra. She wore tight leggings that accentuated her curves.

"Hey, how are you doing?" Jake asked the woman.

"Hey," she replied with a smile.

"Can you show me how to do those squats you were just doing?" Jake asked.

She grinned, turned around, and placed a lightweight on her shoulders. She positioned one leg behind her, bent her knee, and lunged forward, demonstrating the move. Jake watched her backside and then exchanged a knowing glance with Pedro, who smirked back.

Jake furrowed his brow, deep in thought. *If I ask for her number and she gives it to me, how do I get her to answer when I call?* Years ago, he had gotten plenty of numbers, but when he called, no one picked up. *But if I don't ask, how will I ever see her outside the gym?* Even if he got her number and they went on dates, how many dates would it take before they had an intimate relationship? He was unsure.

When the woman finished her demonstration, she turned around and smiled at Jake. He returned a flirtatious smile.

"You seem like a cool person. I was wondering if we could hang out sometime. What's your phone number?" he asked.

"I'm sorry, but I already have a man," she said in a sudden Southern accent.

Jake immediately sensed she was putting on a fake voice, which only irritated him more.

"That's cool. Nice meeting you," he said, walking back to Pedro. Jake knew he always had good manners, even when people were rude to him.

"Access denied," Jake muttered.

"You'll meet someone at some point. Not all the women in the world have boyfriends," Pedro reassured him.

"Maybe it's just the people in this state. I'm kind of ready to get the fuck out of here. My voices are acting up again," Jake said, a defeated look on his face.

It was incredible. He had spent six years in college and never had sex with any woman—just foreplay with one. Maybe if he had been in a serious relationship, none of these mental health problems would have surfaced. Maybe if he just found a steady girlfriend who looked like Rachel, he'd be okay. But deep down, he knew that wasn't the case. He could see his organization becoming a force in the country, making a difference, making appearances. But could he really go to bed at night believing that everything he had endured in mental hospitals was just preparation to work within the so-called mental health system? Besides, his new friends had problems that sex alone wouldn't fix.

"Well, that pretty much wraps it up. I'm going home to make a quick phone call before sleeping."

Jake and Pedro went their separate ways. As soon as Jake got home, he pulled up Rachel's contact and called her.

"Hey, Jake, what's up? I've been looking at some of the presenters for the NAMI convention. Some of them have good things to say, but others are just so ambiguous with their words," Rachel said.

“Rachel, tell me the truth. Do you actually follow and understand what they’re saying?” Jake asked.

“No.”

“Don’t get mad about it—I don’t either. It’s almost like they’re trying to be confusing on purpose.”

“I don’t think the audience they’re speaking to is the average American. Certain presenters cater to a specific crowd—professionals in mental health.”

“Yeah, you could be right. You know what, Rachel? I’ve been thinking, and I don’t think I can be the leader anymore.”

“Don’t give up, Jake. Don’t let your symptoms get the best of you. I have voices, too. They make me feel crazy, low and confused most of the time. But we’re actually doing something here—helping people. There’s something really sick about this whole mental health problem.”

“Hypothetically, take someone like Jamal from Southside Chicago—he can’t afford $300 a week for therapy sessions. And because of his financial situation, he can’t even afford a mediocre therapist.”

“Well, yeah, you’re right. Poor people can’t afford even an average therapist. But from what I see on the list of speakers at the NAMI convention, some of these people are real angels. They’re actually making a difference. But they have a marketing problem. Take the Yellow Tulip Project, for example. I don't think you've heard of them, but they have something good going on," Rachel said.

"Yeah, I've heard of them. I found them while browsing the NAMI website. A lot of the projects and programs they have—I didn't even know they existed until I stumbled upon them," Jake replied.

As he spoke, he felt his tactile hallucinations flare up again. Every time he said something to Rachel, he saw a face as if it were telling him to get to the point. He clenched his fists, frustrated. He didn't see Rachel as a sex object—she was an intelligent woman with valuable insights—but the voices, or whatever they were, made him feel humiliated as if he were the dumbest person alive, broadcasted for the world to see.

"My voices are acting up. I'll talk to you later, Rachel. I need to get some sleep. Goodnight."

"Goodnight, Jake."

Chapter 17

Despite everything, he felt proud of his conversation with Rachel. It seemed like they were on the same page about the NAMI convention. He went upstairs, ate some Ugandan food his mother had made, took a shower, and climbed into bed. But as he went through these simple activities, he had the distinct feeling that he wasn't alone—like he was two selves sharing one body and mind.

How was that even possible? It had to be him doing it. But then, how could he be doing it without realizing it? His eyesight was getting worse, too. When he paused to focus on something, his vision shifted. He called it "perception change." If he stared at a towel or a wall, it was as if someone else was looking through his eyes. He could feel the shift along with the voices in his head.

On top of that, he had an eye disease called keratoconus. His corneas weren't concave, distorting his vision. Without contacts, he struggled to see both near and far. Each lens costs about $600. Once, he broke one and had to wait two weeks for a replacement. His right eye, though dry, had better vision than his left. If he covered his left eye, he could see almost 20/20. Still, he sensed something was off. The blurriness was strange, but when he relaxed for about five minutes, he could see more depth in it—as if something vital was missing. It was like the soul of what he was looking at wasn't there. Was it a sanity issue or a real vision problem? The more he thought about it, the more he concluded that it was emotional.

And this was with the contacts.

Last night, when he went to sleep, he saw a devil staring at him in his consciousness. It wore lipstick, but it was undeniably demonic. The sight shook him. If he saw it again, what would he do? He didn't know. But somehow, he believed he would bounce back—like he always did. The emotions these hallucinations triggered weren't always strong enough to make him consider self-harm, but sometimes, they were.

What if his diagnosis was really schizoaffective disorder? Would he be trapped in a unique kind of hell, one he couldn't fathom forever? Because it felt like, over time, something in his mind was diminishing. He didn't know what it was—maybe the foundation of his short-term memory. One thing he was sure of, though: his concentration was deteriorating. What if he could no longer have an intelligent conversation without seeing that demonic face over and over?

The only thing that seemed to help, even a little, was Wellbutrin—at least, he thought it did—and large cups of coffee. He preferred French Nescafé, mildly dark. It was the best instant coffee he had found.

It was Saturday, the day of the convention. Today, Jake and his friends would finally see what was being done about mental health problems in the country and how they could help. Jake noticed the face-mimicking thing that his voices did to his face, but they weren't talking that morning.

Perspective

Jake could use his mom's car today, so before driving to the convention, he went through his morning ritual and said his usual prayer. The news reported that everything would go as planned at the convention. All his friends from the organization called him, confirming they would meet him at the NAMI convention.

Jake knew it was important to listen to the speakers, but he also felt that he was going to hear something special today—something life-changing. There was an unshakable feeling in the air as if this day would alter his life forever. He thought about the NAMI website and the presentations he had seen. It was true—he was impressed. There were people who genuinely wanted to help with mental health issues and were taking action. But why weren't they on CNN or the front page of YouTube?

Jake would cross-reference the names of speakers from NAMI with their YouTube videos, only to be surprised at how few people engaged with their content. One particular man had only 83 likes for his presentation, while a Young Thug video had 1.7k likes. More and more people were seeing therapists these days, yet mental health still wasn't a primary news topic. If someone's mental health deteriorates, how can they solve other problems in the world?

Arriving at the convention center, Jake saw the parking lot was packed. Frustrated, he found a spot at the very back and walked toward the front gate. A huge grin spread across his face when he saw his friends waiting for him.

Pedro looked sharp in his dress shirt and tie, giving Jake a half-smirk. Ayn, dressed in jeans and a wife beater, smiled at Jake, trying to mask her emotions about their date and the depressed phantom. She put on a strong front, but deep down, she felt like doing something bad to herself—just kind of.

Jake glanced at Jason, who smelled of citrus soap and cocoa butter. He couldn't remember a time Jason ever smelled bad. It was part of Jason's OCD—his constant battle with germs. Rachel looked as beautiful as ever in yoga pants and a tight t-shirt, grinning at Jake like the Cat from *Alice in Wonderland*.

They all exchanged greetings.

"So, what's the plan, guys? There are PhD presenters, authors, psychiatrists, and therapists," Pedro said.

"How about we check out this guy first—Mark Thompson? I read his book. It was mediocre, but it had some good parts about his psychosis."

Holding pamphlets, they made their way to a room filled with people waiting for Mark's talk. Mark stood on stage, chatting with a sound engineer. He looked like any regular guy—denim Wranglers and an AC/DC t-shirt. He didn't glance at Jake and his friends as they entered, but that wasn't arrogance. In fact, he had a carefree, happy smile—one that was hard to dislike.

Perspective

Reading Mark's memoir about his psychosis in Paris made Jake consider writing a book even more. Yes, Mark had been to Paris. And yes, he had a psychotic episode—naked—running through the city, preaching that the world would end that night. Whenever he spoke to someone, they either briskly walked away or ran. The French police tried to put clothes on him, speaking in broken English. When Mark wouldn't comply, they forced him into a car, shoving him inside so roughly that his head hit the roof. He got a concussion, felt woozy, and momentarily stopped preaching.

They threw him in prison, still wrapped in a towel. By morning, he was preaching again—to the prison guards—about the rapture. Later that day, they sedated him and sent him back to America. By then, he was on antipsychotics, calm, and fully clothed. No one on the plane would have guessed he had been running naked through Paris, prophesizing like a frenzied Jehovah's Witness on crack. Once back in the U.S., he was admitted to a psych ward, and from there, the story got pretty boring.

Jake later discovered in a NAMI interview that someone else had written Mark's book—based on an interview with him. This irritated Jake. He wondered if the ghostwriter had exaggerated parts of the story to make it more dramatic.

Mark opened his presentation with a joke. The audience laughed. Then, he shifted into serious mode, discussing mental illness and summarizing his book like he was chatting with friends at a bar. The crowd laughed at his humor, though Pedro wasn't impressed.

When Pedro learned Mark was diagnosed with Bipolar 1—just like him—he thought the whole event was just for book sales. Pedro's own psychotic break had been terrifying. He wasn't sure if he was in hell, the Matrix, or something else entirely. Whenever Pedro talked about the GRE, he spoke fast. His emotions tinged with paranoia—like the Devil had played a trick on him. The GRE had scarred him permanently. It made him feel forever disconnected from "normal" people, just as he had felt during the dreaded test itself.

Mark ended his talk with another joke, and the audience laughed again. Then, he sat at the side of the room, signing books. From where Jake stood, he could see how relaxed Mark was, chatting with each person in line.

I could do that too, Jake thought.

He often romanticized the idea of going from city to city, signing his novel, and giving speeches. Watching Mark, he felt the dream pull at him even more.

Maybe after solidifying his organization, he would be able to write about everything he and his friends had done.

"There's something I didn't tell you guys. I'm about to give a speech in about an hour. I've been emailing a psychologist who's researching people with schizoaffective disorder. I know we don't like labels, but I told him I have it, and he said he'd let me give a short speech after his presentation on what it means to live with this condition," Jake said.

"Jake, you never told us! I have so many questions. Are you going to introduce our organization? Are you going to tell everyone about us? About Mount Zion? Are you going to talk about the good and bad of NAMI?" Rachel asked hastily.

"Some of everything, I hope… I'm going to tell people how it feels to live with this," Jake replied.

"That's really good, Jake. I just don't have the guts to do that right now. My chronic anxiety is still too overwhelming—I don't think I could give a speech now," Pedro said, his voice barely above a whisper.

"Yeah, you don't have to. I'm pretty sure there's something for all of us to do. I won't lie, though—I'm a little nervous. But I feel like I have to do this. I've got to be a voice for people like me. There are people out there going through what I'm going through right now, and they need someone to speak up. Even with that, my hands are shaking, and I'm sweating, especially my palms," Jake admitted.

"Breathe in slowly, then exhale even slower. Make sure your exhale takes more time than your inhale," Ayn suggested.

Jake practiced his breathing while watching people take their seats in the auditorium. Everything was crystal clear, and surprisingly, his voices weren't manifesting in facial or verbal hallucinations. He felt free but terrified of making a fool of himself.

He noticed the psychologist he had been emailing walking toward him, briefcase in hand.

"Hey Jake, how are you feeling today?" Dr. Hugo asked.

"I'm okay—a little nervous—but I'm ready to do what you need me to do," Jake responded.

Jake knew Dr. Hugo needed someone who experienced voices and delusions—someone who could articulate what it meant to have schizoaffective disorder and still function. Unlike some professionals, Dr. Hugo truly wanted to help people. Jake had watched him speak on YouTube, saying this illness was lifelong, genetic, and required both medication and therapy. Despite that, Jake sensed through Dr. Hugo's expressions and demeanor that he genuinely cared. If more professionals put in the effort Dr. Hugo did, maybe there would be more breakthroughs.

The audience settled into their seats. Pedro, Ayn, Rachel, and Jason sat in the front row. The plan was for Dr. Hugo to begin with a brief explanation of the disorder before Jake shared his experience. Then, Dr. Hugo would discuss the current treatments available.

Jake sat behind Dr. Hugo on stage, watching as the psychologist stepped up to the podium, paper in hand. Dr. Hugo was a professional—well-spoken, confident, and thorough in explaining schizoaffective disorder.

Jake glanced at the audience and was startled by how many people were looking at him intently. Their expressions told him they genuinely wanted to understand this disorder that afflicted 1% of the world's population.

"This is Jake. He is highly functional and has schizoaffective disorder. He's going to share what it feels like to live with it," Dr. Hugo announced.

Jake's tall 6'4" frame loomed over the stage as he stood up. He took a moment, thinking briefly about Malcolm X—how he stood at podiums, speaking with vigor and determination about race relations in America. To Jake, Malcolm was like a modern-day prophet on stage, but he was human too. Malcolm had moments of fear, just as Jake did now.

"I've tried everything, y'all. I've tried everything, and those emotions are still there—along with the voices. The only thing I haven't tried is this—standing here, talking to you. And honestly, this scares me less than the voices," Jake began.

"I can't tell you how many therapists I've seen, how many psychiatrists. None of them have truly made a dent in what's going on with me. I used to remember every medication I tried, but now it's a jumble—they've been spread out over so many years. Something tells me I can't live the rest of my life like this, constantly fearing these disturbing emotions that cut to the core of who I am.

"The only things that have helped me are Alcoholics Anonymous, God, and my new friends. I try my hardest to maintain a conscious connection with God, and sometimes,

I feel it. I pray on my knees morning and night—every single day—just hoping to experience one day without hearing a single voice, without auditory hallucinations, or whatever you want to call them.

"I'm not some genius who can read academic dissertations on auditory hallucinations and draw conclusions. I've read about treatments—some things help, some don't. Dialectical behavior therapy helped at first, and it still helps a little, but it doesn't solve the problem. Cognitive behavioral therapy? Same thing—mild help, no solution.

"I want a solution. I want to start a therapy or remedy that actually solves the problem. But from all my Google searches, I haven't found anything. I've read stories about people miraculously cured, but what are the chances that's me? What exact words do I need to say in my prayers? I'm not an atheist—I believe in God 100%—but I'm tired of this bullshit. I've complained about this so many times, and no one knows what to tell me. People just say, 'I wish I could help you.'

"I'm not going to hurt myself or anyone else, but I'm tired of living like this. I read once about someone with my condition who went to a Buddhist monastery and got cured. Should I do that? But then I think—if that actually worked, wouldn't it be all over the news? CNN would be running a headline: 'Schizophrenia Cured in Tibetan Monastery.'

"These voices have been in my head for so long, I'm starting to believe they're a part of my DNA. And that scares me, folks. I can't imagine the fear and pain I'd be living with in my later years if that's true. Imagine my wedding day—when the priest asks my wife and me to say our vows—and I hear a voice telling me I'm the dumbest person who ever lived.

"It's either I'm in emotional pain, or I'm in fear of pain. I may sound selfish, but I need someone to help me. I need help right now."

The room was silent. Jake looked out at the sea of faces, some stunned, some nodding, some blinking away tears. He had spoken his truth—raw and unfiltered. And now, he waited.

I need someone who understands my struggle better than psychiatrists and therapists. I have friends in the audience who aren't diagnosed with exactly what I have, but they deal with extreme OCD, bipolar disorder, depression, and schizophrenia. That last one is kind of like me. I was diagnosed with schizoaffective disorder. I use these labels, but I hate them. My friends are so much more than their diagnoses. They are not their illnesses; they are extraordinary people.

Jake strolls across the stage.

They didn't choose this. I didn't wake up one day and decide it would be amazing to have voices in my head that humiliate me every day. Voices that bully me that read my thoughts and emotions. Of course, I'd love to have a nine-to-five job like everybody else. But at least when I'm home,

I can sleep, distract myself, or pray out loud when I'm having an episode. If I worked at Duke Energy and told them I needed time to talk to my voices to calm them down, do you think they'd let me? When I had an IT job, I talked to my voices, and people thought I was on drugs. They got mad at me as if I could control it. I didn't ask for this.

First of all, the stigma has to change. You can still be an average person and have mental health challenges. Remember what I said about my friends? They have what they have, but they are incredible people. And not to sound egotistical—I'm an incredible person, too. I can't do this alone. That's why I have my friends.

We need a movement. A revolution for mental health. There has to be a new way of looking at it. If this country is so great, why are European countries doing better when it comes to mental health? I read an article once that said people with mental health issues in America are considered more dangerous than those in Europe. With all our advancements, that shouldn't be the case. If our healthcare system is the best in the world, why isn't our mental healthcare?

I've been hospitalized so many times. Please, help me and my friends. Help Rachel, Pedro, Jason, and Ayn stay out of the hospital. If we don't have the answers, we have to try harder. Kind of like what JFK said: "We don't go to the moon because it is easy; we go because it is hard."

Jake stands at the podium for a moment. A round of applause erupts. He scans the crowd and smiles—relieved no one is throwing bananas or oranges at him. Slowly, he steps back and takes a seat behind the podium, still watching the audience. For the first time in his life, he feels like he's making a difference. The only feeling that compares is when he talks to his four friends from Zion. It's possible, he thinks. It's possible. I can make a change.

Money doesn't cross his mind after the speech. He isn't worried about how he'll survive once his parents are too old to care for him. In that moment, God tells him, *You will be alright. You will be happy.* God whispers to him in his subconscious, *Thank you for being my instrument.*

Dr. Hugo approaches the podium as the applause continues.

A man on the edge of the aisle moves quickly toward the stage. He wears a sweatshirt, clutching something inside it. He leaps onto the stage, grabs the psychologist by the neck, and presses a gun to his head.

"Shut the fuck up, asshole!" he screams.

Jake and his friends freeze in shock.

"I want you to shut the fuck up with that bullshit!" The man points the gun at Dr. Hugo, then turns and shouts at someone who isn't there.

"I think he has voices," Jake whispers to Jason. "Did you see how he talked to nobody behind him?"

"We have to do something. He's a voice-hearer who's probably confused. We might need to get out of here," Jason says.

"It's too much!" the man shouts. "They talk to me all day, driving me crazy! First, they told me to kill someone. Then, they told me to kill myself. And now—I know what I'll do! Since I can't kill myself, someone in here has to help me. *Someone make the fucking voices stop!* I've seen psychiatrist after psychiatrist, and they just tell me to see another one. I've tried every medication known to man, and they still humiliate me. Someone in here is going to help me, or this asshole is dead! I've been following him online. If I don't get help, he's dead."

Most of the room empties, but Jake and his friends stay behind, along with a few others.

"I know how you feel, man," Jake says, stepping forward with a hand extended. "Going everywhere and finding no help. But you can't let the voices win."

"You don't know me," the man snarls. "You don't know what I've been through."

"I've been to the hospital. I've seen countless doctors. I'm just like you. I'm tired of living like this, too. I don't want to live like this for the rest of my life. But I can't give up. You're probably right—maybe that guy you're holding *is* a douchebag. But don't let him change who *you* are. I had to look deep inside myself. To remember the love I have for my friends and my family. To remember the good times before the voices—the times when I was happy. I had to keep researching my problem and refuse to give up. God chose us for a reason. We can withstand a lot. We've been through hell."

"You have it easier than me," the man mutters. "My problem is worse."

Jake glances at the man's arm and notices the slash marks. Slowly, he lifts his own arm and turns it toward him.

"Look at my arm," Jake says. "We both have self-inflicted scars. We both tried to put the pain somewhere else. These are our battle marks. But you know what? When I did that shit, the voices only egged me on. It made everything worse."

The man's grip loosens. He kicks the psychiatrist forward and hurls the gun behind the stage.

The man falls to his knees, sobbing uncontrollably.

Jake rushes over and places a reassuring hand on his shoulder. "What's your name, man? I'm Jake."

"I'm Jung," the man with the gun mutters.

Pedro, Rachel, Ayn, and Jason exchange stunned glances, struggling to process what just transpired. The police storm in, securing Jung in handcuffs.

"I'm sorry," Jung mumbles. "I just wanted them to stop. That's all I wanted—just for them to stop."

Jake watches as they haul Jung away. Jason steps up beside him. "Jake, I couldn't leave you alone with that guy—Jung, right?"

Rachel shakes her head in disbelief. "Jake, how did you have the guts to do that? I can't believe what I just witnessed."

Jake watches Jung disappear from sight. "I saw myself in him. If I hadn't met you guys, maybe the same thing could have happened to me. I've searched everywhere—and I mean everywhere—looking for answers. I spent days on the internet searching for cures, but I always came up empty. This man reminds me that there's a war going on. A war of the mind. And if no one does anything about it, it'll only get worse."

A heavy silence settles over them. Pedro is the first to look up. "Do you guys really think we can make a difference? I don't even know where to start."

"Maybe we start with our stories," Jason suggests.

Jason exhales sharply. "I'm still shaken up. Jake, you could've been killed. That guy would have shot you and that psychiatrist."

"I know," Jake admits. "But I had to take a stand. Who better to talk down someone with severe hallucinations than someone who understands them firsthand? A part of me wanted to run, but another part knew I had to do something. I even thought about what would happen if a sniper had taken Jung out—nothing would change. The cycle of violence would continue. The violence people with mental health issues inflict on others, and the violence they inflict on themselves—it has to stop."

Jake walks over to a chair, sits down, and exhales deeply. His emotions finally overwhelm him, and he breaks down. His friends gather around him, embracing him. Thirty minutes passed with him talking to his friends. Reporters burst into the room, thrusting microphones in his face.

Chapter 18

"A man experiencing a manic episode held a psychiatrist hostage at a NAMI convention, claiming to see imaginary people behind him. Another man—also battling hallucinations—managed to talk him down, convincing him to drop the gun and let the psychiatrist go."

The TV screen cuts to footage recorded after Jung was taken away in handcuffs. A reporter stands in front of Jake.

"So, how were you able to talk down the disturbed individual?" she asks.

Jake stares straight into the camera, still crying. Jason wraps an arm around him, leading him away from the reporters. The rest of their friends form a protective barrier, ensuring Jake makes it to Jason's car safely.

Once inside, Jake exhales in frustration. "Man, I'm tired of this shit. I didn't tell you guys, but I need to say it now—when everything was happening, I was at peace. The voices were completely silent. No hallucinations, no whispers. I was scared, yeah, but I was at peace."

Jason's eyes widen. "They were gone? That makes sense, though. Maybe they were scared, too. Maybe they weren't expecting you to do that. Jake, when you were talking to Jung, you were like a superhero. I've never seen anything like it—except on TV."

"Something else," Jake says, staring out the window. "Everything was crystal clear. I was terrified, but I had never seen the world that vividly before."

That night, Jake comes home feeling overwhelmed—excited yet anxious. On one hand, the voices had vanished during the crisis. On the other, he hadn't expected the media frenzy. He checks his Facebook and sees 30 friend requests.

"This is crazy," he murmurs. He had never received so many requests before.

A knock at the door interrupts his thoughts. Looking outside, he sees three cars pulling into the driveway. Reporters spill out of their vans.

"Jake! There are strange people outside!" his mom calls down.

Still processing everything, Jake takes a deep breath. He needs more time to sort through his emotions, but he figures he can answer a few questions.

"Jake, how are you feeling? How does it feel to be a hero?" asks one reporter.

"I'm feeling... okay. A little overwhelmed. I don't feel like a hero. I'm just Jake. I saw someone in trouble and wanted to help," he replies.

"Did your voices tell you to do it?" another reporter asks.

Jake frowns. "No. They were silent—probably from the adrenaline."

"Are your voices telling you to hurt yourself right now?" a third reporter presses.

"No. They're quiet."

"Are your voices telling you to hurt anyone else?"

Jake's expression darkens. Just when he thought people understood, they proved they didn't. Their questions showed complete ignorance of what it's like to be him.

"I'm done," he snaps. "I want all of you off my property. Now."

He slams the door so hard that the walls shake.

His mom peeks her head out from the kitchen. "Jake, who was at the door?"

"Nobody," he mutters before retreating to his room.

"So, you think you're somebody now?" a familiar voice taunts in his head.

Jake stiffens. "What the fuck? I thought you were gone."

The realization hits him: the voices returned because of how the reporters made him feel. But they sound different— less like tormentors, more like old friends. Maybe this is their way of sticking around until he finds the right help. They feel unfinished yet content.

Jake sighs, turning on his laptop. He types his name into YouTube. Sure enough, someone uploaded a video of his talk with Jung. The views are climbing fast.

His phone buzzes.

"Hey, man! You're kinda famous! The local news is airing your whole speech," Jason says.

Jake switches the TV to the news. There he is—front and center.

"Maybe I don't have to do anything," he thinks. "Maybe, through the media, people will finally see how big of a problem mental illness really is. Maybe they'll realize that real change needs to happen."

His phone vibrates again—another call.

"How did they get my number?" Jake wonders, staring at the screen.

He accidentally hangs up on Jason and answers the vibrating phone.

"Hello, Jake. This is Andrew from TED Talks. We were wondering if you'd be interested in speaking about mental illness in Los Angeles. We'll cover your travel, hotel, and all other expenses."

Jake hesitated, weighing the opportunity. This could help the movement for mental health awareness. But what if I'm just a fleeting sensation? It's not about me. It's about people like me who aren't living normal lives, the ones in their own personal hell. I don't even know how the media works. I might as well ride the wave and do my best, he thought.

"Yes, I'll come to Los Angeles. But can I bring four friends with me, all expenses paid?" Jake asked.

"You can bring one," Andrew replied. "I'm part of the NAMI society in Los Angeles. I saw your video and found it compelling—your speech with the psychiatrist and the way you de-escalated that disturbed individual. Too bad he's in jail, but we agree with you—most people with conditions like yours aren't violent. You're a good example, Jake. You've used your struggles to advocate for something greater."

"I've thought about doing things like this before," Jake admitted, "but mostly in a personal way. I need to discuss this with my friends and family before making a decision."

They said their goodbyes, and Jake noticed a call from Ayn. He picked up.

"Hey, Ayn!" Jake greeted her.

"Jake, it's happening! We're being taken seriously. God works in mysterious ways. If you hadn't had that altercation with Jung, none of this would be happening. You're really making a difference!" Ayn said excitedly.

"I just got a call from TED Talks. Someone affiliated with NAMI in L.A. wants me to do a presentation. They're covering travel and expenses for me and one guest," Jake explained.

"I'll go! I mean, if you're not thinking of bringing someone else," Ayn offered eagerly.

Jake paused. He hadn't considered bringing a woman. What would the media say? Did it even matter? It's not like he was running for president. Besides, Ayn was a good person, and they were just friends—though he'd always been drawn to her. Maybe this was a chance to grow closer.

"Yeah, you can come, Ayn. I'd love for you to join me in L.A. We should all meet up and discuss everything," Jake said.

"Okay!" Ayn replied.

They ended the call. Jake exhaled, exhausted. He wasn't sure how famous he was, but he knew he had local recognition, maybe even some national attention. I don't even know how to feel about that. Now I'll be able to get any woman I want, he thought, then grimaced. But what about Ayn? She was with me before any of this.

Jake opened Facebook and saw 200 friend requests. He scrolled through, noticing many attractive women. Maybe this is good. They saw something real in me. I wasn't sugarcoating anything. But Ayn—she saw all sides of me, not just the articulate, confident version on YouTube. She saw the playful me, the shy me. She saw me grow into this. I'll focus on Ayn for now. Maybe I can get her to reconsider waiting for marriage.

Just then, voices at the door caught his attention. His mother was speaking to reporters—people trying to ride the wave of his sudden fame. She came downstairs to find him still wide awake in bed.

"Jake, what is happening? I saw your video. Are you sure you can handle all of this with your mental health?" she asked, concerned.

"It's incredible, Mom. When I was speaking, my voices were silent. No hallucinations. Nothing. I was nervous, but I had total clarity," Jake explained. "To be honest, I was scared as hell."

"Jake, you shouldn't have talked to that crazy man with a gun! You could've been killed!" she exclaimed.

"I was scared, Mom, but I can't keep living like this without something meaningful happening. If I didn't do that, I'd probably end up back in Zion next year or worse."

"No, Jake, don't do that again. That man was a lunatic!"

Jake thought about how his mom labeled him without truly understanding him, but she loves him. He simply said,

"Okay, Mom, whatever you say," and stopped talking. He turned over, attempting to sleep.

It's kinda crazy—I feel a little scared of myself. What if she's right? What if I have an episode while I'm on stage at TedTalks? This crowd would be larger and more distinguished than NAMI. People would be flying in from all over the world. *What if I have an episode on the plane?* He shook his head. *I have to stop catastrophizing. I have to use logic.*

Whenever he was on stage, the voices seemed to quiet. *Plus, Ayn will be there.* He thought about Eva Longhorn, who had done a TedTalk. She admitted to having several voices or entities in her head, yet she still spoke in front of all those people. *Then again, I don't know what's going on in her head. Maybe she practiced for years with larger and larger crowds, making TedTalks easy for her. Plus, she said she could talk to her voices whenever she wanted, even scheduling times to engage with them.* But Jake couldn't communicate with his voices like that. They weren't friends. More often than not, they turned on him, injecting negative, demonic emotions into his consciousness.

"I can't fucking live like this, God," he whispered into the darkness. "I can't live like this, Holy One. But what about all those people who need a voice? What about the people of color who need someone to speak for them?"

Then, a thought hit him like a gut punch. *What if none of this is real? What if I'm still in Zion? What if this is just one big delusion wrapped around the idea of becoming famous?* Plenty of people suffered from delusions of grandeur—thinking they were destined for greatness or that they were prophets meant to lead a world revolution. He used to have thoughts of power, too, of being the President of the United States or some great influential figure. *And now… it's happening. My delusions—or maybe dreams—are coming true.*

He still felt like the same old Jake inside, but something was different. *Am I enlightened?* He didn't want to be fake for the press. He wanted to be honest. He had lived through some truly demonic emotions, and he wanted to share that with people.

Sleep wouldn't come. His mind spun in circles, recycling the same thoughts. *This is real. It's happening right now. But something's missing—some feeling that should give me confidence to speak in public, but it's not there. I'm scared as hell to talk to a reporter, to do TedTalks, or even a NAMI presentation. But there's this tiny part of me that tells me I have to. And that part is stronger than the fear.*

It was the same feeling he had when he spoke at the local NAMI event, talking down Jung. *It's like… God. It only emerges when people are watching me when all eyes are on me.*

How do I make God's emotion stronger so that I don't feel like I'm in the Matrix? The sensation was uncomfortable as if the present moment was both birth and death, hell and heaven intertwined. Maybe the Matrix theory was real. Maybe certain emotions could bring someone to the doorway of the Matrix. He thought back to the first time he entered Zion when he was in a full-blown psychotic state. *I was so scared. So paranoid. Thought after paranoid thought after paranoid thought.*

That was the moment a new chapter in his life had begun—a chapter of beautiful paranoia and utter hell. And yet, he had never really talked about it with a therapist. He wasn't even sure how he had managed to fall asleep back then.

All he remembered was looking into the eyes of an old Black woman—her dark eyes piercing into him, her voice eerily reminiscent of Madea from the Tyler Perry movies. Maybe his mind had assigned her that voice to keep him tethered to reality. After that moment with the Madea Lady, everything blurred. The next thing he knew, he had woken up in a mental hospital, lying next to some other guy in another bed.

Thank God, he thought. *Thank God I didn't wake up still trapped in a paranoid fantasy.*

The memory resurfaced so clearly, clearer than it had been in years. *Yes, this is reality. I'm not in the Matrix. This is real. God was there through all of it—Zion, the mental hospitals—making sure I didn't hurt myself too much, emotionally or physically.*

Maybe I can talk to someone at TedTalks in Los Angeles. Maybe I can tell them about that day when I was 23 years old. God did this for me. Even if I sometimes imagine

I'm becoming famous, this isn't an illusion. Something deep inside me is telling me this is real.

With that thought, exhaustion finally took over, and Jake drifted off to sleep.

When he woke up, he instinctively checked Facebook. Friend requests were still pouring in—hundreds of them. *So, this isn't an illusion. This is real.* He picked up his phone and saw thirty missed calls, mostly from numbers he didn't recognize. Among them, he noticed three familiar names— Jason, Pedro, and Rachel. All three had left voicemails.

Jake pressed play on Pedro's message.

"Hey, man. I hope you got some sleep. I know it must've been hard with all this fame. I drove past your house this morning and saw your mom talking to reporters outside. So… what's our next move? Rachel told me you're going to Los Angeles with Ayn for a TedTalk, all expenses paid by NAMI California. That's amazing. Call me anytime so we can figure out our next steps—if you still want to be a group."

The voicemail ended. Jake sat up, feeling a pang of guilt. *Why would Pedro even ask if I still want to be a group? Of course I do.*

They had been together before all of this. And no matter how fast fame had arrived, it would fade just as quickly. The media would move on. A new story would take over tomorrow or next week. But Pedro, Jason, and Rachel? They were real.

And Jake wasn't going to lose that.

Jake called Pedro, and Pedro picked up the phone.

"Pedro, hey man. I heard your voicemail. I have to say, you guys mean more to me than all this fame. I feel a deep bond with you all—something I've never experienced before, even with my closest friends. We'll definitely meet up," said Jake.

"We can meet at my place. I don't know why I said that... It's just, when I saw you speak at NAMI and the way you challenged Jung—that was the most powerful thing I've ever witnessed. It was you, but at the same time, it wasn't. You seemed incredibly articulate and clear, almost transcendent. If I didn't know better, I would never have guessed you'd ever experienced a single hallucination or delusion," Pedro said.

"I'm not sure what came over me. A lot of emotions were running through me. One thing I remember thinking about was Malcolm X—how human he was, even when it felt like God was speaking through him on that podium. In that moment, I felt like a vessel, as if God was using me to tell the audience that something was seriously wrong with the mental health system, not just here but probably worldwide. I had to say something. It wasn't just me up there—it was something far greater. But I have to admit, I was absolutely terrified."

"Yeah, I can imagine. That had to be overwhelming. I found out that Jung was still in prison, but at least his psychiatrist was able to visit him. His lawyer is considering pleading insanity. Have you ever had thoughts as intense as Jung's? To do something like that?" Pedro asked.

"A few times, but not nearly as often as Jung. He's definitely an extreme case, but when he cried, I didn't see a sick man—I saw someone desperately trying to get well. I felt his pain. I've never been that far gone, but maybe if I hadn't met you guys, I could've ended up like him," Jake admitted.

"Right. Well, thank God no one got hurt—physically, at least. I mean, he had a gun."

"Actually, you're gonna laugh at this—it wasn't even a real gun. It was a BB gun with the top painted black," Jake said.

"Are you serious? He didn't have a real gun? That's insane. He could've been killed," Pedro said, shaking his head.

"Yeah. Can you imagine if someone like him was on our team? I doubt we'll ever see him again, though. Even without him, I know we can make a real difference."

"We'll meet at my place this evening," Pedro said.

They said their goodbyes and hung up. As Jake was on the phone, several people tried calling him. Turns out, his mom had told his aunts, uncles, and cousins about his recent speech. He called a few of them back, having pleasant conversations. Most of his time was spent explaining schizophrenia, though he bent the truth a little about how much control he had over Jung. He framed Jung as a man down on his luck and made sure to mention the fake gun.

His extended family was proud of him, saying he was going places. They had heard stories about his hospitalizations, but they never fully understood what he went through daily. As he spoke with them, his body kept shifting slightly, struggling to stay still. He also experienced occasional face hallucinations—an entity, or whatever it was, smiling at him at intervals. He powered through the phone calls, and before he knew it, it was evening.

Jake put on jeans and a T-shirt and stepped outside. A lone reporter immediately rushed up to him, microphone in hand.

"No, not today. I'm busy," Jake said, brushing past and getting into his car. His phone was still ringing as he drove to Pedro's.

When he arrived, he saw everyone's cars parked in Pedro's driveway. No reporters in sight. Before he could knock, the door swung open. Rachel stood there, grinning.

"Oh, hail, leader Jake," she teased, opening her arms for a hug.

Jake smirked and hugged her, Inside, everyone was gathered in the living room, excited to see him. They greeted him warmly, laughter filling the room.

"You guys, just because I got a little bit of fame doesn't mean I'm abandoning the group. I'm going to use this platform to help solve the mental health crisis—or at least make a dent in it. We need a game plan," Jake said.

"Well, I think your TED Talk in Los Angeles is a good start. It'll solidify you as the leader of our movement," Jason said.

Ayn blushed deep red. She had just spoken to Jake on the phone, but seeing him again in person after the NAMI convention was different. She stared at him with the same excitement as a fangirl watching a boy band like *NSYNC or the Backstreet Boys. She looked as if she might burst.

"Hey, Jake," she said, beaming.

Jake met her gaze, not smiling too much. If he had lighter skin, his blush would've been obvious, but instead, he just grinned from ear to ear, like the Cat from *Alice in Wonderland*.

"Yeah, I'm really excited about the trip—Ayn and I will be going together. I wish the whole gang could come, but our time will come soon," Jake said.

Everyone cheered and laughed.

"We'll help you write a speech—unless you'd rather go freestyle like you did at NAMI?" Pedro asked.

Jake thought for a moment, the weight of their expectations settling on his shoulders.

At that moment, Jake remembered how the entity mimicked demonic voices when he spoke with his people he knew. There was something eerily familiar about their voices, a contrast to the ecstatic emotions that surged through him during his speech when he had confronted Jung.

"Sometimes, I don't know if I can do this, you guys," Jake admitted. "I always feel the voices right next to me, no matter what I do. It's like I have too much responsibility to be the benevolent leader of this group." He let out a deep sigh, running his hands through his hair. Though he didn't cry, the exhaustion from everything—his condition, the voices, and the pressure—was overwhelming.

He had hoped that fame would silence the voices, but instead, they merely changed, adapting in ways he hadn't expected. They still talked, though now their words were more of an annoyance than an outright torment. It made him feel as if he were trapped in a realm of hell he couldn't understand. Maybe he had hung himself, and this was that particular realm.

The thought of the intense sexual emotion he once experienced, the one laced with excruciating pain, crept into his mind. Would it happen again? He had no way of knowing. The idea made him uneasy, just like the prospect of delivering another speech. To be honest, he had felt possessed when giving the NAMI one. The moment it ended, he was just Jake again.

"I thought fame would make the voices go away, but they're still here. I feel a little exhilarating, but mostly, I'm just nervous about having to talk to people. And on top of that, we haven't even established a real foundation for this organization we're trying to build," he said.

"Whenever I research mental health organizations, they never seem to be as big as I hoped," Ayn chimed in. "If these organizations were truly effective, wouldn't they be viral by now? It's like someone gets famous, builds an organization, and then the world moves on to the next trending topic on CNN."

"Let's not get carried away," Jake interjected. "I'm 'minifamous' at best. This is just a conversation within the mental health world. I'm not Obama or anything."

"So, I guess we don't have a plan," he continued. "We know we need to do something, but we don't know what."

"We could join an existing organization and try to make it better from the inside," Jason suggested. "There are a lot of dedicated people out there working hard to address mental health issues."

"Good idea. Here's the plan: You guys research mental health organizations—what they do and why they aren't more well-known. Meanwhile, Ayn and I will work on the speech and head to Los Angeles to deliver it. They want something heartfelt, but we'll have a general outline prepared," Jake concluded.

With that, the group disbanded, sharing a few jokes and casual conversation before heading home. Pedro lingered for a moment, waving as the last of them left. As he shut the door, his heart pounded erratically. He took his blood pressure—it was higher than usual. He was struggling to focus, torn between helping the group and studying for his finals.

He excelled in most of his classes, but 19th-century literature was his weak spot. He had a keen interest in Russian literature, but books like *Moby Dick*—with their poetic prose—left him perplexed. He knew he could pull off at least a B+ if he studied hard enough. Unlike Rachel, whose near-genius mind made academics effortless, he had to put in the work.

Then it happened—his thoughts spiraled into a frenzy of fear, racing faster than a Kentucky Derby horse. Panic gripped him. He took a shower and a dose of Zyprexa—more than usual, the amount he had originally been prescribed in Zion. He lay in bed, paranoid, convinced that with every move, the police would come for him and send him back there. Desperate, he dropped to his knees and prayed.

"God, I don't know what's happening. I feel so paranoid like I can't control my thoughts. Fuuuuck..." His speech slowed, slurred, almost unrecognizable. Then, suddenly, he spoke too fast, barely aware of it.

Lying in bed, his mind fixated on the GRE. *How will I ever take that test again? Will I be completely terrified for the rest of my life?* The memory was pure hell as if the devil himself had been staring him down, forcing his brain onto a hot stove, an adrenaline rush he couldn't contain.

"This is crazy. I needed PTSD counseling or something to deal with this, but my life wasn't even in danger. I need someone to help me understand it so I can make sure it never happens again. I need to dissect every emotion, every reaction, but if it was psychosis… maybe no one can truly understand it. That's what pisses me off—when people say only God can help. Because God isn't talking back." He clenched his fists. "I need someone with a God-level consciousness, someone who has been through this and figured it out."

Pedro wanted to cry but couldn't. It wasn't sadness; it was confusion. He looked up the definition of psychosis: *A severe mental condition in which thought and emotions are so affected that contact is lost with external reality.*

That's kind of true, but not exactly.

He could still see, still touch—his senses were intact. But inside his mind, it was chaos, one paranoid delusion stacking upon another. Yet, some part of him—some solid, grounded part—remained, desperately trying to define reality. *How do I understand what happened unless some part of me was observing the part that was in psychosis?*

Perspective

Slowly, his thoughts began to settle. He felt calmer. He knew he wasn't capable of tackling differential equations like this, but at least he wasn't going to let fear-driven thoughts consume him.

The next morning, he woke up unable to move. He stared at the wall, willing his hand to move, but it wouldn't budge. Panic surged through him—had the Zyprexa paralyzed him? He wanted to cry but couldn't. With immense effort, his fingers twitched, then his arm. Slowly, his body reawakened, and he gasped as if surfacing from deep water. He was awake, but exhaustion clung to him.

Chapter 19

"Hey Jake, how are you doing? I've been thinking about your speech, and I think you should have an outline but also speak from the heart—like you did with Jung. I enjoyed your speech before that, but I was really moved by the way you talked him down," said Ayn.

"I don't know if I can do that again. I don't even feel like going. When I gave those speeches, it was like I was possessed—like other people were speaking through me. Huh, maybe I should just wing it," said Jake.

Jake wanted to talk to Ayn about their relationship. He wanted to know if they were getting closer, if there was something more between them. Part of the reason he had agreed to go with her was the hope of becoming more than just friends.

"So where does that leave us? Are we growing closer, or what? This whole trip feels kind of romantic," said Jake. He decided to throw those words out there and see what happened.

"I don't know, Jake. When I saw you up there on stage, talking like that and taking down Jung, it was exciting. You made me feel like some kind of teenage fan. But I'm still a little scared. I guess we'll see where fate takes us," said Ayn.

Jake felt a flicker of hope, but then Ayn's tone suddenly shifted. It was as if a dark cloud had settled over her. She wasn't entirely depressed, but she seemed to be heading down that road. They said their goodbyes, but Jake couldn't shake the feeling that something was off.

'What if he isn't attracted to me anymore? Maybe he has other girls now that he's a little famous. A lot of women want to be connected to a man who's trying to change the world. What if I'm not smart enough to be part of his revolution? What if he loves someone else? I guess I kind of love him, but I can't compete with those girls he just added on Facebook.'

Ayn couldn't stop her thoughts from spiraling, so she called Rachel.

Rachel picked up after a few rings. "Hey, Ayn Rand," she said playfully.

"I'm not Ayn Rand, Rachel. Though I guess that's a compliment since she was a brilliant writer," said Ayn.

"What's wrong, sugar budgens? You don't sound so good," said Rachel.

"I feel like Jake might not be interested in me anymore now that he's semi-famous in the mental health community. It's messing with my head. It kind of triggered my depression," said Ayn.

"Ayn, Jake is crazy about you. He's liked you since Zion. Why would he go with you to Los Angeles for TED Talks if he didn't care?" said Rachel.

"It's just that when I feel really down, it's hard to think straight. Before my internship, my depression never hit me this hard," said Ayn, her voice gloomy with uncertainty.

"Why don't we have a girls' night out and hit the mall? We can shop for some outfits for LA," suggested Rachel.

Just as Ayn was about to reply, Rachel's phone buzzed with a text. She glanced at the screen, and her expression twisted into a scowl.

Bitch, stop sending me threatening messages. I don't even know who Jason is. If you keep this up, I'm going to the police.

"Bitch!" Rachel muttered under her breath.

"What? Why did you just call me a bitch?" asked Ayn, confused.

"Oh no, not you! Sorry, Ayn. I was talking about this text I just got."

"Is everything okay?"

"Yes, everything is just dandy. Just another bitch trying to get my man," said Rachel, rolling her eyes.

Ayn sighed. "Yeah, I think a trip to the mall would do us both some good. Listen, Rachel, have you ever thought about dating other guys? I don't think Jason is into you anymore. Plus, you're so beautiful, you could get someone amazing—someone who actually deserves you."

Rachel scoffed. "I have my mind set on one man, and that's Jason. I'm surprised you haven't noticed—beneath that tough exterior he puts on for the world, deep down, he still loves me. One day, he'll marry me, and all those jealous bitches will regret ever doubting us."

Later that night, Rachel woke up and checked her messages again. The same woman had sent another text:

If you text me again, I'm calling the police.

Rachel smirked. She recognized the name from a psychology class they had taken together. The woman had once asked Rachel if they could partner on a schizophrenia research project. Rachel, already knowledgeable on the topic, had agreed to help. At the time, she had even wondered if she herself had some form of schizophrenia or just an overactive imagination.

Back then, Rachel had been in the early stages of her relationship with Jason. She often joked about him seeing someone else but would follow up with serious questions. Jason usually brushed it off, thinking she was just playing around. They had their share of arguments, but for the most part, their relationship was driven by intense physical attraction. Their first meetings always ended in heavy sex. Jason enjoyed it, and so did Rachel. Despite being pursued by many men, she had only been with one other guy before Jason, back in freshman year. But there was something about her that made her more alluring than other women—something in her personality that was tenacious and prideful, which always seemed to pull Jason back in.

After several nights of steamy passion, Jason found himself falling for her. He loved how articulate, interesting, and creative she was. They shared the same tastes in movies, music, and even sports. But as time went on, he started noticing her delusions. He gently suggested she get help, but every time, their chemistry pulled them back into bed, and he forgot all about it.

Many of their conversations seemed to revolve around her paranoia—her belief that some woman Jason was supposedly involved with was trying to kill her. Eventually, Jason decided he couldn't handle it anymore and broke things off. That was when Rachel spiraled.

She opened her medicine drawer and, instead of her usual sleeping pills, took an Ambien. She needed something stronger tonight.

The next morning, she woke up groggy but decided to watch some TED Talks about mental illness. She enjoyed all three videos she watched, but she couldn't shake the feeling that she had heard the same messages before. There was always talk about the stigma surrounding mental illness and efforts to erase it. It was nice seeing the support those speakers received, with some TED Talks racking up hundreds of thousands of likes.

One video in particular stood out—it had 858,000 likes.

The video by Elanor Longhorn had 2.3 million views, which Rachel thought was amazing. Elyn Saks had one with 1.1 million views. The only problem with this situation was that Rachel had seen other presenters speak about mental illness just as persuasively. It was difficult to ascertain if Elyn and Elanor truly did better presentations than the others. Still, the presentations were good.

"I do believe the onset of these diseases happens when someone is in their early twenties. The stories they told about themselves were very sad indeed. There was one girl who cut herself because a friend told her that if she did, she wouldn't have to deal with complicated emotions. So she did it. She was diagnosed with schizophrenia, I guess, but she was one of the clearest speakers there. She was doing a one-on-one interview, and she was so down to earth. She sounded so normal. I would have never guessed she had been through what she had. Her recollection of her episodes was impeccable. She once said she thought she was in the holodeck on Star Trek. That's a terrifying delusion because everything in the holodeck seems real," said Rachel.

The holodeck was similar to being in the Matrix—an artificial world where an external force could alter reality at will, introducing a tsunami or any other catastrophe at their leisure. Even people who weren't mentally ill couldn't definitively prove the holodeck or the Matrix wasn't real. There was no way to notice unless one reached a heightened existential awareness. The girl had cut herself several times because she felt numb and trapped. She wanted to feel something, anything. She wanted to be free.

"For me, things get jumbled when it comes to Jason. I think I have all the facts, but when I look back later with a clearer mind, I find discrepancies in my logic. I just don't know if I'm right about Jason's other girlfriends trying to kill me. It feels so real. I can even hear them threatening me, saying they'll kill me if I don't leave Jason alone. But if that's true, how did they communicate with me? I don't have their phone numbers. I'm not friends with them. I've never spoken to them face-to-face. And if I did, where?"

Rachel shook off her thoughts and decided she had done enough research on TED Talks for now. It was time to buy clothes for Ayn's trip to Los Angeles. She picked up her phone and called Ayn.

"Hey, Ayn, are you ready to hit the mall and go shopping?" asked Rachel.

"Yes, I'm ready," Ayn replied.

"I'll pick you up in 20 minutes," Rachel said.

Rachel freshened up, ate her oatmeal cereal, and got ready. As she painted her nails while watching TV, she suddenly heard a voice.

"We're watching you. If you don't stay away from Jason, you're dead meat."

Rachel's face fell. Fear gripped her. Why would someone want to hurt her over Jason? He wasn't rich or famous like Brad Pitt. "If they want him so badly, they can have him," she thought. "But then again, I love him. He's mine. We might get married. He told me he loves me. I can't live without him. But I also can't fight all these women who want me dead."

Her phone buzzed with a message from Ayn: "What's taking so long?"

Rachel was jolted back to reality. But the question lingered—what kind of technology were they using to watch her? And why was she so important that they would go to such lengths? "I'm smart, funny, and beautiful, but that doesn't make sense," she thought. "It's not like I'm Hitler, and the fate of the world hinges on my impending death."

Rachel finished her nails and got in her car to pick up Ayn. As she drove, the voices came and went, threatening her. She refused to cry—she was too prideful to let them win.

Ayn saw Rachel pull up and ran outside. She wore a white tank top and a flowery dress.

"Hey, girl, how's it going?" Ayn asked.

"Someone is threatening to kill me if I don't stay away from Jason. But I love Jason, and he loves me," Rachel said.

"I don't know what you see in Jason," Ayn replied. "Yeah, he's handsome and strategic, but you act like he's Jesus Christ or something."

Rachel frowned and adjusted herself as she passed a green light. "So, Ayn… how are things going with Jake? Are you going to let him have some?"

"For one thing, I'm a virgin, and I'm keeping it that way until I get married. But I have to say, seeing him on that podium at the NAMI event made me a little excited. It's one thing to see him take charge with us, but seeing him in front of all those people, showing them his heart… it was attractive. It's like he believes in something greater than himself. Like he's some kind of savior," Ayn said, her eyes gleaming.

Rachel smirked. "Look at you, comparing your guy to Jesus Christ now."

"He's not my boyfriend. And this trip to Los Angeles is strictly business. We need to keep pushing forward with our movement if we want real change. It's just that when I'm with him or working with our group, my depression isn't as bad. I actually smile. I feel like I'm part of something big. I truly believe that God chooses broken people to fix a broken world," said Ayn.

"I'm with you on that, Ayn. I was on TED Talks yesterday, and I saw some really passionate presenters discussing mental illness. I don't know what organization they're part of, but they genuinely cared about making a difference," Rachel said.

They got out of the car and walked toward the mall entrance. Rachel noticed the way some men looked at her.

"Wherever we go, guys are always after you," Ayn said. "And Jason doesn't even think you two should be together."

"That's not true. Jason loves me, and I love him. And this is me being logical. How can Jason be part of an organization helping people with mental illness and not want to be with me because of mine? If that's true, then maybe I really am schizophrenic. Wait, that sounds confusing. Maybe if I tell him I'm sick, that would solve everything. But I don't feel sick," Rachel said.

"Rachel, you're making my head spin," Ayn said, rolling her eyes. "Anyway, I can't believe I'm going to be alone on a plane with Jake, staying in the same hotel building and watching him give his TED Talk. I guess I could give him a kiss. There's nothing wrong with that. But he really cares about the cause. I don't want our relationship to cloud his judgment. Or maybe it will make things clearer. He talks about sex all the time. Maybe I should…" Ayn trailed off, lost in thought.

"No, Ayn, I was just joking about you giving it up. I like your whole virtuous thing. It proves you have integrity," said Rachel.

They walked through the mall, chatting about clothes and movies. By the time they finished, they were exhausted and ready for bed. Rachel received another message from the same woman who had been threatening her with the police. This time, surprisingly, she texted back, apologizing and saying she was just confused.

I can't always tell when something is real or dangerous when I act on my delusions. Sometimes, I'm so deep inside them that I don't even notice I'm outside the realm of reality. It felt really good going out with Ayn, buying stuff, and just hanging out. Ayn really made me feel better. And being part of something that tries to help with the mental health situation in this country—and the world, Rachel thought.

After taking a shower and slipping into her pajamas, Rachel decided to browse YouTube for speakers discussing mental illness. She found a woman named Rachel Waford, who spoke about the importance of young adults receiving immediate help during their first psychotic breaks. Waford was engaging, occasionally humorous, had great body language, and presented well-researched facts. Rachel looked her up on Google and discovered that she held a Ph.D. in clinical psychology and was based in Georgia.

The only part of Waford's presentation that Rachel disliked was her explanation of psychosis. Waford mentioned sensory problems, but Rachel wished she had elaborated more—maybe given an example of what it actually *felt* like to be in psychosis. The last time Rachel had experienced psychosis, she had felt like her life was in danger. She struggled to trust anyone, convinced that nearly everyone was out to get her so she wouldn't have Jason.

Rachel furrowed her brow, trying to analyze her psychosis as best as she could. She realized that all of her episodes involved Jason in some way. Maybe there was something wrong with how she felt about him. She knew she loved him, but did she love him to the point where it distorted reality? Preventing her from thinking logically?

She was brilliant—a genius, even. She had a 4.0 GPA and hardly studied. So why couldn't she understand this Jason conundrum?

Before going to bed, Rachel called Jake to tell him about Rachel Waford. Though tired, Jake watched the video at the same time Rachel went to sleep. He was impressed. Waford's speech was inspiring. She didn't say it outright, but she implied that there needed to be a cultural shift regarding mental illness. But *how* was that supposed to happen? The media—movies, TV shows, music—paint mental illness as something dangerous and unfixable. Jake had lost count of how many times the villain in a story was portrayed as "psychotic" when, in reality, most psychotic people were more likely to harm themselves than others.

Well, my speech was nothing like Rachel Waford's. She spoke with a structured outline, with precisely timed sections. She's probably so high up in the mental health paradigm that she wouldn't talk to me or my friends, Jake thought.

He continued browsing YouTube and remembered a resource from a book he had read—*NAMI Smart Advocacy.* One of the first search results led to a discussion about mental health. The video was long, but he clicked on it anyway. Twenty minutes in, he was hooked. The panelists were discussing real mental health issues. One speaker emphasized how government funding was misallocated, failing those with severe mental illness. Another woman living in a rural area shared how the nearest mental hospital was 40 minutes away. Mental health crises were rising in her town, forcing people to spend *weeks* in the emergency room. The discussion was intellectually sound and riveting.

Chapter 20

After two weeks of planning Jake's speech, the whole group met numerous times to draft and refine it. They decided to work on it together rather than leaving it solely to Jake and Ayn. They didn't want the speech to be overly scientific—if scientific at all. The core issue was clear: *There is something deeply wrong with the mental health system in America, and there likely needs to be a cultural shift to address it.*

They spent days debating which points to highlight, revisiting Jake's previous speech at NAMI. It wasn't always precise or perfectly timed, but it had *moved* people. In that speech, Jake had spoken honestly about his daily struggles—how simple tasks felt as complicated as rocket science. In the end, they crafted a speech with the same intent as Jake's original message.

At 1 p.m., Jake's parents dropped him off at the airport. They had noticed how busy he had been since his NAMI speech, but he took the time to explain what he and his friends were working on. He told them that something had to be done about the mental health crisis and that he was using the NAMI platform to push for change. He was excited but also nervous. This TED Talk was going to be televised nationally. And Jake knew he didn't have an advanced degree in the subject. He had a degree in electrical engineering, sure, but no master's, no Ph.D., no clinical psychology background.

But he *had* been through the system. Over and over again. He knew what it felt like to be completely and utterly hopeless, searching desperately for the right pill, the right therapy—anything that could save him. He didn't want anyone else to go through what he had endured during his psychotic episodes.

While waiting at the airport, Jake saw Ayn getting dropped off next to him. Her mom stepped out of the car and smiled at him warmly.

"You must be Jake. I've heard so much about you," she said.

"Hello. Nice to meet you. I'm Jake," he replied.

"I hope you knock them dead at that TED Talk. I know what you're trying to do with the whole mental health movement," Ayn's mom said. Then, to Jake's surprise, she gave him a big hug and even kissed him on the cheek. She did the same for Ayn before getting back in the car, exchanging a knowing look with her daughter.

"So, Jake, are you ready to rock and roll?" Ayn asked.

Jake hugged her a little longer than usual. When he pulled away, she looked at him like they were in a high school Romeo and Juliet play, unsure how to conceal their feelings.

"Yeah, I'm ready. Let's get our tickets," Jake said.

As they walked through the airport with their luggage, Jake thought about the visions the voices had given him about his future wife. They told him about all the sex he'd have in the first month, how his wife would be head over heels in love with him. She'd also sing "How Can I Live Without You" by Whitney Houston. They had promised a whirlwind romance, a grand wedding, a love story straight out of a movie. He had never been in a serious relationship beyond college. He had dated and kissed someone, but intimacy had been elusive.

Ayn had made it clear she wouldn't have sex until marriage. Maybe he could wait. She cared deeply about the mental health movement. She *liked* him. Did she *love* him? Maybe love could grow, given the right nurturing. And Jake certainly felt like he was doing just that by going to Los Angeles with her.

Then, suddenly, the voices returned. He could see a distorted, grinning face in his mind's eye as he spoke to Ayn about his speech.

"She's beautiful," the voices sneered sarcastically.

And with that, he felt them settling in, as if they would be with him through the entire trip—through every intimate moment with Ayn. He didn't want the voices to take over the moments he had with Ayn, like it happened when he was having sex with the prostitute. The voice were so pervasive that despite over taking the lead, he had to lie down motionless while the prostitute rode him. His erection would come and go with the voices. Eventually, Jake had to steer his thoughts imagining about Helen Slater in her seductive supergirl costume while the prostitute made him cum.

He wanted to have every moment with Ayn in seclusion. Even if it was a kiss or a conversation. As they moved along the immigration, everytime Ayn looked at Jake, his smile widened. He was also getting a hint that she might be finally leaning in toward him. As they saw their luggage slid out the conveyer belt, he turned to her and asked, "So, Ayn, tell me about your previous boyfriends."

"Umm.. not much to tell. Just one guy I had a crush on freshman year but nothing serious happened."

As they proceeded toward the waiting lounge, Ayn realized that she hadn't taken a refill on her antidepressants. She was too excited for this trip and wouldn't imagine getting a depressive suicidal episode but she never knew. Her mind had always created havoc, creating scenarios of her loved ones being harmed or in danger.

"You tell me. You must have a good ol' list of girls." Ayn asked to get her mind off of those depressing thoughts.

"Unfortunately, not to disappoint you but there was only one. She must be a doctor by now. When we dated, we would very often go on dates to NY pizza, Bojangles. We were also part of this African student union raising awareness about Africans. Now that I think of it, I wasn't in love with her."

Ayn just flashed her widest smile. Jake couldn't help but giggle that finally Ayn was very subtly flirting with him.

They had a lot of time till boarding, Jake asked Ayn if they can stop to eat something.

Jake and Ayn walked over to the restaurant and ordered their pizzas. They sat at a table just outside the store. A Black woman wearing tight jeans and heavy makeup smiled at Jake, but he didn't smile back. When the woman locked eyes with Ayn, who sat next to Jake, her expression turned into a sneer. Ayn shifted uncomfortably, concluding that the woman's reaction stemmed from the fact that she was white and Jake was Black.

I thought we, as a society, had moved past this taboo of Black men dating white women. I'm not trying to steal anyone. I just like Jake as an individual, not as a Black man. As a human being.

Jake felt uneasy too, but not because Ayn was white. He liked her for her beliefs and what she was trying to accomplish through their organization. The taboo element added a layer of intrigue, but for him, personality mattered more.

Ayn frowned and poked at her pizza with a fork, analyzing it like a scientist studying a specimen. "Why did that woman look at me like that? Am I just another white woman stealing a Black man?" she joked.

"Don't worry about her," Jake replied.

Ayn's invisible phantom, unnoticed by others, crept up behind her. She got up to grab a napkin, and as she turned,

Jake caught himself checking out Ayn's figure. It was perfectly shaped making him erected.   The voices in his head smirked at him, acknowledging his reaction. It made him think about how often they interfered, even in his most private moments.

Sometimes, when he watched adult videos, the voices would taunt him. At first, he'd feel normal arousal, but then a male voice would interrupt, making him feel ridiculous. He would try to ignore them, focusing on the woman in the video, but the moment was often ruined. Other times, the voices would say, *That is God,* an eerie cue that sometimes would make him go very hard on his cock pushing him to climax. More often than not, they won, leaving him frustrated and angry at their intrusion.

Jake shook off the thoughts. "Are you okay, Ayn? Is your depression acting up?"

"A little. That woman's look really got to me. It was like I was her enemy. I can't shake the feeling that something is wrong with me. Maybe it's my depression coming back," Ayn admitted.

"There's nothing wrong with you. It's not the 1940s. If she has a problem, that's on her," Jake said.

Ayn gave a small smile. "Are you nervous about your TED Talk?"

"I'm very nervous," Jake admitted. "Last time, I felt like I was possessed by something. And this time, there will be some distinguished people in the audience. I hope I don't freeze. Sometimes, I remind myself that other people have done these talks and survived, and that helps. We all did a good job writing it. Now, I just have to deliver it. Plus, having you in the crowd will help. Once I see your face, I'll be okay."

He exhaled. "What we really need to figure out is what to do with our group. We have no documentation, no recognition—no one even knows who you guys are. They only know me. And I have a feeling my mini fame will fade fast. Every organization I've researched has already tried everything. I also have to say—I've been on edge. The voices are doing their 'face thing' more often, and sometimes I feel like screaming in public. It's like I'm on a mountaintop, struggling to breathe. And honestly, I *am* having trouble breathing."

"Maybe we should all do speeches like you. You make me feel like I could do it too. You inspire me," Ayn said.

"That's actually a good idea. If I talk to the right people, maybe I can put you guys on."

Under the table, Ayn placed her hand on Jake's. It had been a long time since he'd felt something so intimate, and he welcomed it. Ayn was beautiful, smart, and empathetic— a freedom fighter. That was what made her so attractive. In his eyes, she was a superhero. Maybe one day, she'd wear a Supergirl outfit for him.

He motioned for Ayn to walk with him to the terminal. They had two hours before boarding and decided to stay near the dock to be among the first to board. As Jake sat down, he let out a deep sigh, exhausted from the day's chaos.

Then, it happened.

It was hard to explain, and he didn't want to tell Ayn about it. He glanced at her and noticed the dismal look on her face—maybe she was dealing with her own struggles. But for Jake, the hallucination hit hard. It felt like he was alone in an arena, with only the voice and its twisted presence.

"All passengers ready to board," the voice said mockingly. Jake's expression darkened. A wave of paranoia surged through him, feeling new yet familiar. It was a realm of hell on earth. He wanted to cry but felt his facial expressions being manipulated. The voices were controlling his reactions, forcing him into a silent war only he could perceive. His eyes watered, but no one would notice.

He pulled out his phone and texted his mom: *Voices are messing with my face. I'm in the terminal with Ayn, waiting to board.*

The simple act of telling his mother offered a shred of relief. Yet, he could sense the voices watching him type, scrutinizing every word.

"I thought the hallucinations would be less now that I'm becoming more well-known," Jake muttered quietly to Ayn, his lips barely moving.

"What's going on?" she asked, concerned.

"The voices... They're doing the facial hallucination thing. When I look at you, I see them too. It's disheartening. I don't know what to do. I feel like screaming at the top of my lungs for them to stop," he admitted, his face scrunched as he tried to maintain eye contact with her.

The voices continued their taunts, their words intertwining with his hallucinations.

"Where's Jesus? You're not Jesus,"

Jake found himself consciously mumbling the words they spoke, repeating them in his head. Ayn caught on.

"Do that. Repeat what they say. Don't worry about people watching—you can just pretend you're talking to me," she suggested.

Jake followed her lead, whispering fragments of his thoughts mixed with the voices' words. The voices sounded ridiculous to him—like a distorted, nonsensical rambling.

"Where's Jesus? Jesus will help you. You're not Jesus. Not her—talk to Ayn about sex," the voices urged.

He lowered his voice, not wanting to make things awkward. So far, Ayn had been incredibly supportive, unfazed by his episode. He wanted to hug her, but the void between them felt too vast.

Jake tried to ground himself, repeating affirmations as his therapist had suggested. But the voices weren't letting up. They wanted him to hurry, to rush toward something he couldn't comprehend.

What did they want?

He had already slept with the prostitute, but even then, they had interfered. The voices had talked the entire time, turning an already complicated act into an unsettling experience.

And now, they weren't stopping.

Jake clenched his fists, feeling trapped between the voices and the real world, with no escape in sight. They have always interfered with him.

"Jake, are you okay? You suddenly stopped talking."

"I'm doing a little bit better. I feel a little bit on the edge. The voices are just talking nonsense. I call this the wind down when they do this. I was kind of thinking, but I don't want to tell you about it now. It was a little bit of a revelation. With what just happened now I don't know how I'll be able to do the TED Talks with being in this type of fear. I guess, if it's too much I can just walk off stage." said Jake.

"I think you will do fine. I think you're right when you told us that you felt possessed or inspired or something. Or some type of augmented version of yourself. As soon as you see those faces you will know what time it is." said Ayn.

"I was really scared a moment ago. I really felt like I was in some type of psychosis. Reality was all misconstrued and shit. Everything that the voices said seemed to be very important. I was hanging on every syllable that they were saying, and I couldn't have a complete thought. Ever thought that I had, the voices would dismiss it as if I am stupid."

"You're definitely not stupid," said Ayn.

"It's very hard to explain, but when I feel those negative emotions, I feel like I'm the dumbest, most clownish person in the world for that brief moment. Then the emotion leaves behind some sort of residual pain, which I'm guessing comes from a clash of underlying feelings. And there's no way for me to predict when the psychosis will strike. It just comes out of nowhere—no triggers, no warnings," said Jake.

Jake and Ayn continued talking about his voices. He shared his interpretations of them, trying to make sense of their presence. The signal above the terminal came on—it was time to board. At that moment, Jake felt okay. It was as if the voices knew they had caused him harm and were momentarily forced to grant him peace.

He settled into the seat next to Ayn, and they exchanged flirtatious banter. As the plane took off, Ayn decided to take a nap. Jake seized the moment to think about God. It was true—ever since he had left the mental hospital three years ago, he had been spending more time with God. Every morning and evening, he knelt in prayer, always asking for the voices to go away. But they never did. They were still with him, even now, as he sat on a plane with a woman he liked.

"Why won't God make the voices disappear? I haven't done anything wrong in a long time. I even joined AA, which I attend three days a week," he thought to himself.

AA had been instrumental in bringing Jake a sense of peace he never knew was possible. He couldn't fully explain it, but every time he attended the 6:30 PM meeting, he felt better. The AA lingo resonated with him.

"The reason I was reluctant to talk about it with my current friends was because of the traditions stating that AA shouldn't be discussed with outsiders," he mused.

Unfortunately, even with AA, the voices remained. The psychotic episodes still came, attacking him with a force straight from hell. He couldn't quite understand how AA helped him with his emotions and his past obsession with drinking, but one thing was certain—for three years, he hadn't had the urge to take a sip of alcohol.

"If only there were an AA for voices and delusions, maybe I'd be cured of this dreaded disease," he thought. But there wasn't. Not many people heard voices like he did. Even Rachel's delusions and hallucinations were different from his. Now that he thought about it, no one in AA was quite like him.

"It's almost as if my alcohol problem was solved by a miracle. Three years ago, I drank every single day without fail. And now, I can honestly say it feels good not to drink anymore. But I still have to find a way to minimize the acute pain these voices bring. God is helping, but I think I need some other type of professional help. If I were still drinking, my problems would be so much worse. Maybe, if I'm lucky, I'll find a therapist who knows about CBTp or ACT therapy."

Jake had read that ACT (Acceptance and Commitment Therapy) involved acknowledging thoughts and letting them pass. He had also watched two videos about CBTp (Cognitive Behavioral Therapy for Psychosis), and they intrigued him. The idea of a therapist helping to shift his core beliefs away from harmful thoughts made sense. But first, he needed a therapist who could help him identify those core beliefs.

In all his previous therapy sessions, he had never discussed the nature of his voices. He rarely spoke about what they said to him. But the CBTp worksheet his old therapist had given him was eye-opening. It had sections for thoughts, emotions, and behaviors, each with pointed questions:

- "What did the voices say that made you feel uncomfortable?"

- "Do you agree?"

- "If you agree, how so?"

There was something incredibly practical about those questions that he liked. Another question asked, "What does this mean about you?" or "What is the purpose of this thought?" The women who presented the CBTp videos on YouTube were articulate and factual. If only one of them could be his therapist—someone who truly cared about him as an individual—maybe he wouldn't have had that episode in the airport earlier.

"God is good, but there must be a legitimate reason why I have these mental health problems. Or maybe it's just the way my mind is wired. Only God knows how exhausted I am from living in fear, constantly wondering when and where the voices will strike next. This chronic fear isn't healthy."

He missed his freshman year of college. Back then, he had friends. In high school, he had only one or two. He had studied a lot, but he didn't have voices back then.

"What would it feel like to be voice-free again?" he wondered.

Whenever he went on YouTube, mental health professionals painted a bleak picture of his future. They never outright said it, but the message was clear: people with his diagnosis wouldn't lead happy lives.

"How can someone live like that?" he thought.

CBTp terminology made sense to him. He related words like *catastrophizing*—the tendency to assume the worst-case scenario—and *personalization*, where he took everything personally. If a cashier gave him an iced coffee instead of a hot one, he'd immediately assume they had something against him. He also resonated with *generalization*—his habit of simplifying situations or people without considering the nuances.

"If only I could find a therapist who does CBTp," he thought.

One of the YouTube videos mentioned that only two dozen therapists in the entire country specialized in CBTp. That number might as well have been zero. Traditional CBT was common, but he needed something more specific—not just speculation about his emotions, but a deep analysis of his hallucinations and delusions.

"Maybe, if I gain enough recognition, someone will help me," he thought.

He knew that sounded selfish, but it wasn't. He cared deeply about others like him. More than anyone could imagine.

It would be amazing to have a therapist like Dr. Waford. She was incredibly intelligent. Her TED Talks and the book Rachel had recommended were insightful and compassionate. She genuinely cared about people who had suffered a psychotic crisis. The problem was, she was busy helping large groups of people. She didn't have time for individuals like him.

And yet, Jake longed for someone who did.

Chapter 21

Jason woke up at exactly 8:00 a.m. His bedroom was spotless—he had vacuumed the night before and dusted his alarm clock, bookshelf, and other objects in his room. He hadn't been to the gym since before the Zion incident, and he was eager to return. During his session with his new therapist, they had discussed exposure therapy. In a nutshell, Jason thought, exposure therapy involves gradually engaging in activities similar to those that trigger anxiety, building tolerance until one can fully participate without distress.

He had been practicing at home with light sit-ups and pushups, but the limited equipment frustrated him. The gym had everything he needed. Impatient, he had lied to his therapist about continuing his home workouts and decided to go straight to the gym in the morning.

As he mixed his protein shake, he noticed his grandfather sitting at the table. Jason knew his grandfather had struggled with mental health issues at his age. Back then, there wasn't a name for it, but today, it would likely be called bipolar disorder. Jason, on the other hand, had textbook OCD—but maybe there was some overlap between the two.

"How are your therapy sessions going?" grandpa asked.

"They're okay. I'm doing exposure therapy. It should help me handle situations at the gym," Jason replied. "I decided to go to a different gym because going back to my usual one would be embarrassing after the fight. But I have to work out. If I don't, I feel like I'm going to lose my mind."

Jason watched his grandfather go to the bathroom, but he didn't hear the faucet run. His stomach twisted with unease.

Did he really not wash his hands? Doesn't he know how many germs he could spread? What if we all get sick? And it sounded like he did number two because I didn't hear any pee, Jason thought, dismay washing over him.

He eyed his grandfather with disgust and growing anger.

"Grandpa, did you wash your hands?"

"Yes, I did. I just turned the water on very quietly," his grandfather replied.

"Usually, I hear you washing your hands. Are you sure?" Jason pressed.

Maybe his bipolar disorder is messing with him. That's so gross. I feel like throwing up just being near him, touching the same table and chairs. I really don't think he washed his hands, Jason thought. There are all sorts of diseases you can get. Poor hygiene could literally kill someone. I remember those YouTube videos I used to watch about bacteria under microscopes—disgusting living organisms thriving in filth.

"I have to do something in my room, Grandpa. I'll see you later," Jason said, excusing himself.

"I'm heading to the store for more cornflakes and stopping by the bank. I'll be back in about an hour," his grandfather replied.

That's disgusting. He's going to touch the doorknob, shake hands with people, and drive his car with those filthy hands. The thought made Jason's skin crawl. His rage was acting up so he confined himself in his room and checked his messages to distract his mind. There it was, Rachel's message with a picture of hers. No doubt she looked amazing, with a smile that resonated no care in the world.

Once he heard his grandfather's car pull out of the driveway, Jason sprang into action. He rushed to the bathroom, grabbed antibacterial spray and paper towels, and scrubbed the bathroom doorknob in repetitive motions. His hands shook with frustration.

"How could he do that? He knows how I feel about germs. And at his age, he's even more vulnerable to getting sick," Jason muttered under his breath.

He discarded the soiled paper towels and grabbed fresh ones, moving to disinfect the dining table and his grandfather's chair. As he cleaned, he noticed a small gray stain on the table. His jaw clenched.

What the hell is that?

His frustration boiled over. He grabbed a metal sponge and scrubbed furiously, but the stain wouldn't budge. Irritated, he went under the sink for a stronger antibacterial spray. He put more effort into scrubbing, but nothing worked.

With a furious growl, he slammed his fist onto the table, sending pain shooting through his hand.

"What the fuck? Why won't it come out?" Jason seethed.

Desperate, he scrubbed harder, applying so much pressure that the table's surface began to peel along with the stain. When he finally stopped, a noticeable mark had been left behind.

"Well, I had no choice. Who knows what kind of chemical voodoo Grandpa got on this table?" Jason muttered.

Stepping outside, he noticed what looked like splotched white paint on his car handle. His stomach twisted again.

"Well, I have no choice. I have to clean that too. Must be bird shit," he mumbled.

He retrieved car soap and a sponge, scrubbing until his arm went numb but he couldn't stop. Some of it came off, but stubborn spots remained. Frustrated, he ran inside to get the metal sponge. This time, he applied just enough pressure to remove the stain without damaging the surface. He hosed down the handle and grinned triumphantly as the sun reflected off the now-clean car.

"Yatsy!" he cheered.

Satisfied, he returned inside to wash his hands. He scrubbed thoroughly, ensuring every trace of bacteria was gone. But as he dried them, doubt crept in.

The way I'm acting right now… I don't think I'll be able to use the gym unless I go through the same process there.

When I was cleaning, it felt like my life depended on it. Why am I such a clean freak? It was like the world would end if I didn't disinfect every surface. I even scraped the damn table down to its core. Every time I imagine something dirty, the intrusive thoughts come back. It's exhausting.

One of my friends once mentioned that cognitive behavioral therapy (CBT) could help with intrusive thoughts about germs. Maybe if I change my core beliefs about contamination and death, I won't be so obsessive.

Jason grabbed his gym bag, packing his water bottle and protein bars. He also tossed in his towel—but not the antibacterial spray.

Jason took a deep breath and muttered to himself, "So far, so good. I can do this."

He decided to go to the gym and clean the machines just like everyone else—no obsessing over every tiny crevice. Normally, he would scrub the wheel of his car before driving anywhere, but today, he resisted the urge.

"I just have a little bit of OCD," he told himself. Then, he texted Rachel: "Did you find any new information about mental health organizations?" After pressing send, he forced a smile, trying to reassure himself that everything was fine. His hands, however, began to sweat on the steering wheel. A thought crept in—something about sweetness and germs. He envisioned maggots on his hands, eating away at his skin. He imagined his flesh peeling off, and fear surged through him, quickly turning into anger. Sweat beaded on his forehead.

"I don't know if I can go to the gym," he whispered.

Another thought followed: *I'm not the only one. Other people fight germ wars too.*

When he arrived at the gym's parking lot, he parked far away from other cars, grabbed his gym bag, and stepped out. Inhaling and exhaling slowly, he steadied himself. *I got this,* he repeated, walking toward the entrance.

As soon as he stepped inside, a man walked past him, nearly grazing his arm. Though they didn't touch, the sight of the man's sweat triggered a panic.

If I come in contact with anyone, I'll surely die.

At the front desk, Jason avoided eye contact as a staff member explained the gym's policies. He wiped the perspiration from his face and muttered a quick "thank you" before heading toward the lockers. *I'll start with the treadmill,* he decided.

He placed his bag in a locker, took a cloth, and wiped the treadmill once—just as most people did. Then, he began walking. As his feet moved, his mind conjured up horrifying images—magnified germs crawling across the treadmill, penetrating his skin, traveling to his organs, attacking his heart.

This is too much. The bacteria is getting into my heart.

His pulse quickened, not from the germs, but from sheer panic. Abruptly, he turned off the treadmill, grabbed a paper towel, and wiped it down again—this time more aggressively. But cleaning didn't ease the fear. A tear escaped his eye. Then another. Before he knew it, he was sobbing as he scrubbed the surface.

A woman nearby noticed and approached. "Hey, are you okay?"

"Everything's wrong," Jason choked out.

"Why don't you stop scrubbing and sit down for a while?" she suggested gently.

His hands trembled as he let the antibacterial bottle and paper towel slip from his grip. Tears streamed down his face. "I have a condition with germs," he admitted.

"Oh, you have OCD? My brother has that too. He struggles with intrusive thoughts and compulsive cleaning," she said, her voice was unexpectedly smooth and understanding.

Jason hadn't expected such a response. He cracked open one eye, catching a glimpse of her warm smile. Sniffling, he asked, "What does he do to deal with it?"

"Two things: therapy with exposure exercises, and talking about his core values and emotions. It helps him a lot."

People passed by, glancing at them. The woman ignored the looks. "Let's go sit in the lobby. Are you new here?"

"Yeah," Jason replied. "Had a little… episode at my last gym."

"An episode?"

"Yeah."

They sat together, sipping Gatorade. Jason opened up about Zion, his past struggles, and the organization he and his friends were trying to build. She listened attentively, nodding and responding with occasional, "That's interesting" or "That's cool."

Before leaving, Jason asked for her number. "Erica," she introduced herself. He nodded, storing the name in his mind.

Back in his car, he sprayed antibacterial solution on the steering wheel before heading home. Yet, something felt different. A newfound confidence settled in. He was more certain about his mission—what he, Ayn, Rachel, Pedro, and Jake were trying to accomplish.

Before doing anything else, he did something unexpected—he ran a warm bubble bath. As he soaked, he reflected on the day. *Yeah, I cried in public. But those emotions were powerful, overwhelming. I thought I was dying.*

Stepping out of the tub, he felt oddly satisfied. Showing his true emotions to a stranger had been… liberating. He decided not to tell Rachel about the whole ordeal—at least, not yet. Maybe not the crying in public, but definitely not about meeting Erica.

He picked up the phone and dialed Rachel.

"Hi, Jason. How are you?" she asked, as if she already knew what he was going to say.

"I'm okay. Just got back from the gym," he said, sneezing into the receiver.

"You don't sound so good. Hope you're not sick, considering your whole OCD thing and all." Rachel chuckled, her laughter reminding Jason of a villainess in a James Bond movie.

"Don't worry about it. Have you found any new information about mental health organizations?"

"Yeah, I really like the Hearing Voices Network. It's a great place to connect with other voice hearers. The people there are amazing. The facilitators lead discussions well, even when they're struggling themselves. It's inspiring."

"That's great, Rachel. You planning on going again?" Jason sniffled.

"Yeah, next Monday. It's weird—there are similarities and differences in everyone's experiences."

"That's good. You're doing a great job."

"How are you doing, my sweet love?" Rachel purred.

Jason scoffed. "Rachel, can we just have a normal conversation?"

"But I missed you, honey. You weren't talking to any witches at the gym, were you? Speaking of the gym, how'd you even manage to go back after what happened last time? I'd think you'd still be struggling."

Jason fumbled for a moment trying to look for words. Even with all her teasing, she had a way of reading him.

"It was tough, but I managed," he admitted, sneezing again.

"Hey—"

Before she could finish, Jason hung up and smiled to himself.

***

Pedro woke up feeling sluggish, just as he did every morning. Moving felt like a struggle, and his thoughts seemed slower than usual. Without his medication, his mind worked faster, but he knew the trade-off was dangerous. He followed his morning routine and sat down for breakfast with his mother.

"So, you have your literature final this morning. I'm sure you' ll do fine," his mother said.

Pedro nodded. He had prepared well, spending extra hours studying and reviewing the professor's evening study sessions. But the thought of the dreaded GRE crept into his mind. *I'm in a fix. If I take the Zyprexa, I won't be able to think clearly and quickly. If I don't take it, I might end up in the hospital again.*

Memories of that day surfaced. He had felt detached from reality—everything was crystal clear, yet nothing made sense. A waking nightmare. *I have to take it again if I want to go to grad school.*

"I've noticed how much you've been studying. I'm sure you'll do well on your final," his mother reassured him.

"I'm a little scared," Pedro admitted. "Thinking about being timed makes me anxious. It reminds me of the GRE when I was in that psychotic state. Mom, I never want to go through that again. Maybe I should've taken a break from college."

His mother gave him a soft look. "You've come this far, so you might as well finish. But if it's too much, I support you 100 percent."

Pedro thought of how hard his mother worked since his father had passed away five years ago. She took on extra shifts to keep a roof over their heads. He couldn't let her down. The darkness under her sunken eyes told him just how much she sacrificed.

"I'll be okay. This test isn't like the GRE. It's more about memory—less conceptual thinking," he assured her with a smile.

Pedro gathered his books and notes, heading to his car. As he drove, he couldn't shake the memory of his GRE experience. His breathing had been erratic, his mind racing with disconnected thoughts. *That test was a nightmare. It felt like an eternity, like I was trapped in some kind of hell.*

His thoughts took a dark turn. He remembered the World Trade Center attacks, imagining the terror of the people on the planes and in the burning buildings. They had to make impossible choices—fight back, stay seated, or jump to escape the flames. His logical mind told him that his GRE experience was nowhere near comparable, but in that moment, it had felt just as real. His brain had trapped him in a terrifying illusion.

As he parked, Pedro felt his hands sweating. A thin layer of perspiration formed on his brow. But he had taken the Zyprexa today, so he knew psychosis wouldn't take hold. Instead, he felt hazy, detached from his emotions. Everything seemed mundane. The moment he stopped thinking about the GRE, his hands stopped sweating, and drowsiness set in. The medication made him sleep longer hours, and even when he was awake, he felt sluggish.

When Pedro received his test, he quickly scanned the first question—it was easy. He flipped to the last question—also easy. Every question was based on the short stories and book excerpts he had studied in his professor's review sessions. He flew through the test, finishing with an hour to spare. It was nothing like the GRE, and that realization gave him a powerful boost of confidence. Maybe he *could* conquer any test.

That night, he came home beaming and hugged his mother tightly. "I love you."

She smiled. "I knew you'd ace it. You studied so hard. You'll do great on your other exams too."

Pedro had earned mostly A's and some B's on his mini-tests. He was confident about his remaining exams. Unlike the GRE, these tests weren't about speed or heavy conceptual thinking; they simply required knowing the formulas and applying them.

Later that evening, he picked up the DBT book that Jake had recommended. He read about the Wise Mind, Rational Mind, and Emotional Mind. He tried applying those concepts to his GRE dilemma.

Rational Mind: *If I put in more time practicing timed tests, maybe I can get a satisfactory score.*

Emotional Mind: *The GRE was such a traumatic experience. Maybe I should just forget grad school altogether.*

Wise Mind: *I can practice two tests a day under real conditions. Or I can apply to grad schools that don't emphasize the GRE as much. My college's MBA program doesn't even require a GRE score. Do I even want to do an MBA?*

Working on his mental health had opened new doors. Maybe he had a different calling.

Satisfied with his plan, Pedro played video games for half an hour. His mind occasionally drifted back to the GRE, but instead of panicking, he acknowledged the thought and let it pass. Over time, he got better at controlling these intrusive thoughts. Instead of focusing on past failures, he reminded himself that he had done well on his literature exam.

Feeling accomplished, he called Jason.

"Hey, Pedro! How'd the test go?" Jason asked.

"I think I did really well. I'm pretty sure I'll ace the other exams too. But I've been doing some thinking. I'm not sure I want to get an MBA anymore. I really like the mental health work we've been doing. Reading this DBT book made me realize how much these concepts could help people. But it seems like not enough people know about them."

"Yeah, I skimmed it. The Wise Mind, Rational Mind, and Emotional Mind framework is interesting."

"I just used it to process my GRE trauma, and it helped a lot. Have you heard from Jake and Ayn?"

"No, just a text from Jake saying he and Ayn are on a plane. Seems like this trip might bring them closer. I hope their relationship helps both of them with their mental health."

Pedro nodded, even though Jason couldn't see him. "I still don't know exactly what we should do. Every time we think of something, there's already an organization doing it. Maybe we should join one. But if these organizations are so effective, why don't more people know about them?"

"Good question," Jason replied.

"I like the Wildflower Alliance. There's this woman I've been emailing—she genuinely cares about helping people. It's frustrating that people like her aren't famous. Instead, we glorify politicians and celebrities…"

"I had an episode at the gym. I thought I could get through my workout without cleaning anything, but I broke down and cried in the middle of the place. Some lady took pity on me and comforted me. I even got her phone number—but that's beside the point. I still have a problem. It's called OCD.

For a moment, it felt like the world was ending, like I was going to die. It was an unbearable feeling; one I never want to experience again. I could almost see microbacteria coursing through my veins. I don't know why I have these intrusive thoughts, and I sure as hell don't want to do exposure therapy. Man, I'm tired of being like this. I just want to be normal," Jason said into the phone.

"I want to be normal too," the voice on the other end replied. "But don't call yourself sick. It just... feels like I can't function without this medication. Like I need it just to get through the day. One thing's for sure—there's no way I can take the GRE while I'm on Zyprexa."

"I'm sure you'll figure something out. You're smart. You can do it," Jason reassured him. "Man, we sure do have some emotional problems."

"Yeah, we sure do."

"Well, I'd better get to bed. It's been a long day. We'll meet up sometime."

"Later, man."

Chapter 22

The plane soared through the sky, giving the sensation of floating on a hover board. Jake had been alert for most of the flight, but he opened his eyes when Ayn tugged on his arm.

"Jake, wake up. We're almost in LA," Ayn said.

"I'm so glad we made it. With everything we deal with, we still flew across the country. My voices have been pretty quiet most of the flight. They murmured here and there but nothing too alarming. They were really bad back at the terminal, though."

"I just kind of drifted off because of my depression, but I feel okay now."

"Yeah, you were knocked out for about two hours. That must be the city to the right," Jake said, pointing toward the dense LA skyline with a smile. He had never traveled on a plane with his voices before, and it felt good to have done so. It almost seemed like his voices were upset that he had enjoyed the journey. Or maybe they had mixed feelings about making it safely—a conflict of emotions he still didn't fully understand.

"Wow, Jake! I see downtown LA. It's beautiful, but the air looks a little smoggy," Ayn observed.

They both laughed, exchanging intimate glances. Ayn felt good about the trip overall, though a passing thought lingered about the woman who had stared at her in the airport cafeteria. More than that, she was focused on the organization they were trying to build to help people.

She had an idea—a nationwide information session to educate people about mental health organizations. Each of them could share their own experiences. "We'd probably need some training in public speaking," she thought.

"Pedro will talk about his experience with bipolar disorder, Jason about his OCD, Rachel about schizophrenia, Jake about schizoaffective disorder, and I'll speak about my depression. We could have a Q&A session at the end. There are so many people who don't even know what NAMI is. I only found out about the Wildflower Alliance from Rachel—or was it Jake? Even schizophrenia.com exists, and there's HVN, NAMI, and NIMH. We need to spread awareness."

As they landed, Ayn shared her idea with Jake. He nodded in agreement. "We can really help people with this organization, and it's also a way to introduce others to resources we already know about. But we need to get comfortable with public speaking. I'm terrified of doing a TED Talk. I don't even have a PowerPoint slide; I'm just winging it. Hopefully, if we do well, we can get funding for our project."

"Yep, we need public speaking coaching right away. And we need to create an outline to stay on track," Ayn agreed.

Jake hesitated before asking, "This is kind of random, but how does it feel to be one of the four people in the U.S., statistically, who have a mental illness?"

"I hate that term—it sounds so slimy and gross. But I guess if I didn't have what you call a mental illness, I never would have met you."

Jake grinned widely, his brown eyes locking with Ayn's blue ones. He was excited but also nervous. He had never had romantic feelings for anyone before. The emotions he had for Ayn made him feel vulnerable. One moment, he felt like he could jump to the moon when she looked at him like that; the next, he feared he might break if he ever saw her hurt, sad, or worse, depressed.

"So where does that leave us? What are we, exactly?" Jake asked.

Ayn leaned in and kissed his cheek—not quite a peck, but not overly eager either.

"I see," Jake murmured.

He reached up to retrieve their luggage, then walked through the tunnel with a spring in his step. Ayn followed closely behind, as if he were the leader and she, the teammate.

The airport was bustling. A man in a suit and tie rushed by, checking his watch obsessively. Did he have a mental illness? A mother wiped tears from her son's face after he tripped and scraped his knee. She looked strong and sturdy. Did she have a mental illness? A group of high school basketball players walked briskly toward the food court. Which one of them would be diagnosed with OCD or depression in college?

Just by looking at someone, it was impossible to tell if they struggled with something unseen. People only shared their deepest struggles when they felt safe. And even then, many wouldn't.

Since Ayn had kissed him, Jake noticed his voices had changed. They still spoke, but their presence wasn't as dominant. They even seemed happy for him, though they weren't sure how to process the moment. For the first time, Jake felt a bit more in control.

Ayn, meanwhile, felt flustered but steady. A shadowy presence—her own phantom—hovered above her. It felt like an old sadness, a quiet but persistent force. She wanted to throw herself into Jake's arms and have him hold her tight. For the first time in a long while, she felt like she was doing something meaningful.

Yes, her studies were important. But this—what she and her friends were building in Zion—this could change lives.

Jake, on the other hand, felt nervous but undeniably happy. He had never imagined his life taking this direction. With his electrical engineering degree, he had struggled to find a job due to his GPA. He had no connections in the industry to help him land an opportunity. But now, doing this work, he was about to help far more people than he ever could as an engineer.

True, if he worked for a power company, he would contribute to providing electricity to thousands. But with this initiative, he might save even one person from taking that final step toward suicide. He could give someone hope that they could live with their mental health conditions.

Not that he liked thinking this way, but maybe he'd meet high-profile people. Maybe, one day, he'd even meet Barack Obama and have an intimate conversation about his presidency, his struggles, his triumphs. Maybe a man like Obama could share some secrets to life. And all Jake had to do was be himself and keep helping others.

He imagined himself engaged to Ayn. They'd have passionate love, work side by side in advocacy, build a life together. They'd have a beautiful home in their home state, and people would write to them, inspired by what they were doing. And all they'd be thinking was, "This is happening, and we're just being ourselves."

"It's nice to dream," Jake said aloud.

"What were you daydreaming about, hotshot?" Ayn teased, glancing at her phone. She was texting her mom, who was relieved Ayn had made it to LA without any major episodes.

Yet, despite everything, Ayn felt an unshakable sadness, like a dark cloud lingering just out of reach. Even when she thought happy thoughts, the sadness remained, like it was woven into her very being.

"I feel happy," she admitted, "but there's this backdrop of sadness I can't escape. Even when I kissed you, it was still there, just hovering."

"Maybe if we both have kids, they'd have a hybrid of sadness and voices. They'd be superheroes," Jake said, smiling at Ayn.

"Don't get ahead of yourself, buddy," Ayn replied.

Deep down, Ayn felt conflicted. How was it possible to feel both happy and sad at the same time? It wasn't neutral—she knew that much. She thought back to her last appointment with her therapist. The doctor had told her she had a disease, something treatable but lifelong. He'd rattled off a list of antidepressants she could take, neglecting to mention their addictive properties, the weight gain, the mania, or the insomnia they could cause. Then, as if it were nothing, he'd suggested that if things got too bad, she could take antipsychotic medication. That terrified her. She didn't want her brain chemistry permanently altered. She knew Jake and Rachel took those meds, but she didn't have delusions or hear voices.

Jake's phone rang. He picked it up.

"Hi, how are you? We just landed in LA and are getting our luggage. About to grab an Uber to the hotel," he said.

"I'm glad you made it," Paul, one of the board members of NAMI Los Angeles, replied. "We're all having dinner in the hotel cafeteria. There'll be some people from other organizations, plus a few NAMI board members. Once you're settled, meet us there."

"Sounds good. We got some rest on the plane—it wasn't a long flight."

"Great. See you soon."

Click. Then the dial tone.

"Looks like we're having dinner with NAMI and a few other groups," Jake told Ayn.

A tall, blonde man approached, staring at Jake for a moment before stepping closer.

"Well, I'll be damned. You're that guy from YouTube—the negotiator. You talked that insane guy down from killing a psychiatrist," the man said.

Jake shifted slightly. "I wouldn't call him insane. He was going through serious mental health issues."

"I'm Albert. So, you must be famous or something, coming to LA."

"I'm not here to be an actor or a leader. I just hope to push people to take mental health more seriously—to inspire some great minds to think."

Albert kept a neutral expression before glancing at Ayn. "Sounds like bullshit. So, is this your girlfriend?"

"This is Ayn. She's part of our group for effective change," Jake replied.

"She's hot," Albert said.

Ayn blushed.

"Well, it was nice meeting you," Jake said, shifting the conversation. "We have to get to the hotel. Time to grab an Uber."

"Don't bother with an Uber. I'm picking up a friend from the airport. I can drop you off," Albert offered.

Jake hesitated and glanced at Ayn. "What do you think?"

"It's up to you," Ayn replied.

"Alright, we'll go with you," Jake agreed.

After collecting their luggage, they waited for Albert's friend. A heavily tattooed man with three nose piercings and a teardrop tattoo on his cheek approached.

"Hey, dude. How's it going? Who are these guys?" the man asked.

"This is Jake and Ayn. And this is Hobbs," Albert introduced.

"Hey, dude! How you doing?" Hobbs greeted, pulling them both into a tight hug. "This is the schizo guy who talked down the other schizo guy on YouTube."

"Oh, that's rad," Hobbs said. "You were like some first-class negotiator. I don't know if I'd have the guts to do that."

Jake explained the situation to Hobbs as best as he could while they walked to the parking lot. They found Albert's beat-up 1999 Buick, its exterior scarred with marks and a broken taillight. After loading their luggage, they began the 30-minute drive to the hotel.

A few minutes in, Hobbs pulled out what looked like a cigarette and lit it. Jake sniffed, recognizing the scent of cannabis. As the minutes passed, the smell grew stronger. Memories hit him like a wave—how paranoid he'd gotten the last time he was high, the voices of distant people whispering to him.

"What are you smoking, Hobbs? Is that weed?" Jake asked.

"Yeah. Want a hit?" Hobbs grinned.

"Can you not? I get really paranoid. My hallucinations get worse," Jake said.

"Please, Hobbs," Ayn added, her voice earnest.

"Nope," Hobbs said flatly.

"Albert, can you tell your friend to stop?" Jake pleaded.

"I can't do that," Albert said. "But I can open the windows."

"Nah, man, I'll lose my buzz. I need the haze," Hobbs retorted.

Albert rolled down all the windows, which helped a little. Jake stuck his head out, fuming. The memory resurfaced—smoking at a bar with a guy, calling his mom to pick him up, paranoia twisting his thoughts. Voices told him to kill himself. He became convinced his mom was secretly taking him to a mental institution. He'd bombarded her with questions, trying to determine if she was really his mother. When he got home, his dad was on his computer, concerned but passive. No hospital visit. Instead, Jake had taken a couple of antipsychotics, which thankfully countered the paranoia. That night, he swore off weed for good.

When they arrived at the hotel, neither Jake nor Ayn thanked Albert. Ayn flipped off Hobbs as they walked away.

"Knock 'em dead, buddy," Hobbs called sarcastically.

Jake wasn't high—thank God—but his head felt fuzzy. The hotel loomed before them, majestic with polished mahogany counters and smooth marble floors. The air smelled fresh and clean. Jake caught glimpses of the hallucinated faces he sometimes saw, their spectral smiles flickering in and out of sight. For once, he didn't try to ignore them. He smiled back. Business or not, he wanted to savor the beauty around him.

At the reception desk, Jake handed over their invitation.

"We're with NAMI Los Angeles," he said.

The receptionist smiled. "Welcome. Paul said to meet him for dinner at 6:00 p.m."

Jake glanced at the room keys. His room was right next to Ayn's. His mind raced. One dusky night, a knock on her door… history in the making. He looked at Ayn, and she smiled back knowingly. How could she possibly read his thoughts? She wasn't acting like an angelic virgin.

They followed the bellboy to the third floor and entered their rooms.

"I guess we have time for a quick shower before dinner," Jake said.

Ayn nodded. "See you downstairs."

"I'm really excited to meet them."

"Me too."

Ayn went into her room and took a deep breath. She sat on the chair and glanced around the hotel room. The king-sized bed dominated the space, taking up most of the room.

"Damn! I can't believe I forgot my medicine," she muttered to herself while unpacking her toiletries. The sadness seemed distant but ever-present, lurking like a shadow waiting for the right moment to take over. Maybe one of the advocates would have extra pills to spare.

She tried to focus on the upcoming dinner—the only thing keeping her mind occupied. Yet, the sadness clung to her, as ancient as time itself, a relic of past generations. If it weren't there, she thought, she could think more clearly. But for now, she had to deal with the hand she'd been dealt.

What did the advocates want to talk about? What did they do for a living? What were their hopes for the future of mental health in this country? So many questions, so little time, she thought.

A knock at the door interrupted her thoughts.

"Hey, Ayn, I'm ready. I took my shower and everything. We should get going now," said Jake.

"Hang on, let me take a quick shower," Ayn replied.

"What were you doing this whole time?" Jake teased. "That's okay, I'll wait."

Jake returned to his room and started answering messages on his phone. Suddenly, a voice emerged from nowhere.

"You seem to be rising up," it said.

Jake turned sharply, his eyes landing on a sinister grin. A wave of self-doubt washed over him, making him feel like he wasn't supposed to be there. It took an immense amount of focus and willpower to push back against the feeling.

He mouthed the words, "I'm not stupid. I'm intelligent."

The affirmation helped. He exhaled slowly and texted his parents to let them know he was safe in Los Angeles. As he was responding to more messages, his phone rang.

"Hey, Jake, I hope you made it to your hotel room. We're all downstairs in the dining hall waiting for you guys. Everything alright?" Paul asked.

"Yeah, everything's fine. I just need to take a shower, then we'll be down," Jake replied.

Ayn knocked on his door. "Hey, Jake, hurry up! We're going to be late for dinner."

Jake chuckled and opened the door. Ayn looked stunning in a dress that accentuated her athletic figure. She had a toned physique, and Jake couldn't help but notice how effortlessly beautiful she looked. Feeling a sudden warmth, he hugged her. Ayn smiled and flushed slightly.

"Let's go, Ayn," he said.

They took the elevator down to the lobby, then walked about twenty feet to the dining hall. As they entered, Jake spotted Paul, who quickly approached him.

"The man of the hour!" Paul said with enthusiasm. "Hope the plane ride was smooth. Come on, let me introduce you to the others."

The first woman they met appeared to be in her mid-twenties. She had long, lush black hair and deep, dark eyes that seemed to hold the mysteries of the universe. Her gentle smile revealed perfect, straight teeth. She wore black sweatpants and a blue NAMI t-shirt.

"Hey, you must be Jake. I'm Rebecca. I saw your YouTube video—you're amazing! You look taller in person. Oh, and is this your girlfriend?" Rebecca asked, smiling at both Jake and Ayn.

Ayn shot Jake a quick, questioning glance. Rebecca's tone felt a little too familiar.

"Hey, Rebecca. Nice to meet you," Jake replied. "This is my friend Ayn. She's been my rock through this whole process and has helped with the videos."

"Hi, I'm Ayn. Nice to meet you, Rebecca. Are you an advocate for NAMI?" Ayn asked.

"Yes, I am, and—" Rebecca started, but before she could finish, another woman stepped forward.

An African American woman with beautifully sculpted hair moved in front of Rebecca. She was about Ayn's height, with radiant dark skin, full lips, and expressive eyes. She wore a vibrant, rainbow-colored NAMI shirt with a pair of jeans.

"My name is Liz. I saw your video. I thought it was incredibly thought-provoking, and I think you're on the right track with your speech. I noticed a few grammatical errors, but I'm sure the one you're preparing for TED Talks is well-polished. I'm with an organization adjacent to NAMI in

Massachusetts," Liz said warmly, shaking Jake's hand with enthusiasm.

Jake smiled. "Nice to meet you, Liz."

Another woman stepped up, extending her hand to Jake. She wore a blue NAMI shirt and light blue jeans.

"Hey, I'm Claire," she said.

Jake expected her to say more, like the others, but Claire remained silent. She didn't smile. Her expression was serious, almost cold. She appeared to be in her fifties, and Jake suspected she was a board member. Paul seemed to be around the same age.

Ayn stood quietly beside Jake, feeling slightly out of place. Noticing this, Paul gestured for the last two women to introduce themselves to her. They exchanged pleasantries, and then Paul clapped his hands together.

"Well, now that introductions are out of the way, let's find a booth to sit at."

Once they were seated, Claire leaned forward, her eyes sharp and focused.

"So, Jake and Ayn, how do you feel about mentally ill individuals in the criminal justice system?" she asked, her tone precise.

Ayn didn't hesitate. "I think the system needs to be reformed, especially for those who weren't in their right mind when committing a crime. What people need to understand is that most individuals with mental illness are more likely to harm themselves than anyone else."

"You sound like a tape recorder. What I was getting at is that I think their charges should be dropped if the psychologist determines they were in an unstable state of mind," said Clarie.

"But how can you determine that? In the heat of the moment, with adrenaline coursing through their veins, anything can happen. It depends on the situation," Ayn said earnestly.

"That's true," Clarie replied with a sly smile before turning her attention to the menu.

Liz glanced at both Jake and Ayn, then smiled as if she had noticed something amusing. She exchanged a knowing look with Rebecca, who smiled back.

"So, where did you two meet? On YouTube, people in the comments are saying you're an item. Is that true?" Liz asked.

Ayn looked seriously from Rebecca to Liz before speaking. "We met at a mental institution where we got acquainted. A few of us decided to team up and fight the mental health stigma of our times. We did go on something like a date once," Ayn added with a chuckle.

"I knew it! You both seem shy, but you're also totally bashfully eye-fucking each other," Liz teased.

"Enough of that, Liz. If it weren't for all the wonderful work you've done, I'd say you sound like an adolescent teenage girl with that kind of language," Clarie said.

The waitress arrived and asked if they were ready to order. Liz told her they were still deciding. They all turned their attention to the menus for a few minutes.

"Stigma remains a significant problem in the world of mental health. People still perceive those with mental illnesses as abnormal, as if they can't live functional lives. What do you think should be done about that?" Paul asked.

"There needs to be a cultural shift that destigmatizes mental health issues. I once read about a study where a man was given the option to sit next to either someone with schizophrenia or someone who was an alcoholic. He chose the alcoholic, believing that person to be less dangerous. The psychologist conducting the study explained that, statistically, people with schizophrenia are actually less likely to be violent. Other tests confirmed that many people wrongly associate schizophrenia with aggression," Jake explained.

"That's remarkable. I've heard of similar studies, but not in that form. That's amazing," Paul said.

"I also think global cultural change is needed. The shows we watch, the movies we see, and even the YouTube videos we consume all shape our perceptions," Jake added.

"Since one in four people will experience a mental illness, excuse me, Clarie, for sounding like a tape recorder, there should be classes in high school and college that discuss mental health objectively rather than subjectively. Increased awareness might lead to cultural change," Ayn suggested.

"That's profound, Ayn. The challenge, though, is getting the government to implement such changes in public schools," Paul pointed out.

"And convincing Hollywood to stop portraying the lunatic with a gun or a bomb as schizophrenic instead of an alcoholic would be just as difficult," Clarie added.

At that moment, Jake saw the familiar hallucination—the faces of the voices smiling at him. For a brief second, he felt transported back to that void-like arena. The eerie grin unsettled him, and he struggled to shake it off. Ayn noticed the concern flicker across Jake's face and half-smiled at him.

"Hopefully, the government can remove this chip from my head so I can finally feel my full range of human emotions," Liz said.

Paul, Clarie, and Rebecca remained expressionless, as if unwilling to react. Ayn looked at Liz, confused. Then, after a few moments, realization dawned on her. She understood that Liz wasn't joking; this was a core belief, a delusion.

"I don't usually share this with many people because I get weird reactions—like the confused look I just saw on your face, Ayn. The government is monitoring me. When I was hospitalized, they performed experiments on me. I was unconscious for a few days, and they implanted a chip in my head to track my telepathic abilities," Liz explained.

Jake struggled to focus on Liz's words. The voices distorted reality, making every syllable feel crucial. He had to ride it out.

"Liz, there's nothing wrong with having those beliefs," Paul said gently.

"Shut the fuck up, Paul. I saw how you hid your emotions when I talked about the chip," Liz snapped.

Paul remained unphased, showing no sign of anger or surprise.

"Liz, you didn't have to say that. Paul was just trying to be nice," Rebecca interjected.

Liz sighed. "I'm sorry, Paul. I just get frustrated when people don't affirm what I'm saying. I really believe the government is watching me. Sometimes I wonder if it's true or not. Logically, I doubt it based on people's reactions, but emotionally, it feels real. That's why I don't share it at NAMI meetings or board meetings—people give me weird looks. But some people believe me. I found an online chat room full of others who feel the same. There's a lot of technology out there that we don't even know about."

Hearing Liz say "fuck you" snapped Jake back to reality. Though the facial hallucination lingered, he managed to focus again.

"I met a guy in a hospital who claimed the government implanted a chip in his body to track him," Jake added.

"See? I'm not the only one," Liz said triumphantly.

"Well, I guess if they could put a man on the moon with the primitive technology of the past, they could implant a chip in someone's body," Clarie remarked.

After ten more minutes of discussing modern technology, their food arrived. Jake bit into his hamburger while Ayn ate her macaroni and cheese.

"The hardest part for me," Jake admitted, "is not knowing if my beliefs are real. Sometimes they feel undeniably true; other times, they don't. Take my belief about Jesus, for example. It contradicts everything I was taught before I started hearing voices. The Jesus in my mind is cruel, rude, impatient, mischievous. He's not a good person. He only appears when I'm in a good mood, just to tear me down. He's a demon, not Jesus. And the devil in my mind—he sounds like the one from TV shows, with that deep, husky voice. They claim to be helping me, but they make me feel small. Sometimes, we laugh together about outside events, but even laughing hurts. They want me to focus on them in some void-like universe. Just now, while you were talking to Liz about her experiences, I was seeing hallucinations and hearing voices. When they do this, I feel temporarily insane," Jake said.

Liz, flustered with glee, turned to Jake. "What do you mean by temporary insanity?"

"I mean I'm disconnected from reality. My emotions, the very thing that anchors me to the real world, vanish. Part of my consciousness shuts down, leaving me trapped in some distorted dimension," Jake explained.

"That pretty much sums up my psychosis," Liz said with a knowing smile.

"You know it is really unfortunate that you guys have to go through this. Most people at NAMI bump into someone who has a somewhat similar experience or knows someone who has it. It's like the line separating reality and illusion is blurred for you guys," said Paul.

"It is actually very ignorant of people to dismiss such feelings. I used to get hurt when nobody believed that Devil is talking in my head, and most of the time fake Jesus is the one who puts intrusive thoughts in my head," said Jake.

Jake began to chime into Liz's theory of delusion but he refrained as it would've aggravated her further. She realized herself that there are loopholes in her story but her ego didn't let her confess it.

"I don't have any issues like you guys are facing but a lot of people at NAMI could relate to what you and Liz are going through," said Claire with a stern face.

"Jake, you have two days till your TED Talk is scheduled. A day is scheduled for any final revision for your speech. I feel what you did at the NAMI convention was truly commendable and with this talk I hope you gain more recognition to further your cause." With that, everyone chatted and enjoyed their dinner.

Bidding adieu to the NAMI people, they walked toward their rooms. Ayn was talking arbitrarily, commending the cleanliness of the hotel. She was admirable of the fact that they were vacuuming the carpeted hallways every thirty minutes. As Ayn was talking incoherently, Jake was lost in his own thoughts. As they reached their rooms, Ayn looked up at Jake. "What happened, Jake? Since we left the dining hall, you have been all quiet. If you are getting jittery about your TEDTalk, then I know you will do an amazing job."

Jake gazed into her deep, blue eyes. He couldn't tell Ayn that all he wanted to do was pick her up and press his lips on hers.

He wanted to pick her up and throw her onto the bed. He wanted to make love to her with raw desire, driven by both her beauty and the desperate hope that it would silence the voices tormenting him. But he knew, deep down, that even if they did this, the voices might not stop. He thought about the prostitute. They hadn't stopped then. But still, he wanted Ayn, and he wanted her badly.

"Maybe if you're not tired, we could watch TV or something," Ayn said, smiling at Jake flirtatiously, her expression that of a playful, angelic.

Jake was taken aback. He could hardly believe his ears. Ayn actually wants to spend time with me in my room? The possibility of what might come next made his heart race. He needed to play this just right, careful not to ruin the moment. He flashed her a wide, confident smile.

"Alright, we can chill together," Jake said. "Let me freshen up first. I'll meet you here in fifteen minutes."

After showering and applying an aloe-fresh scented lotion to her skin, Ayn knocked on Jake's door with an expectant smile, as if waiting for something monumental. Jake opened the door and grinned.

"Well, come on in. We can watch TV or something," he said.

"That sounds cool," Ayn replied quickly.

Perspective

The massive king-size bed faced the television. Jake leaned against the headboard, resting on a pillow. To his surprise, Ayn sat right next to him. She smelled incredible, and her skin seemed to glow. When she had climbed onto the bed, Jake had caught a glimpse of her round, firm buttocks, all plump and luscious denting the mattress. She didn't have the wide hips he usually preferred, but her athletic frame more than made up for it.

Ayn flipped through the channels and stopped at a scene of a couple walking hand in hand through a colorful park, exchanging lingering glances.

"Jake, I know you're going through a lot, but just remember, if you ever need to talk, I'm here for you," Ayn said softly, placing her hand over his.

Jake felt a surge of emotions. He liked Ayn, both physically and emotionally. But his mind was plagued with worry. What if the voices interrupted him like they had before? The last time, with the prostitute, he hadn't even been able to enjoy it—he had felt like he was on a mission.

Yet, since Ayn had agreed to come over, he hadn't seen or heard the voices. He sent a silent prayer to God before turning to meet Ayn's deep blue eyes. At that moment, it felt as though they were communicating telepathically.

Ayn was telling him: "You can do anything in the world you want to me."

Jake was responding: "You are so beautiful. I can't resist you anymore."

He leaned in slowly, deliberately, pressing his lips against hers. Ayn responded, closing her eyes, reciprocating the kiss. Jake's hand moved to her thigh, brushing it in slow, sensual strokes. Ayn reached for his shoulder, pulling him closer. Their kisses deepened, time slipping away as if they were long-lost lovers reuniting.

Then, suddenly, Ayn turned aggressive. She grabbed Jake's shoulders and pushed him onto his back, climbing on top of him. Her hand found his hardened dick protruding through his pants.

Jake's mind briefly flickered back to his fear—that the voices might return at any moment to ruin this. But they didn't. He wrestled Ayn playfully, flipping her onto her stomach and smothering her entire body with kisses. He sniffled her neck, licking, biting and sucking, leaving marks up till her ear. Gripping her waist, cupping her perfect ass he slid her pants down, then her panties. Her perfectly shaped backside sent a fresh wave of desire through him making him harder.

He discarded his own clothes and positioned himself behind her, entering her in a slow, deliberate motion. Ayn gasped and moaned as he thrust into her. He wasn't wearing protection, but he didn't care. He'd pull out before finishing. Holding her hands behind her back, he watched her arch for him, the sight alone intensifying his pleasure.

The warmth, the tightness—it felt incredible. Just as the pleasure reached its peak, he pulled out and released onto her backside, his body trembling. With a deep sigh, he collapsed beside her. Ayn wiped herself off with her pajamas before turning to Jake, a satisfied smile on her lips.

"Did your voices bother you?" she asked.

"No, they didn't. I had my alone time with your attractive self," Jake said, grinning

Ayn chuckled. "You really like my butt, huh?" she teased, laughing in a way that was both playful and sultry.

Jake stared at the ceiling, his mind still spinning. Maybe the voices won't come back, he thought.

That was amazing. I want to do this every day for the rest of my young adult life. It felt so good to be inside her. And I actually like her—emotionally. That made it even better. Maybe I should drop this whole mental health crusade. But what if the voices return? I have no guarantee they won't. Still, maybe things will be easier now. Maybe all they ever wanted was more sex.

Ayn lay beside him, equally satisfied. She had never had sex before. Being with a man she loved, feeling him inside her, knowing he wanted to satisfy her just as much as she wanted to satisfy him—it was incredible.

"So, are you ready for the TED Talk?" Ayn asked.

Jake exhaled sharply. "To be honest, I'm terrified. I've never spoken on a platform like that before. A lot of important people do TED Talks."

Ayn turned to him, her blue eyes filled with conviction. "You're important too."

Jake hesitated. "You think so?"

She nodded. "I know so."

They kissed deeply, gazing into each other's eyes for a lingering moment. After dressing, Jake moved behind Ayn, wrapping his arms around her before they both drifted into sleep.

Jake woke up to find Ayn in the shower. He lay back on the bed, relishing the quiet, grateful that the voices hadn't intruded during their night of passion. But just as he began to savor the peace, he sensed the familiar presence—smiling at him. Frustration surged through him.

"Damn. What am I going to do?" he muttered aloud.

The face had appeared a few times, but the voices only mentioned they were processing emotions, insisting that things had changed. Jake doubted that meant they were diminishing in power or shifting focus entirely. Given how things were going with Ayn, he assumed they'd be together again soon.

So why were the voices still here?

The anger was sharp, but beneath it, there was a strange sense of relief. The insanity that usually bubbled beneath the surface felt subdued that morning. He could still hear the voices, but they seemed... content. Like him. Even so, he couldn't imagine living with them forever, no matter how much weaker they became.

It is what it is, he thought. I know I'm not the only one going through this.

He turned on his computer and pulled up his speech. Objectively, it was well-written—structured with the right pauses, perfectly timed. But something about it felt off. Too polished. Too detached. It read more like a book report than a heartfelt testimony.

When he spoke at the NAMI event, he had spoken from the heart. No complex jargon, no pretentious phrasing—just raw, lived experience. That was what resonated with people.

His thoughts were interrupted as the bathroom door opened. Ayn stepped out, wrapped in a towel, her damp hair curling against her shoulders.

"Ayn, how would you feel if I scrapped the speech we worked on and just spoke from the heart?" Jake asked.

She frowned. "You've already memorized it. We fine-tuned it to sound like someone who really understands mental health."

"But that's the problem. Most people don't understand it that way," Jake argued. "I want to reach everyone—not just those who already know the DSM definitions. Half the country thinks bipolar disorder means split personality. If I speak in clinical terms, I'll lose them. But if I tell them what it's really like, maybe they'll listen."

Ayn studied him for a moment before a small smile played on her lips. "You might be onto something. If you're going to improvise, at least work in some of the key points. You're not just ranting on a street corner—you're doing a TED Talk."

Jake chuckled. "Yeah, I'll mix it in."

He spent the rest of the day revising his speech, injecting more of his own soul into it. Meanwhile, Ayn called her Zion friends and family. For once, she didn't feel the familiar weight of depression pressing down on her. When her mother reminded her about her missed medication, a flicker of fear surfaced, but she pushed it aside. She focused on Jake, on their plans, on the excitement of tomorrow. The suicidal thoughts lingered at the edges of her mind but felt more like ghosts than threats.

A stray thought disrupted her fragile peace—she had glanced at Jake's Facebook page and noticed a flood of friend requests, many from women.

I sound like Rachel. This is insane. I'm not Rachel. She shook her head. Of course, Jake has those requests. People admire him. He wouldn't change.

The phantom presence in her mind stirred, prodding at her insecurities. But she countered it with rational thought, pushing back against the irrational jealousy.

That night, after dinner at a nearby restaurant, they made love again. Jake enjoyed it, but his mind kept drifting to the TED Talk.

What if the voices come back while I'm on stage?

He reminded himself that every time he had been in the spotlight, the voices had stayed silent. Still, anxiety gnawed at him.

After Ayn retreated to her room, Jake picked up his phone and called Chris a college friend. To his surprise, Chris answered.

"Jake! How are you holding up? Hope you're still sober with all the chaos going on."

"I'm still sober," Jake assured him. "Just nervous about the TED Talk. This is the biggest thing I've ever done. What if I end up like those viral YouTube guys? Famous for a week, then forgotten."

Chris laughed. "You don't care about fame. You care about change."

Jake exhaled. "Yeah... I just want to make a difference."

"Picture The NAMI speech," Chris said. "You're sharing."

Jake laughed. "No one's as wise and funny as you, Chris. All hail."

Jake was silent for a moment. "Remember when my psychiatrist told me I was broken?"

Chris sighed. "Yeah. That messed you up. But you bounced back. You realized you're not broken. You're somebody. That inspired me."

Jake swallowed. "He said it like... like my entire existence was screwed up."

"And yet, here you are," Chris said. "Now I'm a telephone responder for people in crisis, and I love my job. When I help someone in their darkest moment, it's like I'm connected to something bigger than myself—something I call God. You'll do great, Jake. You're not broken."

Jake closed his eyes, letting the words settle in his mind. Maybe, just maybe, Chris was right.

"I guess you're right. Maybe I will be okay. If it weren't for friends like you, I wouldn't have made it this far. I wonder if I'm dreaming. It feels like I'm being catapulted into a life full of open doors," Jake said.

"We're the lucky ones—not dead, not in jail, and not locked away in a mental institution like before," Chris replied. "Let's say a Prayer before you go to sleep."

Together, they recited:

"Lord, make me an instrument of your peace:

where there is hatred, let me sow love;

where there is injury, pardon;

where there is doubt, faith;

where there is despair, hope;

where there is darkness, light;

where there is sadness, joy.

O divine Master, grant that I may not so much seek

to be consoled as to console,

to be understood as to understand,

to be loved as to love.

For it is in giving that we receive,

it is in pardoning that we are pardoned,

and it is in dying that we are born to eternal life.

"Jake, I love you, man. I believe in you," Chris said.

"I love you too, man. Goodnight," Jake replied.

With that, he removed his contact lenses and went to sleep—peacefully. No nightmares, no voices, no humiliation, no demons. He rested with his head nuzzled in God's world.

Chapter 23

Jake woke up early in the morning, said his prayers, and thanked God for guiding him in the right direction. He chose a synthetic button-up shirt paired with brown khakis and secured them with a black belt.

Ayn greeted him at his door, wearing a blue dress that complemented her figure. Together, they went downstairs to meet Paul, who was elated to see them both.

"So, are you going to eat any breakfast, Jake?" Paul asked.

"No, I'm not. I don't want to risk any stomach issues from unfamiliar food," Jake replied.

"I understand. I just hope you have enough energy for the day. We'll meet Liz, Claire, and Rebecca at the TED Talks venue," Paul said.

"That sounds like a good plan," Jake agreed.

Ayn, Jake, and Paul stepped outside and got into Paul's small Honda Civic.

I guess people in mental health don't get paid much, Jake thought.

Ayn was feeling fine, but her mind was occupied. She imagined giving a speech about depression. *It would be great, but I'd have to be in the right emotional state. If I'm too sad, I wouldn't have the energy to deliver it. But if Jake can do it, and he's close to me, then I can too. Ever since I met my friends from Zion, I've felt an urgency to help with mental health issues—not just in this country, but maybe even globally. I don't know exactly what needs to change, but something has to.*

"So, Jake, how are you feeling? Are you ready for your TED Talk?" Ayn asked.

"Yes. In a strange way, I feel ready. My voices haven't been too active lately. I've seen faces smiling at me here and there, but I think I'll manage," Jake said.

His right hand was sweating, and he felt faint. He knew he was nervous. But he also realized that his speech could help people who didn't have a voice. There needed to be a cultural shift in how society viewed mental illness. Even the word itself hurt. He had a general idea of what he would say, though much of it was subconscious.

Paul drove steadily, keeping a static hold on the gas pedal. He cheerfully told Jake and Ayn about some of the attendees. Jake and Ayn recognized a few names from mental health books they had read, but most were unfamiliar.

When they arrived at the venue, they saw a long queue of people waiting to enter. However, Paul, Ayn, and Jake were directed through a separate entrance, where they received badges and assigned seating.

Inside, some attendees eagerly introduced themselves to Jake. One woman, a clinical psychologist, approached him with excitement, her eyes gleaming.

"I'm thrilled to meet you, Jake. I'm Dr. Clearwater. If you're looking for a new doctor, I can help you find the right fit. Your case is unique—you're incredibly resilient. Despite the severe abuse you've endured, you still manage to help others. Many people, even without your challenges, struggle with public speaking. I wanted to ask..."

Before she could finish, another woman pulled Jake by the arm.

"Hey, Jake! I'm Sara, an intern from England. I'm giving a speech about mental health in the UK," she said.

Sara was stunning. Her long, curly blonde hair framed her face perfectly. When she turned to greet someone else, Jake noticed her curvy waist and perfectly shaped figure in her black Speedo pants and low-cut blouse. She was clearly flirting with him.

Ayn approached with a suspicious look, her expression darkening. "Jake, there's someone I want you to meet," she said, clearly annoyed.

"Nice meeting you, Sara," Jake said as he stepped away.

"I'll be seeing more of you later," Sara said with a sly smile.

"Hey, Jake, I'm Dr. Applewood. I'm leading a new online CBTp class for people with hallucinations and unusual beliefs—though not necessarily delusions. I'd really like you to join. It could be incredibly beneficial for you," Dr. Applewood said.

"That sounds interesting, but how is your class different from individualized therapy sessions for CBTp—if those even exist?" Jake asked.

"Well, if you'd like, I can help you find a therapist trained in CBTp..." Dr. Applewood began, hesitating.

"You want to help me because I'm on YouTube. But what about a young man in South Side Chicago with schizophrenia, no good insurance, and no connections? How would he get individual CBTp sessions?" Jake challenged.

"Ah, well... it's just that... I mean..." Dr. Applewood stammered.

"Exactly," Jake said, unimpressed.

Paul spotted Jake across the room and walked over. As he explained the day's schedule, Jake half-listened, lost in thought.

I could really get help with these voices and strange beliefs. It seems like these people genuinely want to help me. Maybe it's because of how people saw me when I debated Jung. And I do have my own hallucination problems. Maybe I should drop all this mental health advocacy and focus on myself. But I can't abandon my Zion friends. They need help, and they want to help others. I want to give them a platform too. And I still care about those who go through what I do, along with others suffering from mental illness. At least for today, the voices have been almost nonexistent. They haven't been bothering me much. I see a face here and there, but I can manage.

Jake and Ayn followed Paul to their seats in the middle of the hall. They had a clear view of the stage.

The first speaker was a renowned neuroscientist who discussed the genetic makeup of people with mental illness and how it differed from the general population. Some of the information was familiar to Jake and Ayn. The scientist made a joke about apples and oranges while explaining different neurons in the brain. Jake and Ayn exchanged knowing glances.

It's true some of this could be genetic, they thought, *but there's no way a magic pill will ever be the solution.*

The neuroscientist emphasized that antipsychotics and other drugs remained the primary treatment for mental illness. When he finished, the audience erupted in applause.

Jake, Ayn, and Paul clapped, but they were not entirely satisfied with the speech. They have heard similar jargon from zillion therapists and psychiatrists they visited. Next up was a girl discussing depression, followed by Paul, then Jake. Ayn remained in the audience, intently listening to everything the girl said.

"My name is Amanda, and I was diagnosed with severe depression when I was 18. I had just started college, eager to meet new people and begin a new chapter in my life. I met some great people, but I often found myself feeling inexplicably sad, even during exciting conversations. Struggling to integrate into social settings, I started isolating myself, thinking it would help me focus on my studies and achieve good grades.

Initially, I did well, but after the first month, I found it increasingly difficult to concentrate. One day, while studying for a test, I realized I was merely scanning the words on the page without absorbing anything. My mind became saturated with negative thoughts: that I was dumb, abnormal, and a waste of existence.

I remembered a scene from a movie where a woman cut her arm to find relief. That idea lingered in my mind, and I eventually bought a pocket knife. But I never had the courage to use it. Instead, I spent weeks lying in bed, staring at the ceiling, not eating, missing classes. My roommate noticed and asked if something was wrong. I admitted that I felt sad all the time but couldn't pinpoint why.

She suggested I might have depression and encouraged me to see the school psychiatrist. When I finally did, I told the psychiatrist that I didn't feel human. Even funny internet shows couldn't make me laugh anymore. She asked if I had thoughts of harming myself or others. I hesitated before admitting that, sometimes, I felt like hurting myself.

She diagnosed me with severe depression and prescribed an antidepressant. For a few weeks, it helped. I was able to socialize a bit more, keep up with my coursework, and attend classes. But soon, I started developing bizarre thoughts—that Google was an evil corporation brainwashing the world and that I needed to hack into their system to save humanity.

When I shared my thoughts with friends, they laughed, thinking I was joking. One friend, however, was more direct and told me I needed help. I insisted that I had already sought help and was simply trying to warn people. Eventually, I wrote a long, erratic Facebook post, claiming Google was enslaving humanity and that I would sacrifice myself to save the world.

That night, the police came to my dorm and took me to a mental hospital. There, I told the doctors about my medication, and they explained that the antidepressant could have triggered a manic episode. After further evaluation, I was diagnosed with bipolar disorder. I was prescribed risperidone, an antipsychotic, which I still take to this day.

That medication saved my life. It stabilized me. I graduated at the top of my class, got a job in healthcare, and am now a mother of two beautiful daughters. My message is this: no matter what you're going through, there is help out there. Don't give up.

Thank you, everyone."

The audience erupted in applause, some even whistling. Amanda smiled and stepped off the stage.

Ayn, however, was furious. *That might as well have been a commercial for pills solving all mental health issues. And why was she diagnosed with bipolar disorder for life when it was obvious the antidepressant triggered her mania? That makes no sense. I've tried medication, and it doesn't work. The only thing that truly helps is my friends from Zion. The support we give each other is immeasurable compared to standard therapy and psychiatric drugs. We have a chemistry that works.*

Ayn's expression shifted to a slight smile as Paul took the stage. He started with humor, joking about the previous speech.

"Well, I guess I'll get my antipsychotic to fix all my problems," he quipped.

A few people chuckled, but most remained quiet.

Paul quickly countered his own remark, emphasizing that while medication helps some people, it does nothing for others. He discussed NAMI and other mental health organizations, including websites like depression.com and schizophrenia.com. He stressed the importance of changing cultural attitudes to reduce the stigma surrounding mental illness.

He also highlighted the role of spirituality in his son's bipolar disorder. His passion and enthusiasm captivated the audience, drawing them into every word. By the time he finished, the applause was deafening—louder than Amanda's. Smiling, he stepped off the stage.

Jake, waiting at the side, was impressed.

"Paul, that was amazing. That was the best TED Talk I've ever witnessed. You had everyone at the edge of their seats," Jake said.

Paul nodded. "It came from the heart, my friend. My son has seen countless therapists and psychiatrists, and it drained him mentally. But ever since he embraced Buddhism, he has found peace. He's been stable for two years now. I'm not saying Buddhism can heal all mental illnesses, but it's healing my son."

Jake was about to respond when the stage manager signaled for him to go on. Taking a deep breath, he stepped onto the stage. He had no PowerPoint, no scripted speech— just his raw, honest experience.

The voices were silent. His mind was clear. No hallucinations. No grinning phantoms lurking in his peripheral vision. He took a moment to absorb the expectant expressions of the audience, many still buzzing from the previous presentations.

"I'm Jake, and I love literature," he began. "I've read all the *Harry Potter* books, of course, but my favorites are *The Autobiography of Malcolm X* by Alex Haley and *Invisible Man* by Ralph Ellison. I love when a book pulls me into someone else's mind, taking me on a journey through their world. The characters, the plot, the scenery—it's all incredible."

He paused, then continued, his voice steady.

"In 2013, I was diagnosed with schizoaffective disorder. The doctor spoke as if it were a life sentence. But it wasn't. I've had good times and a lot of bad times. I've been hospitalized about fifteen times, mainly due to mixing alcohol with my symptoms.

The voices started off harmless but grew cruel over time. They humiliated me, filled me with rage, made me want to hurt myself. I also have visual hallucinations—a face that superimposes over my own. It makes me feel like there's always someone else with me.

On top of that, years of antipsychotic use have left me with tardive dyskinesia."

Jake exhaled, steadying himself. The audience listened in silence, waiting for his next words.

That makes me tense up my neck, squeeze my stomach, and blink uncontrollably. It's disturbing enough on its own, but combined with the voices, visual hallucinations, and the overwhelming sense of an invasive presence, it becomes unbearable. The presence makes me feel exposed—violated, even. Perhaps the best way to describe it is humiliating.

I've cut myself before and attempted suicide more than once. Recently, I was admitted to Zion, a mental hospital in my home state. There, I met four other young adults who also struggle with mental illness. Despite our different diagnoses, we found we had more in common than we didn't—despair, happiness, life goals, failures. We shared a connection that transcended our individual conditions.

Some of us had been in and out of psych wards, seen psychiatrists and therapists, yet never found true closure. In that moment, we decided to support each other emotionally and to explore ways to improve mental healthcare in this country. We are strong, wise, and powerful together. We believe we can create an organization to help others with severe mental illness. One of our goals is to raise awareness of lesser-known nonprofits that provide crucial assistance, ensuring that those in need can access the help they deserve.

These four individuals helped me through some of my darkest moments in that hospital, just as I was able to help them. There is hope. People with mental illnesses are warriors. They can change the world. They can uplift others who share their struggles. Like my friends, there are extraordinary individuals working to solve this complex issue," Jake spoke passionately."

He stood still for a moment, scanning the crowd. A weight had been lifted. He had spoken his truth. There needs to be a cultural change in mental illness. How we perceive it as a society needs to change. The crowd erupted in applause; some even whistled. Strangely, his mind drifted to *Invisible Man*—specifically, the narrator's first speech before a large crowd. Though he couldn't recall the details, he remembered the way the narrator had seen the audience—as a massive, insatiable beast.

Jake allowed himself a brief smile before it quickly faded. He had done it. His speech would be televised and streamed online. He knew people saw him as *the schizo who talked down another schizo*, preventing Jung from a violent confrontation with the authorities. Jake recalled the sheer terror he had felt that day—how he had spoken as though possessed while Jung cried before him. He had been so scared he could have been shot. He could have been killed. And yet, in that moment, he had felt something deific guiding him. He had to end the stigma against those with mental illness—especially those who hear voices. He had to tip the scales, to make someone like him—the one who hears voices—a superhero.

As he stood on stage, soaking in the applause, he *felt* like a superhero. Like some kind of *super advocate*. Walking offstage, he reminded himself that a little bit of pride was okay—but he couldn't let his ego consume him. He was on a mission. A mission that couldn't be stopped.

As he spoke with the stage manager, his mind returned to Ralph Ellison, his favorite author. Despite *Invisible Man*'s impact, Ellison had given only two interviews. His book spoke for itself. Ellison had waged a war on race relations; Jake's war was on mental health stigma.

"That was a powerful TED Talk," the stage manager said. "You really got straight to the point. You didn't sugarcoat anything. I had no idea people like you go through that. I always thought hearing voices was like listening to a TV or a phone. I had *no* idea how emotionally damaging and disturbing those voices could be."

Jake nodded. "It's impossible to explain the daily pain of this condition. If it's true that about 1% of the world hears voices, I wouldn't be surprised if most of those voices are negative. We have a lot of work to do."

They shook hands, promising to meet again. As Jake passed by the next speaker, the man shot him a look—one of anger, almost disgust, as though Jake had committed some unspeakable act. Something about the man's demeanor seemed... off. He looked troubled, as if his entire world had come undone. He passed that guy and found his seat beside Paul and Ayn.

"I'm Steve, folks," the man announced as he stepped onto the stage. "I talk to aliens from another planet."

The audience exchanged wary glances. Some chuckled, assuming Steve was leading up to something grand.

"They *probe* me," Steve continued. "I've had sex with a couple of them, and it was *gross*. Some of their anatomy is similar to humans, but most of it is... very different. They abduct me all the time and run experiments on me. They have this machine that circles my eyeballs using nanotechnology to squeeze my eye muscles and conduct tests. They feed me chemicals that make me shit out purple liquid and throw up green sludge. They give me things that make orange bumps appear on my face."

Murmurs rippled through the audience.

"I'm a master student of *Life* and have a PhD in *Alientology*," Steve declared. "The aliens are everywhere—in the government, the FBI, CSI. The person sitting next to you could be an alien in disguise."

By now, the audience was whispering, their expressions shifting from curiosity to concern. Steve wasn't talking about mental health anymore.

"What's this?" Steve suddenly screamed. "They have something *on* me! Some kind of chemical—GET IT OFF!"

He ripped open his button-down shirt, sending buttons flying. His bare chest heaved with frantic breaths. Then, in one swift motion, he unbuckled his belt and tossed it into the crowd. Security rushed forward as he yanked down his pants, standing in nothing but boxers. Then, to everyone's horror, he pulled out a small knife.

"It's okay, Steve," said the largest security guard. "Drop the knife. You'll be okay."

Steve stood naked, brandishing the weapon, his eyes darting wildly. He was *well-endowed*, but this wasn't the place for nudity—this was a TED Talk, where intellectuals discussed pressing issues, not some derailed porno-gone-wrong.

"They're taking over!" Steve shrieked. "We can't let them win. Save the children first! *Save the children!*"

"You're right," the security guard said smoothly. "The aliens are here, but we need to get you to a safe place. You're too important."

Steve hesitated, his expression flickering with doubt. Did the guard *believe* him? Before he could decide, another guard tackled him from behind, covering him with a jacket. The audience erupted into chaos. People rushed toward the exits.

Ayn, looking disgusted, turned to Jake. He, in turn, felt a wave of frustration. *After everything I poured into my speech, now this TED Talk will be remembered as the one where a guy stripped naked on stage.*

"I can't believe that just happened," Jake muttered as they made their way out. "That man must be deeply disturbed. And to think—I thought I'd done *everything*. I've never done *that*."

"Hopefully, he gets the help he needs," Ayn replied, facing Jake. "I wonder if the rest of the talks will go on."

The lobby buzzed with conversation. Some people were still in shock at witnessing a severe mental breakdown firsthand. Others were already leaving the building.

Then, the intercom crackled to life. "The situation has been neutralized. The individual is in custody. This is a stark reminder that many are in dire need of help. Presenters who wish to continue may proceed to the back of the stage. Again—the situation has been neutralized."

"They are right. We shouldn't let one incident impact the entire talk. Let's go back inside," said Ayn.

"You are seriously thinking to go back inside?" said Paul, furrowing his eyebrows a little concerned.

"Yes," said Jake and Ayn in unison and they all merged with the crowd inside the hall.

The crowd was relieved to return to the structured and professional atmosphere of a TED Talk, although half of the audience had already left. Jake, however, remained on edge, half-expecting another disruption. But the audience was composed, and the speakers carried on smoothly. One presenter even jokes, "Now you see why we need major changes in mental health—when even a TED Talk can have an episode."

After the presentations, everyone gathered in the lobby for refreshments and discussions. Ayn, Jake, Paul, Claire, Liz, and Rebecca engaged in insightful conversations with notable professionals and advocates.

A middle-aged white man with a blonde mustache and wavy blonde hair approached Jake just as he finished speaking with a clinical psychologist.

"Hey, Jake. I'm Jacob Jackson, a radio talk show host. I'm putting together a special on mental health featuring professionals and advocates like you. I wanted to see if you'd be interested in joining the conversation," Jacob said.

Jake responded immediately. "I'll only do it if my friends can join. They're advocates too and deserve recognition for all the work they've done. They have severe mental illnesses but are incredibly intelligent and would add a lot to the discussion."

Jacob hesitated. "I don't know… we were just looking for you. I'll have to check with my boss and see if that works."

"Well, you can't have me unless you have them too," Jake said firmly.

Jacob nodded and continued chatting with Jake about his presentation and personal experiences. As Jake spoke about his severe mental health episodes, Jacob listened intently, nodding and responding with the occasional "interesting" or "uh-huh."

"Alright, Jacob. It was nice meeting you. You have my number—let me know what your boss says."

Jake then walked over to Ayn, who looked exhausted from the day's events. Paul was deep in conversation at the far end of the lobby, while the rest of the group mingled throughout the room.

Feeling drained, Ayn agreed to grab a bite to eat with Jake and Sara, who was practically glowing with excitement at seeing Jake again. Ayn was so worn out that she didn't immediately notice the flirtatious glances Sara was shooting at him—or the way her hand lingered on his shoulder. But as the evening wore on, Ayn felt a familiar weight creeping in. It wasn't a full-blown depressive episode, but it was enough to pull her away from the conversation, leaving her staring blankly and contorting her face slightly in discomfort.

She couldn't quite pinpoint the sadness. The TED Talks had been good—except for that one about prescription drugs, which she disagreed with. She knew, deep down, that even if she took her antidepressants, this mysterious, creeping depression would still be there. It came without warning, without cause.

Jake noticed her shift. "Ayn, are you okay? You look kind of down."

"I'm not feeling great, you guys. I think I'm gonna head back to the hotel and take a nap," Ayn said, shooting Sara a sour look.

Jake was confused. Just the other day, they had been so happy together. They had been intimate. She had enjoyed the talks. So why this sudden shift?

Ayn wasn't sure why she was leaving Jake alone with someone like Sara, but she had to go. As she waited for her Uber, she thought hard about the overwhelming emotions.

Am I going to have to live like this forever—never knowing how I'll feel from one moment to the next? I can't do this every day. But I won't take antipsychotics. I already feel like an old woman, my body aching in my twenties. Maybe I don't have depression. Maybe it's bipolar disorder. But I've heard of people with depression who struggle like this, too. Now Jake's going to think I'm too sick to be his girlfriend.

She sighed, tapped at her phone, and ordered an Uber.

From across the sidewalk, Liz called out, "Hey, Ayn! I didn't know you were still here. Are you okay? You don't look so good."

"I'm having one of my depressive episodes. My body aches, and I don't feel like doing anything. It just hit me out of nowhere," Ayn admitted. "Maybe I do have some sort of chemical imbalance."

Liz shook her head. "Don't worry about that. You're just processing everything. You might be crashing from all the excitement. I've got my own issues, but when I feel depressed, it's like I'm trapped in a hole I can't climb out of. I scream in my head, but there's just silence."

"That's exactly how I feel," Ayn said. "I can't think clearly or even experience my senses properly. It's this numbness that won't go away. My mind is sluggish, like I'm trying to recall the presentations, but I just go blank. It's like my brain is caught in some kind of trap. My neck feels stiff— like something inside me is forcing it to be that way, making me as uncomfortable as possible. My whole body aches, but my neck feels like a tree trunk. How can I be an advocate when I feel this sick? Am I going to be like this forever?"

Liz placed a hand on Ayn's shoulder. "Don't think like that. I'm sure there are plenty of advocates out there who struggle with their own issues and still do amazing work. Try thinking about your heroes—that helps me. Who's one of yours?"

"Harriet Tubman," Ayn said without hesitation. "I know she was just a person, but I love the way people called her

Moses, like she was some kind of goddess. She helped so many people."

Liz smiled. "That's a good one. She never gave up, no matter how hard it got. Now, let's get up and go find your man."

Ayn burst into laughter and hugged Liz. "You're not as crazy as you let on."

Liz chuckled cynically. "Oh, trust me. I am."

The two of them turned back toward the street, where Jake and Sara went. Ayn pulled out her phone and called Jake.

Chapter 24

Jake took a bite of his burger and laughed at one of Sara's jokes.

My internship has been instrumental in helping me feel better about myself. I spent countless sessions with my psychiatrist, trying to quiet the voices in my head, but the pills just made me sluggish—like some kind of zombie. When I joined my internship, I met people like me. We talked openly about what was happening with our voices.

I was sexually abused as a child, and not long after, I started hearing the abusive voice of the person who hurt me. Eventually, I learned to reconcile with it. I realized the voice was scared and alone, just like I had been—it wanted to share my story. When I finally opened up during the internship and heard others with similar experiences, I started to heal. People in the program shared coping techniques, and now, I have lifelong friendships with other voice hearers from all over the world," Sara said, finishing with a bright smile.

Jake nodded, setting his burger down. "When I was little, my parents argued a lot. It got so bad sometimes that I had trouble sleeping. I remember going to school exhausted and miserable. This was around the time I started middle school. Before that, in elementary school, I was the class clown—Mr. Funny Guy. But in middle school, I became quiet, withdrawn. I didn't talk to many people or hang out much.

I started hearing voices when I was twenty-five. I don't know what triggered it. But when I was twenty-two, in college, I was really depressed. I spent a lot of time alone, drinking, and, well... feeling sorry for myself. I guess I kind of wanted a girlfriend," Jake said, ending with a chuckle. But there was two times many years later after. I saw a deliverance minister. He made me cry with paralyzing emotion, and my voices said I was molested when I was 5 years old. The deliverance minister said that was the cause of all my problems.

Jake's phone rang, breaking Sara's hypnotic gaze. He quickly picked it up.

"Oh, Hi, Ayn. Are you feeling better? Where are you?" Jake asked.

"I'm heading your way with Liz. She helped me feel better. What restaurant are you at?" Ayn replied.

"We're at the burger place on the corner," Jake said.

"We'll be there in a few minutes," Ayn said before hanging up.

Jake looked distracted. "Ayn will be here soon—with Liz. I think you've met her before." His voice held a trace of frustration.

"Oh, that sounds like loads of fun. I'm looking forward to it," Sara said, though something in her tone made it seem like she had been caught in the middle of a plan.

A few minutes later, Ayn and Liz walked through the front door, laughing at something between them. As they approached Jake and Sara's table, the mood shifted.

"Hello, Ayn. Hello, Liz. It's so nice to see you again. Jake and I were just chatting about mental health. Why don't you grab a couple of chairs and join us?" Sara said, her tone warm and inviting.

Liz and Sara exchanged a look—one that seemed to acknowledge exactly what Sara had been trying to do with Jake. Ayn, too, eyed Sara suspiciously before offering a polite smile. Then, something seemed to dawn on her: Sara was a fellow mental health advocate, fighting the same battle.

Jake caught Ayn's gaze and smiled as if he could read her mind.

They all settled in, shifting the conversation to the upcoming TED Talk event.

"Yeah, Ayn, I was talking to a radio host who wants to interview me along with a psychiatrist, a board member from the Zyprexa corporation, a therapist, and maybe a few others. I told them I wouldn't do it unless I could bring you guys—maybe you, Pedro, Rachel, and Jason, too. This could be a great opportunity for all of us," Jake said.

"That sounds like a good idea," Ayn replied, smirking. "It does seem like you're getting all the limelight."

The table erupted into laughter—some more than others

Pedro sat in the waiting room, anxiously waiting for his psychiatrist to call him in. He had been worrying about Zyprexa and didn't want to take it anymore because it made him feel sluggish. But at the same time, he feared experiencing another episode like the one he had during the GRE.

From his research online, he knew that most medications—especially antipsychotics—came with side effects he didn't want to deal with. He was also reconsidering his career path, reflecting on his friends and their struggles.

The psychiatrist appeared at the door.

"Hello, Mr. ... You can follow me to my office."

Pedro followed the psychiatrist into a neatly furnished room and sat down on a very comfortable couch.

"So, how are you doing?" the psychiatrist asked.

"I'm not doing so well. When I take the Zyprexa, I wake up in the morning and can't move for a few minutes. During the day, I'm constantly drowsy. I even tried lowering the dose, but I still experience the same issue, just for a shorter period..." Pedro trailed off.

"You shouldn't change the dosage of your medication unless you talk to—Wait!" the psychiatrist interjected, alarmed.

"Sorry about that. I should have called you or something," Pedro admitted.

"That's okay. We'll put you on an even lower dose," the psychiatrist replied.

"You can go lower than that? Wow."

"Is there anything else going on?"

"I keep thinking about the episode I had during the GRE. It's driving me crazy. I don't know if I'll ever be able to take the test again after what happened. It was like a living nightmare."

"Don't worry. With medication, that won't happen again. Do you want an antidepressant to help ease your anxiety about it?"

"I think we're finished here," Pedro barked.

He stood up abruptly, scolding the psychiatrist before storming out and slamming the door behind him.

Jake and Rachel are right. All these people do is prescribe more and more medication. I have to get in contact with them. This is insane. It's like there's an underground network of psychiatrists whose only solution is to drug their patients. There's history that has to be dealt with, personalities that need to be understood. That takes time. Slapping medication on the problem doesn't fix anything.

Pedro pulled out his phone. *I'd call Jake, but he's busy in California. I'll call Rachel.*

He rarely spoke to Rachel on the phone, but he reasoned that since she had experience with medications, had dealt with psychosis, and was a psychology major, she might be able to help him with his constant rumination.

"Hola, amigo! What's good?" Rachel answered cheerfully.

"Hey, Rachel. You and Jake were right. These psychiatrists just want to solve problems with medication.

But I have an issue—I can't stop thinking about the GRE episode, and it's driving me crazy. I don't know how to put it to rest."

"Well, do you even want to take the test again? Just don't take it."

"It's not that. I'm scared it could happen in another situation."

"Why don't you tell me more about it?"

"It's hard to explain. It felt like I was in some sort of hellish realm, and the devil was watching me, entertained by my fear. It was like I was being forced to walk toward an electric chair where I would die—a horrible death.

"As I sat there, looking at the test answer sheet, adrenaline surged through my veins. My mind screamed at me to do something—anything. I wanted to stay still and just write my name, but the adrenaline had to go somewhere. That's when the hypothetical scenarios started.

"I had this one thought—I was in a mental asylum, imagining the whole test. If I bubbled my name wrong, I'd cut my wrists. If I wrote my birthdate incorrectly, I'd get a lobotomy. It was like being in *Saw*, where I had to either cut off my foot or endure unbearable pain until I died. The fear sliced through me like a hot knife through butter.

"I'm trying to remember everything, but there's this fog, like quicksand, keeping me from fully grasping the experience. What I do know is that it was the most terrified I've ever been. It's like my brain doesn't want me to remember, like it's protecting me from reliving it. And honestly, I kind of understand why."

"I think you explained it pretty well," Rachel said. "You need to figure out a way to remember in a safe way and understand how to prevent it from happening again."

"How do I do that?"

"I don't know, but there has to be a way."

"Maybe if I focus on one thing that stands out... Oh my God! Now I remember what I was thinking about before the GRE episode. I can't believe I did that. It was just an experiment with my thoughts, but it must have gone wrong somehow."

"What was the thought? Even if it was bad, it's not that unusual. Everyone has intrusive thoughts sometimes," Rachel reassured him.

"Yeah, but it wasn't just a random thought—it was the way I did it. I don't know exactly how it triggered the episode, but I'm certain it played a role. I've never thought like that before."

"What was the thought?" Rachel pressed.

"I was thinking to myself that maybe the devil isn't who he really is. Maybe if I imagined a scenario in my head, it would help me think better on the GRE. I remembered a movie or something about someone who sold their soul for money or prestige. It seemed kind of stupid but also kind of logical at the same time. I wasn't going to sell my soul, but

I wanted to play around with the idea, just to see how it would feel. If it felt too uncomfortable or scary, I would stop.

So, I decided to execute a loved one in my imagination slowly, just to see how it felt. I pictured my mom standing up, and I pointed a loaded handgun at her head. I held the gun in front of her face for a moment, studying her expression. Then, in my mind, I pulled the trigger.

First of all, it didn't make me think any faster like I had expected. Instead, I felt an overwhelming sense of guilt for even imagining it. Then, I saw a vague image of a devil in my mind, and that was around the time when my symptoms started. After that, it was a roller coaster. I couldn't control my emotions anymore." Pedro said.

"That sounds pretty intense, but I don't think it's a reason for complete concern. I've had thoughts of killing the women I thought were surveilling me to get to Jason," Rachel said.

"It's just that… Rachel, I've never been so scared in my life. I was out of my mind with fear, and I didn't know what kind of hell I had entered. Whenever I think about that day, I realize there are things in this life we are not meant to experience—things we are not supposed to know about. But what I really want is to be able to remember them without falling apart. If that's even possible," Pedro said.

"We'll work on it, but you don't have to figure it all out in one day. Maybe your brain needs time to process everything, bit by bit. Whenever you want to talk about it,

I'm here for you. And so is the rest of the gang. We have to help each other survive in this wilderness of America. Ha ha ha!" Rachel laughed hysterically.

"Yeah, we have to help each other," Pedro agreed. "You guys give me hope that I can reconcile with my past. You're all amazing people, fighting your own battles but still standing up for what's right. When I get better, I'll always keep you, Jason, Jake, and Ayn in my heart. I just hope we all heal and don't have to deal with these problems forever. Have you heard from Jake and Ayn? They should be on their way back from Los Angeles by now. I wonder how the TED Talk went. It's incredible that Jake got to give a speech. I can't wait to hear about it."

"Yeah, me too. I can't wait to hear what they have to say," Rachel said.

***

Jake was alone in his hotel room. He would have slept with Ayn, but she had been on the phone with her mom for hours. Even though she enjoyed being with Jake, her depression played hide and seek with her emotions.

Jake went through the meticulous process of removing his expensive, medically necessary contact lenses. Using suction cups and a magnifying mirror, he carefully placed them in their mini chambers. He woke up the next morning already resigned to the blurry world that awaited him without them.

He had keratoconus, a condition where the cornea thinned and became cone-shaped over time. The doctors had told him it would stop progressing by the time he turned forty, but that only made him angrier. He already struggled to see without contacts—how much worse would it get before he felt completely blind? Now in his mid-thirties, he resented the idea of worsening vision during a time in his life that was supposed to be his prime.

With his contacts, he could see clearly—mostly. But he had been having persistent problems. One time, his left contact had been slightly misaligned, causing the edges to scratch his eye. The discomfort had sent him to the doctor multiple times for adjustments. Other times, he suspected his eyes were drying out because of how the lenses fit. His brother had mentioned it, but Jake couldn't always tell if he was experiencing the same issue. His left eye, in particular, felt dry a lot of the time, sometimes so subtly that he barely noticed.

Then there were the tiny marks that sometimes appeared on his lenses. The doctor had once referred to it as "fuzz," but Jake didn't know if it was that or something else. He was meticulous about caring for his lenses, so how a mark appeared remained a mystery. He currently had a small mark on his right contact, but his vision was still clear. His warranty had expired, and he couldn't afford another $600 for a replacement pair, especially when the same problem could happen again.

The biggest issue, though, was his left eye. No matter what he did, he saw the world slightly blurry through it. He had been thinking about it on and off for months, but recently, the realization had hit him harder. He would never see clearly through his left eye.. again. Maybe with a miracle no matter how improbable.

Everything that had happened with Jung, NAMI, and TED Talks had kept him too busy to process it fully. But as he put in his contacts that morning and closed his right eye to test his left, the blurriness was undeniable. The reality of it settled in his mind like a weight.

It reinforced a feeling he had tried to ignore: the feeling that he was somehow handicapped. Some kind of monstrous cyclops. In his mind, he pictured himself with a black patch over his left eye, relying only on his right.

But then he thought about Rubin "Hurricane" Carter. He had been in prison when one of his eyes had failed him, yet he still became a powerful advocate for criminal justice. He had written a beautiful book, with Nelson Mandela even contributing to the foreword.

If he could do that for criminal justice, I can do this for mental health, Jake thought.

Yes, his eye condition was one thing, but his mental health struggles were another beast entirely. The voices he heard had terrified him in ways he couldn't even explain. They had hurt him with their cruelty, twisting his emotions in ways that tested his humanity. The way they warped faces in his mind disturbed him beyond measure. It was like someone hijacked his deepest, most personal emotions, leaving him exposed and powerless.

Even though he had no idea if these problems would ever go away, he knew he had to keep fighting. He had to push for better trauma-based research. Too many therapists and psychiatrists had failed him. Maybe someday, when all of this was behind him, he would write a book. Maybe by then, he would have helped bring real change to the mental health system. Maybe, by then, people would finally get better therapy instead of just pills with side effects.

A knock on the door pulled him from his thoughts.

Ayn stood outside.

"Hey Jake, how are you doing? Good morning!" she said with a smile.

"I'm not doing so good. I have to tell you something."

"What?"

"You know I have an eye condition called keratoconus. The last couple of days, I've noticed my left eye getting considerably blurrier. I can still see detail with my right eye with contacts. The last time I saw the doctor, he said a cornea transplant was the only option. He didn't offer any reassurance or alternatives. It's hard to accept that my left eyesight is deteriorating, and there's nothing I can do to make it as good as my right."

"That doesn't sound good. I had no idea you were going through that. Are you sure the doctor can't do anything else?"

"From the way he talked, he's done all he can. I've had contacts for a year and a half, and in the first six months, there was no issue with my left eye. It feels like it's getting worse quickly. The doctor said the cone in my left eye is more irregular than the right, which is probably why the vision is worse. I'm struggling to accept that my left eye is blurry," said Jake.

"I don't know what to say. I've never experienced anything like that. When I get really depressed, I feel like hurting myself. Sometimes, the pain is so overwhelming I think about shifting it elsewhere—like losing an eye. But I guess for now, you have to realize it could be worse. At least you can still see clearly with your right eye. And you still have some vision in your left. What helps me sometimes is making a gratitude list. Like, you don't have a life-threatening disease. You don't have cancer. Plus, you're still handsome."

"That helps a little. I do that sometimes, and it does make a difference. It's just that this eye issue affects my whole life. I'm in my thirties. I already struggle with mental health issues, and now this. It feels like a law written in my mind: Thou shall not see clearly through my left eye forever. I know people who have similar problems."

***

Jake and Ayn's plane landed back in their home state. Jake felt proud that he had managed to deliver his TED Talk despite everything he was going through. When he finished speaking, the audience erupted in applause. Now, he wanted the rest of his friends to have the same opportunity to speak in front of a crowd. He smiled at Ayn as they disembarked, feeling an extra sense of pride knowing she was now his girlfriend.

As they left Los Angeles, Ayn kissed Jake on the lips, catching him off guard. The moment made him feel like he was on top of the world. It was only the second time a girl had kissed him, and he savored it. His voices didn't bother him much during the flight, though they had smirked at him a few times when Paul drove them to the airport.

"It's so nice to be home. I'm exhausted and just want to sleep," Jake said to Ayn.

Ayn gave him a mischievous smile, but before Jake could respond, his phone rang. He answered.

"Hey Jake, this is Jacob, the radio host I told you about. Good news—you and your friends can all come on the show. My boss thinks it'll be great to get multiple perspectives from people with mental health conditions. The discussion won't be biased at all. We want you to speak freely. There will also be a representative from the Zyprexa corporation, a psychiatrist, and a CBT therapist on the panel. It should be an interesting conversation. We have to do it in five days at the YPR newscast building. It'll be set up like a podcast and will also be aired on YouTube. This is a great opportunity for your friends. Does that work for you?"

"Yeah, Jacob, that works. We'll meet you at YPR in five days. Thanks for the opportunity," said Jake.

"Great. See you then," said Jacob. There was a brief silence before Jacob finally hung up, as if he were waiting for something else.

"Who was that?" Ayn asked.

"Jacob, the radio host I mentioned. Looks like we're going to meet him at YPR in five days. Should be good for you guys—since I'm famous already," Jake joked.

"You're not famous yet, Mr. Denzel Washington," Ayn teased. They both laughed, and Jake put his arm around her as they grabbed their bags and headed outside to wait for their ride.

***

"…And boom, he was naked on TV, screaming about the alien invasion, waving a knife at the guards—with a gargantuan cock!" Rachel exclaimed, grinning.

Ayn, Jake, Jason, Pedro, and Rachel sat in Pedro's living room, eating pizza and rehashing the TED Talks event.

"I still haven't processed what happened at TED Talks," Jake said. "I remember being on stage, delivering my speech, and then suddenly, that guy was naked and waving a knife. I wouldn't be surprised if it made national news. Of course, they can't show the footage, but it must have been terrifying for the guy who was speaking about aliens."

"Yeah, it must have been," Rachel agreed. "The internet has full coverage of his speech right up until he pulled out the knife and became naked. I can't imagine how his therapist feels. She probably thinks she failed him. His psychiatrist will probably increase his antipsychotic meds."

"It's insane. Of all places, it happened at TED Talks," Jason added. "It feels like there's a psychological cold war going on. He must have been struggling in the days leading up to it. In his mind, he was probably trying to help in his own delusional way. Is he really a bad person if he was trying to save us from an alien invasion? Even if it was just an illusion?"

"If you put it that way, he's a hero," Pedro mused. "I hope they don't hurt him. I laughed, but I know how it feels to have an illusion distort reality."

"I don't think medication will help him," Rachel said.

"I don't think so either," Ayn and Jason agreed in unison.

"So, are you guys ready for the podcast tomorrow? I don't think we really need to prepare. We just have to show up and be honest," Jake said.

"Yes, sir! I'm ready, sir!" Rachel saluted with a smirk.

Jake turned to Pedro. "How are you doing? You look a little down."

"I've been having a hard time getting over the GRE episode. It haunts me every time I think about it. I talked to Rachel, and she helped, but I can't stop wondering what I'd do if it happened again. During that episode, I had suicidal thoughts. I could have easily jumped off a building or in front of a train just to escape the terror. I've never been so scared in my life. It happened so quickly, yet it felt like a lifetime. I remember bits of what I was thinking before it happened and some of the reasons behind it, but to fully understand, I'd have to relive that moment—something I never want to do," Pedro said.

"I had a similar experience," Jake replied. "I saw a strange figure. A devil or something like that. Then, after that, my memory goes blank."

"I was at my sister's apartment with my mom, dad, and brother, sitting on the couch. And then, all of a sudden, I stood up—stiff as a board. My back was rigid, my arms stretched straight in front of me. Thoughts were racing through my mind, faster than I'd ever experienced. I remember thinking the world was one giant competition— everyone fighting for jobs, money, status—while others were left behind, just waiting to fade away. But at that moment, I didn't feel like I was rising above anything. I needed adrenaline to outthink people, but I wasn't functioning.

"Somehow, my family got me to sit down on the floor with my back against the couch. I was hyperventilating, gasping for air like I was struggling to survive. I was in a full-blown psychotic panic. It felt like an eternity before the ambulance arrived. I barely registered them—just their uniforms. One of the paramedics was young. I could see his face, but I wasn't sure if he was a threat or just something I needed to be wary of. His facial expressions shifted ever so slightly, and I thought I could read his mind through them. He seemed confused.

"They walked me to the ambulance slowly and told me to lie down. My dad was there, trying to talk to me, trying to calm me down, but it was hard for him. When we got to the hospital, somehow, I managed to settle," Jake finished.

Ayn stood up and wrapped her arms around Jake in a slow, warm embrace.

"Wow, Jake, that was so similar to my story. The racing thoughts, the suffocating adrenaline… I know exactly what you mean," Pedro said.

"Yeah," Jake nodded. "As I was telling it, I felt some of the emotions again. But most of them are buried deep in my subconscious. They're too painful to deal with regularly."

"Alright, guys, we should probably get some rest. We have to meet with Jacob and everyone at YPR tomorrow, so we'd better sleep if we can," Jake added.

"Yeah. What a way to end the day. It would've been nice if we could've wrapped up with a good joke," Jason sighed.

"Why did the chicken cross the road?" Jason asked.

"Get the hell out of my house, Jason," Pedro said.

They all laughed, grabbed their belongings, and headed home for the night.

Chapter 25

Rachel was the last to arrive at YPR. The others were already seated in a room with Jacob, who was visibly excited about what was to come later in the day.

Jason glanced out the window and noticed a man in a black suit and tie sitting in the backseat of a limousine. The vehicle parked at the far end of YPR, and the man stepped out, scanning his surroundings with an air of sophistication. Taking out his phone, he muttered, "Yeah, I have to do this damn interview with some sick people. Looks like I have to sell our brand to the public the best I can. The boss says I need to push the message that we're trying to help people, not give them diabetes. If I pull this off, I'll get that bonus and finally buy that speedboat I've always wanted."

The window was open, and Jason was the only one who heard him. The rest of his friends were engaged in conversation with Jacob, oblivious to the exchange.

A knock sounded at the door, and Jacob answered it. The man entered, extending a handshake. "I'm Mr. Birk with the Lily Organization," he introduced himself. As he surveyed the room, his face contorted slightly at the sight of Jake and his friends. He attempted a polite smile but failed. Taking a seat far from everyone, he resumed his phone call, giving orders about the placement of his new furniture.

The next person to enter was a middle-aged woman with gray streaks in her hair. She beamed at Jacob, radiating such warmth that even Ayn, despite her struggles with depression, found herself smiling back. Approaching Jake first, she said,

"You must be Jake. The mental health community is very excited about you. It's a pleasure to meet you. I'm Dr. Graceland."

"I'm Jake. I think I saw you at a TED Talk, but I didn't get a chance to speak with you. So many people wanted to talk to me after my speech," Jake replied.

"Are these your friends?" Dr. Graceland asked, making her way around the room, greeting each person. When she reached Mr. Birk, his expression darkened. The tension between them was immediate, as if they were natural adversaries. Though they had never met before, something about each other set them on edge.

The last person to enter was a short, middle-aged Jewish man. "I'm Dr. Figgit, the psychiatrist called in for this discussion," he announced. Jacob shook his hand with the same enthusiasm he had shown the others. Dr. Figgit introduced himself to the group, maintaining a neutral demeanor.

Jacob clapped his hands together. "Alright, ladies and gentlemen, we're heading into the podcast room for our discussion. I hope everyone is well-rested because we'll be here for a while talking about mental health. There will be water and snacks, and we'll break for lunch before resuming."

As Jacob spoke, Mr. Birk stared at Jake with a scowl, as though recognizing him from somewhere.

Everyone rose and followed Jacob into the podcast room. Nine chairs faced a central chair where Jacob would be facilitating the conversation. Each seat had an expensive-looking microphone in front of it. Mr. Birk claimed the chair closest to Jacob, positioning himself as the most important person in the room. The others took their seats, with Jake and his friends sitting together.

"No, don't put the picture above the kitchen table—put it in the living room!" Mr. Birk barked into his phone.

"Excuse me, Mr. Birk," Jacob said firmly. "We're about to start. Could you please get off the phone?"

Mr. Birk shot him an irritated glare but ended the call.

A makeup artist moved through the room, powdering faces while the cameraman adjusted his equipment.

"Is everyone ready?" Jacob asked.

"Finished," the makeup artist confirmed.

"Ready," the cameraman echoed.

A stage manager stepped up. "Starting in three… two… one… action."

Jacob leaned into his microphone. "Hey, this is Jacob with YPR's newscast, broadcasting live on the radio and YouTube. We have something special for you today—a panel of unique individuals discussing mental health affairs in America. Joining us is Mr. Birk, an executive with the Lily Organization. Their drug, Zyprexa, is commonly prescribed for psychotic disorders but is also used to treat severe depression and anxiety. Recently, concerns have arisen about its potential to cause significant weight gain, increasing the risk of diabetes. Mr. Birk will be addressing these claims today."

Jacob continued, "Mr. Birk holds a degree from the University of Wisconsin and an MBA from Stanford. Before joining Lily, the company behind Zyprexa, he served as the President of Operations for McDonald's in the Midwest, where he doubled revenue by implementing aggressive business strategies, raising wages, and increasing employee benefits."

During the recession, Mr. Birk managed to keep McDonald's serving billions of people below the middle-class wage bracket. He employed more immigrants than any other fast-food chain in the Midwest, expanding the company's reach into new rural areas.

One day, he attended a conference hosted by Lilly on doubling the sales of Zyprexa. His presentation showcased an archetypal strategy that projected a significant increase in sales across the Midwest sector. His projections were so precise that he was invited to join Lilly's board of directors. Since then, his innovative advertising techniques have generated millions in revenue.

"Hello, Mr. Birk. Very happy to have you here," Jacob said.

"Thank you, I'm pleased to be here. Ha ha ha. But I'm not just about making money. My goal is to provide Lilly's products to the public so they can be free of mental illness," Mr. Birk replied.

"We'll get to that in a moment. Let me finish the introductions," Jacob continued.

"Next, we have Dr. Graceland. She earned her undergraduate degree in psychology from the University of North Carolina at Chapel Hill, followed by a master's and Ph.D. from the same institution. Her dissertation focused on therapy methodologies for severe mental illnesses, such as major depression and extreme schizophrenia.

Dr. Graceland currently runs a practice in Atlanta, Georgia, where she provides consultations for patients with a wide range of diagnoses. She helped spearhead a nonprofit organization, *My Brother's Keeper*, which brings mental health resources to low-income communities. She has hosted several webinars on mental illness in America and the effectiveness of modern therapies.

She is also widely known for her YouTube video through *My Brother's Keeper*, where she discusses Cognitive Behavioral Therapy for Psychosis (CBTp) and its potential to help individuals struggling with severe mental illness. The video gained significant traction, leading to her appearance on *TED Talks*, where she delivered an in-depth presentation on the importance of training therapists in CBT and CBTp.

In addition to her advocacy, she is the author of *The Essence of Severe Mental Illness*, available on Amazon. She is deeply committed to transforming the way society perceives and addresses mental illness.

"Hello, Dr. Graceland. It's a pleasure having you here with us," Jacob said.

"I'm happy to be here. I hope I can contribute to this important conversation," Dr. Graceland responded.

"Next, we have Dr. Figgit. He is a distinguished psychiatrist in this county, treating patients with conditions ranging from mild anxiety to severe schizoaffective disorder. He firmly believes that the best patient outcomes stem from the right combination of medication and therapy.

Dr. Figgit has spent over 20 years prescribing psychiatric medications and tailoring treatment plans to meet his patients' individual needs. In his published work, he outlines the connections between symptoms and the medications that provide the most effective relief.

Beyond his career, he is a father of two sons attending Duke University. His wife, also a psychiatrist, met him in medical school, where they bonded over their shared passion for psychiatric medicine. Dr. Figgit proposed to her in a moment of triumph—right after successfully persuading a severely psychotic patient in an asylum to take life-changing medication, something no other doctor had managed to do.

Following his internship and graduation from medical school, he worked at the same asylum, where he learned the importance of being headstrong, logical, and ethical when treating patients. He saw firsthand that many individuals arrived confused and lost, in desperate need of a professional who could guide them toward recovery.

Dr. Figgit takes great pride in his work, finding fulfillment in changing his patients' perspectives and helping them build robust recovery plans. He is acutely aware of the dangers of overmedication and "zombification" and is committed to prescribing the right balance of medication to alleviate distress without dulling a patient's mind. He describes psychiatry as both a science and an art—one that requires an understanding of symptoms, medications, and the complex psychological landscapes of his patients.

"Hello, Dr. Figgit. It's a pleasure to have you here," Jacob said.

"Thank you. I'm happy to be here," Dr. Figgit responded earnestly.

"Finally, we have Jake. He holds a degree from State University and is an avid reader of literature. He has been in and out of hospitals with a diagnosis of schizophrenia. When he was first institutionalized, he was diagnosed with Bipolar I Disorder. A few years later he was diagnosed with schizophrenia. Over the years, he has seen countless psychiatrists and therapists, yet none have truly been able to help him.

Despite his struggles, Jake has found solace in advocacy. Speaking out about mental illness gives him a sense of purpose and peace, allowing him to navigate the complexities of his condition while helping others do the same."

Perspective

He was known for talking down a severely confused mental patient who was about to shoot a psychologist at a NAMI event. Jake managed to calm the individual and peacefully turn him over to the police. He had also spoken at TED Talks in Los Angeles about his struggles with hearing voices and experiencing abnormal beliefs. After his speech, a disturbed individual took the stage, undressed completely, and pointed a knife at the audience and security guards. Once the man was apprehended, Jake remained to watch the rest of the presentations. That was where I first met him—in the lobby—this sincere young man named Jake.

The conversation that followed included four of Jake's friends, all of whom he had met at Zion Mental Hospital. It was there that they realized something was deeply flawed in the mental health infrastructure of this country. They wanted to change the cultural perception of mental illness and the nature of existing treatment methods.

Among them was Rachel, diagnosed with schizophrenia; Pedro, diagnosed with bipolar disorder; Jason, who struggled with obsessive-compulsive disorder; and Ayn, who suffered from severe depression.

"Welcome to the program, you guys," Jacob said.

Jake and his friends were excited to be part of the YouTube special. Across from them, Mr. Birk sat stiffly, his expression barely concealing his disdain, as if he viewed them as insects that needed to be crushed. He was only there because the board members had made it mandatory, but he would have much preferred to be at his new house, overseeing the movers as they arranged furniture and hung pictures.

Meanwhile, Jason stared anxiously at the microphones. He hadn't seen anyone sanitize them. His face twisted in disgust. Who knew how many people had spoken into them or what kind of germs they carried? The thought alone made his skin crawl. He needed the sanitizer in his car. If he could just clean the microphone, he'd feel a little better. Instead, he took slow, controlled breaths to calm himself. The discomfort gnawed at him, threatening to unravel his sense of security. Sweat formed on his brow. He glanced at Rachel, who smiled at him, and that small reassurance grounded him. If she could be happy to be here, why couldn't he?

Jacob cleared his throat. "Let's start with you, Mr. Birk. There have been reports of people developing diabetes after taking Zyprexa. Many patients have complained about significant weight gain—"

Mr. Birk cut him off. "You can stop right there, Jacob. Zyprexa is a safe drug. The benefits far outweigh the risks. It has brought peace and stability to many patients. If someone gains weight, they should see a nutritionist, hit the gym, or watch their diet. Besides, diabetes has a genetic component, so some people are just predisposed."

"I agree," Dr. Figgit added. "I've prescribed Zyprexa to many patients, and while weight gain is a potential side effect, its effectiveness in treating psychosis is undeniable. The sedative properties alone can be life-changing for those who are, to put it simply, out of touch with reality."

Pedro shifted uncomfortably. His voice was barely above a whisper. "Can I say something?"

"Of course, Pedro," Jacob encouraged him.

"I've been on Zyprexa for a while, and it does help control my psychosis," Pedro admitted. "But I've gained a lot of weight. I don't think like I used to—I feel slowed down, like my mind is foggy. And in the mornings, I wake up unable to move. My arms and legs feel like stone. It's terrifying. Even at a lower dose, the problem persists."

"Everyone responds differently to medications," Mr. Birk said dismissively. "Not everyone has those issues, like… what's his name over there."

"Well, I had the same problems," Jake interjected. "I gained a lot of weight, and I also experienced paralysis in the mornings. I'd lie there, completely unable to move, and after a few minutes, I'd finally regain control."

"That sounds terrifying," Jacob said, frowning. "There seems to be a real connection between Zyprexa and sleep paralysis."

"This isn't something to be alarmed about," Dr. Figgit replied smoothly. "If one medication isn't a good fit, there are other antipsychotics to try."

Jake clenched his jaw. "I've tried several different medications. None of them fix the voices. They just make me feel worse. The only thing they do effectively is slow me down—my thoughts, my reactions, everything."

"In that case," Dr. Figgit said with a knowing smile, "I'd recommend a combination of medications tailored to your needs." He looked at Jake as if he had him all figured out.

Jake's eyes darkened. "When does this stop, Dr. Figgit? There is no perfect combination. I've been on different mixtures of medications for years, and I'm only getting worse. Just admit it—you don't know how to fix this." His voice was sharp, his frustration palpable.

Dr. Graceland had been quietly observing the conversation with a half-smile. Nothing she had heard so far surprised her—not from Dr. Figgit, not from Mr. Birk, not from Pedro or Jake. But she found Jake's passion admirable.

"The problem," she finally said, "is that many psychiatrists are trained to believe that the only solution to mental health issues is a handful of pills. But I believe in focusing on the nature of the problem. I want to talk to patients about their voices—what they say, how they make them feel, who these voices seem to be. It's important for patients to feel heard, to know that their thoughts matter. Too many psychiatrists tell patients to ignore their voices, to write them off as meaningless. But what if, instead, we engaged with them? What if we approached them with compassion?"

Her words hung in the air, challenging everything that had been said before.

Rachel liked what Dr. Graceland had to say. The only problem was that it was hard for her to be compassionate toward the voices—especially since they were so prosecutorial. Sometimes, they sounded like real people trying to hurt her, and Rachel couldn't bring herself to feel compassion for someone who seemed to be putting her life in danger. Since she wasn't sure whether the voices were real or not, she decided it was best to stay quiet and simply listen to what Dr. Graceland had to say.

"For instance, with Jake, I start by asking what exactly the voices do that make him feel his privacy is being invaded. Then, we discuss what they typically say and what they want. The most important thing is ensuring that the person I'm speaking with feels comfortable at all times. If they're having a particularly bad day, I steer the conversation in a different direction. I've found that voice hearers are more willing to talk about their experiences when they feel the voices won't punish them for speaking. In many cases, the voices are deeply connected to a person's emotions and core beliefs. Sometimes, the voices even seem to have input, leaving the individual confused about their reality," Dr. Graceland explained.

Both Rachel and Jake, as voice hearers, smiled in agreement. They felt Dr. Graceland was on the right track.

"Wait, wait. That's all well and good," Dr. Figgit interjected. "But when I worked at a mental hospital, if a patient was erratic, violent, confused, or suicidal, they needed heavy-duty medication. In those cases, I had to give them a sedative—some kind of tranquilizer. I couldn't risk someone hurting themselves or others." His frustration was evident.

"I understand, Dr. Figgit," Dr. Graceland responded calmly, "but there are ways to de-escalate a situation through conversation. Certain words can trigger a person, while others can calm them down. The way you speak, your tone, even your facial expressions can make a difference. Jake isn't a professional, yet the way he talked down Mr. Jung was admirable. He instinctively used many of the same methods I would in that situation."

Mr. Birk looked bored at this point. He felt he had already made his point, so he tuned out the conversation, texting on his phone and occasionally glancing up with feigned interest.

"Dr. Graceland, I wish I had you as my therapist," Jake said earnestly. "You seem insightful, caring, and understanding. I haven't had great experiences with most therapists I've encountered, and my experiences with psychiatrists have been even worse. I need someone who asks the right questions—someone who helps me manage the symptoms my voices create. A lot of the time, they act like demons, but then there are moments when they do things that remind me they aren't real entities. I want to understand what makes them tick. If I can figure that out, maybe I can have some power over them." His voice grew more animated as he smiled at Dr. Graceland.

"And that is exactly what my team and I are trying to help people achieve," she responded.

"I really believe there has to be a way to feel less anxious and fearful of the voices," Jake continued. "There has to be a way to either coexist with them or make them disappear. It's just… I've been searching for so long, and I'm exhausted. And I'm tired of seeing other people go through the same thing—or worse."

"This is all fascinating," Rachel chimed in, "but why is it so hard to find people like Dr. Graceland? I'd never heard of her before today, and she's amazing. There should be some kind of search engine that helps people connect with professionals like her—people with big ideas and real solutions."

"Have you tried Google?" Mr. Birk said dryly.

"Asshole," Rachel shot back, turning to face him. "Just sit over there and count your billions. Think about all the people you've condemned to using insulin for the rest of their lives."

"Whatever," Mr. Birk muttered, going back to his phone.

"Pedro, you want to weigh in on this?" Jacob asked.

"I like what I've heard from Dr. Graceland so far," Pedro said. "I had a psychotic break, and it's been really difficult to recover from. I was in a dark place, and I don't ever want to go back there. I want to understand what caused it so I can prevent it from happening again. I've tried to piece it together on my own, but all I get are fragments—I don't have the full picture. My friends have helped a lot, but I'd love to talk to someone like Dr. Graceland about my thoughts and emotions—about what led me to that breaking point."

"You just need the right medication to help with your problem," said Dr. Figgit.

"Stop the shit, Figgit. Not everybody wants to be a zombie their whole life," Rachel snapped.

Dr. Figgit's expression remained calm and composed despite Rachel's outburst. She was still mad at him, but even angrier at the voice in her head that called her a **"bitch."**

"If you keep talking, we're going to kill you. Didn't you hear us say before that Jason is ours?"

The voice was deep, filling every part of Rachel's consciousness. She felt paralyzed. She wanted to scream at them, to tell them she was in the middle of an interview and didn't have time for their nonsense, but they wouldn't stop. It was the voice of a girl from her college history class, someone she used to talk to.

"We're going to kill you nice and slow," the voice hissed.

"I wish you'd shut the fuck up," Rachel muttered under her breath—quiet enough that only Jason and Jacob noticed.

Jacob wanted to make sure she was okay for the interview.

"Excuse me, Mr. Figgit, we're taking a fifteen-minute break. We'll be back soon, ladies and gentlemen."

The cameraman called, "Cut," and everyone moved to the break room. Jason followed Rachel and sat beside her, looking serious.

"It's the voices again. What did they say? You can trust me, Rachel. You have to tell me the truth—I might be able to help," Jason urged.

Rachel hesitated but finally admitted, "They said they're going to kill me. One of them sounded like a girl I used to know. And they said they want you." She looked exhausted, her face drained of color.

Jason's expression softened. "Rachel, I don't know where we stand in our relationship, but what I do know is— I love you. And I don't want anything to happen to you. I'll protect you, no matter what."

"You really mean that? We're boyfriend and girlfriend again?" Rachel asked hopefully.

"I won't go that far," Jason said with a slight smirk. "But I'll tell you something—it could happen. You've amazed me with your hard work and your heart for this organization. You really care about something bigger than yourself, and I find that beautiful. I don't know how much you believe your voices, but part of you knows something isn't right."

"That's true. I get confused sometimes. But when I really think about it… the voices don't make sense," Rachel admitted.

"Come on, let's go to my car and grab the sanitizer so we can clean my mic when we get back," Jason said.

Rachel grinned. "That's my love—being a clean freak again."

"Didn't you hear what I just said? We're not a… whatever," Jason muttered, shaking his head.

They walked outside to Jason's car, retrieved the antibacterial spray, and returned to the building. Meanwhile, the others chatted about various topics—except for Mr. Birk, who was glued to his phone.

When they walked back in, Jacob stepped in front of Rachel.

"Are you okay? I could tell you looked a little disturbed. Was it your voices?"

"Yeah, but my good friend Jason helped me feel better," Rachel replied, smiling at Jason.

Jason raised an eyebrow. **Friend?** He hadn't expected that.

Jacob clapped his hands. "Alright, time to head back for part two of the interview."

Everyone returned to their assigned seats. Jason finished wiping down his mic as the cameraman counted down.

"Action," the stage manager called.

"Okay, Dr. Figgit, you can finish what you were saying," Jacob said.

Dr. Figgit straightened. "I just wanted to say there are many different medications available, and I've prescribed a lot over the years. They can really help—"

Rachel cut him off.

"Do you have a soul, Dr. Figgit?" she asked bluntly.

The room went silent.

"I mean, do you actually listen to your patients? Do you ask them about what makes them laugh or cry? Have you ever formed a real friendship with one of them? Have you ever finished a session and thought, 'I truly love this person as a human being'?

"Pills can't make you love a book. Pills can't make you love a person. That comes from deep inside us.

"Right before the break, I had a voice in my head threatening to kill me. Part of me felt like it was real. Part of me knew it wasn't. But I didn't take a PRN to numb myself—I turned to my support system.

"My friend Jason saw my face and knew something was wrong. He asked me what the voices were saying. And with some simple, kind words—showing me love and understanding—he calmed me down. Not a pill, Dr. Figgit. Love.

"It was hard for me to tell him, especially since my voices were talking about him, but the moment I did… something changed. I felt free. I felt a connection. And just like that, the voices stopped—at least for now.

"Try loving your patients, Dr. Figgit. Before you drown them in a cocktail of medications."

Dr. Figget was stunned. This little blonde woman, who looked like an airhead, had just said something so profound that it shook him. A part of him felt like a demon being vanquished from God's presence, screaming, *Noooo!*—but that same demon clung to his ego, refusing to let him verbally agree with Rachel. Yet, he knew she was right. He had always seen his patients as subjects, not people. More than once, he had even told them they were broken, that only medication could fix them.

"Well played, young lady. Well played," Dr. Figget said, offering a modest half-smile. Rachel, looking triumphant, met his gaze.

"I've been diagnosed with severe depression," Ayn began, her voice steady but filled with emotion. "Sometimes, it feels like I'm trapped in a dark cave, unable to climb out. But with support from my friends, I've experienced moments that remind me why life is worth living. When I'm in a slump, I tell my friends how I feel as best as I can, and even if I don't always get to the root of the problem, it helps. Someone once told me, *a problem shared is a problem half-solved*, and I believe that with all my heart.

"Depression is a relentless condition. There are times I want to isolate myself, times I've even felt suicidal. But my friends have shown me that, no matter how dark it gets, there's a light inside me that can't be extinguished. Working with them for mental health advocacy has helped me step outside my own mind. Since meeting my friends in Zion, I no longer feel like I'll be stuck in this darkness forever. I believe I will get better.

"I may not fully understand what's hurting me, but I know that with my friends, I'm closer to the truth than I could ever be on my own. So, I'll keep fighting for mental health awareness. I have to believe we are stronger together. I have to believe there are answers—answers to why my friends and I suffer the way we do.

"Pedro doesn't want to relive his psychotic episode during the GRE every time he closes his eyes. Jake doesn't want to see faces that aren't there. Rachel doesn't want voices whispering that her days are numbered. Jason doesn't want to be chained to the compulsion to clean everything he touches. And I… I don't want to be tormented by suicidal thoughts anymore."

Ayn turned her gaze to Mr. Birk, who was typing on his phone.

"Mr. Birk, do you remember a time when your wife cried, when you saw the sadness in her eyes? Maybe you didn't know exactly what caused her pain, but you felt it, didn't you? That's what we have in our group. A deep love. A bond. We don't just sympathize—we *empathize*."

A single tear rolled down Ayn's cheek. Mr. Birk kept his expression unreadable, his face a perfect poker mask. He couldn't let the world see—especially not on YouTube Live—that he had been touched by an angel.

"There needs to be a cultural shift in how we view mental health," she continued. "Yes, some people laugh at those with mental illnesses because they act 'abnormally.' But there's another way to look at it—through empathy. If we actually cared about our cousin, our classmate, that stranger struggling on the street, instead of writing them off, we could make a difference. We could save lives.

"Our country is advancing in technology, medicine, and science, yet when it comes to mental health, we're still failing. Why do we glorify stories where someone with a mental illness turns violent? Why don't we have movies where a person with a mental health condition *saves the day*? Why isn't a therapist like Dr. Graceland famous for her groundbreaking work? Why do more people know the Kardashians than someone like her? That's not logical.

"I've had OCD for years. Right now, I *want* to clean every microphone my friends have used. My illness has transformed—I don't just fear germs for myself, but for them too. I don't want them to get sick and die. I *understand* them. When they tell me their emotions take control, when they say they feel handcuffed in an endless cycle of pain, I *get it,*" interjected Jason.

"There *has* to be something more we can do. Sure, we have commercials urging people to call a suicide hotline, but we need more. We need to teach people how to recognize the warning signs within themselves. We need real intervention.

"My friend Jake has gone from psychiatrist to psychiatrist, therapist to therapist, and gotten nowhere. And me? I can't stop obsessing over germs. I *see* them in my mind before I touch anything. It's *hell.* If I don't clean an object, I feel like the world will end. I feel like *I'm* about to die. I even get tactile hallucinations—I *feel* the germs crawling on me. I want to scream so loud that the whole world hears me. Not because I want to scare anyone, but because I need *help.*

"The only real help I've ever found is in my friends. They're the only ones who understand. I live in constant anxiety, feeling like germs are always trying to kill me. It's exhausting. I can't relax. I can't think. I can't *be.*

"And the worst part? There's *suicidal ideation* mixed in. I won't kill myself, but deep down, I feel like death is always knocking at my door. And I don't even understand *why* I have this fear. Maybe it stems from my childhood, but no therapist has ever asked me about that. No psychiatrist has tried to help me get to the root of my pain.

"I don't want to just manage symptoms. I want to understand *why* I am the way I am. I want someone to help me unwind my mind so I can be *free.*"

Jason's voice broke, and a heavy silence filled the room.

Dr. Figget and Mr. Birk avoided eye contact, as if embarrassed to be there. Meanwhile, Dr. Graceland wiped away silent tears, sniffling quietly as she listened.

"I want you to be free, Jason. I want you and your friends to break free from your mental health struggles. When you were speaking just now, you sounded so powerful. You really touched my heart. I admire how much love you show your friends, even while facing your own challenges. You and your friends are truly remarkable. Sometimes, I wonder if the support you give each other helps more than anything else.

Cognitive Behavioral Therapy can help with your OCD, too, Jason. I know people get tired of hearing about different therapies—they can seem overwhelming—but finding the right therapist makes all the difference. Someone who truly cares. Someone who's willing to work with you, to explore how your thoughts connect to your emotions and behaviors..."

Dr. Graceland's voice was calm yet firm.

"Stop right there, Dr. Graceland. I've heard that before—on YouTube," Jason said, his expression earnest. "How exactly are *you* going to help me with my OCD?"

"Well, we start by identifying the thoughts that trigger your compulsions—the ones that lead to excessive cleaning. That's the first step. But therapy isn't just about strategies. There has to be a connection between us. You let me in, I let you in."

Jason considered this, then smiled. "That's a better answer. You're not pretending to have a clean-cut solution, but you're still willing to get to the root of it. I like that."

Rachel glanced at Jason with a warm, friendly expression—not flirtatious, just understanding.

Dr. Graceland hesitated for a moment, as if debating whether to say something.

"Dr. Graceland, is there something you want to add?" Jacob prompted.

She exhaled, then nodded. "Yes. I just want to say that there *is* hope. Jake and his friends have been through a lot, and they're fighting to create change in how mental health is viewed. But they shouldn't lose sight of their own healing.

There are people out there who can help—not just professionals, but individuals who've been through similar struggles.

Mental health support works best in a community, but it's also deeply personal. At some point, each person has to look inward and ask themselves: *Who am I?* I know this sounds simple, but I truly believe that changing how you think can change your mental health. It's incredibly difficult, but giving up on therapy isn't the answer.

Yes, therapy is expensive, and insurance doesn't always cover it. But that doesn't mean you stop searching for help. Even the internet is better than nothing. You've probably Googled your diagnosis before—read the first ten search results and called it a day. But don't stop there. Dig deeper. Read research articles, even the verbose ones. Find coping strategies that resonate with you.

Most of all, be your own advocate. Fight for your freedom. Fight to break free from the cycle of recurring emotions. Some people will support you; others won't. But above all, don't give up on yourself. Believe that an answer exists, somewhere.

What you're doing is hard, and there will be times you feel like quitting. But this world is huge. There are millions of people out there. *Somebody* has the answer, or at least a way to make things better.

I charge my clients for my services, but that doesn't mean I don't care about those who can't afford therapy. I know I can't save everyone, but I do what I can. I genuinely care about the future of mental health in this country. It doesn't make sense for someone to be hospitalized for mental health crises two or three times a year, only to come out without proper treatment. Jake, you and your friends are right—there has to be cultural change in the mental health system.

One in four people take antidepressants. If that's the case, shouldn't there be more awareness about the societal pressures that lead to emotional distress?"

Dr. Graceland's expression was passionate, illuminated by conviction.

Jake and his friends listened intently. Jake thought she was amazing, but he wasn't sure he could afford her as his therapist. Plus, with all the time he poured into advocacy, he wasn't sure he could even commit to sessions.

"That was an insightful discussion," the host said. "We at YPR are grateful to have had Dr. Graceland, Mr. Birk, and Dr. Figget with us today. Also, a huge thank you to Jake, Ayn, Rachel, Pedro, and Jason. We hope our listeners learned something valuable and that this sparks more conversations about mental health—maybe even at dinner tables across the country."

Jacob signaled to the cameraman and sound crew to stop recording.

"Hey, Jake. I'm really glad you guys came. We got quite a few hits on YouTube Live, and we're leaving it up so more people can watch." Jacob shook Jake's hand. "You have my number—call me anytime if you need anything."

Jake smiled. "Yeah, I'm happy we came. Hopefully, this gets people talking about mental health in a real way."

After saying goodbye to the doctors and Mr. Birk, Jake and his friends gathered in the lobby to reflect.

"Rachel, you were incredible. And so were you, Jason," Jake said. "Jacob told me we had quite a few live viewers, and once word spreads, even more people will see it."

"Everyone did great," Rachel said, then smirked. "Speaking of someone who made an impression—look who's coming over."

Dr. Graceland approached, slightly out of breath.

"You guys are *amazing*," she said. "I support you one hundred percent. I truly believe you're going to change the future of mental health—not just in this country, but in the world. I have my own projects, but I'll help however I can. I'd love to work with each of you as clients, but I already have a full schedule with patients managing a range of mental health conditions. Still, don't hesitate to call me if you need anything. That goes for all of you."

With that, she left, and the group huddled together again.

"She's really something special," Rachel said. "Like one of those angels trying to change the world."

"She sure is," Jason agreed. "So... what's next?"

Jake hesitated, then spoke. "I haven't been to church in a long time, but I want to go. There's a Black megachurch near my house that I used to attend. I'd love for all of us to go together. We may not all be religious, but I think it could be good for us."

"I'm in," Rachel said.

"Yeah, I'll go," Jason added. "Some of the things I deal with feel *very* spiritual. This whole looming-death thing... Maybe it'll help. I'm basically an atheist, but I'll give it a shot."

They all agreed—Pedro would pick them up, and they'd go to church later that week.

Chapter 26

Jason was the last one picked up at his house by Pedro. Irritation was written all over his face. The entire morning, intrusive thoughts of impending doom had plagued him, and they refused to subside. He couldn't explain why, but deep down, he felt as if his fate was sealed—an inevitable end approaching within months. He wasn't sick; he had no terminal illness something like cancer, no rare disease. Yet, something in his gut told him his days were numbered.

If time was slipping away, he wanted to spend it with his friends—those who had stood by him through both hardships and joy. Being part of their organization felt like belonging to something greater than himself. They were gaining popularity and could genuinely help people. Still, Jason couldn't shake off the gnawing worry.

Dark thoughts crept in. He imagined his own funeral— his family gathered, his friends grieving. And then there was Rachel. She still loved him—almost to a point where it is more of an obsession. How would she cope with his death? It would destroy her. The thought of her spiraling into despair unsettled him. He questioned what would become of her mental health when he passed. If he passed. If there was even an afterlife.

How would he die? His mind conjured images of an excruciating end. "Maybe an infection, something debilitating, something that numbs me completely," he thought. "I'd be bedridden, unable to talk, trapped in my own body. Suffering before death would be unbearable, but at least I wouldn't be the first to endure it. But this is me—my death, my suffering. It feels so final, so terrifying."

He didn't want a painful death. A quick one seemed preferable, yet even that thought terrified him. Would he feel an instant of excruciating pain before slipping into nothingness? And then what? Judgment? God deciding whether he belonged in heaven or hell? The uncertainty gnawed at him.

"What if I go blind first?" He shuddered at the thought. "I take my sight for granted. Jake has keratoconus, and his left eye is already blurry. He doesn't dwell on it much, hasn't even cried over it. Maybe his brain refuses to process the finality of it." Jason couldn't imagine such a reality. And yet, he was convinced that something far worse was coming for him.

The thought spiraled into madness. "What if I get an organ infection, unbearable pain coursing through my body? Or worse—a lung disease. Struggling to breathe, strapped on machines, drowning in my own body's failure. I know what suffocation feels like. Holding my breath underwater too long—lungs burning, the unbearable pressure, the panic. That's what dying must feel like. And with every tick of the clock, I feel it closing in on me."

Jason felt as if he had already witnessed his own death, a vision creeping toward him with absolute certainty. Perhaps it wasn't death itself but the fear of it that tortured him the most.

"Maybe the church will help," he thought. "Maybe the preacher will say something that eases my mind. Maybe an angel will come to me, whisper reassurance, tell me I have time—that I don't have to fear this. I've heard stories of atheists encountering angels, finding comfort in their presence. Maybe it could happen to me. Maybe someone—something—can convince me I'm not about to die."

Yet, he struggled to believe it. His mind had been conditioned to worry, to overanalyze, to catastrophize. It would take Jesus himself to shift his perspective.

"I need a brain transplant," he thought bitterly. "Some kind of surgery to make me feel different. Because this? This is unbearable. Sometimes, I think about ending it myself—just to escape the constant worrying. I'm afraid of disease, but it's this fear that's truly making me sick. Maybe I need to talk to someone."

Jason exhaled sharply and finally spoke. "You guys, I don't know what's causing it, but I can't stop worrying about death. I keep having these intrusive thoughts that I'm going to get an infection and die from some life-threatening disease."

His voice cracked as he continued, "I also feel like I'm going to suffer a great deal before I die. I can't get it out of my head—it's driving me crazy."

Ayn glanced around the car at everyone, her expression uneasy. "Well, you're right about one thing. We're all going to die someday, one way or another. And I get it—I know what that fear feels like. I don't want to go through anything like what I felt during the internship ever again. I understand your fear, Jason."

She hesitated before adding, "I don't want to throw generic advice at you—like 'listen to music' or 'exercise'—because I know how frustrating that is. I don't know what to tell you, honestly, because I worry too. And I can't stop either. But at least you know you're not alone in feeling this way."

Rachel nodded. "She's right. Don't worry, sugar, it's going to be okay. You have all of us. Alone, we might feel small, but together—we can be a lot."

I sometimes wonder what it would feel like to die, but I realize I'm not alone. As difficult as things may seem, there has to be someone out there going through the same struggles. With millions of people in the world, and with how similar we are in so many ways, certain experiences are universally shared. I believe there must be a way to find comfort in hardship. I may not know what it is, but maybe the church will help.

"I know you're an atheist, but you can always become a born-again Christian," Rachel said.

They pulled into the church parking lot, only to find all the spots occupied.

"We can park in the lot across the street and walk over," Jake suggested.

Pedro nodded in agreement and drove to the adjacent lot. After parking, they all stepped out and made their way across the street. The sound of praise music filled the air, harmonizing beautifully. Rachel did a little dance to the rhythm, making everyone laugh.

"I've never been to an all-Black church before. I guess there's a first time for everything," Rachel said. "But honestly, church is church, no matter where you go."

"The important thing is that you're here, and God's message is in this place," Jake replied.

"That's true," Pedro added. "It may be a Black church, but they won't shun you or tell you to leave. I've seen white people here before, and judging by their praise, they receive God's message just the same."

As they entered the church lobby, they noticed a crowd mingling—chatting and sipping coffee. Jake hadn't been to church in years. In fact, the last time was four years ago, and if he was being honest, it was mostly to meet women. After a Wednesday service, he struck up conversations with a few attractive women, but he had also enjoyed the pastor's sermon. The pastor had a unique way of tying scripture to everyday life, often using humor, which Jake appreciated. The only part he found odd was when the pastor spoke about praying for business success—it never quite made sense to him.

They found seats toward the back middle section of the sanctuary. Ayn sat next to Jake, Jason next to Rachel, and

Pedro to Jake's right. Ayn felt a bit down, though she hid it well. She thought back to times when she would pray for happiness. Even when everything seemed fine, she couldn't shake the sadness. She would watch her favorite TV show and still feel empty. She'd talk to a close friend on the phone yet remain hollow. Sometimes, though not often, she would cry while praying, and strangely, that was the only thing that brought her some relief. But the problem with crying was that it pushed her closer to the edge of despair, into a place where thoughts of suicide lurked. She never truly planned to harm herself, but during those moments, all hope seems lost. And yet, somehow, she always rebounded—she didn't know how, but she did.

Now, sitting in church, she found herself drawn to the praise team. Their voices were powerful and sonorous, filling the room with an overwhelming presence of God. They sang about hope, about renewal—mirroring the very process she experienced after her lowest points. Triumph filled her heart as she recognized that familiar pattern: she always made it through.

Jake reached for Ayn's hand and gave it a gentle squeeze. She smiled. He, however, was still grappling with fear—the kind that crept in uninvited, lingering at the edge of his consciousness. Then, there was the face. That disturbing, demonic presence that loomed over his mind's private space, pressing in closer at times like this. It seemed angrier when he was in church, as if resentful of his attempt to seek faith.

Whenever he stared at someone too long, the face appeared—superimposed over his own reflection, twisted and contorted. It was his face, but wrong. And the more he focused on it, the stronger its presence became. It was suffocating.

His left contact lens was also bothering him. Three months ago, he had gotten a new prescription, so his cornea shouldn't have changed since then. Maybe it was the way he removed his lens at night—suctioning it off with his tongue slightly wetting the tool. But he had top-tier, durable lenses; they shouldn't be this uncomfortable. Still, the discomfort wasn't constant. The real problem was the voices and the face. They were what pushed him toward the brink. They were what tormented him the most.

Ayn squeezed his hand a little tighter, and a small wave of relief washed over him.

Meanwhile, Pedro was lost in thought, reflecting on his own struggles. He bowed his head a few times, silently asking God for peace regarding the GRE ordeal. That test had felt like a personal version of hell—an inescapable, contorted nightmare. Maybe there really had been something demonic at play, something that burrowed into his mind and stirred those unbearable emotions.

Now, in church, he hoped for clarity. Maybe God, an angel, or even Jesus himself would provide answers—would reassure him that it wouldn't happen again. The praise team was already lifting his spirit. Their voices were electric, especially the lead singer, whose presence seemed to make his soul rise. It had been years since he'd set foot in a church, not since middle school.

And yet, beneath the uplifted feeling, a shadow remained. The sadness. The dwindling confidence. Something dark lurked, feeding off his emotions, whispering that he wasn't like normal people.

I know I'm not alone. Right now, I'm with friends who have been through even worse than I have. Jake, for instance, has endured unimaginable hardships. And there are people all around the world who have experienced struggles like mine yet still manage to lead good lives. I have to find a way to cope, even if it means reading a thousand books.

I prayed to Jesus about it before, but nothing happened. I once heard someone say that you have to surrender your whole heart, mind, and soul to Him for Him to work wonders. Well, I did. Or at least I think I did. So why isn't He helping me? I need His help now. Thinking about this all the time is driving me crazy. I need some reprieve. He helps others—He has to help me.

Pedro sat deep in thought as the preacher stepped onto the stage, clad in armor and gripping a sword in his right hand. He surveyed the crowd with the intensity of a fearless leader rallying soldiers who were losing confidence in battle.

"Praise the Lord!"

"God is good!" people shouted in unison.

The preacher's gaze swept over the congregation as if he recognized future world-changers among them. He raised the sword high in the air and roared, "I'm not afraid of you, Goliath!"

The crowd erupted. "God is good! God is good!"

"David wasn't afraid of Goliath, my friends," the preacher continued. "He stood firm because he knew God was on his side. All he needed was his slingshot and faith. Goliath feared no one—he was over nine feet tall! But David remembered how God had helped him defeat a bear with that same slingshot. And so, he aimed, released the stone, and struck Goliath in the forehead. The giant fell dead on the spot. David then cut off Goliath's head and presented it to his people as proof of God's power.

"The lesson is simple: If God is with you, no trial can defeat you. No matter what you're facing, believe in Him. Know that He loves you, even in the depths of your suffering. Evil cannot stand against His presence. Build your faith. Pray, read His word, discuss Him with others, and most of all, praise Him. There are countless unseen blessings God provides daily—your beating heart, your sight, your ability to hear. Never doubt His presence."

The preacher's voice softened. "I once met a man who had cancer, was blind, and suffered from schizophrenia. A nurse asked him, 'How are you still smiling and joking?' He replied, 'Because even with all my struggles, I can feel God's presence giving me the strength to live.'

Perspective

"That man was me."

The room fell silent.

"I first developed schizophrenia in my twenties. The voices were relentless, whispering vile things about my family and me, urging me to end my life. I tried. I harmed myself, desperate for relief. Sleep was impossible. I was hospitalized multiple times for suicide attempts or for simply losing control. Each time I left the hospital, I was slightly better, but the symptoms always returned.

"I can't count how many times I begged God to heal me. At times, I cursed Him, questioning why I had to go through this. I hadn't done anything wrong. Then, one day, I stumbled upon testimonies on YouTube—people who had been cured of schizophrenia through Jesus. So, despite the constant demonic presence I felt, I immersed myself in the Bible. I read the Old and New Testaments. I studied the Gospels of Luke, Matthew, Mark, and John repeatedly. There, I found God's love.

"In scripture, I saw how God led His people through impossible situations. They had to follow His commandments and resist idols, yet despite their failures, He still loved them. That realization changed me. Even with schizophrenia, God loved me more than I ever understood.

"The more I prayed and studied His word, the less I found myself in the hospital. I got into less trouble with the police. I was healing.

"Then, I started coughing up blood. I went to the doctor, and they told me I had cancer. I couldn't believe it. As if the voices weren't enough, now I have cancer too. How much could one man endure? I prayed for a miracle, read the Bible, and continued my chemotherapy, hoping for healing.

"Two years later, something else happened. My vision began to deteriorate, month by month. Another doctor. Another diagnosis. A rare eye condition. I would eventually go blind. If I lost my sight, how would I read the Bible? How would I take care of myself? Through all of it, the voices tormented me, their demonic presence suffocating. They did the worst thing imaginable—they made me feel as if I was being molested, though I never had been. It was pure evil.

"I was losing faith. I decided to give God one last chance. I begged Him to heal me, to show me a sign before I ended my life.

"Then, a knock on the door.

"My mother answered. She told me that a group of people were going door to door, offering prayer walks. They wanted to pray for me."

I told them about all of my problems, and one of them placed a hand on my shoulder and prayed for healing. At first, I didn't feel anything, but then a warm sensation stirred in my heart. After they left my house, I continued listening to the Bible audiobook. That night, when I went to sleep, I didn't hear a single voice or feel the overwhelming demonic presence. Instead, I felt the presence of Jesus comforting me, whispering, "You're going to do great things in my name."

The next morning, I woke up and realized my vision had improved slightly. Each day after that, I could see a little better, until, eventually, I was able to read the Bible again. Not only did the voices and the demonic presence fade, but one day, my doctor told me my cancer was gone.

I won't lie—there were many nights of crying and rage when I was suffering. But when it all disappeared, I knew I had to spread the word of Jesus to those in need of healing. After those miracles, I felt genuine happiness, a deep joy from God's presence. Jesus told me, "Because of your faith in God, you will feel the Holy Spirit wherever you go." And indeed, wherever I go, I feel God's love in abundance.

Of course, I have had days of anger and sadness, especially when my mother passed away. Despite all the hardships, a part of me never lost hope in God. I was scared many times, my emotions erratic, the voices pushing me toward suicide. On top of that, I was blind. At times, I welcomed cancer as an escape. But Jesus saved me. I believed in Him with my whole mind, heart, and soul.

Faith is a fragile thing—it comes and goes. But when you hold it in your heart, it becomes the most powerful force known to man. My message to you all is to never lose faith in God, no matter what you are going through. If you believe, He will pull you out. His will is sovereign.

I suffered from schizophrenia for six years, blindness for one year, and cancer for 24 months. Yet, that little part of me, deep inside, believed I would be okay—that I would be saved. When I prayed with that man and asked Jesus to forgive my sins, the Holy Spirit entered me and began a deep healing.

Now, I am a preacher with a church in Chicago, and I never tire of sharing this story. I know it reaches people. Sometimes, I feel like crying—not just for the miracles, but for the way God gave me joy even in my darkest moments. There were times when I couldn't see my mother's face, but God would tell me jokes to make me laugh. My mom would ask what was so funny, and I'd tell her, "God is making me laugh."

Some say I endured unimaginable suffering. But when I felt God's presence, I knew I would be okay. So, no matter what your circumstance is, don't lose faith in God. He is a living God! A graceful God! A gentle God! He loves you and wants a relationship with you. Never stop praying and worshiping. Everything He does is for your own good. But you must have faith.

As the visiting preacher finished speaking, he asked everyone to bow their heads, offering a prayer for all in attendance. The deacons moved through the aisles, collecting offerings. When the bucket reached Jason, he smiled and passed it to Jake, who was sobbing quietly. Jake sniffed, staring at the floor, whispering, "I've been trying so hard to pray to Jesus to take away this demonic presence, but it's still there. It still tortures me. But if that preacher could go through all that and still preach, maybe one day Jesus will deliver me."

After the offering, the preacher dismissed the congregation. As they walked out, Rachel appeared flustered but satisfied, especially with the part about schizophrenia. Pedro looked as if he had just seen Jesus speaking on stage. As the preacher exited, Pedro maintained eye contact, his expression one of awe. Ayn squeezed Jake's hand, offering a half-smile as they walked together to the car.

"Wow, that preacher was incredible," Pedro said. "It's amazing how someone can endure so much and never lose faith in God. It makes my own struggles seem insignificant in comparison. He was truly inspirational."

"He really was," Jason agreed. "I may not be a full believer in God, but it's true—things do happen. Maybe I'm wrong, and God does exist." said David.

"He touched a lot of people," Ayn added. "Jake, are you okay?"

Jake exhaled deeply. "I pray every day, but the voices are still there. Sometimes, I feel like God isn't listening. But I know He's there. If He could help that man and all the people I've seen testify online, maybe He can heal me, too. Maybe Jesus works through different methods— medications, psychotherapy. Whatever it is, I have to keep pushing for change in mental health awareness. So many people have given up and taken their own lives because they can't handle the daily torment. The demonic presence in my mind sometimes pushes me toward that dark place, making me believe there's no way out." He sighed. "I don't know why I go through this. I've done everything the voices asked of me. You guys, I don't know if I can be your leader anymore. It's becoming too much."

"Jake, don't you remember what we've been through together?" Rachel urged. "The interviews, the negotiations, the TED Talks, NAMI—we can't give up now. People are listening to us."

"She's right," Jason added. "There are people out there who didn't commit suicide because they heard your story. You gave them a glimmer of hope. Focus on the lives you've changed."

Jake nodded slowly. "Maybe I need to go back on the Invega injection. It makes me feel strange, but it helps sometimes. I have an appointment with my psychiatrist tomorrow, and I'm seeing my therapist right after. I'll talk to them, see if they can help."

"There's nothing wrong with that," Pedro reassured him. "After that, we'll figure out our next move."

Chapter 27

Jake drove to the psychiatrist's office, tears streaming down his face. But when he cried about the demonic presence, his emotions would shift—rage would take over, and he'd feel an overwhelming urge to scream or harm himself.

He also noticed that when he was on the phone or alone at home, his face would twitch in strange ways, making him uncomfortable. His head still had a tendency to tilt downward, despite his efforts to pull it up. In public, he masked this by placing his hand under his chin as if deep in thought or concentrating intensely to suppress the movement.

When he met with the psychiatrist, he shared most of his concerns, though he withheld his self-harm urges, fearing hospitalization.

"What you have is tardive dyskinesia. It comes from taking antipsychotics for a long time," the psychiatrist explained.

"But why do I still have it even when I stop taking the medication for a while?" Jake asked.

"It becomes independent of the medication," the psychiatrist replied.

"So what can I do? I need to get back on antipsychotics because they help sometimes, but the TD is really hard to deal with."

"I'm going to prescribe you a medication called Ingrezza—it should help. But you'll need to be patient; it takes about three months to work. I'll also give you a 154mL injection of Invega Sustenna for the hallucinations."

Jake broke down, sobbing. The same medication that was meant to help him was also the cause of his debilitating tardive dyskinesia.

"I know this is tough," the psychiatrist said gently, "but you're making the right decision. Give the medications some time—they will help."

Leaving the office, Jake drove to meet his friends.

"How are you doing?" Ayn asked. "You don't look so good. Have you been crying?"

"The psychiatrist diagnosed me with a bad case of tardive dyskinesia—these involuntary movements—and my voices seem to be getting worse. The demonic presence is really disturbing me when it intensifies. I start having terrible thoughts," Jake admitted.

"What kind of thoughts?" Pedro asked.

Jake hesitated. He didn't want to say he was thinking about suicide or self-harm, so he simply said, "I feel like screaming and breaking things."

He paused, telling himself that he needed to trust these people—his friends, his partners in this campaign they were building together. Then, with effort, he confessed, "Sometimes, I feel like hurting myself. When the presence is strong, the urge to end everything gets overwhelming. I thought working on this campaign with you guys would help, and sometimes it does—when I'm giving a speech or caught in a heated discussion. But it's always there, watching my thoughts, my movements. Pushing me. Once it starts, it doesn't stop until I'm drowning in suicidal thoughts.

I also get these episodes where the voices mock Jesus in a condescending way. It's disturbing because I love and respect Him, but they twist my thoughts. Sometimes, the voice pretends to be Jesus, and it shakes me to my core. Then, there's this other thing—the sexual emotions. It feels like something is forcing itself on me, like an invisible force pushing an unwanted sexual experience on me. It's horrifying. When it happens, I feel this overwhelming urge to grab a knife and stab myself."

Tears welled up in Jake's eyes, but as he tried to cry, his face locked up. A tightness gripped his eyes as if something inside him refused to let him show his pain. It hurt—more than he could explain—because even in this storm of emotions, he couldn't release them. Suddenly, rage bubbled inside him. That's what the entity wanted—to push him into fury. He sobbed again, but even his crying felt controlled, manipulated.

"I saw something flicker across your face—like you were feeling something else," Ayn observed.

"That's the rage," Jake admitted. "The voices don't want me to cry, so they twist my emotions, forcing me into anger. But deep down, I just want to cry. The rage comes from somewhere deep inside, and when it surfaces, I feel like hurting myself. I haven't in a long time, but with these invasive emotions, it becomes unbearable."

Tears streaked his cheeks as he sniffled.

Ayn stepped forward and hugged him. "I love you, Jake. You're not alone in this. I've had suicidal thoughts too. I don't hear voices or demons, but my own thoughts pull me into a dark pit. It feels like I'm drowning in self-pity, sinking into quicksand. I lose all confidence. Even when I watch my favorite shows, I feel nothing. It's like a phantom sucking the energy out of me. They call it major depression, but that term doesn't even come close. It's more than that—it's part of me. My happiness is tangled with my sadness, like a seesaw."

"Don't say that, Ayn. You seemed happy when we were in Los Angeles," Jake said.

"Maybe you just need to be around Jake more," Rachel teased. "He seems to make you happy."

Ayn's face turned crimson. Seeing her blush ignited something in Jake—a quiet confidence. The presence still loomed over him, but for a fleeting moment, he felt wanted. He wasn't just a loner. Knowing Ayn had deep emotions—and that he might be part of them—gave him strength. He stopped trying to cry. He felt solid. He felt like a man.

Ayn half-smiled at him, and through some miracle, he managed to smile back.

"I guess we all have our struggles," Jake said.

"For me, it's the GRE," Pedro admitted. "I just can't go through that again. It was demoralizing. The fear sank so deep into me that even thinking about it shakes me. I don't want to die, but I also can't live with that fear hanging over me."

"How do you feel now?" Jake asked hesitantly.

"Better. Just saying it out loud helps," Pedro replied.

"That's it—we should tell the truth more often," Jake said. "People get scared when the topic of suicide comes up, worried about being reported. Let's make a pact—we won't do that to each other."

They all agreed.

While Pedro was talking, Rachel had been texting. Suddenly, she perked up. "I just got some good news. My mom has five free tickets, hotel included, for the Bahamas. I know we're all going through a lot, but maybe getting away for a bit would be good. What do you guys think?"

"Are you serious?" Ayn asked.

"That sounds amazing," Pedro added.

They all exchanged glances, nodding in agreement.

"Looks like we're going to the Bahamas," Jake said, a small smile breaking through.

They were all due to go to the Bahamas in a week, but each of them was preoccupied with their mental health issues and how it might affect the trip. Ayn thought about the sunshine and the beautiful places she would see, but the dark phantom always hovered over her. She didn't know to what extent it would drain the happiness from her.

When she fell into depression, it felt like sinking into quicksand. The more she thought about anything, the deeper she sank into negative emotions. The depression seemed to stop only when it wanted to. Jake had a way of making her see life differently, but even with him around, the phantom still lingered. She laughed at Jake's jokes, but beneath her laughter was a solemn face.

They had slept together a few times before the Bahamas. The sex brought her to a momentary high, but as soon as it was over, the phantom returned, hovering over her. Eventually, she decided to take antidepressants after praying to Jesus one day. When she didn't feel Jesus helping her, she made a deal with herself to take the pills. The first few days left her feeling both manic and depressed, but as time passed, she started to feel more stable. However, she didn't feel like her old self before the depression. There was an artificial quality to it—like she was different, but her subconscious kept trying to pull her back into despair.

She flirted with the idea of overdosing on antidepressants, but thoughts of Jake's face would stop her. Shame and guilt would wash over her for even considering it. Mornings were the worst. She wanted to stay in bed longer, but an acute wave of suicidal thoughts would hit her. She could sense them coming, and though she tried to pray, the moment she opened her eyes, she would feel wide awake, robbed of sleep. She hated waking up to suicidal emotions; they played havoc on her mind. More than anything, she just wanted to be normal.

She thought of Rachel but quickly dismissed the thought—Rachel had schizophrenia, and Ayn couldn't imagine what she was going through. But the mornings had to change. The cycle started when the first rays of sunlight peeked through her window, lingering and dragging her into a pit of despair—suicidal despair.

Rachel, on the other hand, was wondering if she would get some time alone with Jason and whether a change in location would shift his feelings toward her. She also felt an underlying sense of competition. The beach would be filled with beautiful women in bikinis, tempting Jason. Rachel tried to think logically, reminding herself that they weren't married or even in a committed relationship, and that there were other men out there. But deep down, something told her otherwise.

"No! Jason is the ultimate male—he loves me. I'm just afraid he'd rather be with someone else instead of me. I knew about Jason's OCD before all those bitches."

"He's mine, bitch. And you're dead," said the voices.

Rachel was startled, though she had heard that voice before. It belonged to a woman from her P.E. class in college. Yes, she was beautiful. Before Rachel could rationalize where the voices were coming from, she blurted out, "No, he's mine, and I'll call the police if you try to talk to me again."

She briefly wondered if her room was bugged, but why would someone go through so much trouble to spy on her? And why would this person want to kill her? She hadn't done anything to anyone. For a few moments, she was convinced there was a speaker hidden in her room. She searched around her desk where the voice had seemed to originate, but she found nothing—no device, no explanation.

Rachel had once acknowledged that she had a problem with hearing voices, but she had also learned to bounce back from the hallucinations. Whether they were real or not remained uncertain. Maybe they came from some realm in hell. Or maybe some hyper-jealous woman had indeed bugged her room. Either way, she was determined to finish reading *Overcoming Distressing Voices*.

The book contained useful insights. It explained that voices stem from negative core beliefs, which gain strength from negative experiences. But if one developed alternate core beliefs supported by positive evidence, they could feel better about themselves and lessen the distressing impact of the voices.

She also read that voices were linked to low self-esteem. If you feel low about yourself, the voices gain strength, making you feel even more uncomfortable. The book included surveys to assess self-esteem levels. At times, Rachel agreed.

Pedro, on the other hand, couldn't stop thinking about his future and the GRE test that had caused him so much distress. He was in a place back then that he couldn't revisit. He would have to be Jesus Christ himself to relive that day and make it turn out normal. The fear was so intense that he couldn't remember ever being that terrified before. The setting had been dark and suffocating, as though the devil controlled his emotions like a puppet, jerking him in every direction. He thought about how he couldn't even write his name. Each letter he bubbled in felt like Hiroshima. Each stroke of his pencil symbolized another piece of him dying. It was as if hordes of demons were pushing him toward the edge of a cliff, where only a fiery abyss awaited.

"Why did I have to go through that?" he thought to God. "What sense does it make? Am I supposed to help someone else facing the same struggle? How can I, when I haven't even come to terms with my own situation? My thoughts are still scattered."

He recalled attending a bipolar-disorder support group and leaving more frightened than when he arrived. "Am I cursed with these thoughts forever?" But there had been one moment of connection. Hearing a middle-aged man recount a similar experience at work had sparked an unexpected feeling of camaraderie. He remembered the man's downcast eyes, fixed on the floor, the weight of his words pressing on everyone in the room. What that man described was pure hell. But the more Pedro thought about it, the more he saw the truth.

"If I can somehow make peace with the dreaded GRE experience, maybe I can help others get through similar struggles. Maybe the fact that I'm still alive means I have a testimony to share. That I haven't given in to the endless cycle of reliving it. I wouldn't wish this on anyone—not even my worst enemy. Well, maybe Hitler. I guess he deserves it. But I didn't."

Jason, on the other hand, had found a way to manage his OCD for now. When thoughts of impending doom crept in, he reminded himself that everyone dies eventually—he wasn't alone. He had also been practicing deep breathing exercises, which helped him stay calm when intrusive thoughts threatened to take over.

"I'm not alone," he reminded himself. "There are others like me. They clean every plane after each trip. Plus, it's not a big deal if I bring a sanitary wipe in my carry-on."

Jake, meanwhile, was doing well. He was seeing Ayn regularly, though he sometimes struggled to make her smile.

She wasn't a Debbie Downer, but she carried a quiet weight. Still, being with her lifted his self-esteem higher than it would have been on his own. The sex was great, but more than that, they had deep conversations, each asking the other meaningful questions.

Jake's voices had started to change, too. The presence he once feared was less alarming, and the voices spoke less frequently. When he gazed into Ayn's blue eyes, they looked so angelic that he sometimes felt like crying. She, in turn, looked into his deep brown eyes as though seeing something divine.

Whenever Jake was away from Ayn, something felt missing, and a dull sadness crept in. The voices would start whispering again, and the face hallucinations would return, but for now, he could handle it. He had scheduled surgery with a doctor in Los Angeles. He knew he would undergo Holcomb cross-linking to stop his corneas from distorting further. He had wanted Intacs, but his previous doctor had warned that his corneas were too thin for the procedure.

Intacs are used to spread out the cornea. This disappointed Jake because he wanted his cornea to change so that he could wear glasses. When he met the doctor, the doctor asked about his expectations. Jake replied that he just wanted to wear glasses—no more contact lenses. When the doctor told him that he couldn't get Intacs, Jake cried. He had been counting on the procedure, hoping to be like the people he had seen on YouTube who got Intacs and achieved good vision results.

He spent most of his time with Ayn, reading books about voices, schizophrenia, and related topics. It was true—whenever he took off his contact lenses, his vision was terrible, and it seemed to be deteriorating more rapidly. But he thought about the people he could help by sharing his story and the lives he might change for the better.

He talked to his group of friends over the phone about the next steps once they returned from the Bahamas. They all agreed to attend the trial of Jung first, though they didn't really have a choice.

The prosecutor wanted Jake to testify in the Jung case, and Jake figured it would be a nightmare. Jung was guilty, but he was also struggling with mental health issues—problems that the average person would find difficult to understand. Jake saw this as an opportunity to shed light on the struggles people with mental illnesses face daily. He figured he would have more time to discuss that with the defense. He didn't know how his voices would behave during the trial, but he also had no idea what to expect in the Bahamas. That trip was supposed to be a relaxing break with his friends before they launched their agenda.

The day finally arrived. Jake's mom dropped him off at the airport, where he met up with his four friends. Rachel was the first to arrive, looking as gorgeous as ever, followed by Pedro, Jason, and, lastly, Ayn. When he saw Ayn, he hugged her and kissed her on the lips—she looked beautiful too.

"Oh, you guys should keep it PG-13 with just a hug. There are kids all around this place," Rachel teased.

"I'm happy for them," Pedro said. "I think they both need a connection."

"I know, I'm just joking," Rachel replied. Then she turned to Jason. "So, Jason, are you going to give me a wet one?"

"Not in this lifetime, Rachel. We're done. We're just fri—" Jason started, but Rachel cut him off.

"Yeah, I know. Friends. Well, we'll see what you think when you see me in this swimsuit," Rachel said, smirking.

Jason blushed and hesitated for a moment. Rachel was undeniably attractive, but he couldn't deal with her constant accusations that he was cheating on her. He understood that it was part of her mental health struggles, but the more he stayed with her in an intimate relationship, the worse her issues seemed to get.

Everyone noticed Jason's hesitation and laughed.

"Well, let's all check in at the front desk. I hope everyone has their passports and tickets. Just kidding—I have the tickets," Rachel said, pulling them out.

"You will never have him," a voice whispered in Rachel's head.

Rachel grimaced for a split second but quickly composed herself. She had heard the voice loud and clear. It was the same as that girl from her psychology class—the one she despised.

Logically, Rachel knew there were no speakers in the airport that could have transmitted the voice. There was nothing in her luggage either. Still, the thought of that girl made her blood boil. Maybe Jason and that girl knew each other. But how? Had they taken a class together at some point?

She shook her head, refusing to let her thoughts spiral. Taking a deep breath, she distributed the tickets to her friends.

The check-in line wasn't too long, so they passed the time talking about the Olympics from a few months ago. Soon, they checked in their luggage and carried their personal bags toward the terminal. As they walked, Pedro's mind drifted to the GRE. A sudden thought hit him—what if he had an episode on the plane?

There would be no one to take him to the hospital in the air or give him oxygen. It would be utter hell. The passengers on the plane might think he was a terrorist, screaming something in Arabic—maybe "Allah" or something like that. If he stood up and started shouting, people might kill him on the spot.

'I wasn't even screaming during the GRE. I was just shaking, breathing profusely. I couldn't control my breathing. Remember that, Pedro,' he thought. The thoughts racing through his mind didn't make sense. 'Well, I brought Zyprexa, so that should help keep my nerves from spiraling out of control.' Even now, when I think about that day, I can only recall bits and pieces. I'm really scared about getting on this plane. I don't know what's going to happen. Logically, whenever I take Zyprexa, my thoughts don't race like that— I just feel sleepy. Like right now, I feel more tired than anything else. I got ten hours of sleep last night, but I still feel exhausted. Maybe it's because I decreased my Zyprexa dosage. I just hope I don't end up sleeping the whole day,' thought Pedro.

"Is baby Pedro anxious about the big, scary GRE?" Rachel teased, smiling at him.

"Shut up, you crazy bitch."

"Hey, hey, hey! You guys, we're on the same side. We all have our problems, and we need to support each other. One for all and all for one, right?" Jake interjected.

"I'm sorry I said that," Rachel said, her voice softer. "I kind of just heard a voice in my head, and I was on edge. Please forgive me, Pedro."

"All is forgiven," Pedro replied.

Readers, you have to understand—these young men and women are battling severe mental health challenges. I don't like using medical terms, but each of them is experiencing the extreme end of their diagnosis. So, it's understandable when things slip out in conversation.

The woman at the terminal speaks over the intercom, "All first-class passengers boarding for the Bahamas, please line up."

Ayn is giddy with excitement, though it doesn't show on her face. She wears a poker face, her emotions locked away. She is happy, yet a part of her remains trapped. Everyone else smiles in anticipation as they get in line, thrilled about their long journey from the East Coast to the Bahamas.

Once on board, Jason discovers he's seated next to Rachel.

"Rachel, you did that on purpose, didn't you?" Jason mutters.

"No, it's fate. That's how we meet fate," Rachel replies, grinning from ear to ear.

Pedro takes a seat next to a woman and her child. 'Well, I doubt this plane would crash with a baby on board. That would have to be some cruel god to let that happen. I'm still a little angry about what Rachel said. She made it sound like I wasn't man enough to handle the GRE. It's not my fault that happened. Or maybe it was. The days leading up to it, I was anxious. I remember barely passing the practice tests. I'm just going to pop a Zyprexa and sleep through this plane ride. I'm a man—I don't know what Rachel was talking about,' Pedro thought.

Meanwhile, Jake and Ayn sit together, both vying for the window seat, which rightfully belongs to Jake. Settling in, he looks into Ayn's big blue eyes as if searching for something.

"Are you alright?" Jake asks, flashing his signature grin.

"I'm okay. My depression is still there, pushing against me. I love you, but it feels like there's this chronic sadness inside me. Maybe it stems from childhood trauma. I know I went through some things, but I only remember the emotions and fragmented thoughts. Lately, I've been considering eye movement therapy. The psychologist said it could help bring out the details of traumatic events," Ayn confesses.

"I've heard of that," Jake says. "With everything I've been through, I know it could help me too. I've thought about taking that psychologist's advice, but I feel like I need to focus on dealing with the more horrific aspects of what we all have. Plus, when I do those speeches and talk to people about mental health, it actually helps me more. I realize that when I'm with you, my problems are less worse. But when I'm alone, that's where they attack me more. I've been seeing these videos of a Sudanese American man who had schizophrenia and he went through a year and half of deliverance. He said in his video that Jesus delivered him from schizophrenia. And he sounds so logical and animated I can't even imagine that he used to be homeless and say things like "Can I sell my soul to the devil in the banks." He was really in deep trouble, but Jesus apparently saved him and made him a new man. There has to be a way to get these voices off me. Maybe Jesus can do it. But then again there are so many people who pray to Jesus to lift off these diseases and they don't get answers back." said Jake.

"So Jesus saved him from schizophrenia. It was a miracle!" exclaimed Ayn.

"Yeah, you know what they say—schizophrenia is incurable. But he received a promise from someone through God, then went through a process of expelling demons. Now he helps others overcome schizophrenia. He's very vibrant and knowledgeable about Jesus and the Bible. He's really into spiritual warfare. I don't think I told you, but I saw several deliverance ministers in the past. Two of them, in particular, made me cry because what I was going through was so painful with the voices.

This man on YouTube, Tethliach Chuol, has several videos where he talks about spiritual warfare. He uses terms like intergenerational curses, strongholds, and demon names like Jezebel. He also leads renunciations, where you repeat after the preacher to break curses and demonic possession. He cares so much about helping others experience what he has. He says he has delivered some people from illness. I'm happy for him, but I don't understand why I haven't been delivered yet. I believe in Jesus. I believe He died on the cross and rose on the third day. I read the Bible. So why is it taking so long? I don't know if I can go on like this.

Do you notice that my eyes keep blinking? It feels like someone is forcing them shut, and it's really annoying. Actually, it's disturbing," said Jake.

"Well, I don't notice your eyes doing that," said Ayn.

"My eyes keep blinking, and I can't stop it. Sometimes they close for too long, and I struggle to open them. When it happens, I feel a burst of fear as I try to force them open," said Jake.

"I'm having a hard time concentrating," said Ayn. "Sometimes, when you're going through this, I feel it too because I care so much. I'm extremely empathetic, so when you feel discomfort, I do too. I keep beating myself up for being depressed. I just don't want to go back to the psych ward. It's not a place I ever want to return to. I think I'm also too dependent on people meeting my expectations. When they don't, I feel depressed."

"Am I part of your expectations?" Jake asked.

"No, you're not, because I understand you have your own issues. I always feel like I'm not doing enough, like I could do more, but something holds me back from fulfilling my full potential. You make me feel better. Ever since I met you, my depression has changed. Sometimes, I feel so happy I don't know what to do with myself but this," said Ayn.

Ayn kissed Jake on the cheek. If Jake were white, he would have blushed.

"Can everybody please buckle your seatbelts? We are getting ready for takeoff," said the captain. The flight attendant walked down the aisle, ensuring everyone was securely strapped in. The plane backed away slowly and taxied to the runway. Then, it accelerated faster and faster until it lifted into the air.

Jake looked out the window the entire time, gripping Ayn's hand tightly. Once they were airborne, he took a deep sigh and smiled at Ayn. "Here we go to the Bahamas. Hopefully, we can all have a good time despite our mental health problems," he said.

"I have all my eye solutions and stuff in my carry-on, so I don't have to worry. I hate taking them off every night, waking up to a blurry morning, and putting them back on. These contact lenses are a hassle. I wish the doctors could just fix my corneas so I wouldn't need glasses or contacts. Well, I can't use glasses anyway. I won't let my eye condition stop me from having a good time with my friends. And on top of that, I have mental health problems—the presence thing and the face hallucinations superimposed on mine," thought Jake.

"I think we're all going to struggle a bit with our mental health on this trip, but I truly believe we'll have fun," Jake said, turning to Ayn. "We'll have moments of happiness. I'm really looking forward to going to the beach."

"I can't wait either! I'm going to have a margarita—oh, I forgot, you don't drink," Ayn said.

"That's okay. I've been around friends who drink, and it doesn't bother me. The obsession with alcohol is gone. I have no desire to drink at all—at least for today. I don't even miss it anymore," Jake replied. "Through AA, I got a miracle from God. Maybe if God could give me a miracle with my drinking, He can do the same with my voices. AA is incredible. It helped me see life differently, to step outside of myself when I can. It's a selfless program where people do service work without spiritual pride. It's the best thing I've ever been part of. If I could adapt it for people who hear voices and struggle with extreme emotions, that would be amazing. But I think everyone's experiences are too different for a single program to work for all. HVN is helpful."

"Rachel was telling me about a book called *Overcoming Distressing Voices*—she said it was really good."

"Yeah, I read it a while back. It's helpful, but it mostly works around the edges. They do mention it in the book, but it's incredibly difficult to change negative core beliefs, and I'm sure I have some that feed my voices." Jake paused for a moment, then smiled. "Wow, it feels so peaceful up here, above the clouds. It's like we're floating."

"It really is beautiful," Ayn agreed. "I haven't read many books on depression, but I know there's some great material out there. I find mindfulness really comforting—just focusing on an object, describing how it feels, how it smells. It helps. There are a lot of books on depression that could be useful, but in pop culture, depression doesn't seem as 'sexy' as schizoaffective disorder. And I mean that in a bad way. People associate schizophrenia with criminals or insanity, but when it comes to depression, they just say, 'Do what makes you happy,' or 'You just need a vacation.' It's so dismissive. Luckily, there are people out there working hard to develop new therapies." She glanced at Jake. "Are you familiar with acceptance therapy? It focuses on acknowledging your problem instead of resisting it. The more you accept it, the better you can manage it."

"Yeah, I know about it—it's really interesting. There are some good approaches, like DBT and CBT. They both help, but when I'm having an episode, I don't think they work as well. Maybe if I did the worksheets in the middle of an episode, it would be different. I should bring them with me— just in case. My therapist gave me some that focus on CBT for psychosis, and honestly, every time I do one, I feel better." Jake suddenly noticed the screen in front of him. "Look, we can watch a movie on these."

He put on his headphones and started *American Fiction*, based on *Erasure* by Percival Everett, a book he had read. Jake hadn't been watching many movies lately, but he was looking forward to this one. Meanwhile, Ayn selected Lady Gaga from the in-flight playlist and leaned back, lost in the music.

Pedro, sitting nearby, felt sedated. He was almost certain he wouldn't have a GRE attack, but the drowsiness made him uneasy. He hated sleep paralysis—the sensation of waking up, unable to move, terrified him.

Pedro struck up a conversation with the woman next to him, who was holding a baby. He learned that the child's father was sitting a few rows behind them and that they were traveling to the Bahamas to celebrate his recent promotion—a substantial raise, at that. Pedro quickly found her boring and kept looking for an opportunity to end the conversation, but she wouldn't stop chatting.

He tried to force her out, his mind drifting to the beach they were all headed to. Then, he thought of Rachel. *She could be schizophrenic, like John Nash, with two people always around her. I know she hasn't admitted to having visual hallucinations, but maybe she's lying because she doesn't want us to feel sorry for her. Either way, I forgive her. I just don't understand where her comment came from. She was obviously going through her own episode and took her anger out on me.*

Finally, the woman turned her attention to her child, giving Pedro the break he needed. He put on a movie—*It's Kind of a Funny Story*, about a young man who ends up in a mental health facility after expressing suicidal thoughts. Pedro didn't find it funny. He found it deeply sad that these people had to use humor to cope with their struggles and socialize. Even the romantic relationship between the main character and the girl seemed premature to him. But still, he couldn't stop thinking about his own stay in Zion and how lost he had felt before meeting Jake and the others.

And, of course, the "booty juice" they had given him—that shot had calmed him down. The first day felt like a haze, his mind racing, yet he was acutely aware that he was in a mental hospital. *I really love my friends,* he thought. *Ayn, Jake, Jason, and Rachel. They supported me when I was in that hospital. Some of them have been to others, but that was my first. And I don't plan on going back to Zion. It was so cold there. I can't forget how cold it was. And some of the nurses were just rude. The doctors were fine if you saw them once a week, but once every two days wasn't enough for two weeks.*

Meanwhile, Jason was listening to Rachel ramble on. He found her discussion of the good and bad parts of DBT and CBT interesting, but when she started rehashing their past encounters, he mentally checked out. Instead, he began wondering whether the flight attendants actually cleaned the seats and armrests between flights. That thought unsettled him, so he reached for his luggage in the overhead compartment, pulled out some hand sanitizer and wipes, and meticulously cleaned his entire seat and armrests.

As he glanced at Rachel, he noticed her slipping into one of her dream-like trances, reminiscing about the good times they'd had. He decided to interrupt. "So, Rachel, are you on any medication?"

"I'm not on any meds. They make me feel squirrely, like a shell of myself," Rachel replied.

"I take Valium when my anxiety gets bad. It helps," Jason said.

"Well, if it helps you, keep taking it," she responded, shifting the conversation to a woman she had heard in the checkout line—someone from her class. Jason, uninterested, shook his head. "I don't know her," he said before putting on his headphones and selecting a movie—*The Hills Have Eyes*. He'd seen it before, he was in the mood for some death and destruction.

Rachel, noticing his disinterest, fell silent. Doubt crept back into her mind. *Maybe the woman I heard in my room and at the airport was just a hallucination after all. But I don't feel crazy. And I know women hit on Jason all the time. I remember walking through the mall with him—girls would smile at him as if I weren't even there. Maybe I imagined it. Wow, I feel confused. I think I'll watch a movie too.*

She put one on. The whole gang alternated between talking, watching movies, and listening to music until the pilot's voice came over the speakers: "We will be arriving in the Bahamas in ten minutes. Please fasten your seatbelts."

The flight attendants moved through the cabin to check compliance. Most of the group buzzed with excitement. They were finally here.

Ayn was excited but slightly apprehensive about her emotions. Jake gazed out the window in awe, watching the vast ocean stretch below. He felt the plane descend, the wheels extending, and then the sudden jolt as they touched the runway. The aircraft sped forward like a bullet, pressing him back against his seat before gradually slowing down.

"Welcome to the Bahamas, everyone," the pilot announced.

The first-class passengers were the first to disembark.

Chapter 28

"So, how is everybody feeling?" Jake asked.

"It wasn't as bad as I thought, but I was sedated with Zyprexa. I enjoyed the landing, though," Pedro replied.

"Me too. It was surreal," Jason added.

Rachel smiled on the outside but was secretly frustrated that Jason wouldn't always listen to her. *Maybe my situation is more serious than I realize. Maybe this illness—whatever it is—is worse than I suspected.*

They headed downstairs to collect their luggage. As they waited, each of them exchanged small smiles, the excitement of their trip momentarily outweighing their worries.

"We're in the Bahamas, baby!" Rachel cheered.

Remarkably, despite their mental health struggles lingering in the back of their minds, they managed to embrace the moment, looking forward to relaxation. After waiting what felt like an eternity at the conveyor belt, they finally retrieved their luggage and made their way to the shuttle bus that would take them to the hotel.

As the bus rolled through the city, they passed slums where people sat on the streets, their faces worn by hardship. *I wonder how many of them hear voices or struggle with something my friends and I deal with. It's so sad. I'm lucky—*

I grew up in a middle-class home with some resources. If I had been born into poverty like this, I'd be screwed. Jake's thoughts raced as he stared out the window. *I've heard they use witch doctors for mental health issues here. I wonder how effective their treatments are compared to modern medicine. Zyprexa just makes me gain weight and increases my risk of diabetes—at least, that's what it does to me.*

A flicker of something caught his eye—a brief hallucination, just for a moment. He clenched his fists, willing the voices to stay silent. *I hope they leave me alone so I can enjoy this trip. It didn't linger, so I should be okay.*

"Once we check into the hotel, we're all getting massages," someone announced.

A ripple of excitement spread through the group. The hotel was extravagant, with an exotic charm that immediately impressed them. A bellboy approached to collect their luggage and lead them to their rooms.

To Jake's surprise, his room was directly across from Ayn's—just like in Los Angeles.

"See you later, big boy," Ayn teased before disappearing into her room.

Jake grinned and stepped into his own, setting his eye solution and eye chamber on the desk for easy access. He felt an unfamiliar lightness, a momentary escape from his usual tension. The thought of the upcoming massage thrilled him. He often found himself clenching his neck involuntarily—a side effect of tardive dyskinesia. He had been on Ingrezza for a while now, but it didn't seem to help much with his neck stiffness.

Oddly enough, when he spoke in front of an audience, none of it mattered. In those moments, he felt powerful, untouchable—like a superhero.

Later, they all gathered downstairs in their bathing suits, ready for the massage. Jake, having been on a diet for some time, was looking leaner. Ayn, as always, looked stunning. Pedro was his usual self, but Rachel and Jason stole the show. Rachel had a youthful face, perky breasts, a slim waist, and a V-shaped definition at her hips and legs—she was undeniably beautiful. Jason, known for his dedication to fitness, sported six-pack abs and sculpted arms.

"Wow, Jason, have you added more abs to your body?" Rachel teased, reaching out to touch his stomach.

Jason scowled and smacked her hand away.

"Well, that's okay—maybe later," Rachel said with a smirk as she walked toward the massage chairs.

Jason shifted uncomfortably, fighting an involuntary reaction as he watched her walk away. He quickly composed himself.

Rachel lay back, fully immersing herself in the moment. Her body glistened with massage oil as she let go of her usual concerns. For once, she didn't worry about Jason or whether other women were after him. Instead, she focused on the here and now, practicing mindfulness.

"Don't forget the glutes," she instructed the masseur.

The man, sweating slightly, remained professional despite her flawless physique.

Jake, meanwhile, found himself struggling with the tension in his neck throughout the massage. But to his relief, the voices remained silent, and no hallucinations disrupted his peace. He especially enjoyed the deep pressure on his shoulders and back, where knots of tension had built up over time. The masseuse's strong hands worked through them with expert precision.

So this is how the rich live, Jake mused. *I could get used to this. If I had a massage every day, my life would be so much easier. My mind already feels more at ease just from my body relaxing.*

Despite the challenges they faced, despite their struggles being more extreme than most, they could still enjoy a vacation. The media often painted schizophrenia as a condition that robbed people of happiness, but in that moment, Jake felt truly content.

I'm happy. Really, really happy. And after this, I'm getting some grilled meat. I wonder how everyone else is feeling...

Jake glanced at the rest of them. They all seemed to be enjoying themselves, their faces relaxed and content—except for Jason.

I wonder if they cleaned their hands before giving me this massage, Jason thought. *These are lower-class people doing this, so who knows if they sanitize? They have to be clean—people pay a lot of money for these massages. Gosh, Rachel's mom must have a fortune. I don't know what kind of deal she got, but it was really nice of Rachel to share this package with us. Ohhh, my calves—that feels amazing.*

After an hour, they all got up from their massage beds and prepared for dinner on the beach.

"How's everyone feeling?" Rachel asked.

Everyone agreed it was the best massage they had ever received. They returned to their rooms to change for dinner at an outdoor restaurant. The meal was good, and after enjoying their evening, they each retired for the night.

When Jake went to remove his special contact lenses before showering, a wave of depression hit him.

I hate this eye disease—keratoconus. My corneas are too thin, bulging out. To anyone looking at me, my eyes seem normal, but these lenses are driving me crazy. Every night, I take them out, and every morning, I wake up to a blurry world. It's a miserable way to start the day. First, I feel overwhelmingly depressed, then I have to drag myself out of bed only to be greeted by a distorted, blurry mess. Sure, I can see a little, but everything is still out of focus. I try to remind myself that others have it worse—some need cornea transplants, which take forever to get. The woman from the Intacs company said my vision isn't bad enough for a transplant, and honestly, I don't want someone's dead cornea in my eye. I'd have to use eye drops constantly. No thanks.

My condition scares me, but I found a doctor who does Intacs implants. He must have some advanced technology to make it work. I just don't want to rely on these massive contacts forever. What if my vision gets so bad I can't even wear them anymore? I researched Intacs, and it seems like the right choice. This doctor is well-known—he should do a good job. The last cornea specialist I saw was blunt, almost rude. If I hadn't suggested Intacs, he wouldn't have even mentioned it as an option. I don't know exactly what custom implants or technology this new doctor will use, but I'm willing to try it.

Sometimes, I think about ending it all because of my eyesight. But then, another thought counters it—I can't let my vision be the reason I give up. If I ever reached that point, it would be because of the voices or that strange presence I feel. Still, I have too many problems. I don't even like sleeping with Ayn without my contacts—I can't see her face clearly, and it makes everything feel disconnected.

A miracle seems far-fetched, but people do get them. Maybe God will see how hard I try to help those struggling with mental illness and grant me one. That guy on youtube named Tethliach Chuol says several times before that there is no cure for the voices I.E. schizophrenia. But he was cured. He even talks about people who were blind and were given miracles and they could see clearly all the sudden. I want to see clearly without these damn lenses. Just thinking about taking them out every night and putting them back in every morning makes me angry. Most people just wear glasses and go about their day. I have faith, but doubt creeps in. What if my eyes stay like this forever?

What kind of technology are they even going to use to fix my corneas? I can't go in the ocean with my contacts— they could fall out. And my left eye barely sees 20/40, even with the lens. My right one might be 25/20 at best. One time, the ophthalmologist tried different lenses, and I saw 30/20 with my left eye for a brief moment. But when the contact arrived in the mail, it didn't work the same. It felt like some higher power let me see clearly for a moment, only to take it away. Or maybe it was something sinister. Who knows?

Anyway, this new cornea specialist is going to run tests on the first day and do surgery the next. And I'll be awake the whole time.

Jake carefully removed his $600-a-piece contact lenses and placed them in their chambers, exhaling deeply.

He could barely make out the soap, but he found it. His feet were just as blurry—fuzzy shapes in the dim light. Still, he washed up and went to bed.

When he woke up, he reached for his contact lenses. He managed to put in the right one, but the left got stuck in the corner of his eye. Squinting at the mirror, he carefully removed it, then tried again, this time keeping his eye wide open.

Heading to the bathroom, he noticed a bubble in his right contact. Annoyed, he went back to his eye station, removed the lens, rinsed it with saline solution, and put it back in.

Dressed in a silky button-up shirt and khaki shorts, he stepped out just as Ayn opened her arms.

"Hey, handsome!" Ayn exclaimed, greeting Jake with a bright smile.

But she was putting on a front. Deep down, she felt the familiar weight of depression settling in.

Yes, reader, people can feel depressed even in vacation spots like the Bahamas.

She tried to focus on her friends and on Jake, but the sadness remained. She remembered reading once that thoughts are like luggage on a conveyor belt—one passes, then another, and another. But that idea didn't help. Then she imagined her thoughts as leaves floating by in an autumn breeze. That helped, at least a little.

Still, the depression felt like a stone lodged in her mind. She wanted to understand what kind of brain chemistry was making her feel this way—why it never truly lifted. This wasn't a passing sadness; it was deep, relentless. She tried to reason with it, reminding herself it was just an emotion and that it would pass. But it never did. It stayed, anchored in her head.

As she and Jake walked down the steps, darker thoughts crept in.

Maybe I should overdose on antidepressants. Maybe that would help. But I'd probably die.

She doubted it would truly help. But was death better than feeling this over and over again? The relentless ache, the exhaustion?

It's hard to be confident when I feel like this. The meds don't seem to be working right now. Depression feels like quicksand—the more I fight it, the deeper I sink. Actually, it's worse than that. Even when I do nothing, I still fall deeper. It's like a demon that drains all the positive energy out of me. It doesn't speak, doesn't show itself, but I know it's there. Wreaking havoc. Right now, I feel suicidal. Maybe I should go to a hospital—just to be watched.

"Ayn, are you okay? You don't look so good." Jake's voice broke through her thoughts. "You look miserable."

"My depression is acting up," she admitted. "I'm thinking about going to the hospital. I'm having suicidal thoughts."

Jake tensed. "What were you thinking of doing?"

"Overdosing on antidepressants," she admitted. "It wasn't an impulsive thought, but it was strong. Stubborn." She took a slow breath. "Let's try deep breathing…" She exhaled. "That helped a little. But the thoughts are still there."

"I don't know the perfect thing to say," Jake admitted, "but don't isolate yourself. Being with loved ones helps. And you're safe with us. No one's calling the police on you—we've all been there."

They reached the bottom of the stairs, where Pedro, Rachel, and Jason were waiting.

"You guys," Ayn said, voice shaky, "my depression is making me feel like killing myself. It's like it's lodged in my brain, clouding everything." She let out a long sigh. "Well… saying it out loud helped. It's still there, but not as strong."

"Did something trigger it?" Jason asked.

"I was just thinking about going to the beach, and suddenly it felt like a phantom hovering over me, draining every positive thought. Slow breathing helped a little, but forcing positive thoughts didn't push the darkness away."

"That sounds a lot like my intrusive thoughts—those feelings of impending doom," Jason said. "Your emotions seem intrusive in the same way. But remember, Ayn—you're in control of your body."

"Try doing something—stretch, color, call someone," Rachel added. "There are so many ways to ground yourself. Infinite ways."

"That's good advice, Rachel. It's just hard to think that way when I feel like I'm sinking in quicksand. But you guys gave me some good ideas, and I'm glad I came downstairs instead of staying in my room with those pills," Ayn said, her voice tinged with sadness.

"These suicidal feelings seem to be something we all deal with," Pedro added thoughtfully. "When our symptoms worsen, we become vulnerable to those thoughts. There must be books on this, but maybe it's different for everyone. I just can't find the courage to go through with it. I know people are more likely to attempt it if they've had previous attempts."

"Well, I've had a couple of attempts, but I'm not going to let that define me. Let's eat!" Ayn exclaimed, trying to shift the mood.

"This seems to be a recurring struggle—this suicidal ideation," Pedro continued. "Whenever we experience overwhelming emotions, we seem to fall into this mindset. We should talk about it more. For me, it's the constant anxiety about the GRE. The fear is consuming me. I wonder if being suicidal would make me lose my fear of that day. I read somewhere that people feel this way when they believe there's no way out, but there's always a way—it's just incredibly difficult to see."

Perspective

"Well, I mostly feel homicidal toward the voices I hear," Rachel admitted. "They sound like people I know or have met before. I doubt I'd ever act on it, but the voices sound so real, like they're coming from a speaker outside my head."

"I'm going to get a little deep here, guys," Jake said hesitantly. "When I feel the sensation of someone molesting me, I want to kill myself. That feeling is so invasive, so suffocating. It consumes every part of me. Usually, I just feel suicidal, but sometimes I also feel the urge to hurt myself. It's like I'm searching for relief from the emotion."

"I just want relief from my depression," Ayn admitted. "It feels like being trapped in a dark hole, desperately trying to climb out. It's so hard to hold onto happy thoughts when I feel like that. The depression blocks out every attempt to feel even neutral."

"It's like we've all had these dark thoughts," Jason added. "When I get intrusive thoughts of impending doom, I feel like ending it just to make them stop. But a few times, that feeling only made the doom seem even worse. Life can feel like hell sometimes."

They all sat in silence for a moment, staring at their menus while continuing to process their thoughts.

"And there are no pills that can make it stop completely," Ayn murmured. "The thoughts just keep looping, like someone planted them in my head."

"I think I'll have the grilled beef ribs," Jake said, breaking the tension.

The rest of the group made similar choices, all opting for something grilled. Rachel also ordered a margarita.

"Are you sure you should have that margarita if you have homicidal thoughts?" Ayn whispered cautiously.

"I'll be fine," Rachel reassured her. "It's mostly when I'm alone or under extreme stress. Anyway, I've never wanted to kill any of you guys."

Everyone laughed, though Jason chuckled a little less enthusiastically—he knew some of the people Rachel had mentioned before.

"So, I guess we can either watch a movie or just head back to our rooms," someone suggested.

The restaurant was stylish, with a tropical ambiance. They ate their meals in silence, enjoying the food. No one wanted to talk about suicide or homicidal thoughts while eating.

They played volleyball outside before taking a walk along the beach. When they returned, each went back to their rooms. Ayn walked beside Jake, nudging him playfully with a smile. Jake responded by grabbing her hands, pinning them against the wall, and kissing her.

Ayn reached for Jake through his pants, feeling his arousal, while using her other hand to open the door to her room. They made passionate love, as if caught in a trance. When they finished, Jake sighed and said he had to return to his room to remove his contacts. He wanted nothing more than to stay in bed with her, holding her close all night, but his doctor had instructed him to take his contacts out every twelve hours.

Back in his room, Jake prepared for the night. He set out his pajamas, towel, soap, and clothes, knowing he'd struggle to find them once his contacts were off. After rinsing his lens container and filling it with solution, he carefully removed his contacts using suction tubes—placing the left lens in the blue chamber and the right in the white one. Without them, his vision was severely impaired. The reality of his eyesight issues always unsettled him. He knew he needed surgery; otherwise, even handling his contacts might one day become impossible without help.

Despite this fear, he had never felt more alive than when delivering his TED Talk and NAMI speech. In those moments, his vision problems faded into the background. Even during his radio show, he hadn't thought about his condition. He knelt by his bed and prayed, asking for Ayn's depression to be lifted and for miracles to touch all his friends. The thought of divine intervention for so many people seemed improbable, but he still believed.

At that moment, he didn't feel the usual presence or the strange face he often saw in his mind—not as intensely, at least. Lying in bed, sleep eluded him. He was too excited about his relationship with Ayn, too eager for another day at the beach after another massage.

'I hope the sex made Ayn feel as good as it did for me,' he thought. 'Maybe it even helped with her depression. My voices were silent during it. But I need to do something to weaken them further. I should use some CBTp techniques. I need to gather evidence for when my self-esteem dips.'

The next morning, Jake woke up and put in his contacts. For a few moments, he felt strange, but the presence wasn't bothering him, nor was the face in his mind. Excited for the day, he put on his swim trunks and a silk T-shirt before knocking on Ayn's door. To his surprise, Ayn looked vibrant—not sad or withdrawn as she sometimes did. It was as if her depression had lifted.

The phantom was gone.

Yes, reader, I know this is hard to believe, but God works in mysterious ways.

Ayn's face glowed with happiness. Dressed in a full swimsuit, she looked stunning. They walked downstairs to the lobby, where they met the others. At that moment, Pedro wasn't filled with fear over the GRE event. Jason wasn't consumed by thoughts of impending doom. Rachel, despite her dark obsession with a woman she believed wanted to steal Jason from her, felt fine.

"How is everyone feeling emotionally?" Jake asked.

Everyone murmured that they were doing alright.

"See?" Rachel grinned. "I told you guys a vacation would do everyone good. Right, Ayn?"

"I feel alright. I don't feel depressed right now," Ayn said brightly.

Jake frowned. "How is it possible for everyone to feel alright at the same time? Jason, how about you?"

"I just want to research that massage lotion they're going to use on us, but other than that, I'm doing fine," Jason replied.

They headed to their massage chairs, lying on their stomachs as the masseuses worked. Jake found today's massage even better than yesterday's—his neck, finally, was relaxed.

He felt a flicker of the presence a few times while talking to Ayn, but nothing too intense. In fact, he felt more than good. He felt elated.

They all did.

After their deep tissue massage, everyone felt loose and relaxed. They grabbed their towels and sunscreen, then took a cab to the beach, just a mile away. They set up their beach chairs, with Jake sitting in the middle. Jason felt so good that he even put sunscreen on Rachel. Though still hesitant about pursuing a relationship with her, he appreciated the gesture, especially considering Rachel had gotten them tickets to the Bahamas with all the perks.

"I'm scared of getting too close to Rachel because she really has issues. And I'm part of her mental health struggles. The closer I get, the worse her hallucinations and paranoia seem to get. The truth is, I really do love her—but as a friend, not as a romantic partner. She gets too jealous— jealous to the point that her sanity seems compromised. But lately, I've noticed she's been acting better. The books she reads about voices—she actually enjoys them. She'll be okay. The group is helping her a lot. She's getting so much support." Jason thought.

"He actually rubbed sunscreen on me… He touched me. He hasn't touched me in so long. Maybe something can happen between us on this trip, but I'm also hesitant, given my mental state around him. I think about him all the time. I really love him, but I wonder if he's slowly destroying my world. But he actually put sunscreen on me!" Rachel thought.

"The sky is so beautiful with the sun shining and the clear water. I might just take a dip in there soon. I don't know if it's because of yesterday's conversation about suicide or just the fact that I've been here for two days, but everything feels so relaxing—it's like I'm in paradise. I know I shouldn't drink a margarita with the Zyprexa I'm taking, but right now, I really feel like having one. The massage and the food were amazing. I didn't even need to do any breathing exercises to feel calm. Everyone here seems so relaxed. Why can't I be relaxed too? Why can't I feel clear-

headed like the other vacationers? For now, I'll allow myself to be okay. I'll figure out what happened with that GRE event another day. Today, I'm going to live in the moment." Pedro thought.

"Who wants to take a dip in the water?" Everyone jumped out of their seats and ran toward the ocean. Ayn hesitated just before going, then stopped and looked at Jake.

"Don't forget your contacts!" she exclaimed. "You can at least go knee-deep in the water!"

Jake smiled, took Ayn's hand, and walked with her to the shore, his feet just brushing the water. At that moment, Jake felt everything was right. He even forgot about his schizophrenia diagnosis. He was with a woman he loved, in a beautiful place, and almost completely relaxed.

On the last day, they sat together at a restaurant over dinner, discussing their week and laughing at jokes.

"Well, it looks like our time here is coming to a close soon…"

"Tomorrow we'll be back on the plane home. I love you guys. I had fun," said Rachel.

"Yeah, I had a great time too," Ayn responded. Everyone else in the group agreed.

"We need to make a agrement," Rachel continued. "Before calling anyone, like a therapist or psychiatrist, we need to talk to each other first. Especially when it comes to things like suicide. If you talk to the wrong people, you could end up in the hospital. We haven't talked about it since the second night in the Bahamas, so I assume everyone is doing okay?"

"I suppose the Jung case is next on the agenda?" Pedro asked.

"Don't worry about that now. We'll talk about it when we get home," Jake said.

With that, the conversation turned back to their vacation, and they shared more thoughts on how great it had been.

When they finished talking, Jake was walking upstairs with Ayn. He noticed his eyes were blinking unusually fast, as if something was trying to keep them shut. It was unsettling, and he felt a sense of anger, frustrated that his vacation was ending on such a strange note. He tried to resist, but his eyes kept closing on their own. He didn't feel like spending the evening with Ayn; instead, he wanted to take out his contacts, take a shower, and go to bed.

The next morning, Jake woke up from a dream. He had been in Uganda, the place where his parents were from. He had been at a large wedding, and when he looked at his clothes, he realized he was the groom, and Ayn was the bride. His heart swelled with excitement. His parents, uncles, aunts, and cousins were all there. Ayn looked stunning, her blue eyes shining, her figure elegant and graceful. There were traditional Ugandan dances, their bodies shaking in ways that looked almost mechanical, and the music at the after-party was a blend of hip-hop and Afrobeat—Jake's favorite. Ayn even had some pop songs mixed in. There was dancing, delicious food, and a feeling of joy that Jake couldn't explain. He wasn't sure how he could afford such an extravagant wedding, but somehow, he had.

When Jake woke up, he felt a mix of frustration and happiness. He had been so content in that dream, imagining a future with Ayn in Uganda, surrounded by his family. He smiled, even though he was annoyed the dream had ended. The idea of marrying Ayn felt real, even if both of them still had unresolved issues. Maybe he didn't have to wait. Maybe a wedding could be possible, after he had a bit more money. He met up with the others in the lobby, and as they talked, Jake thought to himself, *Soon, I'll be a witness for Jung at his trial. I already have over 100K views on the NAMI video, and the phone's been ringing off the hook with advertisers trying to partner with me. The only ad I've accepted is the one for NAMI, though. I still care about that, to some extent.*

They all got into the cab back to the airport, feeling sad that their vacation had come to an end but also eager to get the trial over with. They checked their luggage, received their tickets, and made their way to the terminal to wait for their flight home.

"If I had more money, I'd take a month-long vacation," Rachel said.

"That's alright, we had a great time in just one week," Pedro replied. "My problems haven't been bothering me much. The GRE stuff is still in the back of my mind, but I managed to be present. Maybe that's what I need more of—self-care when I get back to my routine."

"Well, I doubt I could get a massage every day or go to the beach, but I could watch a movie or catch a funny comedian now and then."

After an hour of this lighthearted chatter, they were called to board their flight. Jake ended up with the window seat again.

Not only is the Jung case on my mind, but I've got eye surgery next week. I'm not sure exactly what the procedure will involve, but I know it's to stop the deterioration of my eyesight.

They won't let me do the normal cross-linking, Jake thought.

"Everything will be alright, honey!" Ayn said, offering comfort.

When they returned home, Pedro's mom picked them up and drove each of them to their respective houses.

Chapter 29

In three days, Jake was scheduled to undergo testing for his eyes. He and his mom were going on a trip back to Los Angeles for the Intacs surgery. Jake had found the only doctor in the country who could do it, but his mom would have to cover the cost of the plane tickets, car rental, and the surgery itself—all out of pocket. How his mom came up with the money, Jake didn't know, but they had it.

When Jake first learned that his primary cornea doctor couldn't perform the Intacs surgery because his corneas were too thin, he cried the entire day. He talked to his friends, who helped him feel better, but the sadness lingered. He also found out he couldn't undergo crosslinking either, which he had been certain he qualified for—but again, his corneas were too thin. The reason he cried was because on YouTube, it seemed like anyone with a cornea problem could get crosslinking—unless it was a rare case. When he learned that his condition was too advanced, he was in shock.

In L.A., they would check the demographics of his eyes and run additional measurements. Then, Jake was supposed to undergo the Intacs procedure followed by Holcomb crosslinking to stop further deterioration. The next few days leading up to the trip weren't too bad. He talked to Ayn and saw her a few times. He also caught up with the rest of his friends and talked about the Jung case.

On the day they left for L.A., Jake felt surprisingly fearless. For some reason, *the presence* was still there—even though he was about to have eye surgery. He read the entire

Gospel of Luke focusing on the story of the blind man whom Jesus healed. Jesus had made mud with His saliva, placed it on the man's eyes, and told him to wash. Afterward, the man—blind since birth—could see. Jake held onto that story closely.

He had been watching this doctor on YouTube. The doctor had helped people with difficult cases before. Jake's previous doctor had said Intacs wouldn't be possible due to the thinness of his cornea, but the California doctor, after reviewing his records, believed he could do it. Jake wrote to his original doctor, who replied that the doctor in California must have access to special technology.

A few months earlier, Jake had created a GoFundMe account, but it didn't raise enough. His mom somehow came up with the money. After a long flight from the East Coast to the West Coast, they rented a car and drove to the hotel. With some time to spare, they went to Disneyland. It was amazing. *The presence* and *the voices* still haunted him, making his life a living hell even there, but he still had moments of genuine happiness with his mom.

The next day, they headed to the doctor's clinic. Jake underwent several tests before he and his mom filled out paperwork in the office. The doctor took Jake to a back room and asked what his expectations were. Jake said, "If I could just use glasses, that would be big—without needing contact lenses." The doctor, without emotion, told him that based on the tests, he couldn't get Intacs.

Perspective

Jake broke down in tears. He had spent hours on YouTube researching Intacs and felt confident it would work, especially after getting what seemed like confirmation from the doctor. He had seen a video of a little girl with a severe corneal issue getting both Intacs and Holcomb crosslinking. He'd also read a book with people who had extreme cases and still got the surgery. Jake had no idea his condition was *that* bad.

His vision without contacts was nearly impossible. The doctor then said he was eligible for ICLs—implantable contact lenses. Jake didn't know much about them or their risks. The doctor played a 3D video about the procedure, and Jake felt a little more reassured when he learned he'd be able to see better—especially in the dark.

Jake agreed to the procedure. The doctor said more tests were needed and that his mom should talk to the secretary about costs since ICLs were more expensive than Intacs. During one of the tests, Jake had to stare into a flashing light that blinded him while more images of his eyes were taken. When they were done, his mom told him everything had been paid for. The secretary informed the doctor that Jake would have both the ICL and Holcomb surgeries the next day. The doctor instructed Jake not to wear his contacts, to avoid scratching his cornea.

The next day, after enduring blurry vision without contacts, his mom drove him to the hospital clinic. They prepared him for surgery, putting him in a gown and placing a head covering on him. The whole ride there was a blur— literally.

479

As Jake entered the surgery room, he kept thinking about the Gospel of Luke, the blind man, and how everything was in Jesus's hands. The eye procedure took about ten minutes. The doctor taped his eyelids open and instructed Jake to look at a red dot on the machine. They started with his right eye. For a moment, Jake saw the doctor holding an incision tool and something else.

Oddly, the doctor was *mean-mugging* him. The day before, he'd kept pressing Jake's mom about Jake's job. She said he did DoorDash, though Jake barely did it. The doctor repeated "DoorDash" like it was a disgusting word, like the job was beneath him. Jake figured that was why the doctor gave him that look on the table. It scared him—this man was about to operate on his eye.

The assistant applied a generous amount of numbing gel to Jake's right eye. Then Jake felt a prick on the side of his eye. He watched as the collagen contact was pushed in and flattened out. The doctor finished by closing the incision.

And then the doctor did the same thing with Jake's left eye, which was a bit more difficult because Jake started lowering his head and couldn't see even a trace of light on the machine. As the doctor poked his eye, it shifted slightly to the side. But after a few moments, the doctor repeated the same procedure on his left eye as he had done on the right. He told Jake to get up and used a magnifying glass to inspect the inside of the eye to ensure everything went well.

The doctor stood up and walked off to do something, and Jake noticed his vision seemed a little better. He looked toward the doctor and saw him smiling—as if he believed he'd made a significant improvement in Jake's eyesight.

Next was the Holcomb cross-linking. In the standard version, the epithelium is scraped off before riboflavin and ultraviolet light are applied, causing excruciating pain for two weeks. But with the Holcomb procedure, the epithelium is left intact, and the pain is mostly confined to the first day. The doctor applied riboflavin to both eyes and set the custom ultraviolet light, which wasn't too bad—except it made Jake's vision slightly blurrier. The process lasted thirty 30 minutes.

An attendant gave Jake an eye mask that he'd need to wear while sleeping for two weeks. When Jake returned to the hotel, he was in a lot of pain, so he rested the entire day with his eyes closed. Ayn called a few times over the first few days, which cheered him up even though he could barely see. He couldn't make out his mother's face or anyone else's.

Because his eyesight was still adjusting, Jake wasn't allowed to wear contact lenses for two weeks. He had to apply three different eye drops daily during that period. Since his vision was severely impaired, he clung to his mom like she was a guiding angel—especially at the airport and wherever they went. He flew home without his contacts, vision blurry the entire time, which was frightening.

Once home, Jake passed the time on the phone and watched Teliach Chuol on YouTube—still with blurry vision. He also attended some HVN (Hearing Voices Network) meetings but had to bring the computer screen inches from his face. Reading anything on his phone meant holding it right up to his eyes.

The doctor who performed the ICL surgery had done a very good job. He called Jake the next evening, and although Jake didn't have much to say, he thanked him for the procedure. The day before Jake left for the airport, the doctor had him read a vision chart. Jake hadn't been able to see it at all with his right eye before—and not much better with the left. The doctor kept emphasizing that the surgery was a success.

When Jake got home, he took his pills, put on his mask, and tried to sleep. The next morning, he woke to find his friends gathered in the living room, happy to see him. Though he couldn't make out their faces, he recognized their voices.

"Your mom let us in, fearless leader. How are you doing?" asked Rachel.

"I can't see your faces. Everything's blurry. I can't wear contacts for two weeks. My vision's a little better, but not by much. The Holcomb cross-linking might reshape my corneas a bit. I hate wearing those contacts," Jake replied.

"Well, you're not alone. A lot of people have your condition and find ways to manage," said Pedro.

Jake acknowledged Pedro was right, though he couldn't look him in the eye. They chatted a bit more before his friends left—Jake's discomfort with the blurriness was less alarming.

That night, he talked to Ayn on the phone. She comforted him well. He passed the time listening to AA tapes and watching blurry AA meetings online.

When the two weeks were up, he saw the contact lens specialist. He was told to wear his old contacts for now—even though they still left everything blurry. The doctor ran tests using his eye machine and told Jake he'd soon be seeing 20/20 in both eyes. Jake was thrilled—he had been seeing 20/60 in his left eye before surgery. The doctor also mentioned his corneas had flattened.

That evening, Jake joined a mental health online meeting at 5:30 PM and excitedly shared that he was going to see 20/20 in both eyes. But he still had to wait another week for the new contacts, and the wait was difficult. Not only was he struggling with poor vision, but the face hallucinations returned—vivid and intrusive. At times, the molestation-themed hallucinations were so disturbing they made him feel suicidal. One night, he woke his mom because he was afraid of harming himself if left alone.

Finally, one of the new contacts arrived at his house the next morning. The long wait was almost over. He could now see his mom's and Ayn's faces a bit more clearly—although only the left contact had arrived, and even that didn't give him sharp vision. Reading was still difficult. His right contact was due the next day.

He returned to the eye doctor for adjustments, and the doctor used the eye machine to refine the prescription to help Jake read more clearly with the left contact. A new left lens was being made and would arrive in a week and a half.

When Jake finally received his right contact, he could see clearly with it—though close-up reading remained tough. Still, Jake felt like himself again.

In a few weeks, he was headed to Washington, D.C., with friends for the Jung case. By then, he would have both new contacts. A congressman had even offered to pay for their hotels—he wanted to meet Jake about something special he was planning.

The week finally arrived, and the group set off for the nation's capital.

"Jung had the psychologist at gunpoint and said he was going to kill him," Ayn explained.

"Yeah, that's true—but why? He may have to do some time for what he did, but not that much. He was pushed to the edge of what a man can endure with those voices. He looked for help in so many places and nobody could help him—not even NAMI. So he took matters into his own hands, in a really dumb way. I know what he did was wrong and he should be held accountable, but he has a serious mental health problem. He hears voices too. And even though I never wanted to be homicidal, I've felt that same loss of hope from the voices before. It's not a fun emotion," exclaimed Jake.

"Yeah, that's true. There are a lot of people out there who can't afford fancy therapists or mental health retreats. So they take matters into their own hands," said Jason.

"I heard on the news that his voices were so bad, he couldn't even read sometimes. Now, if you can't even read simple things, that's major," said Pedro.

"He was kind of handsome, though. What happened to that naked guy at the TED Talks from Los Angeles?" said Rachel.

"Let's just deal with one mental health crisis at a time. Do you guys think he's going to plead insanity?" said Ayn.

"Of course they are. His voices made him deranged. He wasn't thinking straight. Unfortunately, I'm going to help his lawyer plead that case. I just hope he gets the help he really needs, because going to a criminally insane asylum might just confine him, not fix what's wrong. I heard he found some solace listening to sermons online. That must've helped. And he listened to the Bible on YouTube. I heard he really connected with the words of Jesus—they were eye-opening for him. Sometimes, they even quieted the voices," said Jake.

"Do you guys know that much about him?" asked Ayn.

"His voices started when he was a freshman in college. First it was random phrases, and he ignored them. But then they started to sound like the devil, telling him to kill himself or his girlfriend. The voices kept saying it, so he dropped out and went to Zion. They put him on medication, but it didn't help. Reading the Bible seemed to center him in the hospital, so he was discharged. But even on medication, the voices kept commanding him to hurt himself. He gave in and cut himself. The voices didn't stop, so he checked back into Zion, where again, he got no real help.

"They eventually put him in the TV room because he was acting aggressively, and they had to restrain him so he wouldn't harm himself. He prayed, screaming at the top of his lungs—and that seemed to quiet the voices for a bit. They gave him heavy meds that turned him into a zombie. He slept a lot but couldn't function. The voices were still powerful. One day he placed a knife on the table and asked his girlfriend to sit with him. He said he was a changed man— but his eyes looked strange. She looked at the knife, looked at him, and left.

"When his parents were home, he held a knife to his arm and screamed that if the voices didn't stop, he would cut himself. His mom called the police, and they took him to the hospital again—for the third time. He would be in and out of hospitals over twenty times. Smoking weed and drinking only made things worse. He went to a few NAMI meetings, but they didn't help much. For some people, they work—but not for him. His voices kept giving him commands. So finally, he went to a NAMI convention and staged that scene—to get help by force," Jake said.

"So, are you guys ready to go to Washington, D.C.? Everything's been arranged by the congressman," said Ayn.

Everyone said yes.

They were leaving in two days to support Jake as a witness in Jung's trial and to meet the congressman for a special surprise. They decided to drive from their home state in Pedro's spacious car.

When the day came, Ayn wasn't feeling well. She was sinking into a quicksand-like pit of depression. Her medication wasn't working anymore, so she turned to meditation exercises. Sometimes they helped; other times, they made her feel more anxious. She brought along Sudoku and crossword puzzles to keep her mind occupied, hoping to distract herself from the emotional weight. Still, the depression felt like a phantom, hovering above her and draining all the happiness and faith she had, leaving her hopeless.

As she got into the car, she felt a dark, suicidal pull.

I guess it's okay to have suicidal thoughts once in a while, but if they happen too often, I might need to go to the hospital. I don't want to kill myself. I love Jake and the rest of the gang too much to go through with it again. Suicide sounds tempting right now only because the emotion is stuck—I can't move it out. I wonder what it would be like. I don't remember my last attempt, but I do remember feeling like an empty shell. It felt like God wasn't there... but people say He is—even when you don't feel Him. I'm just tired of having these thoughts. They feel like they're coming from inside me, not from the phantom. There has to be another way to get rid of this depression.

With that, Ayn turned to Jake in the car, kissed him on the mouth, and smiled.

Jake noticed Ayn looked worried but figured something about his presence made her happy again.

They were all excited to go to Washington, D.C., to support Jung at his trial. Jung was likely pleading insanity—and he'd probably get it, given his history of mental illness.

In the car, they talked about the books they'd been reading—Kay Whitfield and Elyn Saks in particular. They really admired Elyn Saks. Despite her schizophrenia, she became a top-tier lawyer, even when doctors told her she'd never do better than a minimum wage job.

They also talked about a book called Schizophrenia, which featured a Black man on the cover who was also the author. Jake liked the book because the author was a person of color. However, he felt the book lacked depth. He wanted the author to explore more of what it means to have schizophrenia—why he believed he had it, and what traumatic events may have led to it.

They had an extensive discussion about HVN and what it meant to each of them. Rachel had been going because she'd been diagnosed with schizophrenia several times and frequently heard voices. Jake attended as well. At the events, everyone knew and liked him a lot.

"Well, we finally made it to Washington D.C. Now we just have to find the hotel," said Jason. After a pause, he added, "Do you guys... do you think we'll ever be cured? That someone out there knows how to make all this go away?"

"I believe in miracles, Jason. If I can be cured of alcoholism, then I can be cured of schizoaffective disorder," said Jake. "We just have to stick to the plan and spread the word about the challenges of living with mental illness. People will help us—and more importantly, help others. My phone's already buzzing non stop since the NAMI event, the TED Talks, and the radio show. But honestly, I've been so focused on helping you guys and coming up with ways to support others that I haven't spent time helping myself. Once things settle down, we'll all be able to get more in-depth help. It sounds selfish, but with all this attention we're getting, there have to be people willing to help us—without charging five hundred dollars a session."

They talked a bit more about their mental health as they arrived at the hotel. They found a parking deck, unloaded the car, and grabbed their bags from the trunk. Rachel looked happier than usual, for some reason. They were all in good spirits—except Jake.

As soon as he stepped out of the car, he started seeing the face again.

The hallucination carried a flood of emotion, as though the entity inside him was filling his entire consciousness with negativity. When Jake saw the face, it became difficult to think clearly. It was strange to explain—but it felt like some part of him welcomed the voices and the face, yet when they came, the emotional pain was overwhelming and suffocating. It bordered on demonic. The aggression in the emotion was almost taunting—like something in his mind was baiting him to call on the voices just so they could enjoy his suffering.

As soon as Jake took the bait, he'd feel an initial rush—like he was about to share some twisted joy with the voices. But within a split second, it would shift into an all-consuming, crushing negativity.

Inside the hotel, Rachel approached the front desk and gave the clerk the code word from the congressman to retrieve their room keys. They each received their keycards, and Jason noticed Rachel walking behind him.

"Rachel, why are you following me?" he asked.

"We must have rooms next to each other," she said, smiling brightly.

It was hard to explain, but somewhere in Rachel's mind lingered that old desire for Jason. She believed, irrationally, that he had feelings for her too. Deep down, she knew she had a problem. The facts didn't support her fear that Jason had secret lovers trying to kill her to get to him. But the love she felt for him was her undoing. It was love entangled with convoluted thinking.

Rachel was smart and charismatic, but her paranoid delusions—especially those involving jealousy—kept resurfacing. She believed that other women were after Jason sexually and would harm her to get to him.

"Rachel, I'm going to sleep. It's been a long day," Jason said flatly. "Nothing is going to happen between us. I think being near me might be what's triggering your delusions."

With that, Jason opened the door to his room and stepped inside.

"Who isn't delusional?" Rachel muttered sarcastically before entering her own room.

Chapter 30

They were all sitting inside the McDonald's, eating breakfast. They noticed people walking past, saying hello and asking for selfies with all of them—especially Jake.

Jake hadn't looked at the YouTube video views of the NAMI event, the TED Talk, or the radio interview in a long time, but lately, he'd noticed more people recognizing him on the street.

"Did you know this case made national news? It's on CNN. I saw Jung's face all over the TV last night in the hotel," said Rachel.

"No, I didn't know that," Jake replied.

A very attractive blonde walked up next to Jake.

"Can I get a picture with you, Jake? What you did at the NAMI event was admirable. You really cared about that guy," she said.

Jake got up and took a picture with her.

Ayn scrunched up her face in irritation. "So admirable," she said sarcastically.

"Is someone jealous?" Rachel teased.

They finished breakfast and headed to Pedro's car parked outside. A few blocks later, they arrived at the courthouse. News crews surrounded the entrance.

"Jake, can we get a statement?" shouted one reporter.

"Are you friends with Jung?" asked another.

"How long have you been mentally ill? Do you take medication?"

"I think we'd better not talk to anyone and just get inside," Pedro said.

"That sounds like a good idea," Jason agreed.

Everyone else nodded.

As they walked into the courtroom, people turned their heads, whispering about Jake and his friends. A few clapped and whistled.

"There's Jung up front," said Pedro.

Jung turned slightly, scanning the source of the noise. When his eyes met Jake's, he gave a small half-smile. Jake smiled back, but apprehensively.

They sat down in the middle of the audience. Jake wasn't familiar with courtroom layouts, but he knew he'd be called as a witness. He had spoken with Jung's attorney a few days earlier and knew what to expect.

The judge banged the gavel repeatedly. "Order, order!"

That's when Jake saw the face again—smiling at him.

He had hoped that with all the chaos, the entity might leave him alone so he could focus on his testimony. But it was relentless, hunting for weakness. Jake felt a secondary, haunting emotion—like someone pretending they didn't want to be there. It was sharp and invasive, clouding his imagination. He grew angry.

Oh no, this is the worst time for this. I hope Jung stays clear-minded when he takes the stand, Jake thought.

The prosecutor stood and began his opening statement.

"It's terrible what the mentally ill go through. But how do you measure how ill Mr. Jung really was? Sure, the gun was fake—but what if it hadn't been? Jung should go to jail for pretending to have a gun and putting lives in danger.

"The psychologist was just doing his job—respectfully. He's not to blame for having a weapon, even a fake one, shoved in his face. He was there to educate the public about mental health.

"The defense will argue insanity. But what does it truly mean to be insane?

"The day before the incident, Jung quit his job and bought his parents McDonald's. He painted the tip of the BB gun black to make it look real. He's held that job on and off for a year. For that whole year, he didn't go to the hospital, even though before that, he had been hospitalized several times a year for five years.

"Yes, he has mental health issues. But he wasn't morally stabilized. He wanted revenge on NAMI for not helping him—when really, he should've helped himself. We all have our own versions of self-care. It was his responsibility to manage his anger toward NAMI and talk to his therapist about it.

"I believe Jung was in his right mind and should be held accountable for what he did. That is all," said the prosecutor.

He sat down.

Jake's hallucinations started lingering longer. The faces didn't just appear—they molested him. It felt like a man was sexually touching him. He felt strangled.

Humiliation washed over him, sharp and unbearable. He wanted to cut himself to escape the emotional agony.

He looked around. His friends were focused on the trial, but Jake could see the cracks forming in their expressions. Jason looked on the verge of a breakdown. Pedro kept reaching into his pocket—probably for one of his Zyprexa pills, Jake guessed.

Why do they always surprise me? Just when I think they won't do anything, that's when they hit the hardest, Jake thought. *I just cried a little—without anyone noticing. I hate that. Sometimes when the hallucinations are strong, I cry quietly. Lately, I've been feeling the full weight of the emotion—with the suicidal thoughts right alongside it.*

Thank God I don't own a gun. If I did, I might've played with it and accidentally shot myself in the face.

Now, the voices began. The same two—one claiming to be Jesus, the other the devil.

"That's not Jesus. Jesus is in heaven," Jake muttered to himself.

"He is not in heaven! You're not Jesus! Stop saying you're Jesus. You're not. I want the devil. I want Jesus!" the voices argued.

They went back and forth, senseless chatter. But every time they spoke, Jake felt pain—physical, emotional, unbearable.

He couldn't leave the courtroom. If he did, he'd have a breakdown—the voices, the hallucinations, the feeling of being touched—they'd all come crashing in.

He mumbled back at the voices. What he said made no sense, but it helped him cope.

"Wait for help," the voices echoed, commenting on his thoughts.

Jake knew what that meant. When they said that, it usually meant the worst had passed. They would start to fade—for now.

Jake turned to the defense lawyer, who was in the middle of his opening statement—Jake had missed the beginning.

"If it were up to me," the defense attorney said, "I would argue that my client doesn't even need an insanity plea or to end up in a facility for the criminally insane. What he needs is real help—professional help from someone who knows what they're doing.

"My client, Mr. Jung, has attended countless NAMI meetings. He spoke openly about his condition. He heard suggestions on how to stop the voices commanding him, but none of them worked. He would meet with his therapist and psychiatrist the following week, trying new medications each time. He tried them all, but nothing helped. He even studied schizophrenia to better understand his illness, but no solution eased his suffering.

"He and his therapist worked on CBT, but it wasn't particularly effective. When the voices were loud, he had trouble focusing on the CBTp worksheets. He tried everything—even converted to Buddhism. For a while, he found temporary relief, but then the voices returned with a vehement wrath, urging him to hang himself.

"He found a job—minimum wage—but a job nonetheless. He began reading the Bible, which sometimes calmed him. He returned to a Christian church, and there, he began to feel a little better. He had faith, and that faith was helping to quiet the voices.

"Even before this trial, Jung read the Bible and told me about it. He said he finally understood what Jesus meant when he said that those who follow him would be persecuted like him. And despite everything—despite the chaos at NAMI—Jung still loves Jesus.

"He just didn't know what else to do when the voices got the upper hand. He found out there was a NAMI convention in town, and in desperation, he went there with a fake gun, hoping to force someone to help him.

"And let me repeat to the jury: the gun was fake.

"Yes, he took the psychologist hostage—but he needed help. Right then, right there. Because at that moment, he believed he had to do anything to stay alive. It wasn't a smart way to get help. But his mind was unraveling under the pressure of the voices. So even though I believe he should be released outright, I'll settle for the next best thing: a plea of insanity.

"That is all."

The defense lawyer sat down next to Jung, turned to him, and smiled—an assuring gesture that things were going to be okay. Jung offered a faint smile in return.

Meanwhile, Jake's voices stopped—those piercing, emotional voices. What remained was just the face. It flickered in and out of focus. Usually, it appeared distorted, mimicking Jake's own expression in a stupid, exaggerated way. Jake sat with his mouth slightly open, biting his tongue—an involuntary tic, a symptom of tardive dyskinesia. The entity inside him twisted his features in his mind into a grotesque cartoon. It made Jake feel humiliated and powerless.

He didn't know how to make the face go away. So he pulled out his phone and began texting Ayn, telling her how he felt. That helped—a little.

Several months earlier, Jake had called 988 during a suicidal crisis. As soon as he made the call, the voices began insisting that 988 was a mystical force. But the face softened, the voices grew quieter as Jake messaged the 988 responder, explaining the hell he was going through.

The responder kept trying to dispatch a mobile crisis team to Jake's home. But Jake always refused. The last time he accepted, he ended up in the hospital. Ever since then, something changed—when Jake texted, the voices and the face became less aggressive. It was like the phone gave him a shield.

As Jake and Ayn continued texting, the psychologist took the witness stand.

"You're a respected psychologist, aren't you, Mr.—" the prosecutor began.

"You can call me Mark," he replied. "I've been a psychologist for about thirty years."

"You received an email from Jung, asking for help—or else something bad would happen?" the prosecutor pressed.

"I checked my email after the hostage situation," said Mark. "I get so many emails, I don't check them daily. I usually just read those from colleagues or research funders. But when I saw Jung's email, I felt terrible."

"Did you know you had a gun pointed at your face?" the prosecutor asked.

"I thought it was real. People were screaming, running from the room in panic. He could've killed me. And all I ever tried to do was help people with psychological issues."

"Did you understand what he was shouting at you?" the prosecutor continued.

"He said if he didn't get help to stop the voices, he would blow my head off. He sounded pretty coherent to me," Mark answered.

The prosecutor turned to the jury. "Yes, we understand Jung has some medical issues. But he had intent. He is not completely insane. He knew exactly what he was doing—at least what he was staging. And let me remind you, even pretending to have a gun and causing mass panic is a crime.

"Jung knew what he was doing. He was angry because he had voices—and most people don't. All he had to do was keep looking for help. He didn't have to endanger the life of a respected psychologist. That's all."

The defense lawyer rose again and approached the witness stand.

"Mark, what kind of research do you do?" he asked.

"I'm working on new therapies for people diagnosed with schizophrenia. It's a form of ACT—Acceptance and Commitment Therapy—where patients learn to accept their condition," Mark began, before being cut off.

"So your job is to help people like Jung?" the defense lawyer pressed.

"Yes. We focus our research on people like him."

"Jung told me he read your research and wanted to participate in one of the trials. But he said he couldn't, because he had Medicaid—and Medicaid doesn't cover research trials. Is it true you only accept participants with high-end insurance?" the defense lawyer asked.

"That is true. We only accept people who have certain types of insurance—not government-issued Medicaid," said Mark.

"So basically, insurance for the poor. If you're poor, you can't participate in the fancy research," the defense attorney remarked. "Jury, I must remind you—Jung is an incredibly intelligent man. He's done extensive research on schizoaffective disorder. He's one of those people who hears voices that never stop, no matter what. These voices urge him to kill himself for seemingly no reason."

"Jung could hardly function. He was even kicked out of his church for going too intense with speaking in tongues. He searched everywhere for medical assistance to help with his debilitating condition, and no one had any answers. How can he get the help he deserves? That is the question."

The defense attorney sat down. The psychologist stepped down from the witness stand with a sly smile.

"Next, I would like to call Jake __________ to the stand," said the prosecutor.

Jake glanced at Ayn and his friends. "I'll be alright," he reassured them. As he walked to the front of the courtroom, he stared at the prosecutor. For a moment, a hallucinated face flashed over the prosecutor's, triggering a wave of discomfort. Jake wanted nothing more than to escape.

He sat on the witness stand, eyes darting between the prosecutor and Jung. A sudden dizziness washed over him. The hallucinated face and voices intensified, keeping him on edge. But when the prosecutor said his name, everything went silent. The voices stopped. His mind cleared. The invasive sensation that focused his awareness on his own body vanished.

"Jake, you've made quite a name for yourself. You managed to talk down Jung and save the day. When you spoke to him, was he coherent?" asked the prosecutor.

"I identified with him. My voices were attacking me just before I came up here. They were disturbing—relentless. I've been where he is: searching for help, finding none. I wouldn't have done what he did, but I understand the despair…" Jake began, before being cut off.

"Just answer the question—were you able to have a coherent conversation with him?"

"Yes. We both got emotional," Jake replied.

"Do you believe he had a gun?"

"Yes. I wanted to ease the situation. He looked desperate, like he was searching for a way out. Forget insanity or jail—he needs real help. His voices are demonic. Do you know what it feels like to have voices commanding you?"

"No, I don't," the prosecutor said. "But I know there are people with schizophrenia who have jobs and contribute to their communities. He reads the Bible and goes to church. How can he be that sick?"

"I don't have an answer. But I believe someone can appear functional and still be suffering. 'Insane' is a harsh word. For me, I feel both sick and intelligent—sometimes at the same time. If you or anyone else were in his shoes, you might've taken your own life or someone else's. And Jung wasn't planning to hurt anyone—he didn't even have a real gun."

"During your conversation with Jung, while he held the fake gun—did it appear real? And would you say Jung is intelligent?" the prosecutor asked.

"Yes, it looked real. And yes, he's intelligent. He realized he'd made a mistake and started crying. I don't think it was just because he had a psychologist at gunpoint. He was heartbroken that he couldn't get help. From what I've researched about him, he doesn't have the money or insurance to attend those expensive mental health retreats with 24/7 therapy."

"Were you scared he might shoot you?"

"Yes. I was scared. But I was also tired. Tired of all the pain. I knew he was like me. I knew before he spoke that he was going through something huge. I didn't know if he knew the psychologist personally, but I knew he needed help."

"I'm tired of reading about people online who've been in and out of hospitals three times a year. Tired of hearing about five suicide attempts because of relentless voices. Tired of people having hallucinations—demons, aliens— that drive them to self-harm or violence. Tired of seeing so many end up in prison, many with mental illness."

Jake's voice grew stronger. "People need help. You remember the school shootings? People like that—those are cries for help. I'm not saying all people with mental illness are violent, but they can become a danger to themselves when life gets unbearable."

A burst of applause erupted from the audience. Whistling and calls of "You're speaking the truth!" echoed through the courtroom.

The judge banged the gavel. "Order! Order in the court!"

The crowd settled into a whisper, then silence.

"I just have one more question," said the prosecutor. "Don't you think he should be punished for what he did?"

"No," Jake replied firmly. "He's already suffered enough. He doesn't belong in a place for the criminally insane. He needs to be in a retreat for schizophrenia, funded by NAMI, the government, or a private organization."

Whispers rippled across the courtroom.

"Order, I say! Order in the court!"

The room fell silent.

The defense attorney stood and approached Jake methodically. "How are you doing, Mr. ________? I'm sorry you're struggling with the voices right now. Jung just told me that his voices were attacking him earlier, too. In fact, they were telling him that no matter what happened in this courtroom, he should kill himself."

"But back to the event—I don't know all the details of your conversation with Jung; the camera was muffled at times. But I understand what you mean when you say someone can be intelligent and sick at the same time, or at different times. I hate that we're pleading for insanity, but I have to ask: how would you gauge Jung's emotional state at NAMI?" asked the defense lawyer.

"He was erratic and scared," Jake said. "He knew what was going on around him, but it seemed like he was also listening to something else while talking to me."

"He told me he was talking to me and to his voices at the same time. They were telling him to kill himself. I knew he was tired—tired of looking for help and not finding it through the means he had. Tired of his voices constantly telling him to end his life. Most people don't understand how that feels. He was tired of waking up every day in hell."

Jake's voice trembled.

"When the voices speak, and it's just him and them in a void—where no one else can reach—it's suffocating. In that emptiness, he'd scream in his mind, sometimes out loud, begging for help. And all he'd hear was silence. He was isolated, tormented by that devilish voice. I'm thankful he found Jesus—he helped him a little. Maybe, with divine support and some real outside help, he can find something better."

"I'm not knocking Jesus—there's a reason why people like Jung and I go through what we go through. But something has to change. Going in and out of hospitals isn't the answer. Taking so many pills you become a zombie isn't the answer. Making plans to kill yourself isn't the answer."

Jake paused, his hands clenched slightly. "I'm loved. Jung is loved—by his mother and father. They care about him. They don't want him to kill himself or end up in a mental asylum for the rest of his life. He doesn't want to undergo repeated shock treatments that turn him into a mindless vegetable."

"From what I've researched, at one point, he was reading the Bible every day—along with a ton of literature on schizophrenia and voices," said Jake.

There were a few whispers in the courtroom. The Judge scanned the room with a cold, silent stare, and the murmurs ceased.

"It seems that you and Jung formed a bond. You two must share some things in common. Would you consider yourself insane, Jake?" the defense lawyer asked.

Jake smiled, eerily reminiscent of the Joker, and looked at Jung, then back at the lawyer.

"I don't know—sometimes. If the voices, face hallucinations, and the emotional residue from past abuse from the entity weren't there, I wouldn't feel insane. But when I constantly see a face superimposed on mine, layered with twisted emotions—the pain is suffocating, blinding, consuming, and demonic. I wouldn't wish it on anyone."

He took a breath.

"When I think about it, I feel trapped—not quite suicidal, but definitely not normal either. But I'm not insane. Even with those symptoms always there, I've maintained relationships. I can read. I've done interviews. I've given TED Talks. How many people can you say have done TED Talks?"

Jake gave a half-laugh.

"I guess you could compare me to Elyn Saks or Eleanor Longden. I also gave a speech at NAMI—even though it kind of went haywire. I've done all of these things while hearing voices. Sometimes, they were there right before I spoke or gave an interview, but I still managed. So, yeah, maybe someone could say I'm a little insane—but I also have emotions like any other red-blooded American."

He shifted slightly, then continued, "Talking with Jung, I found him to be unique. But his voices lead to outbursts, repeated calls to suicide hotlines, breaking glasses and plates. Even if he's not completely insane, there is something inside him—something fractured—that pushes him to these extremes."

"Let me ask you a hypothetical question," the lawyer said. "With all the research you've done on Jung, and everything that happened at the NAMI convention, can you imagine him having a family, kids—a 401k and a solid 9-to-5 job?"

Jake looked at Jung for a long moment, then turned to Ayn, then to the lawyer. A single tear rolled down his cheek, followed by another, and then his whole face was drenched in tears.

As he cried, he spoke.

"He needs help. I need help. Living like this is hell ! I know what he's going through, and no one can see inside his mind to understand the torment. He needs real help—help from someone who actually cares and understands."

Jake sobbed, his voice cracking. "That's all. I'm done," said the defense lawyer.

Jake stepped down from the witness stand, sniffling. He wiped his face and walked to the back of the courtroom, where Ayn, Rachel, Jason, and Pedro stood waiting. They all embraced in a group hug. Though anguish and despair still weighed on Jake's heart, he felt a warmth—more than physical. It was spiritual.

Jake felt God's presence for the first time.

He felt safe, like everything was going to be okay. That somehow, things would work out. Despite all the cameras pointing at him, Jake felt a deep sense of Power, Love, and Self-Control from God.

"Order! Order, I say—order!" shouted the Judge.

There was talk from the front of the courtroom, but Jake couldn't make out the words—he was in a moment with God.

Jung stood up and took the witness stand. The Prosecutor rose, smiling like he was facing a long-lost adversary.

Jung's face was flat, exhausted. He looked like he just wanted to sleep.

"So, Jung," began the Prosecutor, "how often do you hear voices?"

"I hear them 24/7, most of the time. When Jake was crying, they told me to kill myself—said there was no hope left," Jung answered.

"What do your voices usually talk about?" asked the Prosecutor.

"They usually say I'm going to hell because I'm bad. Sometimes they just repeat my thoughts back to me—which is really disturbing. They don't always tell me how to kill myself, but they push me toward it. They consume me. They're powerful—really powerful—and I haven't figured out a way to weaken them. Only reading the Bible helps, sometimes."

"Have your voices ever asked you to hurt anyone?" asked the Prosecutor.

"Yes, my voices tell me to hurt people. They're telling me to hurt you right now," replied Jung.

"Jury, how do we know it's not Jung's own thoughts that want to harm me? He's probably angry because I'm the prosecutor. Have you ever, yourself, felt like hurting someone?" he pressed.

"Yes. Sometimes I hear voices that sound like people I've met or known, and then I kind of feel like hurting them. But most of the time, the voices want me to kill myself," said Jung.

"So, you have homicidal tendencies. Not just voices—you, yourself," the Prosecutor said, eyeing Jung like he was a wild animal. "Have you ever hurt someone specifically?" he continued.

"I was going to stab my ex-girlfriend, but part of me didn't want to. The voices said I had to either kill myself or kill her. I felt stronger urges to hurt myself. I called her over to my apartment, put the knife on the table in front of me. I was going to ask her to sit near me, then grab her and slit her throat. I really didn't want to do it. I knew something was wrong with my thoughts. I mostly end up in mental hospitals because I'm suicidal," Jung confessed.

The Prosecutor scanned the Jury's faces, then looked back at Jung. "That's all," he said sharply.

The defense lawyer stood. "I really don't want to pursue this insanity plea. You read the Bible more than most Christians I know, and you've done extensive research on your mental illness. But I have no choice but to ask these questions. How often do you think about hurting others?" he asked.

"Not all the time, but sometimes. I was just thinking about stealing that officer's gun and taking the Prosecutor hostage—demanding a helicopter to escape to some deserted island or something. I'm not going to do it, but lately, I've had more thoughts of hurting myself. I wanted to hang myself in the jail cell, but there was nothing to hang from. I managed to chip off some stones from the wall and tried to cut myself with them, but they were too blunt," Jung said.

"How often do you feel like hurting yourself?" the defense lawyer asked.

"Every day. With the voices, I get suicidal thoughts constantly. They give me commands daily, and I feel an urge to follow them. I've had quite a few attempts. I tried hanging myself once, but the lamp broke. I've overdosed on pills multiple times. I used a knife once but couldn't cut deep enough," said Jung.

The Jury looked weary and sympathetic. They seemed to feel more pity than fear—less like they were seeing a killer, more like they were witnessing a man broken by his mind. The defense lawyer glanced around the courtroom in dazed exhaustion.

"That's all from me."

After some brief procedural language, the Prosecutor rose for his closing statement, as if the entire trial were some kind of performance.

"Ladies and Gentlemen of the Jury. You've all witnessed that this man is dangerous. Regardless of what he says about his voices, he had the intent to kill his girlfriend. He even staged a fake hostage takeover, which could have led to real harm. He planned out what he wanted to do at the NAMI convention and bought a fake gun that looked real. It doesn't matter why he did what he did. Mark is a respected psychologist and never should've been put in that situation—no one should. Jung should be incarcerated with no chance for parole. He admitted himself that he had the urge. If he's released into the public, it's only a matter of time before someone gets hurt. These documents in my hand show he actually tried to purchase a firearm but failed. If we don't act, it could be your son or daughter next. I rest my case."

He sat down with unsettling satisfaction.

The defense lawyer stood for his closing, visibly shaken and disturbed by the spectacle the trial had become. He felt as though divine forces had already passed judgment, and that the Prosecutor was merely a puppet.

"Ladies and Gentlemen of the Jury. Jung has been diagnosed with schizoaffective disorder. Unfortunately, medication hasn't helped him. I worry more that he'll harm himself than someone else. But what he did, he did. I'm pleading with you to consider placing him in a proper mental health facility—not a criminal asylum where rehabilitation is nearly impossible. Yes, what happened was wrong, but the voices he heard that day weren't just symptoms—they were demons. Jung wanted help. He wanted to be free from the endless, tormenting chatter in his mind. Voices that violate and humiliate him, that question his every thought and focus only on his worst impulses.

There are too many people in the criminal system who never received the help they needed. Many end up worse off in prison, deprived of the medical care they could have had on the outside. I just don't want to see this Christian man locked away forever.

Case closed."

The defense lawyer returned to his seat and quietly reassured Jung, "Everything's going to be okay."

There were a few words the Judge said that Jake couldn't quite make out—something about jury deliberation.

Most people began to stand and exit. A few approached Jake.

"What you said was very inspiring. I have a brother with schizophrenia who's struggling to get help. He's tried every medication out there, and none have worked. What you said deserves the highest esteem," said one man.

"Thanks, I appreciate it," Jake replied, blinking uncontrollably as the Judge gave his final remarks. It felt like someone else was closing his eyes—like a malfunction deep in his brain. He'd been taking antipsychotics and believed they were causing the involuntary blinking. It was hard to keep his eyes open unless he concentrated hard, or got lucky and the spasms stopped.

Outside the courtroom, Jake and his friends were quickly surrounded by reporters shouting questions about the trial.

Jake ran with his friends to Pedro's car, carrying their things on his back, and they drove to the hotel.

"That was some court case. Jake, what happened up there was amazing," said Ayn.

"Yeah, it was," Jason agreed.

"I hope they let Jung go. He needs proper medical treatment, not to be locked up in a cell for the criminally insane," said Rachel.

"I did the best I could," Jake replied. "There were times I thought about it. I didn't have a solid plan, but I considered going to a renowned psychologist's house and begging him to help me with my mental illness. It's hard to find help out there. Jung was desperate."

"We're going to visit him and make sure he gets help, no matter where he is," Ayn said with resolve.

Since Jake had increased his antipsychotic dosage, he'd been dealing with tardive dyskinesia—his eyes blinked uncontrollably. Still, he pushed forward. He called his psychiatrist and said he would reduce his antipsychotic dosage. The doctor agreed and prescribed a higher dose of Ingrezza to manage the side effects. That night, Jake took the extra dose, hoping it would calm his constant eye-blinking.

After dinner, they all retreated to their rooms, feeling uneasy about the Jung case. The next morning, they headed downstairs to the hotel lobby for breakfast. Guests approached Jake, saying things like, "Good job, Jake," and "I'm so happy about what you did on the witness stand."

Within minutes, reporters stormed the breakfast area, eager for interviews.

"Let's make a run for it to the car," Pedro said.

They sprinted to his vehicle, chased by reporters, and drove to the courthouse for the hearing. Even more reporters awaited them there.

This is what it feels like to be famous, Jake thought.

"No comment. I have to get into the courtroom. Sorry, you guys," Jake said to the reporters.

He took his seat next to his friends, in the same place as before. His neck keeps tensing up, making him uncomfortable. At first, he blamed the voices, but then he recognized it could be tardive dyskinesia. Maybe the Ingrezza needed more time to work.

Suddenly, the face hallucination appeared again—superimposed on his own—and an overwhelming wave of negativity washed over him.

Meanwhile, Rachel beamed with a wide smile, even though deep down, she wasn't sure what the outcome would be.

Jake missed the beginning, but the jury leader stood to announce the verdict.

"We, the jury, find the defendant Jung not guilty. However, he should receive serious help. He will not go to jail or be sent to a criminal asylum."

Jung jumped up and hugged his lawyer. He turned to Jake, his face radiant with joy. Jake snapped back to reality, returned the smile.

The crowd erupted in celebration, but the judge quickly called for order.

"Order, order!"

The prosecutor looked furious and muttered, "He could have had a gun."

Outside the courtroom, Jake and his friends gave a few interviews.

"So, Jake, how does it feel to be the hero of the witness stand?" asked one interviewer.

"I just saw something wrong and wanted to help. Jung needs help, not a jail cell. He's lucky—his fame might get him that help. But what about the people who aren't famous? I'm fighting for them. For those who don't have money or insurance but still need help."

"What's next for you and your friends in D.C.?" asked the reporter.

"We're going to see Congressman Peters. He has a surprise for us," Jake replied.

"I hope it's a million dollars. You deserve it!" joked another reporter.

"We're not doing this for the money. We want real change," Ayn said, grabbing Jake's hand.

A female reporter rushed up to Ayn. "Are you Jake's girlfriend?"

"Yes, I am. And we're going to keep pushing this mental health issue until we see real, effective change. We want the entire infrastructure reformed—whatever it takes," Ayn said with a smile at Jake.

"…Well, that's when I knew there was…" Rachel began, but Jason gently pulled her toward Pedro's car. They all returned to the hotel and gathered in Jason's room.

"Wow, Jake! You're super famous, and now we're kind of famous too," Jason said. "We all had interviews out there!"

Jake's phone rang. It was the defense lawyer's number.

"Hey Jake, it's Jung. I just wanted to thank you for everything—your talk at the NAMI event and your testimony. You really helped me. I already have a Zoom meeting scheduled with one of the top psychologists in the country. He said he'll do whatever it takes to help me with the voices and other issues."

"I'm so happy you're free," Jake replied. "I can relate to what you're going through. Keep reading the Bible. I'm sure more people will step in now that you're famous—ha ha."

"Ha! That's funny. You should get world-class help too—you're famous now!"

"I would, but I've got to keep spreading the message. The mental health system is broken. Going in and out of hospitals isn't a solution."

After a pause, Jung said, "Well, let's talk later. Maybe hang out sometime. Peace, man."

"Yeah, we can do that. Peace," Jake said.

The group, who had been listening in, erupted with joy.

"Yes! Jung is free. I know what he did was wrong, but jail would've made things worse. Any one of us could've been pushed that far under the right pressure," said Jason.

"Yeah, I'm just glad he's getting real help," Rachel said with a wide grin.

"We're all happy," added Pedro.

"Tomorrow we will see the congressman. From what I hear, he really cares about mental health. I think he'll have good news," Rachel said.

"You guys, what are we going to do to fix this infrastructure?" Ayn asked.

"I don't really know," Pedro admitted.

"Well, we might not know exactly what to do yet, but something has to change. We need to inspire people to help others dealing with mental illness," said Jason.

"On that note, we should call it a night and see what this congressman has to say tomorrow," Jake said.

Back in his room, Jake grew concerned. When he covered his right eye, vision through the left was still blurry. The idea of a cornea transplant terrified him. His eye specialist had promised 20/20 vision in both eyes—but only the right one was delivered.

Frustrated, Jake got on his knees and prayed about his eye. Then he went through the usual process of removing his contacts. The suction cup got stuck, making it a struggle, but eventually, he got it out, said another short prayer, and went to sleep.

Chapter 31

They all met in the lobby, where even more reporters had gathered that morning. Without time for breakfast, they rushed straight to Pedro's car. He drove them to the Congressman's office. It took a while to find a parking spot, but eventually, they did. Once parked, they walked up to the front door, where a security guard stood.

Rachel gave the code name, and they were all let into the office.

"Nice to finally meet you, Jake—and all your friends," said Congressman Peters.

"Hey, so why did you want to see us?" asked Jake.

"We want you to give one of the inaugural address speeches for the new President of the United States," said the congressman. "You'd be perfect. Right now, you're the face of mental health advocacy. And I'm working to secure more funding for new therapies and medications."

He paused for a moment, looking sincere.

"My son has schizophrenia," he continued. "Even with all my resources, I haven't been able to find the right care for him. I know this is big—but think about it. You'd be like Amanda Gorman, who read her poem at the last inauguration."

"She's the one who wants to be president one day," the congressman added.

"I love her," said Rachel.

Jake pulled his friends into a huddle, like a football team discussing a play.

"What do you guys think? This would put us even more on the map. Rachel, do you want to do the speech?"

"No, Jake, you should do it," Rachel replied. "A tall, handsome, charismatic guy like you is exactly who they need."

"You really think I should? This is huge. The President is going to be there!" said Jake.

They all nodded in agreement.

"We'll help you write the speech," said Ayn, though she had a feeling he might wing some of it.

"Okay, I guess I'll do it," Jake said. "This past half-year has been like a rollercoaster, but yeah—I'll do it."

They turned back to Congressman Peters.

"I'll do it," Jake said. "I believe in the need for better mental healthcare in this country—and it's not just about medication. We need innovative therapies. And I believe you're trying to make that happen."

"You all like pizza?" the congressman asked. "I ordered some."

They agreed enthusiastically, and within 29 minutes, pizza had arrived. Over slices, they talked about how mental health funding would be distributed.

"The inauguration is next month," said Congressman Peters. "I'll cover your travel, your clothes—everything. Just show up so Jake can deliver the speech. The President already has her speech prepared but is looking forward to meeting you all today."

"The President of the United States?" Rachel gasped. "She's going to be amazing!"

"Yeah," the congressman nodded. "She's seen your YouTube interviews, heard Jake's TED Talk, and knows about your work with NAMI. She's excited to meet you. She'll be here in about an hour."

Jake could hardly believe it. Soon, he would meet the next President of the United States and speak to the entire country about mental health. Part of him felt like he was dreaming, but as he looked at his friends around him, it all felt real. A delusion couldn't be this complete.

His dream was finally within reach. He was going to help millions.

He thought about his own mental health—how much he cared about others, too. He wondered how the voices would react to all of this. Would they show up when he met the President? But during the entire conversation with the congressman, he hadn't heard a single voice. Hopefully, they wouldn't return at the worst moment.

There was a knock at the door.

The security guard answered it, and two men in sunglasses entered. They frisked Jake, his friends, and everyone else in the room. Then they inspected the space for any hidden threats.

"All clear. She can come in."

When the President walked through the door, Rachel burst into gleeful laughter. Pedro and Jason grinned from ear to ear. Ayn and Jake tried to keep their cool, smiling politely.

"I've heard so much about you, Jake—and all your friends," said the Vice President.

Before anyone could respond, Rachel stepped forward.

"I've heard about you too, Madam President! It's such a pleasure to meet you. Can I get a selfie?"

"Well, it's nice to meet you too," the President said with a warm smile.

She shook hands with Jake and each of his friends, then spoke about her plans for mental health reform. She asked if they'd be interested in becoming official advocates.

They told her they'd think it over—not all of them fully trusted the government.

"I'd like to help fund any organization you plan to build. This will be a new America—one where people like Jung get the help they need."

A Secret Service agent leaned in and whispered something to her.

"I've got to go," she said. "Speech in Pennsylvania tomorrow. But it was an honor to meet you—Jake, Pedro, Jason, Ayn, and Rachel."

With one of her award-winning smiles, she left the room, Secret Service agents in front and behind her.

They chatted with Congressman Peters for a few more minutes, but he had to head to the congressional chamber to meet with lobbyists. So Jake and his friends made their exit, rushing back to Pedro's car to avoid the crowd of reporters.

As Pedro drove, their conversation buzzed with disbelief and excitement.

"This is fucking unbelievable—we just met the President of the United States, and we're on a first-name basis!" Rachel shouted.

"Yeah, it's wild," said Pedro, "but I still don't trust the government. We need to be sure some pharmaceutical company isn't pulling the strings behind the scenes."

"Don't forget what Congressman Peters said," Ayn reminded him. "They're investing in new therapies and trying to make hospitals more supportive than harmful. I'm so happy for you, Jake. This is huge."

***Jake paced around Pedro's table, walking back and forth.
"No, not those words—we need something stronger. Let's focus on our stories. Together, we cover the full spectrum of mental illness in this county. That means we can connect with a broad audience. The stories are what matter most. You guys will be behind me for support. So, for instance, when I talk about Jason, I'll gesture toward him," Jake said.

"How about me? How about me? Aren't you going to mention me?" Jung chimed in.

Everyone laughed.

"We can't forget about you, Jung."

For the past two months, Jung had been receiving therapy from one of New York's top specialists via Zoom. He'd made significant progress, learning to manage the voices in his head—lowering their volume and frequency. His therapist had helped him coexist peacefully with them. Jung had also been reading the Bible and sharing testimonials on his popular YouTube channel. Alongside Jake and the others, he'd been preparing for the inauguration speech and would be standing behind Jake during the address. The experience filled Jung with joy and hope. He believed that one day the voices might disappear completely.

He dreamed of writing a book about everything that had led him to the psychologist at NAMI.

For now, he was just happy to contribute—to help others with mental illness, especially those who lacked the money or fame to access high-level care like his.

Lately, Rachel had started dating Jung. She found him more intriguing than Jason. She still had lingering feelings for Jason—love like that doesn't vanish overnight—but the yoga and spiritual lessons she'd been learning from Jung had helped her immensely.

Jason, on the other hand, had found a book on OCD that helped him manage his sense of impending doom and reduce his compulsive cleaning habits.

Pedro still had flashbacks to the GRE but was working on a short story about the experience—about how so many people, like him, live in fear of a test that supposedly determines their future. Through his online bipolar support group, he discovered that talking about his psychotic episodes not only helped him but resonated with others as well. He was now actively searching for a therapist to help him process the flashbacks.

Ayn and Jake had been spending every day together, basking in their deep love. But Ayn was afraid. Afraid that losing Jake would plunge her into a deep depression. She also feared she was turning him into her higher power. Even though Jake was famous, he never let it get to his head. Urban models sent him friend requests and provocative photos on Facebook, but Ayn didn't realize that Jake only had eyes for her—physically, mentally, and spiritually.

Ayn was still on her antidepressants, but she didn't credit them for her happiness. She believed it was Jake—and their shared mission of advocating for mental health—that gave her joy.

"That's it, you guys. Let's call it a night—we've done some great work for the inauguration speech," Jason announced.

Jake stood at the podium, scanning the crowd. In the front row, sat the newly elected president—victorious by a landslide. Her smile was both commanding and graceful, almost regal.

Jake glanced back at his friends. They stood in a proud line behind him, dressed in formal attire, all beaming—including Jung, whose cheesy grin was unmistakable.

Jake, standing tall at 6'4" in a fitted suit, eyed the twin microphones in front of him. He thought of Barack Obama and smiled. *So this is what it feels like to be important,* he mused.

Before him stretched a sea of people. Giant news cameras were locked onto him—this moment would be broadcast nationwide. As he scanned the crowd, his eyes found his mother and father seated together. A wave of warmth swept over him.

He smiled, took a breath, and began his speech.

"Ladies and Gentlemen, life is hard. But it is uniquely hard when you're living with a severe mental illness…"

My friends and I have all been diagnosed with severe mental illnesses. I've been hospitalized multiple times, tried various medications and combinations, and seen numerous therapists—some covered by Medicaid, others I had to pay $120 per session out of pocket.

I've had suicide attempts.

Once, the voices in my head told me to kill myself. I placed a bottle of Clorox on my table and just sat there. A deep, fake voice—sounding like a distorted Jesus—told me to drink it. I didn't, but the urge was overwhelming. My mom happened to walk past my room and saw the Clorox. She immediately understood what I was about to do. A wave of fear and will to live crashed over me, and just like that, the suicidal thoughts vanished. Had she not walked by, I might have listened to the voices.

My voices are usually deep and husky. Once, I overdosed on caffeine pills. Instead of energizing me, my head turned to sludge. The intensity overloaded my brain, slowing everything down. I remember hearing a voice— sounding like the devil—counting each pill: "ONE… TWO… THREE…" Their goal was clear: to torture me, to make my life a living hell.

There were brief good times, but they were rare. Most of the time, it was pure hell. I had delusional thoughts because of the voices. I felt insane, and my self-esteem was shattered. I've self-harmed before. My family watched from a distance, afraid and helpless. They didn't know whether I'd hurt them or myself.

The voices were screaming, telling me to end my life right then. Sometimes, one sounded like Jesus—but it was really a demon. Other times, the devil took over. They took turns. I couldn't think straight. I cut my wrist three times. The knife wasn't sharp, so the wounds were shallow, but the marks remained. That twisted voice laughed, as if proud of what he'd caused—like he'd been exposed and didn't care.

That night, I ended up in the hospital.

I've never felt more hopeless than when dealing with those voices. I attended countless HVN (Hearing Voices Network) meetings which is amazing. I heard stories I could relate to.

When we talk about suicide in this country, we focus on suicidal *thoughts*, but what about suicidal *emotions*? Don't those come first?

I also went to Alternatives to Suicide meetings, but I didn't find real help there. I was in a strange position: living in what's considered the best country in the world, yet unable to find effective treatment for the voices or the emotions they triggered.

One woman in HVN mentioned that neurofeedback helped her. My insurance wouldn't cover it, so it was out of reach for me.

Eventually, I began drinking to self-medicate. It helped at first, but the relief was short-lived. I joined AA and stayed sober for three years. Still, the depression lingered. The voices played a mechanical orchestra with my emotions. I didn't go a day without suicidal thoughts or feelings—either from the voices or from what I call "face hallucinations," which were just as devastating.

It felt like some demonic entity was overlaying a grotesque, stupid face on top of mine. Even though I knew I was intelligent, the voices twisted my self-perception into something cruel. I can't explain the emotional pain this caused—it felt evil, inhuman. That "face thing" haunted me for years, growing worse with time. As if the entity inside me was losing space in my mind and using my face to express its torment. It made me feel less than human—like some kind of creature.

I wouldn't wish that experience on my worst enemy.

One day, I completely lost control and began destroying the house. Someone called the police, and I was taken to Zion Mental Hospital.

It was there that I met the incredible people standing behind me today. As some of you know, I met Jung later. *The crowd laughs.*

Except for Jung, we all met in a mental hospital after our own personal episodes of horror. The way we connected—the comfort and ease of our conversations—made me love these men and women deeply. They supported me in ways no therapist or psychiatrist ever had. Despite our different diagnoses, we understood one another.

Jason has severe OCD. My girlfriend struggles with deep depression. Pedro was diagnosed with bipolar disorder. Rachel has schizophrenia. I was diagnosed with schizoaffective disorder.

I don't know how to cure them, but I know how to make them laugh or think. I know what moves them to tears. We've built a bond and promised to support one another, no matter what.

We decided to become mental health advocates. Maybe even start an organization to help others like us.

Because here's the truth: My friends have looked everywhere for help. They've found bits of relief but no cure.

Is it taboo to say I want more than symptom management? I want a *cure*.

As a nation, we need to come together and explore new treatments—new ideas—to truly address mental illness. There *must* be something more we can do.

I care deeply about my own mental health, but I also care about others who are suffering silently like me, like my friends. The stigma alone is suffocating—and that has to change.

I'm looking for a world where someone can walk into a boardroom and say, "By the way, I hear voices"—and not be met with silence or shame. Everyone in this country knows someone living with a mental illness. Something needs to be said, because we all know suicide is not a viable option.

Too often, it's young people who feel trapped, seeing no way out, believing suicide is their only escape. I'm tired of hearing stories like the girl who loved Harry Potter and fantasy novels—who took her own life because of depression. Or the man who hanged himself because command voices told him, over and over, to end it.

Each of my friends has struggled with suicidal thoughts. But because of the bond we share, we made it through. We survived.

I believe in people doing the right thing. Take Jung, for example. Despite having severe symptoms of schizoaffective disorder and being on the verge of prison, he made it to the inauguration. He watched the president being sworn in. And doesn't he look... normal? We have to keep fighting for values.

"Being your brother's keeper" isn't just a dead slogan. We need to care more. We need to be empathetic. Living with suicidal thoughts every day isn't easy.

Perspective

Pedro—my good friend—still battles depressive thoughts tied to his psychosis. When he took the GRE, he was terrified. And to this day, no therapist has been willing to truly help him unpack that trauma and lay it to completely rest.

Jason lives with obsessive thoughts of doom. He feels compelled to clean almost every surface he touches. It's not his fault—it's the way his brain is wired. He imagines germs at a microscopic level, and sees them as blood-contaminating monsters. That's his reality.

My girlfriend Ayn falls into deep depressive spells. At times, she says it feels like a phantom is standing on her chest, sucking out every ounce of joy. Even when she smiles, the emotion behind it doesn't register. Most of the time, she doesn't *feel* the happiness she expresses. As beautiful, brilliant, and captivating as she is, she's hit with emotions that make her feel like the dumbest, most worthless person alive.

Then there's Rachel. Looking at her, you'd never guess she has schizophrenia. She looks like a Victoria's Secret model, curves and all. But she hears voices—voices that tell her someone wants her dead because of her past with Jason, sitting just behind me. These voices speak to her through objects in her room, making her wonder if there are speakers hidden there. They whisper when she tries to sleep, invading her in her most private, vulnerable moments.

And yet, despite all this, we've found connection. We've chosen to identify with each other's struggles instead of comparing them. Our diagnoses may differ, but our emotions overlap. It's incredible how someone with OCD can talk to someone with major depression about intrusive thoughts—and they *get* each other.

Me and my friends—we're different, yes. But in the ways that matter, we're the same. We're more optimistic than pessimistic. Just as brave—if not braver—than any renowned leader who's never set foot in a mental hospital.

And most of all, we care about making a cultural change for the future of mental health in this country.

Jake proclaimed these words with a voice that rang out—commanding, almost tyrannical in its intensity. There was a pause. Then the place erupted in applause and whistles.

Somehow, in that moment, Jake felt something shift deep within him. A rearranging of emotion. A release of trauma. And just like that, the voices—along with the "face thing"—were gone.

He felt a godly presence stir inside him.

Power.
Peace.
Love.

He was free.